ERIC LINDSEY

Age of Conflict

First edition

ISBN: 979-8-9873462-0-4

Imprint: Independently published

Dedicated to my late father, John Lindsey.
He passed while I was writing this book, and although he and I discussed it,
he never had the opportunity to read any of the words herein. He would
have been the best editor, co-writer, and valued opinion giver of all.

I hope you like it, Dad.
And thank you for always believing in me.

I miss you dearly.

Contents

Chapter 1

As I lay there, face down in the alley, dust filling my lungs and my own blood pooling in the dirt directly under me, all I could think about was cursing God for making me weak.

"God wanted to give you a head start in life," Mother would always say, referring to my premature birth. But this had never eased my resulting lack of abilities. God may have given me an early start in life, but it came with a debt I was having to pay back the hard way each and every day since.

I heard footsteps approaching again, so I sprung up from the earth with wild abandon and did my best to fight off the attacker. I faintly remember hitting something, but what—or better yet, *where*—it was on the boy so intent on giving me a likin', I could not tell you. But it must have shocked him, or at least stung a little, because he leaped back and shouted, "Why, you yellow-bellied boot licker!"

At that moment, the voices of children watching, and in most cases, applauding my pain, let out a collective gasp. I understood the reason. If Ms. Thompson had heard what Willy just shouted at me, everyone involved in this tussle would surely be held back after lessons. You see, our teacher did not tolerate cursing a fellow Christian and only moderately allowed such language in reference to a Heathen. I, however, did not mind the momentary respite from the attack, as it gave me some time to catch my breath and look around for a hasty escape. My plan to run for it was just about to commence when I heard a voice rising from behind the onlookers.

"Leave him alone, Willy!"

The crowd looked around in wonder and suspicion.

"Who said that?" Willy demanded.

Pohl, the blacksmith's son, and newest pupil attending Christiansburg, Virginia's Schoolhouse, eased through the group and, with an almost reluctant tone, simply said, "Enough."

Pohl, being new in town, was afforded a mystery toward his temper, abilities, and fierceness that, thankfully, my classmates did not want to discover. Especially in combination with his size. Willy scowled, huffed, and turned toward the schoolhouse with a quick, "He ain't worth it, anyhow."

I had never thought Willy to be that smart, but with this retreat, he did gain a small amount of my respect. At least he was attempting to 'hoe an easier row,' as my Uncle Frank would say. Because looking at Pohl, he appeared to be a hard row to hoe.

To be fair to Willy, my being small brought along with it the usual attention of others looking for easy pickins. But what I added to this deficit was contempt and orneriness that bordered on annoyance. That seemed to be the only way people would notice me, and I had to make them. And today, I had again taken it too far with Willy. Mother tended to minimize my character faults by repeating certain phrases often.

"Garit, remember. When God shorted you in stature, he multiplied in spirit." or, "Now Garit, I saw the fire burning in you the day you were born, and it's brighter than the sun. Some people just prefer the shade." The first statement I kind of understood, the second…I wish I

2

could understand how to master this fire because, for some reason, it only seemed to burn others and make them want to feed me knuckle sandwiches.

Pohl, on the other hand, was quiet, reserved, and BIG. The literal opposite of my attributes. He came to Christiansburg halfway through the school year and, up until that day, did his best to keep attention away from his direction. Of course, being ten and almost a foot taller than all the other kids garnered a decent share of awareness, but his preference was to fade into the background whenever possible.

Maybe I sensed this desire to wane into the shadows (or I simply was being my usual indiscreet self), but I always made it a point to at least say hello to him each school day. Looking back, those attempts to edge out of him a response, or my eagerness to be forward, had at some point struck a chord with Pohl, and he stood up for me that afternoon. I needed him, and I suppose he also needed me. He just didn't really know it yet.

As the years ticked by, Pohl grew bigger, and I grew bolder, but most importantly, our acquaintance expanded into a friendship, and I rarely ended up watching my blood pool on the ground anymore. Having the largest kid in town as your friend has its privileges. It was not one-sided, however, and although it would take a lot to pry out of him, Pohl would probably have said what he gained from our friendship was adventure.

Chapter 2

Beatrice Hahne was the prettiest girl in the Shenandoah Valley. Or at least that's what everyone said. I had never been out of Christiansburg, but one look at her and you had to believe everyone was right. Radiant blond hair and stunning complexion. That's what Mother always said about her. I always thought that it seemed like she glided when she walked. Not like any other person's walk I had ever seen. I noticed her early on when we both started to attend the schoolhouse. Most of the trouble I got into was directly related to her. More accurately, trying to get her attention. She surely would never glance my way due to my good looks. I did not have any. But what I lacked in looks, I made up for in personality. A personality that usually resulted in Willy or other boys whopping me pretty good. But it was worth it just to know that Beatrice, or B, as I called her in my own mind, had any inkling that I existed. Looking back now, B was mostly all I ever thought about growing up. She was the reason I demanded to stay in school, even though Mother could have used use more help on the farm.

I did feel bad, of course, but how in the world would I ever get B to notice me or, better yet, talk to me if I was stuck on the farm all day? You see, my father left us right after I was born, and since then, it was just Mother, Uncle Frank, and I to hold down the farm. They did alright between the two of them, and since I was pretty sickly in nature, I always figured I could not help much anyways. I did my best, but tasks that other boys could do easily came hard to me.

Oh, don't get me wrong, Mother would never let me take the easy road or get out of doing chores. Her philosophy was, 'work hard, like working for Lord.' But, I always kind of felt that she knew that without an education, what else would I be good for in the future? Not in a bad way, of course, just in reality. I couldn't cowboy, farm, build or brawl, so I had to focus on learning another way to earn my keep. Schoolin' it was.

And I never complained because I could stay near to my Sweet B. Whether she noticed me or not. I did find out one day when Ms. Thompson asked each pupil to write an exposition about our family history, that B and I shared something in common. And learning this fact put even more of a zip in my step. Both she and I were descendants of Hessians: Germans that were needed by the British to fight against the Colonies in the Revolutionary War.

Although we did not talk about it much (for good reason), in Christiansburg, a lot of the settlers around here were immigrants directly associated with the War. As Mother would tell me, once the War was over, Britain abandoned most of the non-commissioned soldiers and the Colonies had no money to send them back to where they came from. There were also the defectors from both sides that just walked away, never to be heard from again.

Well, both our great-grandfathers were among those left behind. And both of German heritage. Now, other than the family name, my family tried the best they could to put a lot of distance between us and Germany. But, with three generations separating them and me, I always felt entirely American. Uncle Frank probably felt more like eighty percent, but that was only when he had too much to drink. Problem was that it was quite often. Mother, on the other hand, definitely had the 'sternness and no-nonsense demeanor of a German,' as Uncle Frank would say when hitting the bottle.

I overheard him saying one time to Mother that this German demeanor was the reason Father left. I really did not care why he left; I just know that after Uncle Frank said that, later that night, I heard Mother crying in her bed. That made me sad for her, and I vowed not to ask too many questions or talk about Father. It was better that way. Mother did not deserve to be sad, and I could be strong for Mother in this way, even though I was not strong in others. Little did I know that this inner strength would be my most significant trait later in life. I think Mother prayed for that strength in me daily. And I am so grateful that she did.

But let's get back to B, my favorite subject. As we grew older and Pohl became my friend, the annoying and obnoxious behavior I exhibited earlier in life to get attention was resolved. I started to learn other, more favorable ways to get attention in general. Most importantly, B's. Number one – Humor. B loved to laugh, and, more materially, she loved the attention she received when she laughed. Her laughter, combined with her beauty, was a spectacle to witness. And B delighted in the attention of others. She needed it. If there ever had been a person put on this earth to be famous, it was B. Emily Dickinson, the most famous person we knew, thanks to Ms. Thompson's poetry readings, had nothing on B. Just seeing her smile was the highlight of my day. Heck, of pretty much everyone's day.

As I continued to grow in my depth of knowledge, wit, and aptitude of the mind, I noticed that life started to get easier. Not easier regarding chores, physical activity, and life in general, but I started to see a path for my later years. A course that could allow me to stop hoping that B could learn to love me and might even unveil a way to prosper in wealth and provide for B in a way that she was starting to contemplate. She was a light much brighter than Christiansburg could contain. She just did not know how to expand past the town's borders and did not have the means. That was the crevice I was desperately searching for, a way into B's world. Or, more importantly, a way for B to need me. So, math, culture, and adventure became my strengths. When others were toiling each day to bring in the cattle, hay, or crops, I focused on the intangible pursuits of Knowledge.

Mother always said, "Garit, you are going to have to think past your situation," and I was finally starting to see her point. It finally hit home when our pup, Bruno, lost his back leg to what we supposed was a Beaver trap. It took him some time to adapt, but he did not know that he could no longer run. I mean, nobody sat him down and said, "dog, you can't run anymore. You don't have a leg." He just kept moving forward until one day, he figured it out and ran. Three legs and all. Although not as fast, running was running to him, and he never thought that he could not or should not run again. He just ran. So, like Bruno, I was going to start running, in the metaphysical sense, running with my mind.

The mind was never a strong point of Pohl. Now I am not saying he was dim-witted or slow; he was what I thought to be dulled. Not boring or lacking intelligence, just not quick to answer or be known for conversation. He would just rather be in the background or shadows. Not in a deviant way, but just in an unassuming, pure way. He did not like attention, although his size always pushed attention his way.

One day in class, Ms. Thompson showed us drawings of the various animals of Africa. Lions, zebra, elephants, and alligators. Seeing those pictures absolutely floored us with wonder, except for the zebra. We just laughed at that, as it was clearly just a mule with stripes painted on it. This gave me a lot of material to use over the next few days. I am sure Mr. Boyer, the town's stable operator, never understood why each time we walked by the corrals, I yelled out, "Better get the paint, boys. Africa needs more zebras!" I know, stupid, but if you were in the know, hilarious. Ahhh, my gift.

Nevertheless, I always thought back to another picture in that collection of animals from Africa that summed up Pohl to me. It was a giraffe: essentially a huge horse with a neck as high as a two-story house. It was easy to see why Pohl would be compared to this tall animal. All the other kids seemed to have the same thought—which embarrassed Pohl. But what caught my attention even more, was the way the artist presented this wonderful animal. The giraffe was pictured walking into a thicket of trees. Ms. Thompson explained that their long necks made it possible for giraffes to eat the most succulent and abundant leaves near the top of the trees, thus giving them an almost-untouched food source to sustain their massive size. I focused on the parts of the tree covering the giraffe's body. I could see its legs, neck, and head quite clearly, but its body was somewhat shielded. At that moment, I realized that's exactly what Pohl would like to be. In the world, but somewhat shielded from the world or views from the world around him. This is where I stop for a moment and remind everyone that to have Pohl's physical ability, size and strength was such a fantasy for me that it was hard having empathy for the big lug. To have his attributes would have changed my entire existence and made me a complete package to the world and, most importantly, to B. But being Pohl's friend also meant being sensitive to his view of life, and as hard as it was for me to understand it, I tried. Although, I did remind him he was being a wussy anytime I could. Especially when his shyness was in full exhibition toward the opposite sex, all I talked about was B, so girls were pretty much the entire focus of each day and conversation. When I asked Pohl who he was sweet on, he just lowered his head and smiled.

"Come on, you hayseed, who is it?" I would poke at him.

He would just mumble back, "Leave me alone, you blowhard."

He never did tell me his girl, although I tried and tried to get him to spill the beans. That was just Pohl, reserved and guarded. It irritated me to no end, but a friend is a friend, weaknesses and all, right? I sure hoped so, as I happened to be the weakest one in town.

Chapter 3

The morning of May 1st, 1858, was one that came with both excitement and dread. Graduation Day. My final year of education was coming to an end, and all that was left to do was the formality of pomp and circumstance. Although our schoolhouse ended in the ninth grade, this was much more than many of the surrounding towns in the valley.

This was mostly because of Ms. Thompson. She never married and intently dedicated her life to her pupils. I never found out why she never had a husband but pondered that it probably was due to her complete focus on us. There simply was no room for extracurricular activities *vis-à-vis* a suitor. For this, I was grateful, as it allowed me two more years than most other schools to hone my skills and distance myself from my physical detractors.

The dread was associated with the question of what was to be next. Education had always also been my refuge. My way to be normal, or even, possibly, exceed in life when all other options might have resulted in me being a disappointment or burden to others. And, if you don't ponder on the early years when most of my daily life ended with a beating or some sort of public humiliation, the schoolhouse was the best part of my life. Besides, I got to see B most days of the week, and it was where I met my best friend, Pohl. Completing my education was a blessing, as Mother would say. I just hoped that it also was not leading to the continuation of my Curse.

"Garit, get to gettin'. We are going to be late," Mother yelled down the hall towards my bedroom.

She knew I was not out of bed yet, since the floorboards weren't creaking. My room was next to the kitchen, so when the house started stirring in the morning, they definitely heard my movements in my room.

As I lay there in bed, wondering what life was going to bring next, a part of me shook with fear. Call it a loss of innocence, or that my life was finally being shoved into the forefront, no longer getting to hide under Mother's or Ms. Thompson's wing. I guess this bird's gotta fly, so here goes. I jumped out of bed and hastily pulled my things together. A freshly cleaned shirt, brushed trousers, and vest.

Mom had spent the entire previous week making me a new set of presentable clothes for today. The material came all the way from Richmond. Along with a beautiful dress Mother had ordered for herself several months ago. I was happy to have some new duds, but more so for Mother. I had not seen her so delighted in a long time. Having pretty or new things was a rarity for her. Pragmatic was her principle. And that principal had taken care of me my whole life, so I was pleased to see that she did something for herself for once.

"I suppose this will do," she joked upon seeing the dress for the first time. I knew from the slight smile and gleam in her eye that she was thrilled to show off her figure. I guess each of us have vanity wanting to be displayed, but Mother's was much more hidden and suppressed.

As I came into the kitchen, ready to grab some breakfast and talk through the upcoming day, I was taken aback by Mother's beauty. Along with the dress, she had even pulled her hair up with some lace and applied some rouge to her cheeks. She looked almost like a different person. Usually attired in something worn and gray, today was special, and in that instant, my love for her grew even more. I took for granted all the sacrifices she had made in her life trying to have mine be "normal" and successful. It's funny the things you start noticing as you age; call it maturity or awareness. Either one, I was starting to experience them, and it made life a little less hard.

What I mean by that is the little details that I started to notice about things gave me an advantage. The way a person's eyes contained joy or sorrow, the way a person entered a room or handled a compliment. All ways to almost have a magic power. The power of *insight*. Once practiced and honed, it could be my ticket into people's lives—in honorable or devious ways. I tended toward the more devious in nature but found a real pleasure in truly knowing someone: knowing what made them happy or gave them joy. What picked them up a notch and gave them confidence. Again, it gave me satisfaction to bring them this feeling but don't get me wrong, I also was starting to master exploiting these small details to my advantage.

But with Mother, I did my best to elevate her daily, more than most. She deserved it, and it was what I could do for my part. Might not be the best farmer or chore hound, but being quick with compliments or intentional acknowledgments was my gift.

"Why, Mother, you look absolutely radiant. Is something special going on today?" I joked upon sitting down at the table. Her back was turned to me as she was still plating up the biscuits, but I could tell by her posture and the slight turn to her head that she was smiling. That always gave me delight.

"Garit, you know what today is, my boy? The day you become a productive member of society," she poked back.

And at that moment, I sensed that she regretted saying that. I saw her almost wince, realizing what she had said. You see, Mother had always felt guilt associated with my small stature and disabilities. I had heard her over the years, saying things under her breath sometimes. "If my body would have been stronger, you might not have been premature," or "your legs are my fault." Which, when I was younger, confused me greatly. For why did she often say, "God wanted to give you a head start in the world," if she felt it was her fault and not God's provincial plan? As I grew older and more receptive to people's inner feelings, it always made me sad to think she actually blamed herself for my shortcomings. I felt that wasn't right, for if we are to truly believe that "God's plan prevails," as Reverend Foust would say each Sunday, then why did she take the yoke of my physical burdens? That wasn't fair. Was it fair that Father abandoned us so soon after my birth? Was it fair that, until Uncle Frank came to stay with us, Mother fended for herself and kept the farm and life moving forward all on her own? Was it fair that my legs, muscles and lungs did not work as well as others? No. But as I learned so directly, what in life is fair? That was something Mother would also say often to me: "Garit, life's not always fair, but you can get it going your way if you're smart."

I appreciated her way of acknowledging my weaknesses and some-how covering them up at the same time. She knew very early on that the only way I was going to survive and possibly thrive was through my wits and determination. So, she did whatever she could to stoke both each and every day. It was her way of wrestling the scales back to even for me, and for this, she earned my respect, love, and admiration. I realized then I should have truly said thank you before now.

As Mother brought the biscuits to the table, I sensed this was my time. Uncle Frank had yet to come back in from the chores outside, and we had this small time to be alone.

"Mother," I said as I took her hand. "I just want to say thank you. Thank you for all that you have sacrificed in life for me. Thank you for striving each and every day to give me the will to not let my issues hold me back. You have always been on my side, and I love you very much. By the way, why are you so dressed up?" I had to end with some humor.

"Oh Garit, you are a pickle, and no thanks is necessary. God deserves all the Glory, and I am just so thankful to Him for giving you to me." I saw tears starting to form in her eyes as she looked down and brought my hand to her face. She kissed it so gently.

"You are the joy of my life, and I would not have asked it to be any different," she whispered. "Now quit your flattery and eat your breakfast. We are running behind."

There it was. Mother's pension for being straightforward and stern. I would not expect anything different but was so touched to see some softness in her tone this morning. She is truly a beautiful soul.

The front door flew open at that instant, and Uncle Frank came trudging in. He was holding the egg basket in one hand and the lantern in the other.

"Garit, my boy, today's the big day!" he said with a hearty smile. Uncle Frank was my role model for humor and levity. He never seemed to be down or sullen. Always on the edge of laughter and quick with a retort. He bears a great deal of responsibility for my life's perspective and, honestly, keeping our house somewhat jovial. Mother tended to shut down our play or matters not related to chores and work regularly. Uncle Frank balanced the farm in that he always strived to find the fun in things.

He could make a game out of anything. How fast can we plant the rows, who can finish first? Or, who can find the most eggs in the hen house? Those types of contests. I think not only to help the chore go by with less struggle but also, in his way, helping me build a sense of accomplishment, as he would quite often let me win on purpose. He knew I would never be the fastest or strongest, but he did his best to give me bouts of success or triumph. I think he knew my life would be short of those moments, so while he could, he would graciously give me times to feel good about myself. I know that this was the reason Mother allowed him to stay with us. She knew that, in her own ways, she could make me prepared for the world, but Frank could assist her in rounding out my experiences. And, boy, am I happy he was around because, as practical and firm as Mother was, I would have ended up being the town's undertaker or something. Boring, straightforward, and the one person in town you never wanted to meet.

"So, what are you going to say, boy?" asked Frank, referring to the Valedictorian speech I was to give soon. "Going to give any real zingers to folks?"

"No," I said, with a quick glance at Mother and a wink to Frank. Frank let out a slight chuckle as if to acknowledge his approval of my upcoming time to shine. For he knew my wit and quick tongue would never be tied up too long on an occasion such as this. But Mother knew this also and rapidly reminded me.

"Now, Garit, your speech is no place for quips at others' expense. It's not every day you get to formally address your classmates, family, and the Lord above."

"I know, Mother, I will try to keep it respectful," and again, another wink at Uncle Frank. He just smiled and took his first bite of breakfast.

As we made our way into town, the clanking of the wagon reminded me of a time not so long ago when Pohl and I had quite an adventure. Or I should say, I *forced* Pohl to have an adventure. He was always the unwilling—or unmotivated—part of our team. I brought the fever for adventure with me and, most of the time gave my fair share to Pohl.

I do have to defend him a little by saying that his father, the town's Blacksmith, really worked Pohl hard. If Pohl was not in school, he was learning the family craft, and that work was difficult. No wonder by the time Pohl was thirteen, he not only grew taller but thicker. An oak tree had nothing on Pohl.

Our adventure started with the familiar clanking of the hammer against an anvil in his barn. His father was busy making horseshoes for Mr. Boyers' stock. It was a larger-than-normal order since some soldiers had come into town on their way up to Philadelphia. Their appearance was the break I had been looking for so that Pohl could slip away. No doubt, at some point, Pohl's dad would remember that Pohl wasn't around and would call for help, but hopefully, his not responding would be simply brushed off as happenstance.

As we put more distance between the clanging and ourselves, I finally felt safe enough to divulge my plan to Pohl. You see, I had overheard B telling some other girls that they were going for a walk in the countryside near Miller's Pond to pick flowers for their Graduation hats. This was surely a great chance to "run" into them—in a non-cholent manner, of course.

"Garit, I don't have time for this," Pohl exclaimed.

"I know, I know, but we're graduating soon, and this might be our last chance to talk to the girls for a long time," I said as a retort.

"You mean to talk to Beatrice," Pohl shot back. For some reason, he always called her Beatrice and never B, as I did. I did not mind it, of course, as it kind of made B special, just for me to say. And I think B liked it too. Made her feel unique, I guess.

"Yeah, yeah, Pohl, you know me too well, my friend. But Janice, Holda, and C-C-C-Cecilia should be there also," I said, putting a stuttered emphasis on Cecilia.

Cecilia had made it very clear to all that Pohl was going to marry her someday. Pohl was less excited about this union but kind of just went along with the narrative in order to create less drama. Because Cecilia could definitely create some drama when she wanted to. They weren't courting or anything because that's not what Pohl does. It was more like Cecilia had made a proclamation that Pohl was her choice in life, and Pohl just went along with the order. But Cecilia was more than likely going to be a good wife, came from some money, and could wear the pants in the family if marriage ever came to fruition. My issue with the union was that Pohl never let on what kind of fruit he actually liked. He just would not divulge to me after all these years what kind of girl he fancied. He kept it to himself and would brush me off with a "just leave it be, Garit." So, I finally did.

As we rounded the bend and saw the edge of the pond, I could hear some conversation and laughter.

"They're here, Pohl," I whispered and gestured for him to hunker down so that they would not see us. I don't know why, as that was the whole point of coming out that day, but I wanted to talk through the plan with Pohl before venturing into the fray.

"Ok, so remember," I told him. "We are just running into them. We did not plan this, okay, Pohl?"

"Yeah, yeah," Pohl said quietly.

"We are just going to see the girls, act like we are deep into conversation once they see us, and then just keep walking as if we aren't stopping to talk," I schemed. "You ready?"

"Whatever," Pohl grumbled.

So, we took off down the path and did our best to look like we were having an intense discussion about nothing. In reality, I bet it looked like we were arguing a very important Amendment to the Constitution from the way we were letting on. The girls could not help noticing us, but I knew our attempts to gain attention were unnecessary because Cecilia would definitely shout for us to come over once she laid eyes on Pohl. And my highly crafted plan shot into action.

"Look, girls, it's Pohl and Garit," Janice said to the group.

"Pohl!!!" Cecilia squealed out. "What a beautiful surprise," she said as if Pohl had planned to come out and see her directly. She was always playing things up like that.

One time Pohl just happened to be taking some hinges out to the Forrest ranch past Cecilia's house, and she ensnared him like a black widow. He got caught, hauled into the house, and couldn't get out of there all day. He sure did get a whippin' when he got home later that night. His father was *mad*, and Pohl knew the beating was coming, but he was just too shy, scared, or otherwise malleable to tell Cecilia he had to go. Finally, he started saying that it was getting dark, and the poor guy got some help from Cecilia's father, telling Cecilia he had to get back home.

Stuff like that was always happening to Pohl. I really felt bad for him. He was kind of like a leaf, just getting blown whichever way the wind took him. A really big leaf, of course, but one that never was able to find his resting place or give an opinion on where He wanted to go. I suppose this was one of the main ingredients of our friendship. I came up with the plans, and he followed. I think he liked it that way. I was the wind for sure, or, as most people would say, the hot air.

Well, the plan had worked, and we were now in a conversation with the girls, and I was working my way closer to B. Janice asked about Graduation, Cecelia asked about anything she could think of about, and Pohl and B kept searching for flowers, staying just outside the conversation. As I inched closer to B, I noticed that she was mostly picking white flowers. That was my in.

"Why B, those white flowers will compliment your radiant hair quite well," I said, like some sort of woman's beauty expert. She just smiled and kept picking flowers. "I assume you are going to be placing them on a new hat I haven't seen before?" I asked, alluding to her upcoming graduation day outfit.

"Um, hmm," she said quietly while continuing her search. With B, you had to really give her something worth her time to respond to.

You see, each day, she received a compliment, exaltation, or doting comment from almost every person she encountered. It was

18

commonplace for folks to fawn over her; she truly was a beautiful site. She had adopted a sort of pecking order for all the comments. If they were the usual 'Good day, miss, and what an even more beautiful day you have made it,' from a male passerby, she would just give a slight smile and small nod of her head. A comment like, 'Ms. Beatrice, you have such radiant skin, and your smile is like a song,' resulted in a polite, 'Thank you,' back from B. But, at least, this was a verbal acknowledgment from the Queen, which was very rare.

Over the years, I had learned there was only one thing that would usually get her to stop, squint her eyes and start a conversation. Rather than fawning over her beauty, I would say something that intrigued her sense of mischief.

You see, not only did B and I have similarities in heritage and lineage, we were both troublemakers. Rabblerousers, you might say. My skill in this area was developed in order to be relevant in a world that would normally look past me. Hers was because she was simply bored with her high status in life and wanted to have some fun–as long as she was still the center of attention, of course.

"So, did you hear that I am giving a speech at Graduation? I think I will make sure to include my observation that life is more exciting when filled with education, or more directly, having knowledge is waaayyy more important than riches, stature, or beauty." I knew that last word would strike a chord.

"Excuse me, Mr. Garit, but what do you mean, sir?" she said, with her eyes somewhat squinting toward mine. I knew I had her attention for at least a few minutes and was happy with my small position of worthiness for the time being.

"I mean that, without an education, all those other things are just possessions that can fade, wither, or abandon their host throughout life's journey. Wisdom via education continues to grow and prosper as we age," I really thought I was being canny now, and surely B would think me clever as well.

"Oh," she said. "But what about senility? Wouldn't that be an encumbrance to wisdom growing throughout life? Or better yet, foolishness. I have seen the wisest men in the county at a loss for words when beauty shows them the slightest amount of attention."

And that is where she had me. I had seen it with my own two eyes also.

One day, the mayor came and spoke to our class about civil government and the role of the public servant in society. Boring! But B saw this as a great chance to gain some attention from him. And she simply played with her hair while he gave his presentation. I tell you the truth before he could even get three sentences into his oratory, his eyes kept focusing back on B. It was like she had put a spell on him. He bumbled and gaffed like an idiot, rambling on about who-knows-what, until Ms. Thompson cleared her throat loudly as if to say to him, 'Come back to reality, sir, we are all waiting for you.' And so, he continued his presentation with his eyes pointed straight at the floor. Almost like that story about Medusa, looking at B would surely have brought his demise. He knew it; we all knew it. And mainly because out of three hundred and sixty minutes in a typical school day, three hundred and fifty-nine of mine were also spent looking at B. Guilty as charged.

"Well, B," I replied, "I believe a man's intelligence cannot be diverted as long as he is confident in his station in life. If a man keeps his wits about him by wanting or having only the best of everything, he can fly above the ordinary annoyances in life."

Boy, that was good, I thought. And I took it further in for a final jab. "Beauty, unaccompanied by wisdom, is as a flower without perfume."

Man, that one even impressed me, for it came out like I was possessed by a French poet. At that, B stopped, turned, and swatted at my shoulder.

"Why Garit," she said, "you sure don't look like much, but your tongue is like a dagger. Just be careful that you don't eventually cut yourself."

And there it was. A put-down and compliment in one easy statement. The kind of thing that B was a master at. And frankly, so was I. I sensed that B was finally starting to see how much we had in common. Maybe even that I might be the only one in the Valley that could hold a conversation with her without boring her to death by pressing and fawning on her the way most people did. Don't get me wrong, she loved it, but I knew she was growing tired of the pedestal they all wanted to put her on. Almost a look-but-don't-touch piece of art. She craved excitement, and I certainly was not in short supply of that asset, or at least the pursuit of it. I realized that I had made my mark on B and wanted to make a quick exit so that she would be left thinking about me further. I didn't want to mess it up, so I quickly focused back on Pohl and the petting he was getting from Cecilia.

"Oh no," I said, "better go rescue Pohl, or Cecilia will be dragging him home to convince her mother and father that wouldn't a graduation day and wedding day go nice together!" At that, B giggled and batted her eyes at me as if to say, "nice work, kid, until next time." So, I tried to show utmost concern for my friend and trotted over to where Pohl, Janice, and Cecilia were standing.

"Come on, Pohl, we have to get going, or we'll be late," I said. Pohl almost let out a 'hurray, I am saved!' but was able to keep it down to a slight "Yep!".

"Where you goin', Pohl?" Cecilia inquired.

"Oh, nowhere special," I quickly interjected. "Just on a chore for the Blacksmith." I knew this was vague enough and a topic that the girls had no interest in, so it was a safe exit strategy.

"Well, okay. Guess I will see you later, Pohl," Cecilia said, disappointed.

I simply grabbed Pohl's arm and ushered him toward the path. While walking away from the group, I made one quick glance back at B and was surprised to see her looking back at me with a smile on her face. I simply waved and received a nod of her head back as confirmation of our connection.

With that, I just started running like a bolt of lightning had hit me or something. Pohl let out a "What are you running for?" and started after me. He quickly caught up, as my running was more like a fast walk for him, and grabbed my shoulder to get me to slow down. But my gait had nothing to do with my brain and all to do with my heart, so I couldn't tell my body to slow down.

Finally, though and without getting too far out of sight, my lungs gave out, and I had to stop, bend over and gasp for air. Of course, Pohl had caught up and was easily keeping pace. He stopped right with me.

"What was that?" he asked.

I heard the words, but they did not make sense to me, for all I could think about was that I had finally penetrated the armor. And, regarding Pohl's question to me, for once, I was speechless and couldn't answer. Although I am less sure it was that I couldn't gather my thoughts, and more because I simply couldn't talk due to oxygen deprivation. I did look up at him and smiled as I tried to force air into my lungs. He wasn't even breathing heavily at all. Another great example of Ying and Yang, as Ms. Thompson had taught us. I just never understood if I was Ying or Yang. Pohl was whichever was the opposite of me when it came to physical means.

"Garit, did you remember to bring your Bible?" Mother said, breaking my recollection of our blissful previous encounter.

"Yes, Mother," I replied.

"Are you going to quote any scripture in your speech?"

"Probably," I said, but immediately sensed my mistake. Definitely should have said, 'Yes, Ma'am,' with a quick and affirmative tone.

"Probably? Probably? What in the world does that mean, Garit? There is no way on God's green earth that you are not going to quote the Word in your speech. Remember, this is an opportunity for you to share God's divine wisdom with all in attendance, don't waste it, son."

You see, if Mother had her way, I would definitely be the next up-and-coming man of the cloth in town. Not because of any sense that I was filled with God's word and convicted to spread the Gospel around the valley. But more like I seemed to be born for that role. It did not take strong physical caliber, money, or stature to be a reverend. Only the Word and the ability to communicate the Word to the masses. And I fit those attributes to the T. And I probably would have been very good at it, but it was a path I did my best to distance myself from. Without breaking Mother's heart, of course. Just a little sprinkled here and there. Remember, Rome wasn't built in a day!

"I will be sure to have some of Word for reference, don't worry," I assured her.

As we had a few hours before the event, I asked to be dropped off at the schoolhouse while Uncle Frank and Mother went on into town for some other supplies. I was happy for this time alone. Honestly, I had not spent more than two seconds thinking about what I was going to say during the speech. For a person that could have a long and varied conversation with a wooden Indian, I was finding it hard to come up with a theme and structure. I think it really had to do with the fact that I was not sure I wanted it to actually be reality. I did not want this time to come to an end. But I was torn. I did want to move on and race into adulthood, I just didn't know what direction to go. My guess, though, was that all my fellow classmates were feeling the opposite. They saw their future beyond the schoolhouse with anticipation.

"Voila," I said to myself out loud. Sounded like I had the basis for a great speech right there.

As I looked out across the schoolhouse, every face looking back was familiar to me. Pupils, teachers, parents, and siblings all crowded into our institution of learning for the purpose of seeing the toils of all their hard work paying off. Education for their loved ones. A pretty rare thing these days, with so many other hardships tearing away at the opportunity for schooling.

In fact, a number of the classmates that I had grown up with had dropped out here and there throughout the years. Their families either moved away in search of work, or the farms could not function without them on a daily basis, and school was the sacrifice. At that moment, it hit me pretty hard. I really was thankful to my mother and Uncle Frank for everything they sacrificed so that I could stay in school. I had never really appreciated that before then. But these emotions could not have come at the worst time. I was seconds away from starting my speech and, I swear, if I started crying in front of everyone, I might as well just step down from the podium and start walking out of town. There would be no way the ribbing and laughter at my show of emotions would cease, ever. So might as well just leave town.

"All right, Garit, compose yourself," I said quietly. I even pinched my right leg really hard, hoping the pain would keep my mind off sentimental thoughts. Not sure if it worked but...

"And now, I would like to introduce your Valedictorian for the graduating class of 1855, Mr. Garit Hotzmire," Ms. Thompson said as she turned and gestured me up to the podium.

Before I knew it, I was waxing away like a gifted orator with
excellent points, emotional petitions, and making everyone whole-heartedly agree that education was the bedrock of society. Or at least, that is what it sounded like to me. From the reaction of the crowd, they were interested at first but starting to show impatience. They were ready for the real reason they were here, the after-ceremony potluck and dance. So, I thought I should shut this thing down quick—but

with a focused punch. Make it memorable, you see.

"So, it is with great respect I say farewell to my fellow classmates, teachers, and sponsors. And I thank them for making our education a priority. For, without help in life, you are nothing more than a lone wolf in this world, fighting for life each day and continuously searching for your next meal. And with that, LET'S EAT!"

I know this wasn't the most profound of statements, but if there is one thing I know, it's timing. And as I saw the glaze in everyone's eyes start to grow, I knew that the smell of potluck delicacies was turning everyone into ravished animals. This wolf reference would appeal to their carnal nature, and as expected, with my yell of "let's eat" came a roar of laughter, applause, and hoots from everyone, young and old. I started patting myself on the back immediately.

As we all shuffled outside in a controlled rush to get in line for food, Ms. Thompson came over to me and gave me a hug.

"Garit, thank you for being such a good student over the years. I have really enjoyed watching you mature and take your education seriously. I have never brought this up before, but I feel there is something I should say to you now".

"Okay, Ms. Thompson, what is it?" I asked.

"Well, I know your physical abilities are compromised, and by no means am I saying that is a bad thing, Garit. Please don't misunderstand me. Please."

"It's okay, Ms. Thompson. Trust me, I have heard it all before, and it really does not bother me anymore".

"Okay, thank you for that. I just wanted to say that you really have a gift of the mind. I hope you understand that. It will take you on so many adventures in life that your body may not be able to. Don't ever feel like your half a man because of that. Most men I have known over the years may have been strong and able, but their thoughts and actions were limited due to their education. I always looked at you and thought that they were half the men that you could be. I am so proud of you."

With those words, I again got more emotional than I ever thought I would on a day like this or really a life transition like this. Nothing ever really hit my emotions before so I thought I would just sail through this as well. As my emotions came rising into my gut, the best thing I could do was just hug Ms. Thompson in a rush and say, "thank you," as I made a quick exit. I admit I was very confused about all the emotions, and I sure hope Ms. Thompson understood this rapid gesture.

I rushed to the rear of the schoolhouse via the side door and hoped that no one was there as the potluck had been set up out front. There were also no windows on that side of the building, so I could catch my composure in private. Thankfully, as I rounded the corner, all was clear.

"What is going on, Garit? Get a hold of yourself," I said.

Keep it together! I thought. After a few seconds, I started to feel the uneasiness leaving and was thankful that it was a relatively short-lived period. And right as I was getting ready to straighten my coat and head back to the front of the building, Pohl came around the other side and threw his hand up.

"Hey, there you are. Everyone is wondering about you. Why are you back here?"

"I don't know, just needed to catch my breath."

"Are you ok? Are your lungs acting up?"

"No, just got a little hot, I guess," I said, gesturing to my coat. Again, a quick-thinking response that, hopefully, Pohl would accept and just move on.

"Oh, ok, it is a little warm today. Well, let's get back to the line, food is going quickly, and man, I am hungry."

As he turned to go, I stopped him in order to shake his hand.

"Pohl, I don't know if I have ever told you this but thank you for being my friend. I mean it, you are the greatest friend a guy could ask for, and I just wanted you to know that."

"Garit, are you really ok? Don't get all soft on me, man," Pohl laughed off this show of emotion.

"Just thank you, my friend," I said sincerely. Pohl knew what I meant and just winked at me. He knew that without him having my back, I might not have made it through each day, let alone each year. He really was my guardian angel, and although he never held it over my head or made me feel I owed him for anything, he knew it. With that, he pulled my hand and started dragging me toward the potluck. "LET'S EAT!!" he yelled as he did. We both started laughing.

Mother had saved me a seat next to her and Frank, but I really wanted to sit next to B, so I kind of dallied around at the end of the food line. Hoping that I could spot her and see that a seat was open next to her.

As I played with the rolls like I was having a hard time picking just the right one, I glanced around the yard and saw B at the far end. Of course, and as usual, there was a group of people sitting and standing around her. Not only was her entire family there, but her girlfriends and other admirers were gravitating around her. Heck, there were people even standing and eating their food in the group rather than sitting down at open seats at the table next to them. She just absolutely had a gift, I tell you. People acted like she just had an aroma or something that was divine, and they had to be close to her to smell the sweet scent. Or maybe they were just hoping that being in her presence would gift them with some small percentage of this allure. Who knows, but I couldn't blame them. I was smitten by the same elixir.

Seeing that B was fully surrounded and protected by her band of sidekicks, I resigned to sitting next to Mother.

"How's the food?" I asked, sitting down in my seat.

"Garit, my boy, you need to graduate more often," Uncle Frank said with a grin.

"The fixin's here are wonderful. Make sure to get some of that pistachio salad, umm-umm good," he said, as he rubbed his belly with his free hand.

Everyone at the table giggled. That was my uncle Frank, a little unrefined but genuine. People really liked him for that. Mother was looking over my plate to make sure I had gotten the most nutritious items available. She always mother henned me in that way to help my body grow or develop a little bit better than it had. It was her way of showing love, and I appreciated that, even though I did not show it often enough.

"Now, Garit, make sure to eat the meat and vegetables first, don't go filling up on Frank's suggestion," she poked.

"I will, Mother," I said in an annoyed tone. Just then, Ms. Thompson approached again and wanted to thank Mother for raising such a fine boy.

This absolutely made my mother shine like a diamond in direct sunlight. She stood up to say thank you to Ms. Thompson and sort of curtsied as she did like she was being recognized by the King of England. It was funny to see Mother acting this way, but it also reinforced my sense of love toward her. She really had made it her life's purpose to raise me right, no matter what and no matter the weaknesses I possessed. She just stormed forward through every obstacle, and as I look back now, I am eternally grateful for the sacrifice and the faith she had in me. I can also say that I did not do my mother justice for these actions, I should have been a better son. Maybe now I can.

Chapter 4

L ife after graduation was very different. No longer did I have to set out each morning for school or stop by Pohl's on the way into town. The normal daily life that I had lived for all these

years just stopped. I did not see Pohl very much, and I really did miss him. But I missed seeing B even more. The school was my only contact with her, and now she was like a shooting star, I was lucky to see her, and when I did, it was over in a flash.

I had settled into helping Uncle Frank and Mother on the farm and, admit, was kind of adrift in life. I did not know what was next for me. Mother could sense this, but she was so happy to have me around more. Before this, I would leave for school in the morning and do my best to not be home before dark. Heck, scheming to be around B was a full-time job, and now I was unemployed, you might say.

But being around the farm was good at times. A little surreal but good. With me helping out with the chores now, it seemed as if we all had extra time on our hands. We talked more at the breakfast table than before because no one had to hurry off to get the day's work done. Uncle Frank and I played a lot more poker. And now, we even started making bets with beans as coins. We never did that before, and the winner of each hand had simply gotten satisfaction as the reward. But now we had a pile of beans to help hold it over the loser's head.

Although, it was Frank that typically had the largest pile. It got to the point that every time I heard him let some gas go, I would say, "you're winning too many beans at poker Uncle Frank!" He and I always laughed when I said it. Usually followed by Mother saying, "Frank, that's disgusting, *stop it!*" The best was when I would hear her laugh a little, especially when we are all in bed, and Frank would let a big one rip. Shook the entire house, I tell you!

But as the summer progressed, I was able to venture into town a little more. The crops weren't ready to harvest for a few weeks, so we just needed mother nature to do her thing for a while. It was nice to help Mother out with the errands, and of course, I was always willing to pick up supplies at the general store. Almost always, I would stop at Pohl's place and see if he could break free to fish, wander, or just talk a little. That rarely happened, as his father had him completely focused on learning to blacksmith now that school was over.

On one rare occasion, the shop was slow, and Pohl's father let him take some time to go to Miller's Pond with me to fish. Pohl really loved to fish. The isolation of it all suited him perfectly. Although, I would usually break the tranquility of the moment with my comments, questions, or the pondering of life out loud. But he put up with it as he wasn't banging on an anvil and away from it all: the town, people, and life in general. He just liked seclusion in general. During this hazy day of fishing and kicking back, I asked Pohl a question that had been rooting around in my thoughts for some time.

"Pohl, if your father is the blacksmith, and you are training to be a blacksmith, is he going to step back or something and let you take over the shop soon?"

Pohl sighed.

"No, Father is years from retiring, and he has made no secret about it that there is only enough business for one blacksmith in Christiansburg."

"So, where does that leave you? Are you saying you will be leaving?" I asked very hesitantly. I really did not want to know the answer to that question. Not because I would be devastated but because that was just one more thing that was unforeseen in this period of life's transition. I was getting pretty tired of the unknown sneaking up on me and not knowing exactly what was going to happen in my immediate circle of friends and family. Growing up is terrible.

"Well, I have to make a living, and father won't let me stay too much longer. He always talks about how he was on his own at thirteen years of age, and here I am, fixing to turn fifteen. I guess I will have to leave Christiansburg and find a town that needs a blacksmith. Father said that Salem is probably in need of one, as the current blacksmith is getting pretty old, and he did not have a son to carry on the service. I think he wrote to him last week about it."

"Salem! That's like thirty miles from here! That just can't happen, Pohl," I demanded.

"Well, it's better that I am still in the Valley, at least, and yes, it's going to happen, I suppose. It's only thirty miles, Garit, not the moon," Pohl said, trying to lessen the blow.

"Might as well be the moon, Pohl. It's not like I can just skip and jump right over there. And besides, if you're as busy as you have been lately, we will never get to do anything again!"

"Calm down, Garit, it'll be fine. You forget that there, I will be the boss. I can shut down anytime I want, and father can't do a damn thing about it. My shop, my rules."

Now, this was something I was excited to hear coming from Pohl. He was right, and we could probably see each other all we wanted, which made me feel better. But I like that I was hearing a little deviousness come out in that statement.

"The student has become the teacher," I said in a low, authoritative voice. We both started laughing uncontrollably as we both sensed this change in Pohl's thought process. And it was a good thing, especially to me. I now had a true partner in crime as they say, although I admit, if this was as shadowy as Pohl thought, I would still have to be the ringleader. And that was an easy job for me. With that, we continued fishing, and both just knew that everything would be okay.

On the way back to town, though, Pohl was acting like he wanted to ask a question, but just could not bring himself to do it. I knew him too well, so I finally said, "What? What is on your mind, Pohl?"

"Well, my life is sort of moving forward with Salem; what are you going to do?" he asked.

And there it was, the question I was dreading myself. I knew someone was going to ask it pretty soon; I was just not ready to answer it yet. The finality of it was so depressing. Not the actual answer, or actually what I was going to do the rest of my life, for I had no idea, truthfully. It was just the fact that this question was the final nail in the coffin of childhood. Honestly, the last few months had been really good for Uncle Frank, Mother, and me. Especially me.

"I don't know, Pohl, I really don't."

"Well, that's a new one for you, not knowing something," Pohl shot back. "You're always one or two steps ahead of everyone else," he continued.

"I know, I know. But on this topic, I feel like I am sinking in quicksand, my friend. I just don't have a clue what my next chapter should be. And to think of that chapter being farther away from you and B, I am just tapped out, bushwhacked, and worn down,"

"Man, that ain't no good, Garit. I am sorry, bud. It will be okay, though. If I know you, it won't be too long before you are buzzing around with the next best idea. I have faith in that."

And with those words, I really did feel a little sense of calm come over me. I just kept walking and looking down at my feet for a few minutes but finally broke the silence.

"You know, Pohl, you're right. I have been thinking so hard about what is ending that I have not been thinking about what is next to start. What's wrong with me? We are finally in the place where we all wanted to be since starting school, the end. We are free! We can do anything we want!"

And with that last statement, I raised my arms up into a V above my head and yelled out, "Watch out, world, you're fixin to meet Garit and Pohl head-on!"

"Garit, you're crazy!" Pohl laughed.

"Yep, yep, I am, Pohl, and thank you for talking with me about things today. I really appreciate you, my friend."

With that, all felt right with the world again. Yes, things were changing for both of us, but the time to grab hold of it was now. The time to move in whatever direction we wanted was now.

"Carpe diem, you son's a bitches!" I yelled out as we were coming into town. Pohl just looked at me and rolled his eyes while grabbing my shoulder. With that motion, he said goodbye without having to say a thing. I did not know it then, but that was the last time I would see him for almost two years.

Chapter 5

The harvest of 1859 had been one of the largest on record for Virginia and the Shenandoah Valley. Great rain earlier in the year had really helped the planting season, and things were going very well on the farm.

Although, things had changed quite a bit regarding my involvement. I was well into my plan to seize the day and had taken a couple of jobs in town. I no longer helped on the farm daily but did pitch in when I could. Uncle Frank did not mind, and Mother was just happy that she had her old Garit back. The one that shot out of bed each day, ready to take on the world. She had been a little worried about me right after graduation and what I was going to or willing to become. I was happy that both of them really fostered my getting back into the swing of things, and I think they were, also.

My first job, and then soon after, my second, came almost by accident. I had been in town running errands for Mother when the local saloon owner, Mr. Stallsburg, and I crossed paths in the Dobbs General Store. He was arguing with Mr. Dobbs about the amount on his bill. He was just insistent that the total was incorrect. You see, his sister had ordered some fabric from Richmond, and he had several bottles of liquor, candles, and playing cards on this order as well. And it was a sizable one, for sure. Mr. Dobbs said that he went through the manifest several times and was absolutely sure it was correct.

"I don't doubt that the manifest is correct, and it looks like all of my items are here. I am just not sure about the total price. I think there are some inaccuracies, because I have ordered mostly the same order for the last three times, and something is just not right with the total."

"I agree. The difference this time was the fabric your sister ordered," Mr. Dobbs explained.

"I am aware of that, but that amount of fabric could not be more than five or six dollars, and my bill is almost twenty dollars more than normal. There must be a reason."

"I do think that some of the liquor has increased in price, Mr. Stallsburg. That must be the source of the difference," Mr. Dobbs said, with respect but expertise. "The bill is correct, sir," he said with a final huff. I had just set my armful of wares down on the counter next to both of them and happened to drop the box of baking soda on the floor. It fell right next to Mr. Stallsburg's feet. This mistake of mine seemed to break through the stalemate, and they both unlocked their stares at each other and looked at me.

"Why Garit, I did not see you were here, son," said Mr. Stallsburg. "How are you and your mother doing?"

"Oh, we are doing fine, just getting ready for harvest and winter thereafter. How are you and yours, Mr. Stallsburg?"

"Doing fine as well. I hope to see you all in church this Sunday."

You see, although Mr. Stallsburg ran the town saloon, he was a Christian man and felt that his occupation was not relevant to his faith. "For you remember, even Jesus drank wine," he would say with a tip of his hat whenever the question was raised. That still did not persuade the most fervent Bible thumpers but at least bought him some time to make a hasty farewell from their company. And, in defense of him, he did not promote the dancing girls and other sins of ill repute, so most of the church folk gave him a pass.

"Yes, sir, Mother and I will be there, and look forward to hearing the reading of Daniel that Reverend Moot promised last week".

"Yes, yes, I am looking forward to that also. Please tell your mother I am glad you are attending."

Mr. Stallsburg was quite fond of my mother. Not in a rude or foreboding way, but he would often ask about her or try to get her opinion of the sermon on the way out of church each Sunday. I did not know if he was sweet on her or just truly appreciated her opinions, but with him being a widower and she an abandoned mother, it just seemed like something was slowly simmering between them. And to me, it was perfectly fine. Mr. Stallsburg was a nice man, doing well for himself, and would be a fine husband for mother if it ever came to it. Mother would always seem to brush off any mention of the relationship, as she had convinced herself that she was too old or too set in her ways to even think about remarrying. I think deep down, she would have welcomed any advancement by Mr. Stallsburg, but she wouldn't be Mother if she didn't project a granite-like facade.

"Mr. Stallsburg," Mr. Dobbs interjected, "what are we going to do about your bill?" he said insistently.

"Well, it looks like we are at an impasse, my friend. You say I owe this much, and I say the amount is wrong. What do you suggest?" Mr. Stallsburg said back with a smile.

"Well, I am not sure…I guess I could have Mrs. Dobbs look over the bill again, but we have both already done so three times together. Do you want to look it over again?"

"No, no, I have done the same. If I know one thing in this world, it's that you should not waste time on things you don't like doing, as that takes away from the time you have doing what you want to do. So how about this? Let's split the difference and call it a day!" Mr.

Stallsburg proposed.

As Mr. Dobbs raised his hand to rub his chin and ponder this compromise, I blurted out a request that, to this day, I can look back and say changed the course of my life forever. You know, those decisions or actions that you can see absolutely changed your life; you took a detour on the path that, before then, you did not even know was on the map. And it had a monumental, pivotal result.

"You both know I was Valedictorian of my class and the best arithmetic pupil in the valley. Let me take a look at the bill," I said confidently. They both looked at each other, looked at me, and shrugged their shoulders at the same time.

"Can't hurt. Go ahead, son," said Mr. Stallsburg.

So, I took the ledger and started going through the numbers rapidly, line by line. As I did so, I thought that these really were simple mathematical equations of addition or multiplication, depending on amounts, supplied on the left side versus the price per unit on the right. Easy. So, I kept going down the list, and two things stood out right away.

The first was that Mr. Dobbs' handwriting was abhorrent. I had always thought that ever since I had become the errand boy for my mother. He would occasionally send notes home to her with upcoming supplies, materials, or other concerns she would be interested in purchasing in the future. As I tried to read them on the way home, I just shook my head. Ms. Thompson would be appalled at the penmanship...and would certainly have given him an Unsatisfactory on his school marks.

As a result, in going down the list, there were several items that I could easily mistake as a one over a seven or vice versa. That was also possible for the fours and nines. The second item that came to my attention was that some of the math was just plain wrong. Line six said, '17 feet of broderie anglaise at .29 per foot.'

Now I had no idea what broderie anglaise is, but it must be nice. At twenty-nine cents per foot, that was expensive. But what I was really focusing on was the total amount. I completed the numeration in my head. It should have totaled four dollars and ninety-three cents. Instead, the right-side column had a total of twenty-two dollars and thirty-three cents, a very significant difference.

"*Voila*," I said out loud while circling the amount with a pencil from the counter.

"Now, I have not gone the entire way through the list, but I think I have found the main offender. I think someone just simply mistook a one for a seven on this item here," I said as I showed them the ledger.

"Honest mistake, I am sure, but the result is around seventeen and a half dollars doing it quickly in my head."

They looked at each other, eyebrows raised.

"I also saw that one of the other items was just wrong in the multiplication, by just under two dollars," and pointed to that line as well while they looked at it, and then again at each other.

"Well, I'll be," Mr. Dobbs exclaimed. "If that's true, it looks like I owe you an apology, Frank," Mr. Dobbs said. He picked up the ledger and started going through the numbers I had pointed out again.

"That's okay, Herman. Honest mistake, I am sure," Mr. Stallsburg said back, putting his hand on my shoulder. "Sounds like you need to hire Mr. Hotzmire here to be your new accountant," he chuckled.

Mr. Dobbs seemed to slough off that comment as he continued his inspection of my findings. He looked up from the ledger at me, looked back down at it, and then set it back on the counter. He then took his pencil, marked out the total, and put the new total down below it with my corrections included. Sure enough, the total was now down by almost twenty dollars.

"That's more like it," Mr. Stallsburg said and started counting out his cash, thus settling the debate and his bill. After they finished up,

Mr. Dobbs spoke again.

"Frank, I am really sorry for the mix-up, and I assure you it won't happen again."

"Herman, how long have I gotten my orders from you now?" Mr. Stallsburg asked.

"Oh, around nine years, I suppose," Mr. Dobbs answered.

"That's about right. And don't worry, I don't see that changing anytime soon. Besides, with Garit doing your books now, I can sleep in confidence that all bills from this point forward will be one hundred percent accurate, right?"

A little setback, Mr. Dobbs hesitated a moment.

"You bet," he said and turned to me. "Garit, it sounds like you and I need to talk." With that, Mr. Stallsburg slapped me on the back, gave Mr. Dobbs a handshake, and left the shop. On his way out the door, he paused and yelled back at us.

"Garit, come see me when you're finished here, alright?"

"Yes, sir, Mr. Stallsburg, right away." I turned back to Mr. Dobbs, who was looking down his nose and over his glasses at me. I wasn't sure if I was in trouble for making him look bad in front of a customer or was going to be rewarded for butting in. As Mr. Dobbs started pulling all the items I wanted to purchase closer to his ledger on the counter, I prepared myself for the former. I was used to this look of 'boy, you're going to get it now' from my years of being the town punching bag.

As I left the store about thirty minutes later, I was almost in shock. *Did what just happened...really happen?* I thought as I loaded the supplies into the wagon. I played what just happened over in my mind. After tallying up my supplies on his ledger, Mr. Dobbs had simply slid it over to me and asked me to complete the total. No smile, no pleasantries, just an order. As I went through the numbers, I found I was excited to use my mind again for this type of exercise. I had not done anything like this since school ended, and I was surprised to discover that I kind of missed it. Yes, I know what you are thinking. Who on earth finds doing arithmetic fun? Well, I guess I do. I just had never realized it before now.

Another thing you should know is that while I was shopping for the supplies, I was mentally tabulating the cost of each item I added to my haul. So, I had a fairly accurate estimate of what the total bill would be. Mother had only given me the authority to go up to six dollars for all the supplies, with strict instruction to put something back if I went over that amount. Preferably the candy, Uncle Frank's whiskey, or lace, in that order until I was under six dollars. Luckily, I was able to get the entire list and still had fifteen cents or so to go. Before the commotion of Mr. Dobbs and Mr. Stallsburg debating the bill, I was trying to see how many ribbons of licorice I could add to get just to six dollars. I figured I could add about ten ribbons.

But, back to the task at hand. I quickly totaled up my bill and found that the amount came to five dollars and eighty-two cents, wrote that number down, and slid the ledger back to Mr. Dobbs. I had not noticed that, while I was figuring up my numbers, Mr. Dobbs had written down his total on another slip of paper near the register. He picked up his slip, put it on the ledger next to mine, and started shaking his head. *Uh oh, here it comes.* Mr. Dobbs set the ledger down on the counter and turned it around so that I could see. His slip had five dollars and seventy-two cents on it, and mine, of course, had five dollars and *eighty-two* cents.

"Son, you just saved me ten cents," he said. "How about that amount as your daily rate?"

"Daily rate for what, Mr. Dobbs?"

"Garit, I would like to hire you to tally all the bills each day to make sure they are accurate. For this service, I will pay you ten cents a day. With your skills, I don't foresee that task taking more than about an hour or two each morning, except Sundays, of course. You would audit the previous day's sales and make sure I had not made any mistakes. I would bet that you will find more than enough to cover your wage each week. My eyes aren't what they used to be," Mr. Dobbs finished with a hopeful grin on his face.

I thought about it for a few seconds, going through my mind about what Mother occasionally paid farmhands when we need extra help. I was pretty sure that was around twenty cents per day, and it was really hard work. Although I thought ten cents per day would be great for such an easy task and the short time required, I shot back, "Fifteen cents per day, and you've got a deal!"

At that, Mr. Dobbs shrugged his shoulders and motioned for me to shake his hand.

"Deal," he said happily. He then proceeded to walk me through the store and talk about our arrangement. I was fascinated by the inner workings of the store that I had previously been oblivious to. It was a whole new world, and I loved it.

After storing up the supplies in the wagon, I made sure to get right over to the Saloon to see Mr. Stallsburg as he'd requested. As I walked toward the swinging doors for the second time in my life, I must admit I had a sense of trepidation. The saloon was always a place of mystery, one that my mother often referred to as being "the place for sinners." So, growing up, I made sure to stay clear of it, or else. Of course, curiosity often got the better of Pohl and me, and we would sometimes sneak peeks in through the windows just to see what all the fuss was about. Seemed pretty boring to us. Just a bunch of men sitting around at tables and such, drinking what looked to be apple juice and playing cards. Uncle Frank and I did that often, without the apple juice, of course. So what was so 'evil' about the saloon? One time, we had all gone into town together, and Frank had ventured off during Mother and my rounds. When we got back to the wagon,

Uncle Frank was nowhere to be found. We waited a few minutes, and then finally, Mother snapped.

"Garit, go on into the saloon and see if Frank is in there."

"The saloon, Mother? You always told me to stay—"

"I know what I said, son, but go on in and see if Frank is there. If so, tell him to come to the wagon right away," Mom snapped impatiently.

"Yes, ma'am," I said as I stepped down from the wagon. Now, I remember this situation pretty well, and I must have been not much over eight years of age. I tried to act brave and be tough, but this request from Mother had me a little shaken, I admit. Mother had put such a foul impression on me about the place that it was almost like I was walking toward the gates of Hades or something. I was nervous, scared, and, quite frankly, hoping that Uncle Frank would turn up all of the sudden from around the corner. Or just come out of another store, almost on cue. As I walked toward the swinging saloon doors, unfortunately, Uncle Frank was nowhere to be seen.

"Thanks, Uncle Frank," I said to myself. I inched up onto the walkway and stopped to take one last big breath before breaching the doors. As I reached out to push open one side of the swinging doors, the other side came barging open and knocked me clean on my tail. Some man came stumbling out. He was holding a large brown bottle. After seeing me sprawled out on the walkway, he started laughing.

"Always gotta watch that first step, sonny!" he yelled and staggered off down the walk.

"Gee willikers, sir," I complained and started to pick myself back up off the ground. I could hear a faint bell going off in my head as if to signify round two. *Ding, ding, ding!*

So, I went forward again and made it about five feet inside the door without any other drama. It was dark inside, even though it was the middle of the day. Smelled like a combination of sweat, cigar smoke, and wet alfalfa. I just could not understand why people would want to be in a place like that. But I was here to find Uncle Frank, so I pinched off my nose with my fingers and started looking around.

I finally noticed him about four tables back, sitting by himself, drinking some apple juice. And as soon as I did, I yelled.

"Uncle Frank, Mother needs you at the wagon—" and I turned, was running and almost out the doors, finishing with "– real fast." I did not want to be in there any longer, as my air was running out. I just kept running back to the wagon and collapsed on the seat next to Mother upon arriving.

"Well, did you find him, son?" she asked.

I couldn't answer. I was still trying to force air into my lungs. Luckily, shortly after the question, Uncle Frank came running up and stopped just short of the horses.

"What's the matter, Anna?" he shouted, half out of breath.

"You know good and well what's the matter, Frank. I have told you to stay out of there, and now you have gone and made us late getting home. And worse yet, I had to send little Garit in there after you. You ought to be ashamed!"

"Oh Anna, I was just getting one drink, I swear, and then coming right back out. No time at all. You have got to learn to lighten up a little!" Uncle Frank barked back. With that, he climbed onto the wagon, took the reins from Mother, and nothing else was said from that point forward. It was a quiet ride home, and there were no games later that night.

As I got to the door of the saloon this time, things seemed different. It certainly was not as imposing as before, size-wise, and it just looked *cleaner* to me. Not in the sense that it was spic and span, as Mother would say. It just seemed less grungy than I remembered. The inside was brighter, and the smell, although heavy in cigar aroma, did not seem so pungent. "Hmmm, not bad," I said to myself. There weren't too many people inside, so I walked over to a gentleman behind a large expanse of walnut with glasses lined up in a row and asked him if Mr. Stallsburg was around. He just motioned with his head to the left as his hands were busy wiping another glass.

As I looked that way, I could see Mr. Stallsburg through a door leading to the back of the building. It looked like he was unloading the supplies from the general store. I went ahead and started walking toward the door, and he looked up and noticed me after setting down a large box.

"Garit!" he said, welcoming and waving me back. "Or should I say Mr. Hotzmire?" he said, winking as he came forward to shake my hand. "You saved me a lot of money today. For that, you have earned the respect of being called by 'Mr.' in my book."

"Oh, it was nothing, sir; just trying to help," I said shyly.

"Nothing? I think not, my boy. You have a mind for numbers, and that is a rare thing to have in this world. I always knew you were smart, the way your mother bragged about you, but son, you're more than smart; you have a gift."

"I don't know, sir. I just like numbers, I guess," I replied.

"And I think the numbers like you, too," he said quickly back.

"Garit…um, Mr. Hotzmire, I have a proposition for you, if I may," he said. And with that, he grabbed his coat from the hall tree and motioned for me to walk toward another small room off the hall.

As we entered the room, I could see that it was a simply appointed office with a desk, three chairs, and a chess table set up in the corner. What really stood out was the artwork of all sorts hanging on the wall in large gold frames. It wasn't a large room, but it had this air about it due to the artwork. I had never seen pictures like that before. Large and full of color.

"Garit, have a seat." Mr. Stallsburg made his way around the desk to his chair and sat down. As I came to rest, he said, "Now, before my proposition, how did you fair with Mr. Dobbs?" he asked excitedly, yet almost like he already knew the answer.

"Well, sir, he offered me a position auditing his ledger each day. To make sure the numbers all add up and no mistakes were made."

"Well, that seems like a fine job for a man of your talents. Did you accept?" he asked.

"Yes, sir," I responded. "It's only for an hour or two each day, so I am sure Mother will approve. I can work it in around my chores."

"Oh yes, that seems like a fine arrangement, and I share the opinion that your mother will be thrilled to see you gain such employment. And may I inquire about the wage he will be paying you—or would that be too forward of me?" he asked politely.

"Absolutely," I assured him. "He offered me ten cents per day."

"And?" he urged.

"And I negotiated him up to fifteen cents per day." At that, Mr. Stallsburg jumped to his feet and clapped his hands together.

"That's it, that's it!," he shouted. "I knew it. I could see it in you!"

"See what?" I asked, startled.

"You have got the lightning, my son! The spark, the juice, the *je ne sais quoi!*"

"The what?" I asked, confused, as he sat back down in his chair.

"The instinct and ingredients to be something special, Garit. I can't believe I never noticed it in you before. That was my fault. I guess I just wasn't paying enough attention. How old are you, son? Fourteen – fifteen?"

"Fourteen going on fifteen this upcoming January, sir," I responded.

"Nice. That is perfect."

And with that, he leaned back into his chair with his two index fingers pressed up to his chin in the form of a triangle. He looked to be contemplating a big decision. I just sat there. This last hour or so had been a whirlwind, and I hadn't even got a chance to tell Mother or anyone about it yet. Well, I suppose I had just told Mr. Stallsburg about the job with Mr. Dobbs, but he really didn't count. What was so interesting about my last thought was that little did I know how important Mr. Stallsburg was going to be in my life. That day was the day my path in life took a hard right, and went on a journey

that even the map could not course…. right off the edge.

A couple of months had gone by, and things were really going well. The job at Dobbs' General Store was perfect for me. I was really starting to make a name for myself around town. In just a few weeks, I had found several discrepancies in the ledger.

It was both good and bad. From Mr. Dobb's point of view, I caught miscalculations that had saved him from losing money on several transactions. Not only from his customers' bills but from his suppliers overcharging him. I had saved him close to seventy-two dollars in my short time of employment. He and Mrs. Dobbs were thrilled!

On the bad side, I also found several bills that were incorrect, in benefit to our customers. Not a huge amount of money, but it totaled close to twenty-four dollars of overcharges. This was a point of embarrassment for Mr. or Mrs. Dobbs (depending on who wrote up the ticket), but I was very thankful that they stood by their word and made sure to refund anyone that had been mischarged.

On the other hand, they wanted me to present any undercharges to the customers and collect on their behalf. And you can imagine what someone would say when a scrawny bill collector like me showed up on their doorstep a day or two after their visit to the store, asking for more money. It was not a fun part of the job. However, I did my best to explain the situation and show them step-by-step the inaccuracies of the ticket. Nine times out of ten, they agreed and would cough up the difference. I just tried to put myself in their shoes and treat them with respect throughout the entire process. Some could not pay right then and there, so I made sure that they could pay it out over time directly to the store.

Mr. Dobbs was completely okay with that arrangement, but Mrs. Dobbs, I could tell, was not. She did not like giving credit to anyone but the elite in town. She always said, "you cannot trust anyone that does not come from money."

To be frank, I actually found the truth to be the opposite. For, you see, the other job that I had, and have managed to keep from you so far, was in Mr. Stallsburg's saloon. And before I go too much further, my mother only knew about one of these jobs in specifics. They technically were the same type of job; in fact, I could probably have argued that they were *exactly* the same job. They just served two different sets of clientele. Both were heavy on using my arithmetic skills, both were dealing with products and sales, and both were legal exchanges of currency for life's staples. Now, one job involved food, cooking ingredients/utensils, or clothing. The other involved refreshments, entertainment, and the occasional review of an outstanding gambling debt. See, so similar that I can hardly tell them apart!

And this is where Mrs. Dobbs was not at all correct regarding the giving of credit to different socioeconomic classes. I can tell you from complete authority that the most distinguished and elevated of the elite, or "from money," as she would put it, were quite often the ones that were significantly in debt from gambling or bar tabs at the saloon. Oh, what a different world we see from behind the curtain. And I had a front-row seat to it all.

Chapter 6

From my mother's point of view, I was going into town each day for my general store position with plenty of time left to finish my daily chores and be home for other needs and conversations.

It really was the best job ever, and she was happy that I was back to my shoot-out-of-bed-each-morning self. And as the one or two hours at the saloon turned into three or four due to additional duties, I just explained that Mr. Dobbs needed me to handle some more collections or refunds, and that took a lot of time. From the way I made it out, Mother often joked that Mr. and Mrs. Dobbs should start spending some time with Ms. Thompson in the schoolhouse to brush up on their math skills.

"They sure get a lot of tickets wrong," she always said. But on the other hand, she was glad it kept me gainfully employed. And by the way, the money was not bad either. Since I was able to keep my other job a secret, sharing my fifteen-cent salary with Mother was much easier. Giving her a portion of my money really helped her and Uncle Frank on the farm. But it didn't really put a dent in my actual earnings.

Mr. Stallsburg paid me commission for every penny I saved or found. Thirty percent on every dollar, in fact. So, if I found out that the house funds from the blackjack table were five dollars short each morning, I made a dollar fifty. Huge, for an hour or so of work each day.

Monday through Thursday, the tallies were fairly light, and the audit did not take very long at all. Friday and Saturday's take were large and getting larger each week. That would typically take me a few more hours to work through. Again, from Mother's point of view, collections for the general store were just high on Friday and Saturday. It made sense. Those were generally the busiest days anyway. So, I had a good cover, as you might say.

To round back to my income, I had gotten so good at doing my job that Mr. Dobbs gave me a nickel raise less than five weeks into the job. I was making, on average, one to two dollars a day from the saloon. And the townsfolk started to only trust my tickets from the general store. When I wrote them up, they were solid and accurate. I was starting to build a reputation for fairness, accuracy, and, from one particularly special person to me, for having some good gossip on most of the townsfolk. You guessed it, B.

B came back into my life suddenly and out of the blue. I had really kind of moved on from my eternal longing for her, mainly due to absence. The saying "absence makes the heart grow fonder" was the reverse for me. Between not seeing her every day, and being involved in what I found to be a very exciting and fulfilling job (or should I say jobs), really allowed me to move on. Of course, I still loved B in a very infatuated, immature way. But not seeing her just allowed me to drift away from her. I knew she would never approve of me being her suitor, and to be fair, I knew that from the beginning. I just didn't have anything better to occupy me at the time. B was my world, and when that world took an intermission, other things became my B.

I had just finished my daily tallies at the general store one afternoon and was returning home. You see, I had asked Mr. Dobbs if I could come in a little later each day because my mother needed me to handle more chores in the morning than before. I typically would get to the store around 8:30 am each day. They did not open until 9:30, so I had a good hour to get my work done before the customers started showing up.

Well, since Mr. Stallsburg was typically waiting on me to audit the take each morning before going to the bank, I thought switching my jobs around each day made sense. I would get to the saloon by 8:00 am each day and be at the store by 9:30 am or 10 am at the latest. Again, Mr. Dobbs thought I was doing chores. My mother thought I was helping Mr. Dobbs, and neither was the wiser. No issues there, right? Besides, Mr. Stallsburg liked me getting there earlier so that I could finish and he could get to the bank quicker, and I liked that I was in and out of the saloon before most people were mulling around or coming into town. Less chance of being seen and having someone mention it to my mother. If that ever happened, I was going to have to do some quick dancing, if you know what I mean.

But back to B. I came out of the general store looking down at a ticket I was supposed to be dropping off on my way home. The customer was on my way out of town. Mrs. Dobbs had forgotten to give him the 10-penny nails that had been delivered the day before. Delivery Boy had been unceremoniously added to my work title. It kind of seemed like I had been given every job in the store by now, yet I had not received more than the nickel raise and certainly no more time to do it. But I digress. Since I was looking down at the ticket and package of material, I ran smack dab into B as she was walking by. At first, I did not even recognize that it was B. My mind was too preoccupied with all the other numbers I had been looking at that day,

I guess.

"Oh, I am so sorry, ma'am. Forgive my clumsiness," I blurted out without thinking or even looking at the person I had run into.

"Why, Garit Hotzmire! I am no ma'am to you!" she said, irritated. I realized it was B and almost fell down, trying to gain my composure. How in the world could I have mistaken her for some ordinary lady walking down the walkway? I was both embarrassed by what I had said and also that I hadn't recognized the one person in this world I should have known in complete darkness.

"Oh, my goodness, I am soooooo sorry. I just didn't see you. The sun was in my eyes." I tried to salvage the moment.

"Garit, you big dodo, it's overcast, and the sun is nowhere to be seen. Try again, you silly kid."

I took that statement to be more than it seemed. She had not just made a quick and easy statement. She noticed what I had said, really noticed, and came back with an intelligent and accurate response. The sun *was* nowhere to be seen—it looked like rain—but, more importantly, she paid attention to me. She called me "silly kid." I immediately saw that as a win and even some insight into her feelings toward me.

I know, I know you're saying to yourself, "son, you are really grasping at straws here," but I'm serious about this. For most of my life, because of my size and physical oddities, no one really paid attention to me. I could be quoting Shakespeare or yelling "Fire!" and no one seemed to care what this odd little fella was saying. I had grown accustomed to it over the years. So the fact that she actually heard me say what I said was a big deal. Second, she called me a silly kid. Not something she would say to a stranger, or a term she would say to the mayor, had he bumped into her. But something that almost implied endearment. Or a connection—with me and me alone.

In the simple words of that reply, I sensed that she missed my nagging infatuation with her, and she did not just think of me as a passing classmate. I was something better or closer than that. But then again, maybe I was just tired and making it much more than it was. Because, in an instant, B showed me that she was the same old B.

"Garit, you need to watch where you're going, young man. You could have ruined my new dress—or worse, my new hat—had you knocked me down."

So, I went from silly kid to young man?

"Wait a minute, *young lady*," I shot back. "We are the same age for crying out loud!" And with that, we both broke into laughter. I was right, something was different this time, and boy, was I in for a surprise.

Chapter 7

The local hotel was not the most lavish of places, from what I had heard. To me, it was a palace. As B and I sat in the lobby enjoying our tea, it was hard to not keep looking around at how nice everything was. I had never been inside before. I had only heard about it from customers in the general store picking up some "coming into town" or "leaving town" supplies. Some were just passing through, and others had stayed at the hotel and so had firsthand knowledge. Most said that it was decent compared to others they had stayed in, but to me, as I looked around, it was downright fancy. That being said, the real beauty sat across from me, stirring her tea and attempting to make small talk about me and my life.

"So, how have you been since graduation? It seems like eons ago, doesn't it?" she asked with a far-off look in her eyes and a smile.

"Oh, fine, I guess. I really haven't thought about the time going by. It's been almost two years, hasn't it?" I was just trying to sound calm.

"Wow, it just seems so long ago," she said softly.

"Well, it is almost thirteen percent of our lives," I said without hesitation.

"Thirteen percent of what?"

"Two years is a little over thirteen of our lives, being that we are almost fifteen years old. Of all the years we have been alive, we were in school nine years of it, or right at sixty percent, of our entire lives." Again, I spoke very quickly and without emotion.

"What on earth are you talkin' about, Garit?" she said, puzzled. "Oh, I see what you mean now, and I should have known, coming from the smartest kid in school! We are not in math class anymore, Mr. Hotzmire, remember."

"Oh, I'm sorry, Beatrice, just a habit of mine. I like numbers and am constantly doing figures in my head about the dumbest things—like percentages of years in school and such. Sorry."

"No need to be sorry. And what is this Beatrice stuff about? You always called me B," she said, almost sounding disappointed that I hadn't. And again, this was the smallest detail, but it just tugged on me in that split second.

"She likes it when I call her B?" I said to myself. And with that, I started to get very warm inside.

"Oh, sorry, Beatri….B!" I caught myself this time.

"Again, no need to be sorry. I sure have missed you, silly kid," she said with a wink and a swat to my hand as it lay on the table in front of us.

Right as I was about to respond to this show of fun, B's mother came storming into the lobby and marched right up to our table.

"Beatrice Grace, where have you been? I have been looking all over town for you! You just vanished while I was in the hat shop!" she said in a loud but controlled voice. There were others in the lobby, and she wanted to sound mad but not cause a scene at the same time.

"Oh, Mother, I am so sorry. I ran into an old classmate of mine, or I should say, he ran into me." She turned to me and smiled. "And I just got caught up in the moment. I have

not seen him for thirteen percent of our lives, and just had to sit down to chat."

"Thirteen percent of your lives? What on earth are you talking about, Beatrice?" she said very confusedly.

Both B and I just looked at each other and started laughing. It seemed that she wanted to make this our inside joke. I had never had an inside joke like this before—except for the "We better get to painting the mules. Africa needs more zebras" joke from years past. And that was just between the fellas and old Mr. Boyer. This was an inside joke, and it was with a girl. It felt much more special. Oh, how little did I know how special it would become. We parted ways as B left with her mother, and I watched my angel glide down the walkway and into the distance. "Boy, she sure is something," I said to myself.

"Garit, you have a letter!" Mrs. Dobbs yelled from the backroom one morning as I was stocking the shelves with Colgate soap. As I carefully stacked each bar on top of the other the way Mr. Dobbs liked it, I was a little put out at the fact that by noon, all these bars would be gone, and without a doubt, someone would knock my stacks over at some point. Soap was a hot commodity around there. It only came into the store every three weeks or so. I always tried to convince Mr. Dobbs that just putting them in a tub by the front counter would be a lot easier, but he insisted that they be stacked, nice and straight. He once mentioned that a well-executed display increased sales by twenty percent. Okay, but they were all going to be sold out by noon anyway, so I was not sure how much increasing sales by twenty percent would help the situation. Would they all be sold out by 11:00 am instead? Oh well, he was the boss, so soap stackin' it was.

I finished up with my final row and went back to see what letter Mrs. Dobbs was referring to. It was probably from Aunt Sarah, Mother's sister who lived in Pennsylvania. She wrote quite often. But, as Mrs. Dobbs handed me the letter, I was surprised to see that it, in fact, was addressed to me. I had never received a letter before, so this was quite an event. I just stood there looking at it in wonder.

"Who could it be from?" I asked myself out loud, almost dismissing the idea that Mrs. Dobbs was still right beside me, seated at her desk.

"Well, open it up, Garit, and you will find out forthwith," she quipped. Her statement had a heavy helping of "What are you, a dummy?" along with a touch of sarcasm. She was very good at adding those sentiments to most of her daily statements, except for with the more well-off customers, of course. She always catered to them and never gave the slightest hint of her snarky way.

"Oh, you bet, Mrs. Dobbs. Thank you for giving it to me." I turned to head out the front of the store to open this mysterious new arrival. Out front, I sat on the bench a little away from the front door and windows. I wanted to be left alone while I discovered who had taken the time to write to me. This was a special occasion, I had to give it due reverence.

As I pulled the letter out, I caught the faint whiff of perfume coming from the pages of paper. Caswell & Hazards' White Rose, to be exact. I could tell that scent anywhere, as the store was lucky enough to get some in once in a while. Mrs. Dobbs made sure that everyone in the vicinity got to sample the "divine aroma," as she would call it. Of course, no opening the bottle and dabbing any actual perfume on your skin; we were just given the box it came in to smell and enjoy. And it was expensive, but each time we received a case, it was gone in a heartbeat. Mrs. Dobbs would wear the scent, "but only on special occasions," she would say to the customers inquiring about the special concoction. I had a feeling, though, that she had a stash of the stuff somewhere in her house. The bill of lading and ledger never matched when I completed my audits on that specific item. There always seemed to be one bottle missing, if you know what I mean. When I brought this finding to her attention, she just dismissed it.

"You know how fine artisans are absent-minded when doing the numbers. They must have just forgotten the extra bottle," she said as if this was a normal and acceptable business practice of the "elite fine artisans" she ordered from.

"Indeed, with such talent, how could you also expect them to know how to count?" I often said back in my mind when these discrepancies occurred.

But, with the scent hitting my nose, I immediately thought back to the day I ran into B. After her mother had found us, and after I got a proper dressing down for "abducting my daughter" from B's mother, she proceeded to tell B with great excitement that she had finally gotten her hands on a bottle of White Rose. Upon hearing these words B literally leaped off the seat and hugged her mother heartily.

"Oh, Mother, that is absolutely divine! I can't wait to wear it," she said, excited.

"Oh no, my dear, only on special occasions. But here, smell the box first," she said as if Mrs. Dobbs herself were standing in front of us. Emmy, the negro hotel cook, was cleaning a table nearby. B's mother noticed that she was very curious about this rare item in our hands. "Only the worthy can smell it," I could hear B's mother saying in her mind to Emmy. And she shifted slightly away from her direction, so Emmy could not see it anymore. After B took in the lovely bouquet, B motioned for me to take a turn. I just shook her off and said, "I have smelled it before. I'm good." B seemed impressed.

"Oh, a man of culture, I see," she said while poking me in the ribs. I just shrugged my shoulders and smiled.

I unfolded the papers inside the envelope. To say that I was excited to read the contents would be an understatement. As I mentioned, this was the first letter I had ever received. I mean, addressed to me. I had read letters before, of course. But they were just always somebody else's letters. I was a secondhand reader, you could say. This was my letter, and it made me feel very special. And the fact that I thought it was from B just pushed me over the top. What in the world would she be writing to me for? Could I have gone from the annoying peripheral of a classmate to getting firsthand correspondence from an angel? *I must be dreaming*, I thought. As I carefully read the letter, I felt as if I were floating above the bench. Each line unveiled her innermost thoughts and aspirations. All I could keep thinking was, *Why in the world did she write me?* over and over again. But as I continued reading and reached the end, it started to make more sense. It was not a love letter or anything of the sort. It was just a simple request for friendship and communication. But as I recollect now, it contained some slight clues of a possible deeper meaning.

Dear Garit,

I would first like to say I hope you are still not worried about running into me a few weeks ago. No bruising ever developed, and my clothing was not torn or disheveled in any way. I am just teasing you, of course. Second, I just wanted to write and tell you that I enjoyed getting caught up with you and talking about the "old days." Since our meeting, I have been wondering if you would not mind writing me and having me writing to you occasionally so that I can stay up on all of Christiansburg's happenings. I don't get into town very often, and hearing about all the people, excitement, and events you seem to know firsthand was such a nice surprise. I hope this letter finds you well, and I will see you around, kid.

Sincerely, Your B.

As I finished reading the letter, I let it rest on my knee and looked off into the distance toward B's house. She lived about five miles outside of town. A fairly good-sized farm that she and her fairly good-sized family grew corn and raised cattle on. Three older brothers, one older sister, and two younger sisters made up the youngest of the Hahne clan. Her father, mother, and grandmother made up the rest. Being an only child and in a house of only two others, this number of people on one farm seemed like something I would not be fond of. All the coming and going, chitter-chatter, and just rigor of cramming that many people into one house seemed, frankly, appalling to me. I was suddenly grateful for my small three-person family. Even though it meant more chores for each of us, I was okay with that trade-off.

My attention went quickly back to B's letter. I read it probably 10 more times, over and over again. This was fantastic! Not only does she know I exist, but she is also inviting me into her circle of friends, wanting continued correspondence, and ending it with, "Your B." What! "Your B?"

"What does that mean?" I said, looking around like I wanted someone to hear my unspoken words and give their words of wisdom back to me. I was absolutely flummoxed by these last two words. "Your B?" I said out loud.

Just then, Mr. Dobbs came out of the store.

"There you are, Garit. I have been looking all over for you. Are you through with the ledger yet?" he asked.

I didn't answer.

"Garit, are you through with the ledger, son?" He walked toward me. "Son, are you okay?"

All I could do was look at him, clutching B's letter. As he got closer, he stuck his hand down near my face and snapped loudly. This sudden noise brought me back from another world in an instant. I looked up at him in what I am sure was a very confused manner.

"Son, is everything okay?" he repeated.

"Oh, yes, Mr. Dobbs. Sorry, I was just thinking."

"Well, whatever you are thinking about must be a very serious subject to be worth all that contemplation. I am not sure where you were, son, in your mind, I mean," he said, almost in a worried tone.

"Oh yes, I was just somewhere that I have always wanted to be," I said with a smile. *Somewhere that I could never have imagined I would actually get to*, I thought. With my B.

Several more letters crossed paths over the next year, and I was always waiting with almost uncontainable excitement for the next one to arrive. Of course, I would see B in person every once in a while if she was in town. But my jobs had started to get so busy that I was usually head-down in a ledger for most of the day. The general store's ledger was not the offender. That took the normal amount of time each day.

The saloon, on the other hand, was a growing monster that seemed to never be full of my number crunching. Mr. Stallsburg had increased my audit duties to include every aspect of the saloon. The bar, card games, faro, entertainment, meals, and the new brewhouse that Mr. Stallsburg built right next door.

To get more patrons in the door and, more importantly, to get them to drink, we served pickled eggs, oysters and celery, cured ham, and assorted cheeses. I had a special fondness for oysters, not so much for celery. We would give free access to any one of these plates with a minimum purchase of two drinks. Shots, steins, or fancy drinks, it did not matter. Two drinks and you ate free. Not too bad of a deal, in my opinion. And, of course, I oversaw inventory, checked all deliveries and orders, and tried to keep an eye on if the two-drink minimum was met.

Dub, the Barkeeper, had a share of the profits, so he really did not have a motive to give away food to those who only had one, or worse, no drinks. His support staff, on the other hand, I had to watch like a hawk. They would use their position to afford sweethearts, brothers, and friends special benefits all the time. Thankfully Dub helped keep tabs on this. But I also had to watch the games, book and pay for the entertainment and keep track of the brewery inventory. All of this kept me several hours into the afternoon each day. It got to the point that showing up in the morning before going to the general store was simply not realistic any more. Once I was in the saloon and working away, I just could not get away to get to the store.

I kept showing up later and later at the store and was running out of excuses. I almost wanted Mr. Dobbs to ask my mother about all the "chores" I must be doing each morning so that I could just fess up to all this mess. I was getting tired but was getting more tired of lying to Mr. Dobbs and, most of all, lying to Mother. I was growing bored of the store duties, same old same old. But I kept telling myself that if I just loved the process, everything would be okay.

It wasn't okay. I was now almost a year into these jobs, and I was starting to dread going to the general store. The saloon was my muse. Yes, the work was hard, but I loved every bit of the excitement surrounding me each day. I was able to see new and upcoming acts sing, dance, or play music several times per week. I had become an expert at gambling. I enjoyed it so much that I started coming back into town during the evenings to play a little myself (off the books, of course).

A side bonus was if I was ordering drinks (just fancy, nonalcoholic, of course), the food was free. Free food that I was responsible for ordering each week. So if I got tired of one thing, I would just set up a new order and menu to fit my fancy. The patrons liked the variety and change as well. Now, there was one side that I never was allowed to partake in. That was drink. I did start to notice more and more that Mr. Stallsburg was growing ever so nervous about my employment situation making its way back to Mother. If it ever did, I knew he at least wanted to have some sort of defense. "I never let him drink alcohol, not one drop, I promise." I could see him in my mind, swearing to my mother if she ever found out.

Now, Mr. Stallsburg and I never made a pact or even really talked about the fact that we would not tell my mother. It was just kind of an unspoken rule. Both of us knew the wrath that she could unleash. Or at least, we could imagine the wrath.

Although most people thought Mother was stern, chiseled, and straight as hard oak, I really can't say that I ever saw her lose her temper or come undone with anger. Yes, she would get upset with Uncle Frank, but that was just their way. Normally, Mother was just a very polite and respectful person. Don't get me wrong, she was stubborn as the day was long, but she always held herself with dignity.

I wouldn't add grace to that statement. She was not graceful. It was more like she was intentional when she moved. If she was walking to the barn, she just went straight there and did not meander around the puddles or paddies on the ground. Straight there and straight back. But I always kind of thought that it was graceful in its own right. Just not the admired type of gracefulness.

So, here I was, growing weary of the general store, working more hours than ever at the saloon, and on the brink of everything crashing down if Mother ever found out. And that was surely any day now. The one thing that made it better was the letters from B. If I said I was in love with her before, now it seemed I was hopelessly in love with her. At times, I was even sick about it. But sick in a good way, of course. And I know the difference, trust me.

Sunday was a good day for me, as it was the only day I did not have to go into town for the store or saloon. I still had to get up to attend church with Mother. Uncle Frank rarely went these days but riding into town with Mother was always a good thing. We did not talk much, but when we did, it was usually because Mother had asked me about how my job was going, how my friends were doing, or very general questions like "Are you happy with your life, Garit?"

"Uhhh yeah, I guess," I would answer back carelessly.

"You mean YES, not yeah, young man!"

"Yes, ma'am," I would respond.

But these little conversations made me feel good because she wanted to know about me. She loved to hear about my life, and, in a way, I felt my life was an extension of hers. She did not vary too much from her daily life on the farm. Chores, cooking, cleaning, cooking, chores, cooking, cleaning, repeat. Every day was the same, and every day she just did it. No complaining. No drama. Just did it and did it to her high standard. Thinking back, that's why Sundays, specifically our ride into church, were so pleasant. It was the one day that most of the regular duties were put on hold. She got to get dressed up more than usual and had time to think about me, God, and (I hope) herself. I guess we had that in common. Sundays were good for us both.

As we rounded the corner one Sunday, coming up to the church, I felt a deep pain in my chest, and it started to grow. I rubbed at it, I coughed a little without bringing too much attention to myself, but nothing seemed to dissipate the pain. Finally, Mother noticed and asked if I was okay.

"Is it your lungs again, Garit?"

I have had several bouts of pneumonia throughout my life and was almost an expert on that feeling of breathing but just not finding the air, so my answer was easy.

"No, my chest just kind of hurts a little, Mother. It will be okay, though, don't worry." That was hard for my mother, as she has been worrying about my health since the second I was born prematurely.

Before I was born, to be more accurate. First, the doctor said I wouldn't make it past the hour. Then he said I wouldn't make it through the night. After which, he said I wouldn't make it to Sunday. I imagine that poor guy did not know what hit him when he came back out that Sunday to check on me. He left that day and began again: "Mrs. Hotzmire, I am afraid your boy won't make it past"...*slam!* The door was shut in his face. He took the hint and never returned. My mother had had enough of these prognostications from what she later described as "that hack doctor."

She was determined to see me through whatever ailed me or setbacks might come, as she had every time so far. She pulled the wagon off to the side of the road and stopped.

"Garit, tell me what you are feeling," she said with a stern but worried tone.

"I don't know, Mother, just some pain around my heart." It wasn't a lot of pain. It just felt like a burning, something deep inside. I had not told her before, but I had been getting this feeling for several weeks now, off and on. Nothing bad, just an uncomfortable feeling that seemed to get worse when I ate or laid down at night. She asked me to undo the top two buttons of my shirt and started to examine me right there on the side of the path. She did not care who saw, but I sure did.

"Mother!" I resisted and pulled back.

"Not right here. The church is right over there; people will stare."

She looked me in the eyes.

"All right, but right after church we are going home, and you have to promise to let me look at you."

"I promise," I said reluctantly but also in agreement. I was starting to get a little worried as to what it could be.

As we returned from Church, I could see that Uncle Frank was up and sitting on the porch. He usually slept in on Sundays a little. Typically, his night before was full of drink and more drink.

"Top of the mornin' to ya," he yelled out to our approaching wagon.

"More like the bottom of the mornin' back at ya," I yelled back. He always laughed at my stupid jokes. He had the same sense of humor that I did, and that made it fun around our farm. Mother brought the wagon to a stop at the front of the house. That made Frank look at her funny right away.

"Anna, why you stopping here and not over by the barn?" he asked.

Mother did not respond to his question, just proceeded to get down from the wagon.

"Garit, now let's get inside and get on with it."

"Get on with what?" Uncle Frank asked in a very confused tone. She again did not answer and just went in the front door straight away.

"Garit, what's going on?" he said with the hope that at least I would answer.

"Oh, nothing Frank, my chest just hurts a little. It's no big deal," I said, walking past him and into the house.

"Okay, little buddy, I'll put the horses and wagon up, don't you worry," he said, shuffling off the porch with haste and down to the horses.

Frank never moved fast, so when he did, it showed me he was worried. Mom was right inside the door. She had already removed her bonnet and overcoat and was hanging them up in a quick routine.

"Garit, take your shirt off and go sit by the fire," she said, moving over to get her medical bag from the cupboard. This exact scene had played out more times than I care to remember growing up, so I knew the drill pretty well. Shirt off, back straight, and deep breaths in through the nose and out by the mouth. I was already into my third set of deep breaths by the time she came back over and knelt by the chair, listening horn up to her ear, pressing it against my chest. As I took more slow breaths in and out, she continued to listen intently. Finally, she took down the horn.

"Well," she said softly, "I don't hear any crackling, and I can't hear any wheezing, so hmmmmm." She seemed puzzled. "Let me hear from your back. Stand up."

We both stood, and she put the horn to the left side of my back and then the right after a few breaths.

"Well, same thing, everything sounds fine. Tell me again exactly where it hurts." She came back around to the front of me so that she could see where I was pointing. I pointed to an area on my chest just under my heart.

"Mother, it's nothing. I wouldn't worry about it." I tried to calm her.

"Well, is it something *you're* worried about?" she asked back.

"Not about..." I said, kind of leaving the end open.

"Garit, what's on your mind? You have seemed a little distant lately. Is everything okay?" she asked in a motherly tone, pushing my hair back behind my left ear. All I could do was look down. I wanted to tell her so badly about the saloon, about the general store, the gambling, everything. Mostly I wanted to stop lying. I felt the pain in my chest rising again and had to sit down.

"Garit, now I mean it, what is going on? I promise you can tell me anything," she pleaded. She could see that I was in pain but more so in my spirit than physical. Mothers just know that somehow. I sat there for a few seconds looking at the fire that was smoldering from when we started it this morning.

I had always felt that a good fire was one of the most peaceful and calming things there was. I could sit and just look at it for hours, although I hadn't been staring into fireplaces lately. Just entirely too busy. I really missed that. Here I was, barely fifteen years of age and already burnt out and ready for retirement! But I don't think it was really the jobs that had burnt me out. It was the fire of lying that finally burnt my heart. Maybe this pain in my chest was God's way of telling me, 'Son, it's time.'

Just as I summoned up enough courage to talk to Mother about everything, Uncle Frank came through the front door and interrupted my confession.

"Anna, everything ok? What's going on?" he said as he looked at my shirtless silhouette in front of the fire. I turned away and started poking the embers with a stick, trying to bring it back to life. I needed it desperately right now.

"I think he's okay, just had a pain in his chest. Everything sounds okay, so I don't think it's pneumonia," she said quietly.

"Well, that's good, I guess? Garit, you okay, son?" he inquired directly.

I responded without turning from the fire.

"I think so, Uncle Frank, just hurts a little." Uncle Frank made his way over to me.

"Show me exactly where, son."

I showed him.

"I have that same pain," he said. "Must mean we're related." He chuckled.

Mother looked over at him and pursed her lips as if she was thinking about something.

"Yep, I get it anytime I eat, lay down, or am worried about something," he said aloud for both of us to hear. "Doc said it was indigestion or possibly an ulcerated stomach. He gave me some nasty tastin' stuff to drink every time I got it. It helps a little, want some?" he asked, looking to Mother for approval. I also looked back at Mother at the same time. I have her a look that said I was willing to try it if she was. Mother looked at me, then Frank, then me again.

"Can't hurt, I suppose," she said, and Uncle Frank jumped right up toward his room to fetch the medicine. I heard him moving things around and searching for it. I took my chance.

"Mother, we do need to talk. But let me try the medicine first, okay?"

She just closed her eyes slowly and nodded her head. Uncle Frank busted the silence.

"Found it!" he yelled from his room. He hurried back out to me and thrust it in my hand.

He was excited because this was a rare time he knew something about something more than I did. He was never formally educated, so I naturally just had more knowledge about such things. Now, when it came to poker, chores, farming, or around-the-house type things, he was by far the expert. Or at least lately, as I was letting him feel like he knew more about poker. Trust me, I could see his hand coming a mile away with all the practice I had been getting at the saloon. It just did not seem right to pummel him. He so enjoyed having something one up on me. Why not let the man have his joy?

"Now, Garit, you have to take just one large spoonful, no more, no less. I've gotten to the point that I kinda just take a swig of it, but I know what I am doing. You're a greenhorn; gotta take it as Doc ordered." He hurried over to the kitchen and grabbed a medium-sized wooden spoon from the jar. "Here you go, my boy, just the right size. You ready?" he looked at me, eager to set me all up.

"I suppose, Uncle Frank. Does it taste bad?" I asked sheepishly.

"Well, yes and no. Yes, when you first swallow it but then after, it just tastes like flour or something. Not good but tolerable, I guess,"

As he finished the description, he jumped back toward the kitchen, yelling as he went.

"Wait, Wait, Wait…when I first started taking it, I always chased it with some milk. Seems to help the taste and make it go down easier. I'll get you some."

As he poured some milk into a glass for me, I started to pour the concoction into the spoon. It was a thick, white syrup, and just by the way it came out of the bottle, I could tell this was not going to be good. Frank came quickly back, holding the glass of milk.

"Ok, you ready?"

"Yep," I said. His excitement was wearing a little bit off on me. I had not seen him this lively in a while. Knowing this subject over me really made him perk up.

"Ok, down the hatch then!" he smiled. I looked at Mother. She nodded approval, and down it went.

"Ugggghhh, milk, hurry, milk…" I reached for the glass Frank was holding. I spilled a little of it on my face as I forced it up to my lips. I couldn't drink it fast enough, and as I did, I truly felt that it was not helping a bit, but just kept drinking until the glass was dry.

"Well, what do you think, did the milk help?" Frank asked like a five-year-old child. I brought my arm up to wipe my mouth and chin.

"That was horrible! Mother, I need some more milk!" She hurried the bottle over to me. I grabbed it out of her hands and did not even bother pouring it in the glass. Drank it straight out of the bottle.

"Garit!" Mother said, shocked. I did not care; I had to do something to make the taste go away. By this time, Uncle Frank was laughing so hard he was almost bent over. He absolutely loved the agony I was in. I guess he knew what it was like so much that he was happy it was happening to someone else.

After chugging most of the bottle of milk down, I finally pulled it away from my mouth to take a breath. As I did, the image of Uncle Frank laughing started to make me laugh, and as I started, so did Mother. By the time it was done, we were all almost falling down with laughter. Frank actually did fall down when I said, "I guess we are milk brothers now," while holding up the almost empty bottle of milk. For, you see, we had become blood brothers several years before. I had cut myself on some wire, and he immediately came over to make sure I was all right.

Upon seeing the blood, he looked thoughtful.

"Garit, there is something I've been wanting to do for a while now," he said. I just looked up at him, trying not to cry from the cut, and nodded. "Well," he went on, "you know that we are not blood relation, even though I know we both feel that way. I say we make it official, right here and now," he said, hopeful, looking into my eyes.

"Well, how do we do that, Uncle Frank?"

He immediately took his hand and cut it on the same wire I had.

"By making us blood brothers," he said, now very serious. "By shaking hands and mixing our blood, we will be brothers for life and will never leave the other in a pickle....no matter what!"

Between you and me, I thought this was pretty gross, but Uncle Frank was very serious about it, so I just shook my head, grabbed his hand, and the rest is history. That is why when I said the "Milk Brothers" comment, Uncle Frank grabbed his stomach, then the chair, and almost fell on the ground laughing. I was always good with timing for a joke.

A few hours later, Mother came and checked on me as I sat next to the fire. By now, I had gotten it going again and had been sitting there almost in a trance for some time.

"Garit, you feeling better now?" she said softly.

"Yes, Mother, I actually am. I guess Uncle Frank's medicine helped me," I said calmly.

"I think you taking some time by the fire helped also. You don't do that much anymore," Mother said in a knowing way.

"Yes, life has gotten pretty busy, hasn't it?" I said, without looking away from the fire.

"It tends to do that as you grow up. Want to talk about it now?" she asked hopefully.

Just then, Uncle Frank came out of his room and walked right up to me, stooped over, and looked me in the eye.

"You good, boy? Did Uncle Frank fix ya?" he said like a proud doctor.

"Yep, you sure did, Uncle Frank." I smiled. I had to muster some exuberance with the answer; he deserved it. I knew he was really happy that he had helped me out and come up with the solution. He was beaming with pride. And it wasn't a lie; I did feel better. What I didn't feel better about was the second half of the treatment fixing to take place: telling Mother the truth. The whole truth. Uncle Frank messed the top of my hair up with his hand.

"Well, you let me know if you need any more of Uncle Frank's doctorin. But I might have to charge you next time for my services," he said with a smirk as he went towards the door. "Now, what did I do with my little black bag?" He pretended to look around for what I assumed was a doctor's bag.

Mother just rolled her eyes. I laughed a little.

"Uncle Frank, you're silly," I said. He really cut himself up with this special display and laughed all the way out the door and out towards the barn. I'm glad someone was happy in the household. I knew there was a better than ninety-nine-point-nine percent chance that Mother would not be very soon.

Chapter 8

It had been about an hour since Mother went to her room crying and slammed the door behind her. I knew that my confession led to her reaction, and I felt like running away. What Mother said to me was fine. What she said to Uncle Frank was not. He did not deserve this. I thought I would wait for Mother to come out of her room before going after him, but I just couldn't.

So, picking up my coat, I headed out the door to the one place I knew he would be. By this time, it was well after dark. Honey, the beautiful golden-brown filly I had received for my fourteenth birthday, knew the track by heart. Straight to the saloon she went.

As I rode, I could not help but start to cry. It was all my fault. Had I just told the truth from the get-go, Mother would not have been shocked by my words tonight. She would not have said what she said to Uncle Frank.

"It's all my fault," I kept saying. And I knew that night, everything I knew and loved would be changing. My life would be thrust into adulthood, and there was no way to stop it. I was not ready. I did not want things to change with Mother and Uncle Frank. But there was no turning back. I had opened the wound, and nothing could heal it.

"It's all my fault."

I found Uncle Frank at a table in the back of the saloon. He had already finished off one bottle of whisky and was working on his second. As I walked toward him, Dub, the barkeep, motioned for me to come see him. I could hear Uncle Frank.

"You're not blood. You'll never be blood," he said loudly. Oh no, this was worse than I thought. As I got to Dub, he leaned forward and spoke low.

"He didn't have enough money for the first bottle, but he said to put it on your tab. It's up to two bottles now. On you."

"Okay, Dub. Thanks. I'll take care of it. But stop him at two, okay?" Dub nodded and went back to cleaning glasses.

That burning feeling was rising in my chest again. I stood at the bar for a few moments, trying to figure out what I was going to say to Uncle Frank. He was very drunk by now and had gone from taking shots by the glass to drinking straight from the bottle. If only I had been strong enough to tell the truth before tonight. This all wouldn't have happened. I took a deep breath in and started toward Uncle Frank. As I reached him, he looked up at me and smiled.

"Garit, my boy, my blood brother, I'm so glad you're here," he said, slurring. "Your mother just doesn't understand, does she? We *are* blood. We *are!*" he said, shouting toward the end of his statement. He stood up and stuck his hand into my face, showing the scar left behind from our blood oath ceremony. I smiled and did the same, showing my scar. He wrapped his arms around my waist and gave me a huge hug, picking me up off my feet.

"Whoa, now, Uncle Frank, you're going to get both of us hurt. Let me down, and let's talk." He released me.

"You and Anna are all I got. You're all I got..." he said sadly. I guided myself down into a chair and pulled the bottle of whisky to my side of the table.

"Uncle Frank, we both love you. I am so sorry this all happened. Mother didn't mean what she said. It was just that she was very mad at me. And took it out on you."

"No, no, no. She's right; we're not real blood. It just hurts," Uncle Frank said, putting his hand up to his face and trying to hide his tears.

"It's not my fault your Pa ran off. And just because I'm his brother, that don't mean nothing. I am not my brother!" he said through his hands.

"Uncle Frank, I know, and she does too. That's not what she meant, I promise. She was just mad about me lying all this time and about the saloon. Or really, about everything. I messed it all up."

"Garit, you're a good boy. A good boy!" Uncle Frank said, trying to get the bottle back from me.

"Oh, no, don't. You've had enough. We gotta get you home. I have the wagon out front. Let's go," I said. I stood up and attempted to help him up, also. Dub saw that I was going to need some help, so was already headed my way. We both got Uncle Frank up and out the door. Instead of setting him on the seat with me, we just laid him down in the back.

As I thanked Dub for the help, I asked him to let Mr. Stallsburg know that I would be in late tomorrow.

"Yep," he said as he walked back into the Saloon. On the way home, I could faintly hear Uncle Frank humming a tune I had not heard before. And every once in a while, he would say, "We are *blood*" out loud as if he was arguing with someone. I was glad that Uncle Frank got so much whisky in him tonight. That might make it better in the morning. He would often wake up not knowing exactly what happened the night before. I prayed he would forget everything, or at least what Mother had said to him. Uncle Frank was just trying to help.

Mother was upset, I was crying, and he came back into the house right at the wrong time.

"Frank, you are not blood. This doesn't concern you!" Mother shouted when he asked what was wrong. She shouldn't have said that. Uncle Frank, blood oath notwithstanding, has been more of a family member to us than my Pa or any other relatives have ever been. Uncle Frank often visited the farm, from what my mother tells me, to see his brother. My Pa. And from how Mother tells it, he did not drink as much back then and had a place of his own. But, after Pa left, he started coming around more and more to help Mother. He told me a few years back that he was ashamed of how his brother left us.

"He should have stayed around to see how great of a son he had," he would often say to me. That always made me feel better.

Pa left because of me. However, Mother would never admit that or let me believe it.

Uncle Frank picked up Pa's slack and has been with us ever since. He is more family to me than anyone but Mother, and for that, I am so grateful. Now, I have hurt the two people in my life that mean the most to me. I have got to get things straight and make it right. Breakfast is going to be a doozy, but no one ever said cleaning up your own mess was easy. Life has never been easy for me; I guess I just got spoiled by how things were going lately. I forgot the reality of my life.

The next morning, I got up early to check on Uncle Frank. I had left him in the wagon inside the barn. There was no way I could even attempt to carry him inside, and he was used to sleeping in the barn anyway. Mother would not let him in the house while drunk. What started as one or two nights a week ended up the other way around lately. The barn was Uncle Frank's primary residence these days.

Luckily, he had stayed in the back of the wagon and still had the horse blankets on him. I did not want to wake him, though, as the more he slept, the better the chance that last night would not be remembered. I said another prayer for that. After checking on him, I ventured back inside and started to pull together breakfast. That was all I could think to do as a sort of peace offering for Mother. Not sure it would even make a difference, but I was willing to try. And who am I kidding? Some biscuits, coffee, bacon, and such won't cure a broken heart. And that's what I had really done. The lying was bad, for sure. The going behind Mother's back was terrible. But taking advantage of Mother's trust and faith in me was the worst thing I could have done. I broke her heart. Now I must do whatever it takes to mend it.

Mother came out a little later than usual this morning. I could see the night on her face. She must not have slept very much, and the fact that her hair was a mess proved she had lost some of her die hard will. Mother would never let her hair—or appearance in general, for that matter—be compromised. Not from a "fussy" or "high class" standpoint, but a clean, well-kept, and civilized manner. It fit her personality to a T. She just did things right. Everything just the right way. With no compromises that would leave others fighting for some sort of dignity. Mother had dignity in spades, and she fought for it in everything she did. Pride. No matter the circumstances, she would just not bend to the will of any force against her. She stood firm, like the tallest oak tree in the county. Well, this morning I could see she was bending a little. And boy, that did hurt me so. When she realized that I had attempted to make breakfast, she took a deep breath.

"Thank you, son," she said, with a glazed look in her eyes.

That was it. No praise. No surprise. Just a simple thank you. We both sat at the table and ate without speaking a word. Although neither of us had much of an appetite, she tried to eat for me, and I ate just because I did not know what else to do. A ways into breakfast, she finally spoke.

"Did you get Uncle Frank a home?"

"Yes, ma'am."

She ate a little more, then continued.

"It was not right what I said to him last night, and for that, I owe him an apology. That will happen today." I just nodded my head in agreement. She knew she had stepped over the line, but I was not holding her to account. It was my failure that drove her there. I finally gained the courage after a few moments to take her hand.

"Mother, Uncle Frank will be fine. Let's just see what he does and does not remember when he wakes up. But if anyone needs to apologize to you both, it's me."

She looked me in the eye, and a tear appeared on her cheek. She looked away for a few moments, wiped her tear, and looked back again.

"Things are going to change," she said softly. "But we have chores to do first. Once they're done, we will square it all away."

This hurt my heart a little more. She wasn't ready to talk about it. She still needed time to process it all. And if I had to rob Father Time himself, it's time that I would give her. She deserved that.

Later that morning, Uncle Frank started to stir, then came into the house for something to eat. I had saved the rest of the breakfast for him and was waiting to serve it when he arrived. He sat at the table, ate, and tried to wake from his haze. After the third tin of coffee, he started to rub his head and seemed to be shaking off the previous night's persistence to hang on.

"How did I get home?" he finally asked. This was not a good question. It gave me a fear that he remembered why he left home in the first place.

"I brought you home," I replied.

"Oh," is all he said. He continued to drink his coffee. I started to clean up and set things right in the kitchen while he continued to recover.

"Where's Anna?" he asked after several minutes.

"Doing chores," I said.

"Oh," was all I heard back again. I finished in the kitchen and was tending the fire when he got up.

"Well, I 'd better go out and help her," he said as he searched for his coat. I quickly sprung up, retrieved it from the hall peg, and brought it to him, hoping that he would give me some clue as to his state of mind or state of recollection.

"Thank you, Garit," was all he said. He walked out the door. This was not good. Not good at all.

Later that afternoon, I was again tending the fire. Both Mother and Uncle Frank had gone straight to their bedrooms after the chores. No one said a word coming back inside. They simply took off their shoes and coats and walked straight to their rooms. My prayers of a forgotten night and forgiven sin were falling on deaf ears, I suppose. Or, I should say, were being heard but not acted upon. And deservedly so, I reckon.

As I sat there trying to figure out a way to mend things, I heard a horse coming up to the house and a "visitor here!" being yelled out. I sprang up and went out on the porch to find Mr. Stallsburg dismounting from the prettiest paint horse I had ever seen. It caught me off guard because I had never seen the horse before, and it was rare that I saw Mr. Stallsburg riding a horse. Either carriage or plain walking was his usual mode of transportation. And at that, the saloon or church were the only places he frequented. He tied up his horse.

"Why Garit, just the man I came to see," he said. "We missed you this morning, and I wanted to make sure you were okay. Dub told me about Frank. Is everything alright?"

Alright would be a vast improvement. But we were nowhere near all right at the moment.

"Well, Mr. Stallsburg, I think we need to talk," as I motioned toward the barn and started walking that way. "I hope you are ready for a long story," I said as we walked.

Chapter 9

As Mr. Stallsburg mounted his beautiful horse, he turned back to me.

"Well, Garit," as he adjusted in his saddle, "you have gotten yourself into quite a mess. But I understand your dilemma and have contributed to it, so want nothing more than to help you make it square with your mother. I am just sorry that it might mean you having to leave the saloon to do so. You have been a Godsend to me, and I can't say that I am not disappointed in this predicament. You should not have lied to your mother, but neither should I. How about I come back out tomorrow, and we clear all of this up together? Sound good?"

"Of course, Mr. Stallsburg. And thank you for understanding and being willing to help," I said while kicking imaginary rocks on the ground. I was so relieved he was not mad at me for explaining I had to leave the saloon. Mother would just not stand for it now that she knew, and I had a lot to make up for with her. And just as I felt I was in the lowest of lows, Mr. Stallsburg said something that, at the time, seemed to be just a part of the conversation. But it hits me solidly as I look back.

"Son, life can be pretty hard. It sure does not need any help from you being harder. Do better next time, and never lie to your mother again. Words I also need to take to heart, so we will work on it together." And he rode off toward town.

I just stood there for a while. Not because of guilt or regret of what I had done. Not because I was afraid to go back in the house and face up to my deed. But because Mr. Stallsburg had called me 'son,' and it just felt different when he said it to me rather than others. Mr. Dobbs or other older folks would call me that quite frequently, actually. I looked three years younger than I really was, so I didn't blame them. But with my father abandoning us so long ago, hearing it come from a man's mouth seemed to always catch me yearning for it to be real. Not the passing 'Get back to work, son,' or 'Son, you're too small to handle that.' This 'son' seemed to have more care, more substance to it. And I was taken aback at the emotional tinge it gave me when Mr. Stallsburg said it. I needed it more than I knew right then.

I wasn't quite sure what to do next as I came back into the house. Just keep waiting for one or both to come out of their rooms, or should I go get them both for our talk? I wanted desperately to get this behind us. It was getting close to noon, and still no movement, stirring, or nothing.

What the heck is going on? I asked myself while stoking the fire.

It was right then that I hit the floor on my knees and begged God to please hear my plight. Please have mercy on my soul and help me to convince Mother I am remorseful. Sorry. Ashamed. To let Mother have a sense of trust in me again. My heart began to have that feeling again, and I was starting to grow very tired of this place I had brought everyone to.

"God, please make it right, and I will never, ever again do wrong, I promise," I prayed earnestly. Just then, I heard a door open. Springing back to my chair and trying to act like nothing was going on, I saw Mother entering the kitchen with her apron on. She went straight to the stove and seemed to be inspecting her area, as I had defiled it this morning with my feeble attempt at a peace offering by cooking breakfast. This gave me hope. Mother was kind of acting normal. This was a good sign. I just kept stoking the fire, trying to act like everything was okay, but I really just wanted to go over and give her a hug and tell her I was sorry again.

For some reason, I didn't. At that moment, I just sat there, frozen. Knowing what I should do but couldn't. I think back now, and I imagine I was just scared. Scared to think she would not hug me back. Not honor the "white flag of surrender" that I so desperately wanted. Just things to go back to normal. But life is hard that way.

Once you let someone down, you can't get ever get that back. One and done. Of course, you find a way to live through it and move on, but that trust is gone. Common respect. Doubt. It's always there a little bit. Pain. I thought I had felt pain before with all my ailments. This pain was different. This pain never really would leave, and that day is something that I swore to not feel again. From now on, things would be different. Things would be truthful at all costs. Mother deserved that.

"Mother?" I finally summoned the courage to say to her.

"Yes, son?" she softly replied.

"Can we talk now? Can we fix this?" I asked with subdued hope.

She stopped, put her hands on the counter, and took a deep breath in.

"Yes. Go get Frank," she said. I slowly made my way to Frank's room and knocked on his door. I could hear some rustling once I did and a slow "come in" from Uncle Frank. I opened the door and saw him kneeling by his bed. It looked as if he had been praying too, and I must admit, I was shocked by this picture. Uncle Frank was not a churchgoin' man. And frankly, we never really talked about God together before. I just assumed that since he was into the drink and a somewhat simple thinker, he was not religious. I tried to hide my puzzled look.

"Can you come out and talk with us about everything?" I also realized while I was asking the question my hope about Uncle Frank not remembering what had taken place the night before was quickly fading. Why would Uncle Frank be praying today? It had to be because he remembered last night. Everything, including the worst parts. As I walked back to the main room, I said another soft prayer to myself. "Lord, please help make this go smooth; amen."

As we all sat in silence, averting our eyes from each other so as to not make direct contact, I really started to get worried. Who would make the first move? In most of my experience, usually, the first to talk was the first to take the weaker position. In poker or gambling, I learned this skill very well and could tell how a person's facial expressions, arm movements, or "small talk" would give away their hand. I got pretty good at it and had taken many a pot accordingly. In this situation, I did not want to win anything; I just wanted it to get back to normal quickly. But I was not sure that anything would be back to normal. We would get past this, but things will be different for sure. Can't get "normal" back. Oh well, here goes, I said to myself.

"Mother—" and just as I said it, Uncle Frank also said, "It's over."

I paused with my eyes wide open as well as my mouth and just looked at Uncle Frank and then at Mother. Uncle Frank never looked up, just kept his head down and started talking. Without a sense of pause or etiquette to let me continue at all. He needed to get it all out at once. *Here it goes,* I thought.

"It's *over.* No more drinking. No more staying out all night and no more being a burden to both of you," he said, as quickly and as forcefully as I have ever heard Uncle Frank speak before. Although his "forceful" was still kind and reserved. Just as Uncle Frank is. Honest. I about fell out of my chair. It's over? No more drinking? He did not mention one word about Mother or about what had been said. Did he remember? I looked at Mother like, 'What's going on,' and pleaded with my face for her to inquire further. She just looked sternly ahead and winced her eyes as if she was holding something in. Holding something back. And then it came out.

"Frank, I am so sorry about last night. I did not mean it. You are more family and blood than anyone else, and I was disrespectful to you. I am sorry."

Frank looked up finally at her and had a confused look on his face.

"What? Anna, I am not sure what you mean. Family?" He looked at me, very confused. I looked back at Mother with a look of 'I don't know what to do here,' and for the first time in my life, she had the same look on her face right back at me.

"Garit?" Frank said to me. "What is she talking about?"

I had to say something, so I just blurted out, "Oh, nothing, Uncle Frank, just something silly Mother said last night," in hopes it would diffuse the situation and all of us could regroup.

"Well, I don't know what each of you is talkin' about, and that's exactly why it has to stop. I'm not gonna drink anymore. Not today, not tomorrow, not ever – ever!" Frank said, slamming his fist down into his knee.

"You both are the best things that have ever happened to me, and I am ruining it by being a drunk. A darn Drunk!" Frank said, and he quickly looked at Mother as if to say he was sorry for saying darn.

She just looked down quickly but back up at Frank and reached over to touch his face.

"Frank, my dear, it's okay." This changed his expression instantly, and he leaned into her hand and closed his eyes for a moment. Now, this was a huge shock, and not even close to how I saw all this going, but I also know when I just need to roll with the momentum, and that's exactly what I did.

"Uncle Frank, are you really not going to drink anymore?" I asked like a hopeful child. Frank opened his eyes, took Mother's hand, and with his left hand, mine with his right.

"May the good Lord strike me down right here if it ain't true," he swore. "I am done with drinkin', and may the good Lord help me stay straight and strong."

At this, I let out an inappropriate chuckle, but it was all too strange. Here I thought I was going to have to be the middleman in Mother and Uncle Frank being mad at each other while at the same time being done in by Mother for lying about the saloon, and now Uncle Frank has said, "May the good Lord" twice in one sentence. *What in the world is going on?* I could not help but laugh. Thankfully my laughter was contagious, and first Uncle Frank started to chuckle, and then after a few seconds, even Mother began to smile a little and then start a small, softened laugh behind her hand over her mouth. For these few seconds, all was well. All was forgiven. All was right with the world.

But I knew deep inside that couldn't be the whole case. My atonement was nigh and would be soon. But while looking over at Mother during this time, I sensed that she was okay with letting it go for now and allowing this wonderful sentiment from Uncle Frank to continue, as we both were very curious as to where this would end up.

After the laughter died down, Uncle Frank went on to explain that he had been visited in the night by an angel, who'd told him to stop drinking. To start living right and stop allowing the Devil's poison into his mouth. He talked with such excitement and detail that as we listened, we shook our heads in amazement. Uncle Frank was so sure he had been visited that Mother and I started to believe it ourselves.

Kind of. I had the thought that although Uncle Frank could certainly handle his liquor and that drinking almost two bottles of the hard stuff had probably sent him into a state he had not been in for quite some time. He was usually a one-bottle man. And not the good stuff. Liquor was expensive, so his drink was typically the cheapest thing he could get his hands on. I know. I was the one who ordered it for the saloon.

His typical bottle was, as Dub, the bartender would say, "One rung higher than horse piss." Dub actually asked me to stop ordering it once, as he felt it degraded his 'profession,' but of course, I couldn't. It was Uncle Frank's brand. And I at least owed Uncle Frank that much for helping me and Mother out all these years. Plus, Uncle Frank was my friend, and that's what friends do. Look out for each other. Even though that involved buying alcohol for my drunk uncle, I don't regret it one bit. But I should have known that two bottles of the good stuff last night was too much. I was too focused on my lie to Mother that I totally failed on that front last night.

But, in a roundabout way, I actually helped all of us by not interfering. Somehow those two bottles had brought Uncle Frank from the darkness of drink to a redeemed follower of God. Pretty good, if I say so myself. *Thanks for the help, God,* I thought.

As we sat and listened to Uncle Frank extol about his vision and his promise to stay straight, I got the sense that although things had changed drastically last night because of my actions, maybe, just maybe, we were headed in a better direction because of it. One thing I now know is that a narcissist always thinks their actions, however how wrong, bad, or misguided they are, turn out to be the right ones, especially when it comes to being right or helping others discover the right answer. And there I had done it again. My shortcomings actually helped Uncle Frank and Mother. Oh, how I love to help people be better. Even when I am wrong, I am right.

We ended this time of conversation with a big hug, telling Uncle Frank how proud we were of him. He smiled ear to ear. His honesty. His eagerness to please Mother and me was really the best thing to experience. He loved us. Honestly loved us. And in his simple way was the smartest man on earth. This made me proud. Proud of him and proud of our family. As our hug came to an end, I knew that I still could not escape Mother's reconning and was preparing for it. Looking back now, not only was Uncle Frank's newly acquired religion and abstention from alcohol a true miracle, but with my help, of course. What happened next was two miracles in one day. As Uncle Frank started off toward the front door, he called out to us.

"Well, someone's gotta do the chores. It might as well be me," with a huge grin on his face. Mother whispered into my ear.

"We will talk about the rest later." She kissed my cheek and turned to Frank to walk with him.

"Frank, I will gladly join you for the beginning of your new life."

In all the moments I have had in life, that split second, watching them head out that door with such high hope for what was next, and the pride that both of them had in Uncle Frank's decision, I place that moment amongst the highest in my entire life. Although, knowing what I know now, it should've been absolutely first place. No question.

Chapter 10

The next day, Mother did not even mention the saloon or the lie. And this is where I have to point out that my mother was sharper than a serpent's tooth, as old Reverend Moot would say.

She had noticed that I had not gotten up early that morning and was now out helping Uncle Frank with the chores and not running into town as usual. She realized that she did not even have to mention it. It was over. The saloon was no more.

And with that, there was no sense even putting an ounce more of thought or energy into it. Mother was efficient like that. Getting her way without even having to mention a single syllable. She was quite a woman. The problem now was that I forgot about Mr. Stallsburg saying he would come out today in order to make things right with Mother the previous day. As I and Uncle Frank went about our day, Mr. Stallsburg arrived at the house and began talking with Mother. I panicked when, turning the corner from the barn, I saw his beautiful horse tied up out front. Dropping my buckets, I ran as quickly as I could to the house in hopes that I was not too late.

Too late, I was. As I burst through the door, it appeared that he had been here a little while. He and Mother were seated at the table drinking some tea. I quickly tried to assess the gravity of what trouble I was about to be in by analyzing Mother's facial expression. It was eerily calm. Less stern than usual. This frightened me even more. *This had to be a trap*, I thought. But, at the same time, I knew I deserved whatever was to come next. Oh well, here goes.

"Well, hello, Mr. Stallsburg; how are you this fine day?" I said, like some Shakespearian actor. Accent and all.

Mr. Stallsburg just looked at me with a raised eyebrow. "Fine?".

"Stop that silliness, Garit, and come over here and sit down," Mother scolded me.

Shit, I said to myself. I couldn't help it; it just manifested itself in my brain. Thank the Lord I did not say it out loud. The impending civil war would have been just a small skirmish compared to what Mother would have done had I verbalized my thought. As I walked over to sit with them, Mr. Stallsburg tried to bring the mood to a better level.

"Garit, your mother makes the best tea, don't you agree? Here, I will pour you a cup."

Looking back, I think he was also giving me some time to gather my thoughts. He knew by my hasty arrival that I might have forgotten about his visit and was unprepared. Working together for as long as we have had given us this small amount of intuition about each other. He trusted me, and I him. As I sat there trying to figure out what to say first, Mother broke the pause.

"Garit, Mr. Stallsburg and I have been discussing your future and where the saloon plays into that future. Where do you think it fits into your future?" she asked with that "I know that you know the saloon is already absent from your future" tone.

"Umm, I...think...that...the saloon is not in my future, Mother, and I am sorry that it has been a part of my past without you knowing," I said while attempting to give an honest and wholesome smile to her.

"Garit, your mother and I have already discussed our conversation from yesterday. I enlightened her that you had already broken the news to me that your work at the saloon was over. I made sure to give you all the credit for that decision, as that's the truth. I also told her that although I am deeply disappointed that you will not continue, what is more important is that you are taking responsibility and not running from it. Most men would not, and for that, she should be proud of you."

With that, Mother interjected.

"Mr. Stallsburg, I will be the judge of how proud of my son I should be. Thank you!"

"Oh, of course, Anna—uh, Mrs. Hotzmire, I mean," he said with a quiver in his voice. I think he was as scared of her as I was. And he should have been. Mother was tough. Mother slowly bowed her head toward him as if to tell him it was alright and turned back to me. This was unlike Mother. She showed a tiny amount of grace toward Mr. Stallsburg's unintended intrusion. So, what happened next was, to this day, the strangest turn of events I have ever experienced. The world turned upside down and backward instantly. She turned to me.

"Garit, what you did by lying to me all this time is heartbreaking and very disappointing. You have never hidden something from me like this before. I am hurt, very hurt, by this behavior. Mr. Stallsburg, this goes for you also. How can you tip your hat to me every Sunday in church, all the while participating in this rouse with Garit? Shame on you!"

Mr. Stallsburg did exactly what I was doing at the time; just looked down at his feet and nodded his head in agreement. Mother continued.

"Now, I cannot say that forgiveness will come swiftly, but how in the world can I profess to have faith in our Lord and Savior and not find it in my heart to forgive you as he has forgiven us? Again, this will take some time, but I promise that I will work on it."

All that both of us could do was continue looking down and nodding our heads. Everything up to this point was somewhat expected. I will say hearing what I had done to Mother out loud hurt worse than I expected, and I was so sorry for the pain it was causing her. How could I have done it? But just as I was descending into my low of lows, Mother said the shocker of all shockers.

"Now, I will work on forgiveness for both of you, and I promise to not take too long, but until then, Garit will no longer work at the saloon."

Until then? I was confused. I took a split second to look up at her from my groveling obedience pose. She saw this and continued.

"Once this time passes, Garit, you may continue your position with Mr. Stallsburg. As long as I see it is not corrupting your soul or behavior. Do both of you understand me?"

I seriously was about to pass out. As Mr. Stallsburg and I looked up at each other, I could tell he was about to do the same.

"Um, Anna, are you saying Garit may continue working for me after all?"

Mother replied quickly and with her normal sharpness.

"Mr. Stallsburg, you may call me Mrs. Hotzmire. And if you have to ask that question, you weren't listening very well. That proves to me you need my Garit more than I thought. Now, I have chores to do, so be along with yourself. But not before picking up this mess," she said. She motioned at the cups and saucers on the table, then quickly stood up and exited through the front door towards the barn, leaving the door wide open.

Mr. Stallsburg and I just sat there in a fog.

"What just happened?" I finally said out loud.

Mr. Stallsburg just shook his head, put his hand behind his head, and rubbed his neck.

"You've got me, son, but I think we're back in the saloon business together. Is that what you want? To come back when she is ready?"

I was still finding words hard to come by but blurted out my feelings anyway.

"Of course. I love the saloon; I mean, I don't love the saloon; I love working at the saloon!"

"Holy Jesus, I am glad you said that. I need you, Garit. And I must admit, I was panicking at the thought of losing you. But as I said last night, I would respect your decision and you for making it. Family is more important, and I envy what you and your mother have. It would kill me to cause any grief to either of you."

"Mr. Stallsburg, thank you," I said softly. "But you better get out of here before she changes her mind and comes back. We just hit the mother lode of grace, literally!"

He knew what I meant and sprang up, grabbing his hat, and headed out the door, saying, "You'll get the dishes won't you?"

"Of course!" I yelled back. "Now get out of here." I saw him mounting his beautiful steed and riding off. As I gathered the dishes and tea, I couldn't describe the feeling I had. It was partly shock, of course, but it was also partly gratitude, fear, and love. Love for my mother, who, for some reason, was allowing this to continue and not raining Hell down on me for what had happened. *That's what I deserved;* I kept thinking. But I also knew to take fate as it stands. I have been doing it my whole life. I just think I might start to have to factor in luck now because I can't explain what just happened by equating facts. It had to be luck. Facts would have had me grounded until I was eighty. Things were a changin' for sure. I just wish I had known then what I know now, in the magnitude of this change.

Chapter 11

Mother, Frank, and I dove into work the next few days around the farm and did our best to move on from the previous events. I think purposely tried to avoid conversation, except for the occasional "Good Morning" and small talk about the farm. Meals together were the hardest time. We usually cut up, talked about our day, and just had fun while eating. The tone these days was not sadness or gloom, but more of a no one really knew what to do or say. This was new territory for all of us. Taking my situation aside, Uncle Frank giving up drinking was huge, and I certainly did not want to minimize it. Each day was a conscious effort by both Mother and me to support him, keep him focused, and helping him through the withdrawal symptoms. The shakes, the sweats, the clear doubt that he had in his decision. As long as we kept him busy, he seemed to do better.

At night, that was the hardest. The pull of the saloon was strong. Like he had an invisible line wrapped around him and tugging him to go. But Mother concentrated on giving him tea to drink so he could hold something in his hands or use it as a stand-in for alcohol. I did what I knew best: tried to play cards or other games with him to keep him preoccupied. The usual laughter was not present, but I could tell he wanted it to be. He wanted to truly be normal again. I could also see the sadness in his eyes. As if he missed a friend or was grieving an absence. Alcohol had been his partner for several years; now it was gone. What or who else could take its place?

We had been so preoccupied with Frank that Mother and I never really had a chance to discuss what had happened. I was so curious why she might let me go back to the saloon. Really, the real reason, not the "how can I not forgive when God has forgiven me" line. Although I have no doubt Mother was being genuine in her motive. She was what I would call a true Christian and had faith a mile long. But there just seemed to be something else. Something more that was helping her be so forgiving. Of course, there were times we could have talked, but she seemed to want to skim past it, keeping herself busier than normal, and honestly, I didn't want to press the issue. We both let things lie on purpose. I so wish I had not done that now. I regret not having the courage to just ask her straight about it. I really wanted to know. My brain needed the explanation that, unfortunately, I never would receive.

About a week after our meeting with Mr. Stallsburg, things were getting into their typical habits. All woke early, had a small breakfast, and then off to chores. Frank was doing better each day. He really was. I was so proud of him. His sense of humor was coming back, and I could see that the tug of the string around his waist to the saloon was beginning to loosen. There would be the regular pulls throughout the evening, but I could tell that Uncle Frank was learning how to resist them. He simply would get up from his chair, shuffle around the room and ask me a question about poker or cards or some other game. He knew that I had a pretty good understanding of all the saloon games so he would just ask, "How does keno really work?" or "What should someone do when they have three of a kind in fives?" Simple questions, but ones that I could talk him through and that he could concentrate on until the urges passed.

Well, this day again started like normal. We all headed off to do chores separately. I typically took the barn and stall duty, Uncle Frank walked the crop fields and inspected for rot or bug damage as well as moisture, and Mother went to the chicken coup to gather the daily haul and tidy it up.

I was just getting into the second stall and grabbing some hay when I heard her scream. Mother never screamed. In fact, I don't think I had ever heard her scream before this. I instantly knew something very bad had happened and sprung out in the direction of her voice. As I got closer to the coup and gained sight of her, I could hear Uncle Frank yelling, "Anna? Anna?" as he ran in from the field. When I got to the coup, I could see Mother holding a spade and jabbing the ground toward the corner of the coup. Nothing really looked out of sorts from this initial survey, so I slowed a little as I made it to the door.

"Stay back, Garit! It's a snake!" she screamed at me over her shoulder. She made a movement as if to make sure her body was in between the snake and me. She kept jabbing down at it in the hay below. I really could not see the snake, but I took her word that it was in there and I should stay back. Uncle Frank had now made it to the coup. He immediately pushed me aside from the door and leaped toward Mother. He picked her up by the waist and backed out the door. All the while, Mother kept jabbing toward the ground. Uncle Frank set Mother down outside the door and went back inside to make sure whatever had gotten Mother all worked up was gone.

While he was doing this, I simply hugged her.

"Mother, Mother, are you okay?" I yelled, trying to get her attention off the spade as she just kept jabbing the ground, even outside the coup.

Like she was trying to keep killing the snake, even though she was now a good ten feet away from it. I could hear Frank inside, moving the hay around with chickens squawking and moving everywhere around him. But I had to concentrate on Mother and not on the commotion inside. I finally got Mother to stop jabbing at the ground by taking the spade away from her and throwing it down. I grabbed her hands in mine and looked straight into her eyes. That's when I saw it. Two puncture wounds near her left jawline and two small lines of blood going down onto her neck.

"Oh, My God!" I yelled out, and Frank had to have heard it. I instantly could tell that he stopped thrashing around in the coup and headed toward us. As he reached the door, he could see what I had seen and let out a moan as he continued our way. He knew immediately that this was not good. Uncle Frank was not an expert on much, but he was an expert on snakes.

His fascination began when he was a child, and although we did not have a lot of snakes around the farm, he knew every species, variety, and kind. The copperhead, cottonmouth, worm snake, scarlet snake, and many more. I can't tell you how many times Mother has had to literally chase him out of the house while he was holding a harmless kingsnake or hognose in his hand, trying to get a rise out of her and me. He loved handling snakes. I really did not have a problem with snakes *per se*, just knew that I should probably not try and pick one up. And that throwing a stone at a Cottonmouth sunning on a log near the pond was a good five minutes of fun with Pohl when we were younger. Mother, on the other hand, HATED snakes. And of course, would inevitably take a snake sighting into a story about Adam and Eve and the devil as a serpent who ruined everything in God's plan for us. One time I did speak up.

"Factually, it wasn't the serpent that ruined it. It was Eve," I said. "She was the one that picked the apple and gave it to Adam. The snake didn't force her to!"

Well, let's just say I never brought that argument up again after the swat on the backside Mother gave me as a result.

We had gotten Mother back into the house, and I was wiping away the blood from the wound when Uncle Frank went running back out the door toward the coup.

"We have to see what kind it is!" he yelled as he ran.

I stayed with Mother and continued to hold a wet cloth on her cheek. She held her hand over mine as if to make sure I was doing it correctly, but I could tell something was not right. Her head was extended upward and to the right, and her mouth hung completely open as if she was frozen in the expression she had when she yelled out. Her eyes were watering badly, and her right hand was clenched and beating over and over on the table.

"Mother, I have you. It's ok; try to calm down. It'll be all right; it'll be okay, mom." I kept saying over and over.

She did not speak; she just stayed in this pose, pounding the table. I remember this vividly because I was hoping that at any moment, she would snap out of it and give me orders on what to do next, as she always had before.

Mother was unshakable when it came to things like this. She always knew what to do. She always was the first to take up helping anyone in distress. And she always was right in her actions. I needed her to tell me what to do right now, but her pain wouldn't allow her to. She was in shock. Now that I have researched it more, she was in excruciating pain from the hemotoxin that the snake had injected into her. It was attacking the blood and skin around the bite quickly. And, as Uncle Frank confirmed a short time later by holding up the sheer size of the diamondback rattlesnake that had bitten Mother, the amount of venom injected had to have been immense. Although its head was almost severed from its body, the snake measured eighty-eight inches long and was later confirmed to have been one of the largest ever seen in our county. The snake was a foot and a half taller than I was standing up. A true monster.

We had gotten Mother calmed down a little after laying her down on her bed. I continued the wet cloth compress. I really did not know what else to do. Uncle Frank had attempted to suck out the venom, but with each try, I could see in his eyes that it was too late. He went through the motion of sucking in, wincing, and spitting out the mixture of blood, saliva, and what I had hoped to be venom, but he knew his actions were futile.

You see, the snake had bitten so close to the main artery in her neck that the venom was now coursing through her body at a speed no one could stop. She started to develop a fever. The area around her cheek and neck began to turn hot and a reddish-black color. Moaning now started to develop, and the hand that used to be helping me hold the cloth to her cheek was down at her side, fist clinched just like the other.

Frank had left in an effort to ride in and get the doctor, but although I did not know as much as Uncle Frank about snakes, I just had a feeling it was going to be too late. I had never seen Mother like this before. She could handle more pain than anyone I knew. Her not answering me when I called out to her or giving me directions regarding her care was a very bad sign. She started to have what I would call convulsions. Her body writhed in pain, and her mid-section moved up and down from the bed. Her hands would beat the mattress one second and then grab the blankets in the other with overwhelming strength.

I literally had no idea what to do. I was terrified. I just kept holding the cloth on her and concentrated on talking to her.

"Mother, you will be all right, you will be all right," I said over and over again. I don't know how long Frank had been gone, but it seemed like an eternity. Mother was starting to become very weak from the nonstop convulsions. I could see her body losing the battle second by second. Her face had relaxed somewhat, and her mouth had gone from wide open to halfway closed. Saliva poured out of the corner of her mouth.

"Please, God help me!" I called out.

I could see her heartbeat in the artery in her neck. It was strong and rapid before, but now it was slower and slower. I knew this was going to end with my mother's passing, but I tried to ignore it and will death away. I am not very strong, but I just kept picturing the grim reaper coming in through the hallway door to take my mother away and me fighting him with all I had.

That's what Mother would do for me, so I would do the same for her. The main reason I am even here today is that Mother had done that time and time again over my life. Literally willing me to live. Prepared to fight anyone and anything that threatened me. She was a force of nature and will. Never surrendering. Never retreating. But I could see her losing the battle now. Her heartbeat slowed and slowed with each breath. In recollection, I have no doubt that the strongest man on the planet would have already succumbed to the venom. His soul would have already been taken from this earth, and his body cast aside to decompose into dust. Not mother. Her strength had kept her so much farther from death than most. But I could tell she was closer than ever before. And at that moment, her eyes opened wide and straight; she took a breath in and spoke in a shallow whisper.

"I'm sorry, Garit."

Those were the last words she would ever say in life. The last words I would ever hear from her. A few moments later, I saw her heart take its final beat and all the air in her lungs escaped. She sank down into the bed and her fists relaxed. She was gone.

I simply lowered my head onto her shoulder and cried as I have never cried before or since.

My protector. My hero. My mother was gone.

Chapter 12

It had been a few weeks since Mother's death, and life continued to slowly pass by. But how and with what purpose was a mystery to me. Going through the motions each day, I felt numb, but continued as we had rehearsed them so many times before.

Each day of my life since graduation had been relatively the same, but with the general store and saloon, mostly saloon, giving me a bit of change from the mundane life of our farmstead. With both of those jobs now gone or on pause at least, each day had a familiar dullness. And without Mother, not even a bright spot feeling of being cared for by someone else. Loved.

Uncle Frank was doing really good through all of this. Yes, he had slipped once or twice, back to drinking like before, but he would quickly refocus and had now gone six days without alcohol. Since this whole self-challenge was initiated, seven days was his record. I suspect that will become the standing pattern over time.

Much better than before, though, so I was still proud of him. The main issue was each time he broke his dry spell; his demeanor grew darker. Each time he was more disappointed in himself, and each time he edged closer to the hard truth that he would never really be able to quit. I loved Uncle Frank and wanted to help, but I simply didn't have it in me. The haze had taken over, and it just wouldn't allow me to worry about his problems anymore. We were just two lost souls going through the motions. Trying to keep it all together.

Mother's funeral was well attended, and she was buried where I knew she would be happy: in the Church cemetery, close to the large oak tree she always mentioned when we passed. It stood a full thirty or so feet taller than those around it. She always commented on how beautiful and impressive it was. To be honest, I did not like those comments. They seemed to be an unconscious reference to how small and feeble I was. How much more would Mother love me if I was more like that tree or like Pohl, strong and tall?

As I got older, I knew Mother did not mean that. It was only self-pity. She simply was talking about the tree, not me. But I have to admit that the comments about the tree just always seemed to hit me that way. And I am so sorry for it now. Now that she is buried in its shadow each and every day. Quietly sheltering her from the sun's glare. She deserved that. And she deserved a son that could do that also. I would just have to live up to that standard in other ways than stature, I supposed. I would make her proud.

One person who came to the funeral that I wished would have stayed away was Father.

"How big of you," I said under my breath when I first saw him back.

I overheard through his constant bragging that he was now in the Virginia Militia. And a superior officer, in fact. He even went the extra mile by wearing his uniform and sword to the funeral.

All I could think about while watching him as Mother's body was lowered into her grave was *So you can commit to your country, just not to your wife and son. How noble.*

Whether it was because he was a coward or because of me being born crippled, I didn't care why he left us, Mother had always tried to shield me from thinking it was my fault. She blamed herself for being too hard on him. But I knew the truth. My feebleness just gave him a final excuse to leave.

From what I have learned about him over the years, he never wanted to be married in the first place. Being a humble farmer, husband, and father was beneath him. It's hard to brag about how brave, heroic, and great you are when everyone around you knows the truth. So, leaving was his only way to play the role.

I have seen him twice in my entire life. The day I was born, and that day, as I buried the true hero in our family. He tried to speak to me after the funeral, but I just kept walking, not even giving him the benefit of a nod or eye contact. Mother would have been proud of me for that.

Uncle Frank did spend some time with him, though. I could see them talking when I loaded up into the wagon to head home after the funeral. They did not talk long, but even that was too long for what I felt he deserved. But I suppose brothers are due at least one conversation in almost sixteen years.

Mr. Stallsburg rode up to my wagon about that time and extended his hand to mine. I was so focused on my father and Uncle Frank that I must have ignored him for a moment.

"Garit, are you all right, son?" he had to say to get me to focus on him.

"Oh, I am sorry Mr. Stallsburg. I am," I said, quickly looking down again, not even acknowledging his open hand in front of me.

"No problem, son," he simply took his hand and put it on my shoulder.

"I can't imagine what you are going through right now," he said, trying to comfort me.

"When you're ready, I would like to talk to you about your future and what's next. Of course, only when your ready, son," he said, squeezing my shoulder.

A tear slid down my face.

"Hang in there. It gets easier, I promise," he said and slowly rode off toward town.

I made it back to the farm, put the horses and wagon away, and went straight to my room. I don't remember much about what else happened there, and frankly, I don't care either. Sleep was my only refuge from the reality that Mother was gone, and I was alone. Father and Mother had both left me.

Uncle Frank woke me up the next day, I think. I really wasn't sure what day it was, to be honest.

"Garit, I tried to let you sleep as long as I could, but you have to go to eat something, boy," he said as he helped me up and out into the main room.

I still had my clothes on from the funeral. As he sat me down at the table, I saw that he had prepared some eggs, bacon, and grits. I will admit, though, that they did not look very appetizing. I confirmed this as I brought a forkful of eggs to my mouth. They were cold and stale. But I did not care. I was starving. I sat there and ate it all. And I don't even like grits. They were good to me that day, though. Finally, I had the notion to ask Uncle Frank what day it was while sipping some coffee.

"It's Tuesday, Garit. Two days since the funeral. You know the funeral?" he asked, sheepishly trying to see what all I remembered or maybe just how I would react to it.

I didn't react. I just kept sipping my coffee and looking forward. I didn't want to react. If I did, it would make it all real. I just wanted to ignore what had happened. She left me. Just like all of them have. Father…Pohl….and now Mother. I just sipped on my coffee and tried to forget it all. But the sliver of peace that might have given me was fleeting.

"Garit, what are we gonna do now?" Frank asked. "What do you think we should do?"

I really did not want to answer. Just wanted to be left alone. I could feel the rage building inside of me. But I had to quell the anger. The tone in Uncle Frank's voice was one of fear. He truly was scared about what lay ahead without Mother.

Mother was the captain. The leader, for so long that both of us were spoiled to that fact. Spoiled in that we did not have to think for ourselves too much, she simply always told us what to do even though each day was as repetitive as a player piano. Day in, and day out, the same, with only the chores changing with the season. But she would still tell us what to do. And each of us would roll our eyes when she did.

"Did she not think we were smart enough to remember ourselves?" I would often think to myself while listening to her short and precise orders each day. Oh, how I missed those demands. I wished she was here again.

I knew Uncle Frank would not let the question go, so after some more quiet time, I finally answered.

"We will do what we always do. The way Mother would want us to."

He looked me in the eye once I was done with my statement and simply nodded his head. He knew the feeling I was experiencing also and simply wanted someone to tell him the next step. He knew better than anyone what needed to be done on the farm. He just needed a little bit of Mother to help him get off high center.

He stood up, grabbed his coat, and was out the door. On his mission.

On the job. He needed a purpose, and I needed to be alone.

Several weeks had passed, and a routine was starting to take hold. Frank did just about everything, I gave the orders, and he followed. The times alone in the house, while he was out doing chores, were my refuge. Hiding from the world is all I wanted now. I have nothing to give. Or really, I wanted to give nothing. Why should I? Everyone leaves anyways. Why should I even try? This pattern of self-defeat and all the memories of people who have ridiculed me over my life due to size, health, or envy of my intelligence seemed to be keeping me knocked down. Kept me shunning the world and stewing in my self-pity, and I liked it. I had more excuses than most to be this way, and that gave me a sense of entitlement to be here longer. Nothing would stop this cycle, and honestly, I didn't care. It was a dark, dark time.

One day though, a knock on our front door would start to change this. I was sitting in the same chair as always, hiding from the world, when a small commotion on the porch was followed by a slighter knock than usual.

"Garit, you home kid?"

I look back now, and those simple words ended up saving me from myself. I can also say in the same breath that it would save and almost ruin me simultaneously. But saving is what I needed then, so saving is what I took.

As I opened the door, there she was. My B. All dolled up and as beautiful as ever. I could not believe she was there, and this was the first time in a long time that I had care of my appearance or behavior. I was nothing short of a wreck and hated that she was seeing me like this. The path I was going down was dark, and she instantly woke something up in me that I thought was going to continue to wither and die.

"B, what are you doing here?" I found myself shouting. I slammed the door in her face. I could not let her see me this way. Less than my usual non-impressive self. I rushed around, running in circles doing God knows what, trying to clean myself up. But I had not even looked in a mirror for weeks. Not even sure of when the last time I had even bathed. Literally, this was unimaginably bad.

"Garit? Garit! Are you ever coming back to the door?" B said with a touch of whimsy in her voice.

"Uh…hold on, will be right out," I shouted back, feeling terrible that I shouted anything at my B. She didn't deserve a shout. She was an angel. She deserves poetry followed by song. Corny, I know, but man, she had that effect on me. I was completely smitten with her. As I finally regained my composure, took a very quick look in the mirror, and smoothed out my lackluster hair with some spit on my hands, I headed toward the door.

Please, God, don't make her run away when she sees me, I prayed. As I flung open the door, B almost fell straight into my arms. She was leaning up against the door, I reckon, trying to hear me scurrying around.

"Gariiiiit!" she yelled. I caught her before she hit the floor. And, of course, it almost took me down with her. As I helped B back to her feet and steady herself, she started giggling. I could not help but start giggling, also. That giggle turned into laughter as we just stood there looking at each other. Wow, that felt good. I had not laughed in weeks.

"What on earth has happened to you, Garit? You look like you have gone feral!" she whisked while looking around the house. And just then, she caught herself. I could see an almost embarrassed look come across her face as she remembered reality. Mother was gone.

"Oh, Garit, I am so sorry. I should not say those things. You must be really hurting right now, and I have no place making fun. I am so sorry, friend, and I am here to help in any way that I can."

"Oh, it's fine, B. I cannot lie and say that things are okay without her, but it is what it is. I sure miss her deeply, though. I am not sure how to even move forward."

"Well, that is why I am here, kid! And I have a surprise coming later today for you."

I admit I did not know a better surprise than having B here right now, but I was very curious about this other surprise.

"What are you talking about, B? Surprise?"

"Yep, one that I know will cheer you up right away. But that is later. Tell me how you are doing, and don't skip any details," B prodded as she took my elbow and guided me toward the chair.

We sat there for what seemed like hours talking about Mother and how I missed her dearly. We laughed at her sternness and imitated her upright posture. But I did it with love and admitted picturing her look was, in some ways, making me sad. But it was good to laugh again. It was good to see B again and feel some life back in my body. Everything had been gray until now.

With B, things gained color again. My body felt warmth and purpose. I needed this and could not wait for my surprise later. As we continued to talk, Frank came into the house and saw that B was there. Now, he knew about her, but he really had never talked to her and only had seen her a few times before. Frank rarely attended church with us. He had said that was going to change after his angel in the night visit, but then Mother died. He also only went into town usually after dark, so he just never was around when B was.

When Frank came into the house, he was acting very nervous. Like he was shy or something, holding his hat in his hands and his eyes down at the floor when talking to B, even after I introduced them to each other. I had never seen Frank like this before. But had really never seen him talk to a girl either, other than Mother. New territory, I guess. B was, of course, her usual charming self and very properly shook Frank's hand after the introduction. This took Frank off guard as his hands were very dirty. He went to apologize or something to that effect but just kind of stumbled saying it and then quickly went to his room, closing the door behind him.

B just kind of stood there for a second, turned to me, and started giggling. I was also just shocked that he acted like that and just shrugged my shoulders and started laughing. I felt kind of bad for Frank but really did not know why he was so nervous in the first place. I couldn't really explain it to B because I didn't know myself.

"Oh well. Let's go out on the porch, B," I said as I started toward the door. She followed and sat beside me on the bench out front. I looked around and could see that she had ridden out on a very nice chestnut mare.

"When did you get that horse, B?" I asked. I had not ever seen that one before.

"Oh, that's part of the surprise, silly," she said, poking me in the ribs as she did occasionally.

She got me a horse? I was not following the surprise story very well.

"So, the surprise is later, but has something to do with a horse," I said tentatively.

"Yep, you are quite perceptive, kid," she said in a sarcastic tone.

"Well, I am just trying to figure it out, B. What in the world are you up to?"

She just smiled and put her finger up to her mouth like it was a big secret or something. I just smiled back and rolled my eyes. After we talked a bit more, she stood up.

"Well, I can see my job here is done. I have woken you out of your slumber, and you better be back to normal now, Garit! I am so sorry about your mother, but it's time to get back to the real world. It needs you. I need you," she said.

Although the past few weeks had been like living in slow motion, a bad dream, this last statement from B suddenly jolted me to the core. "I need you?" I said inside my head. This seemed like a different B. She said it in a different way. Normally a joking or sarcastic tone had changed to a soft, somewhat needy tone. This was new.

"Well, thank you, B, for coming by. It was just what I needed. I missed you too," I said as I went to grab her hand with mine.

What happened next about made my heart stop and die right there. She kinda shooed my hand away from hers and came in for a hug. I just had to follow as I really did not know what to do. As her face got closer to mine, she kissed me on the cheek.

"Oh Garit, you are so silly!" she said and bounced off toward her horse. I again stood there in shock. I think back now and smile. That is pretty much what B saw most of the time when she was around me, I imagine. A shocked, jaw-wide-open me. She was always leaving me this way. Putty in her hands. But B had that effect on most, and she delighted in it. She relished this reaction and thrived on the excitement around it. She was the kind of girl that wanted everyone to notice her, everyone to like her, or really, everyone to love her. It was her way. And out of everyone, I was the most affected by it. I always had been and always will be.

Infatuation? Obsession? I don't know. My immaturity then called it love. My maturity now calls it myth, voodoo. For now, I know better. If only I could go back and educate my younger self, it would have saved me the pain and anguish yet to come. The raw emotion that I thought I had been through with losing Mother was nothing compared to what my B had in store for me. But for that time, I was smitten and living in a dream. The innocence was nice.

Later that evening, we had agreed to meet up in town so that B could show me the surprise. I was supposed to be out front of the saloon at 6:00 pm sharp. And "wear some good clothes, Garit," was ringing in my head as I was getting ready. B had said that earlier to me. Frank finally came out of his room as I was putting dinner together. I told him I was headed into town. He still seemed very rattled by our earlier guest and was still acting shy or something. Something just seemed off with him.

I could see that he wanted to talk to me about it but was holding back for some reason. He could tell that I was very excited about tonight's meeting and didn't want to muddle it up, I suppose. We just sat in silence as we ate. That was pretty normal these days. The times of joshing at each other and laughing had faded. Most of the time we were just trying to get a rise or a smile out of Mother. That was a daily challenge for both of us. Not only was it fun, but I suppose it was done out of love also. To see her smile made both of our lives better because we loved her. She was our cornerstone, our light. Now, it was dark.

But a spark had reignited again inside me after today's visit. It was pretty small, of course, but was starting to grow. And going to see B tonight was fanning the ember. I simply could not wait. I finished supper up first and started to clean up my place setting when I noticed Frank looked like he wanted to tell me something.

He had hardly touched his food, so I finally asked him about it.

"What's on your mind, Frank?" I continued cleaning up. As I was putting the dishes in the wash basin, I could hear him get up from his chair behind me and walk over to the fireplace. I thought he did not hear my question, so I started to ask it again.

"Frank, what's—" and he interrupted me.

"Garit, you know I love you, right?".

"Of course I do, Frank. What kind of question is that?"

"Well, I just want to make sure you know that before I tell you what's on my mind,"

He stoked the fire a little with his boot.

I turned around and walked over to him. It'd been a long time since Frank had acted this way, and when he did, it was usually something pretty big. Pretty big to him, I mean. He always overreacted, compared to Mother or me.

Frank was genuine, kind, and simple. He overthought the slightest of issues that you or I would just run past. That's okay, though, as he was doing it out of respect or love. And who could fault him for that? Mother and I had had to lean into this when it came up. We would slow down a little for him. And that was okay; we loved him also and would do whatever we could to accommodate.

Looking back, that's what real love does. Whether a large or small act, it's bending your will, pride, or time to be in the moment of others you care about. To be empathetic to their thoughts, feelings, or world. Mother used to quote 1 Peter 3:8 all the time: "Finally, all of you should be of one mind. Sympathize with each other. Love each other as brothers and sisters. Be tenderhearted and keep a humble attitude."

I never really understood this scripture or why she repeated it until then. My main reason was that we had nothing really to begin with. I mean, we had a farm and each other. But in no way, shape, or form did we have anything to not be humble about. Hell, even my health, or lack thereof. Being humble never even got a chance to grow from seed in our lives. We had nothing to be proud of in the first place. Father left us. Every day seemed hard. We had a roof over our heads and food to eat.

But I had the opportunity to witness almost daily the cruelty of being "different" or "weak" in a world that does not prize such attributes. So being humble in attitude was pretty much forced on me from the get-go. Mother knew this, but as I grew up and understood better, she was talking about the things we did have. We had each other; we had Love, Laughter, and a Home. God gifted me with intelligence and thoughts bigger than my situation at hand. Hope. A hope that one day, things would be different. And instead of always being face down in the dirt on account of someone else, I might be the one mightier than them. Metaphorically, of course. Maybe be in a position of power or influence. I think Mother was, in a sense, "warning" me of things to come. But also that Frank would never have those gifts. He was just simple. It took maturity to understand that, especially in these last months without her. What I always looked at as a positive: Frank's honesty, genuine motives, his simple thoughts, was in this world a negative. And now that Mother was gone, I had to look out for that. For him.

As I got closer to Frank, I simply reached out my hand and touched his shoulder.

"Frank, come on, out with it."

"Well, Garit, I just want you to be careful."

"Careful about what, Frank?" I asked.

"Well, now that your mother is gone, you don't have anyone to talk to about things. Things that you are going to have to learn. Things that your mother knew more about than me. Things that…"

I interrupted him. I knew this might go on and on, and I had to get to B soon.

"Frank, it's okay. We are going to be okay. Now, what exactly are you wanting to talk about here?

"Girls," he said quietly.

"Girls!" I said, laughing at this. He got an embarrassed look on his face.

"Now, Garit, I'm being serious. Girls can be very dangerous. That's what your father always said to me, and I took him for his word. I don't exactly know what it means, but I did not want to find out. And with your mother gone now, I don't know how to handle that pretty girl coming out to the house earlier."

I stopped myself from blurting out, "Oh, you think she's pretty, too?" I knew this would embarrass Frank even more. Now was not the time for that.

I simply took a step back.

"Frank, don't you worry none. B is just a friend. No matter how much I would like it to be so, I don't think she wants it to be any more than that with me. Friends."

Now I kind of felt bad for saying that to Frank because it felt like I was lying to him. Just this very day, she had kissed me on the cheek for crying out loud. No other "friend" had ever done that before, so this was new territory for me also, but I had to make sure Frank was not worried about this, no matter how much I had hoped that B would one day be more than friends with me.

I could see it was bringing Frank stress, so I did what I now call Gariterizing. Sometimes leaving out the details or information concerning a certain situation is better for all parties involved. Especially me. But in this case, I did it out of love for Frank. I just did not want him worrying about it. I know he felt a great responsibility now to guide me in the right direction with Mother gone. However, this particular subject was something he really did not know anything about. Why make him fret? It was the right thing to do. Maybe just the wrong way to do it.

"Frank, don't you worry none about B," I repeated.

"We are just good friends. Besides, she could have her pick of any boy in the county. Why in the world would she pick me?"

I figured that statement would help Frank not worry. But as I said it, that sense of hope that she had given me earlier in the day started to wane a little. That spark that was starting to grow seemed to be doused a tad. My own words, meant to help Frank not worry, backfired. They started to make me worry a bit. Frank looked up from the fire's gaze and smiled a little.

"Well, that may be so, Garit, but just as your Daddy always said, girls are dangerous. 'Treat 'em like a rattler. Give em' plenty of space, and don't ever turn your back on them,' he said. And I have done so my entire life," Frank ended with a proud look on his face.

"Don't worry, Frank, everything will be all right," I said and started to head toward the door. "I am headed into town. I'll be back later."

"Oh, okay, Garit. I will be here when you get back and remember what I said. Be careful!"

If only I had really listened to those words, then. Frank always spoke the truth. I just didn't want to hear it at the moment.

Chapter 13

As I rode into town, the gnawing of what I had said to Frank started to grow. How is it that the opposite sex can have you flying high as a kite one minute and then lower than a dung beetle the next? And B didn't even do anything to me. I was doing this to myself.

Doubt. I hate doubt. But it had plagued me my entire life, like a little court jester sitting on my shoulder. Whispering and singing into my ear "you're not good enough. You're too small and weak." In many ways, that jester was absolutely right. But this time, I had to fight against him. B had come to my house to check on me... fact. B invited me into town... fact. B kissed me...fact. Facts had to trump the Jester in this hand. Or at least I hoped they would.

Crossing the creek into town, I started to feel electricity pulsing through my body. It had been a long time since I came into town. With me quitting the General Store and saloon, and of course, Mother's passing, there was really not much of a need to. I really didn't want to see anyone anyway. But I would be lying to myself if I said it did not feel good being back around.

I could hear the piano playing in the distance from the saloon and saw several people walking to and fro. There was even a new store next to the bank. It looked to be a place that sold elixirs and such. Medicine.

And then, as I turned the corner toward the saloon, I saw another shop had sprung up next to the stables. It said 'Blacksmith' on the shingle out front. *Hmmm. Mr. Gobles must have expanded the stables a bit and moved his forge and such out to its own space.* Previously, the blacksmithing had been done inside the stables, down at the far end toward the back. This was a whole new building set aside from the stables and out front where everyone could see it. I supposed that was good. Before I left the saloon, it had seemed like we were getting a lot more requests for blacksmithing and boarding. Not only our customers but also from the increased military coming through town. Mr. Gobles and Pohl's father must have been doing well on account of that and had expanded.

As I continued and pulled up to the saloon, I could see B inside, sitting at a table right up front. Hard to miss her and her blonde hair. She was all made up and seemed to me like a beacon in the dark. I stopped and watched her for a minute or so while I sat up higher than the window on my horse. She was laughing as usual. And several other men with their hats turned back and smiles on their faces were at other tables surrounding hers. Like a grove of trees standing around a pond. She always drew that sort of attention.

B was not alone though. She had another girl sitting beside her, and a dark-haired man sitting with his back toward me. He had his hat off and seemed to be the one causing B to laugh. I really did not pay much attention to that. I was always drawn to B's smile. And for now, it had me under the same spell as it always had.

I dismounted and stood beside my horse for a few moments. Mainly just trying to get myself in order and catch my breath. My weak lungs always reminding me of their presence. I pulled down the sleeves of my coat, straightened my collar as Mother always did for me, and took another deep breath. "Time to join the living again Garit," I said to myself as I stepped up the walkway of the saloon. I placed my hands on the swinging doors. "Here goes."

I walked through and met B's eyes with my own.

B sprung out of her chair like a bee had stung her. She ran over to me. I did not even get two steps inside before she was on me and giving me a hug. Her hands came up so fast I didn't even have time to brace myself. And for the second time that day, I fell over due to B flinging herself onto me. Luckily this time, rather than hitting the ground, we just fell back into the door frame. It stopped both of us from coming in contact with *terra ferma*, as Ms. Thompson had always said.

"We've got to quit running into each other like this," I said, grinning. She started laughing as we tried to steady ourselves back up.

"Garit, you are the funniest person I know, and I love you for that, kid." she quipped back.

We just stood there for a second.

"Well, without further ado, your surprise, Master Garit, awaits," she finally said. She turned me around so that we could both see the table she had been sitting at. As I looked away from her and to the table, I saw Pohl already standing up. And grinning from ear to ear.

"Pohl, what on earth are you doing here?" I shouted. I started hastily walking toward him. He did the same and he met me with a huge handshake that turned into him bear-hugging me off of my feet.

"Garit, my old friend. I thought we would never be back together," he said as he squeezed the life out of me. I coughed like I couldn't breathe. I added some dramatics to it, of course, playing around. But it was somewhat real. That boy was strong. Me, not so much. He quickly set me down and just held both of my shoulders in his hands.

"Oh, I am sorry Garit! I got away from myself. I am just so happy to see you. And be back in town!"

With that, his smile turned, and he looked down.

"I am so sorry about your mother, Garit. And that I could not attend the funeral. I simply could not get free of work to get here. That was wrong of me and I am truly sorry."

"It's okay, Pohl. I understand, and quite frankly, everything has been kind of a blur since then."

"I can imagine, my friend," Pohl said quietly back. "But I am here now and here to stay!" Pohl ushered me over to the table. I wanted to ask what he meant, but he already started up with the introductions.

"And here my good friend is the only other person in my life that holds a candle to you." He took the hand of the other girl seated at the table. She rose to shake my hand.

"Ms. Cora Lee Hazle, my better half and the love of my life," Pohl said.

"Nice to meet you Mr. Hotzmire," she said as we shook hands. "Pohl has told me all about you, and all the trouble you two used to get into."

I looked at Pohl and he still had the huge grin on his face.

"Okay, wait a second" I blurted out. "First, you're back? Second, how on earth did you swindle this fine young lady into being the love of your life? And third, B, you owe me an explanation as to how you knew about this before I did!!

Everyone at the table just started laughing and looking at each other.

"Garit, man, it's good to see you. I have missed that quick wit of yours," Pohl said while grabbing the back of my neck.

With that, all of the "trees" surrounding the B pond realized that her attention would be focused on our table the rest of the night, and they turned back to their own, with a sense of defeat. I had known that feeling all too well. When the glow from B's light ceases to be focused on you and flitters over to something or someone else, it's a rude awakening to life as it was before her.

But I was basking in it right now and it felt as good as ever. Like a drug pulsing through your nervous system. And I would do whatever it took to keep it going.

As we continued to talk and catch up with what was happening in our lives, it seemed like time stood still. One person's story would morph into another's, and by the time we started to pay attention to our surroundings, the saloon was starting to empty, and the staff was starting to sweep the floors.

It was late. Real late. And I didn't remember a time I had not been home by ten before. I got the sudden shock that Frank was going to be really worried about me, but I shoved it aside. There was nothing on God's green earth that was going to take me away from the feeling I had right now, or from B.

As my attention came back to the conversation, I was just happy. Happy that all of us were here and happy for Pohl. Cora Lee seemed to be a very delightful girl and to care for Pohl very much. She was pretty but in a simpler way. She was quiet and composed. She was in most ways, the exact opposite of B, but in a good and pure way. I was glad that Pohl had found her.

As I sat and listened to all that was going on in his life over the past few years, it was very evident that Cora Lee had been the crowning achievement and had brought joy to Pohl immensely. He had been working for his father for such a time that the day-in, day-out process of being a blacksmith and a blacksmith's son had taken a toll on Pohl.

It was then I felt a small sadness come over me. In the past, I had been his partner. His comrade. His fun. Now I had been replaced by Cora Lee. Don't get me wrong, I was so happy for them. It was just a small sense of loss. A feeling that I had felt so much of lately. A small and lonely place I seemed to be stuck in. But tonight, being here, was something of a chasm in that darkness. B's light shone on me, and

Pohl, my best friend, was back in my life. Even if it was probably just for a moment, things felt perfect. The loss feeling would have to be driven back. Driven down. For this moment of happiness might be fleeting. And I wanted all that I could get of it.

As we exited the saloon, we were all having such a great time that we had not really even thought about what our next move would be. We weren't drunk. All of us had barely even had time to drink, what with talking and laughing so much. We certainly were not tired. I sensed that all of us wanted the night to continue; we just had not even thought about the next stage. Well, that is until B spoke up.

"Okay, everyone, stop!" We all just kind of froze mid-laugh. "Now, we must prepare for the next portion of the evening," she said with a very dramatic tone. She swirled around in a ballerina-type dance. We all busted out laughing again and waited for her direction. "We can't take this party to my house. You all know how my mother is. And we can't take this party to the hotel where Pohl and Ms. Hazel are staying. In separate and proper rooms, I might add! I am so proud of you two. No, there is only one place this party can go, and I will simply not take no for an answer." She stopped spinning and looked directly at me.

"Um, why are you looking at me, B?" I said nervously.

Both she and Pohl busted out laughing again. I was obviously very uncomfortable with the destiny B had determined for the group and, most importantly, me. It was usually I who had all the plans. I who had all the secrets of what was to be next. But this time, she had taken me out of my element.

"Well, Mr. Hotzmire, I seem to recall that you are now the king of your castle, head of your household, master of your domain. And as such, your castle seems to be the most appropriate destination, correct?"

B looked around for affirmation from the rest of the group. The thought process was correct and even funny to a degree, but as soon as she finished saying it, I saw Pohl wince.

It took me a second to understand why. But then B also stopped suddenly, her hand over her mouth like she had gotten caught stealing or lying or something. She had just realized what Pohl already knew; the joke about my independence was a little off-color this close to Mother's passing.

I just looked down, away from their eyes. For the last few hours, I had forgotten about Mother, or better said, pushed her aside for a while. It had felt nice. Not nice that she was gone, of course, just nice that I had not had to think about her being gone for once. Pohl and B had forgotten, too. B lunged toward me and grabbed my hands.

"Oh Garit, I am so, so sorry about that. I did not mean…."

"It's okay, B, I understand. You don't have to apologize. We all forgot for a moment. And that's okay."

Pohl put his hand on my shoulder again.

"I am really sorry, Garit. Sorry, she is gone, but sorrier that I was not here for you when she left."

I just gave him a small and simple half-smile.

"Me, too."

After a moment of silence, I shook myself.

"But," I shouted, "what B said is true. I am the master of my own domain now, and I say we head to the house. My house, to be exact!"

I jumped off the walkway and did my best impression of P.T. Barnum himself, walking down the main street before a carnival. He had come through town a few years before, and the pomp and parade that followed him was something from another world. Everyone remembered that and would for years to come.

All of us started laughing out loud again at my imitation and headed to our horses and carriages in an effort to head that way. I, to my horse and Pohl, Cora Lee, and B headed for the stables. I assumed B had her own buggy and Pohl had some sort of buck wagon since he had come from farther away with Cora Lee. As I mounted my horse and turned up the street toward the stables, I saw Pohl entering the new blacksmith shop, with Cora Lee and B waiting out front.

"So, burglary is on the agenda as well tonight?" I asked. I knew Mr. Gobles would not take kindly to Pohl entering his new shop unaccompanied.

Both B and Cora Lee just giggled and looked at each other.

"Does he not know?" Cora Lee asked B. B shook her head with a coy smile.

"Not know what?" I asked.

"Well, that is surprise number three, Garit!" B said, grabbing the nose band of my Honey's harness and petting her chin.

"B, you have already surprised me enough tonight. What on earth is surprise number three?" I demanded.

B cleared her throat and spoke in an announcer-type voice.

"Ladies and gentlemen, I am pleased to announce to the town of Christiansburg that your new blacksmith has arrived all the way from Salem, Virginia! Introducing the strong, handsome, and talented Mr. Pohl Starp and his beautiful fiancé, Cora Lee Hazle!"

She started to bow and clap toward Cora Lee and Pohl, who had stepped back out of the shop onto the stoop.

"What in the world is going on here?" I yelled back.

"Pohl, you are back! And you're engaged!" yelled B.

"Wait for one minute, B; Cora Lee and I are not engaged. Although, dear, I do love you so," Pohl said as he rushed over to take Cora Lee's hand.

Cora Lee just smiled.

"She's just having some fun, Pohl. No need to worry."

But Pohl then looked up at me.

"Yep, I am back, my boy, and the shop is mine."

At this, I jumped down off Honey onto Pohl, who was not expecting this. But he had the strength and ability to hold my weight easily.

"Wooo Hooo!" I yelled, loud enough to begin to cause a scene in town. People began looking out their windows at us.

As Pohl sat me down on my feet, I had to ask.

"But what about your father? Is he okay?"

"Yes, yes, Garit. He is fine. He is just slowing down a bit. He and old man Boyer have been planning this for about a year or two now. I did not want to write and tell you as I was not sure it would actually happen. I have wanted to tell you so badly, though. Then, when I found out it was actually going to take place, your mother had just passed. I didn't think it was the best time to tell you."

"Not the best time! Finding out that my best friend in the entire world was coming back to Christiansburg would have been wonderful, Pohl."

I made a fist and hit him on his right shoulder as hard as I could. It didn't faze him one bit. He just smiled.

"Well, I should have told you before, but now you know. I'm back."

I spun around to B and spoke before thinking.

"B, the only way this night gets any better is if you say you will marry me right here and now!"

This statement shocked everyone, and I could hear Pohl almost swallow his own tongue. I turned to B and very dramatically went down on one knee, extending my hands out in front of me.

"Well, will you make an honest man out of me, B?" Everyone started to laugh in shock. And what happened next was the second most shocking event that has ever happened to me in my life up until then. Like time stood still, and it was all a dream or something. Foggy yet crystal clear. B looked down at me.

"Maybe someday, Mr. Hotzmire, someday," she said.

I fell over and lay flat out on the street, pretending like I had been shot through the heart. Then I immediately looked up at Pohl.

"Did you hear that, my friend? She said *someday*! I have died and gone to heaven!"

"Garit, get your scrawny self up out of the dirt," B yelled at me. "We have got an evening to continue." At that direct order, I jumped up on my feet, ran over and gave her a huge hug.

"Yes, ma'am!" I leaped onto Honey.

"I like that you can follow orders, Mr. Hotzmire. You may be husband material yet," B said while laughing. Pohl and Cora Lee were also laughing and heading back inside the shop. B followed, and for a moment, I was alone. I seriously could not believe what had just happened. It was almost sensory overload or something. My best friend was coming back to town; he had what you might as well call a fiancé, and for that matter, so did I in B. All the pain and depression that had been flowing through my life lately seemed to be draining away like ink from a spilled inkwell.

I looked up at the stars in the heavens and closed my eyes.

"Mother, I wish you could hear what just happened."

But I smiled to myself and thought she already had. A tear had formed in the corner of my eye at the thought of Mother looking down and seeing all that had just happened. She and I really never talked about B and how I pined over her so much. She just knew. Like all mothers just know. I started to get a very warm feeling around my heart and was thankful I was still living in this moment. Thankful for my friends. Thankful for this new hope in a life that, up until today, had been blunted and faded. I was back. And, by God, it would be better than ever. Mother would want that.

"Master of my own destiny," I said to myself and chuckled. "That sounds pretty good."

As I opened my eyes, I saw Pohl driving a carriage out from the stable doors with Cora Lee next to him and B sitting in the back. As I caught B's eyes, she stood up.

"Well, the night's not getting any younger, Garit! Lead the way home, sir!" she yelled.

I spurred Honey and started to gallop to catch up and lead the wagon. Looking back now, that was the start of the most exciting period of my life. Literally, that second was the inception point, the fork in the road, the destiny-changing event that very few people actually get to acknowledge in their lives. Of course, there are some that do. But most people are just victims of circumstance. Their lives evolve and change via the ebb and flow of happenstance. Some choose their destinies. Will their life in a certain direction. I am not saying I am one of those, but I can also certainly say that from that point forward, I would not let life happen *to* me. I would try and force life to happen *for* me. That little ember from earlier in the day had now grown into a fire that night. A fire growing so fast that eventually, it would consume all around me.

But tonight, it was glorious, and all I wanted to do was take down any limitations I could to contain it. Life was good tonight, and be damned; I was going to make it great!

The ride out to my place was full of loud talking, laughing, and the same old jokes as always but was unmistakably different. We all felt grown up. Or at least, I did. Before, we were all just kids and had parents or other reasons to be sheltered from life. We were sheltered by others and did not have to look the world in its eyes if we didn't want to. We were young. Most of us barely even sixteen years old.

Now though, each of us possessed a sense of independence. A sense that our decisions had merit and we had the reigns. Scary in one sense but very exhilarating in another. Pohl had probably already gone through this process by moving off and being on his own for a while. Growing up. B, she was always years ahead of anyone in maturity anyway, so we are probably just starting to catch up to her. Me though, I just had not thought about it. Before Mother's passing, things were looking up. I felt grown up since I was working at the store and saloon. I had responsibilities. But it was never completely on my own. Even though Mother did not know the whole story, I always felt like if things went south, I could always hide beneath her protection. She had my back no matter what. She was my mother. When I told her the truth, I could see that hedge of protection wither a bit. Not that she would ever stop loving or protecting me. Just that she realized I was growing up and would be venturing out of that protection soon. I was starting to have my own thoughts. Not *our* thoughts or plans, as usual. We did everything together. And the fact that I had hidden something from her not only hurt her but made real the upcoming independence I was starting to exhibit. What a difficult situation that must be. To love someone so much. To want to protect them from everyone and everything. But at the same time, know that you have to let go and let them venture out into a cruel and unforgiving world alone someday.

And at that moment, I realized something that shook me to my core. What if she knew all of this would be happening, and her death would make it easier for both of us?

"No, that's stupid, Garit," I told myself. "Stop being such a pansy." I knew I was onto something, though, and I did not want to believe it.

Right then, B shouted up to me.

"Garit, well, what's your answer, sir? Garit!" she yelled again.

"Oh sorry, just was thinking about something. What?" I yelled back. Everyone just started laughing while B repeated the question I had lost while thinking.

"Do you have any alcohol at your said castle?" she yelled.

I stopped my horse and turned it sideways in the road, which caused the carriage to also stop behind me. I pursed my lips like I was in deep thought.

"Well, Frank always kept some in the barn," I finally said. "But he has been sober for months now, and you know Mother would have nothing to do with alcohol. So, we may be in for disappointment."

And just as I said it, I could tell that, even though that was the truth, I should have said something else. It felt like the schoolhouse bell had just rung and recess was over. Everyone just stopped laughing and looked at each other. I should have just said, "well, of course," and the night would have continued its wonderful path unencumbered. But we all kind of came back to reality for a second and that brought down the mood by twenty levels.

"I have a better idea anyways," I shouted out, trying to stoke the flames of excitement again.

"Instead of going to my house, I happen to know of a better, more adventurous place to go." I had to salvage the night after my *faux pas*. If we don't have alcohol, the next best thing was an adventure.

"I happen to recall that Miller's Pond is just around the bend," I said to the group, knowing that this night, filled with memories and stories from the past, would welcome some more. I knew Pohl and B would be excited. I was not sure about Cora Lee. But I had to try something, and that was all I had at the moment. And my hunch was correct. B just stood up.

"Perfect."

Pohl just smiled as he and I shared the same thought about the last time we had visited the pond and were spying on the girls a few years ago. Pohl turned to Cora Lee.

"Is that all right, dear? It really is a beautiful pond, with lots of flowers I can pick for you," he batted his eyelids, trying to win her approval for the plan.

"Of course, Pohl," she said approvingly. "Anytime I can get the promise of flowers and some time alone with you is peaches," she said with a strong southern drawl.

We all started to laugh, and I felt the relief that I had saved the evening. Man, what a feeling. We were pretty close, so it did not take but a few minutes and we were there. B jumped down from the carriage and ran toward the edge of the pond while I tied Honey up to the back of the carriage. Pohl set the brake and proceeded to help Cora Lee down. When she made it, he looked deeply into her eyes.

"I love you," I heard him say.

She just smiled.

"I know you do," she said and pulled his hand to start walking in another direction from where B was. I just stood there, trying not to ruin what looked to be a great time of smooching that was coming Pohl's way. And this made me very happy for him. He was always so shy. Even though every girl around had eyes for him, he did not want any part of it. He simply did not like the attention and frankly would run from every advance. I was happy that Cora Lee had found a way around his shyness, and he was finally experiencing what every boy in the world wanted. Girls! But for that matter, it seems as if Pohl had gotten way far ahead of me in that department, so this might not be the first time he has been with a girl. I sure couldn't wait to find out the next day. There would be an inquisition at high noon if I had my way. And Pohl would tell me anything. He had to. We were best friends.

This left me in a precarious situation. Pohl and Cora Lee disappeared over the hill, and I could see B standing on a small point jutting out into the pond. She seemed to be just standing there, looking out over the water. I could not tell if she just wanted to be alone or if I should go out to her. This was most of my problem for most of my life. I overthought things rather than just acting on them.

"Well, by God, that part of my life is over," I said to myself as I rustled up the courage to go out to her. On the way over, I could hear her humming a song. Not sure which song, but it did not matter; any sound coming from B was as beautiful as if God's angels had sung it themselves. She was an angel. And I happen to be at Miller's Pond alone with said Angel. This was going to be exciting.

"What you humming?" I asked B as I got closer. I did not want to startle her, so I figured this was a good way to break the ice and ease into the situation.

"Oh, nothin'. Just a tune I heard a few weeks ago when visiting Roanoke with my daddy." Roanoke was the largest city in the area, but I have never been there, so it was like a whole other country to me. The fact that B had been there didn't surprise me, and I so wanted to know more about the trip. What a great way to get her into a conversation.

"Wow, Roanoke! What was it like?" I blurted out, like some stupid kid in grammar school. She did not notice. I think she felt the same way as I. Anything outside of Christiansburg, or Montgomery County, for that matter, was alien to both of us. A good kind of alien, though. One that hit both of us square in our hearts for adventure. B and I did not have a lot in common, but excitement or lack thereof in our current lives and our growing desire to pursue it definitely hit a chord with both of us. She could tell my question was genuine.

"Well, it was marvelous, Garit. We only went in because daddy had some cattle he was selling at their sale barn. He says you get a little more per head by cutting out the middleman or something like that. But I was not going to miss going with him for the world. I had to be around those stupid cows much of the trip, but it was worth it!"

"What was the best part?" I asked excitedly.

"Oh, I would have to definitely say the fine hotels and shopping.

There were musicians on the street corners and all the latest fashions. And the people, Garit. There were people from everywhere. New York City, Philadelphia, Boston, everywhere, I tell you. And if my daddy had not been there, I think I would have run off with a few of them, to be honest. It was just so different than here. But anywhere is different than here."

Following that statement, B could tell that I agreed. I was eating up her description of Roanoke, and again, I could tell that she was starting to put two and two together about her and me. We had a lot more in common than we both realized. There had been moments over our lifetime that we both discovered them, but this was the first time we started really adding them up together. We really were a lot alike. This put me at ease, and I think it did her, also. I broke the silence.

"Do you remember the last time both of us were here?"

"Here at the pond?" she asked back with anticipation.

"Yep, old Miller's Pond. Back in school, Pohl and I came across you, Cecilia, Janice, and Holda."

"Oh, my goodness, Garit, I do remember that," she burst out giggling. "And Cecilia was sweet on Pohl," she added as she danced around me.

"Yep, I am not so sure she and Pohl were on the same page about that, but yep, she was sure sweet on him!" I added.

"Oh, what a fun time," she laughed. "All of us were so young, so innocent, not a care in the world. But times sure have changed, Garit. And I am ready for what's next in life." As she looked up to the stars, she said, "there is a whole gigantic world out there, and I have only seen one percent of it so far." With that statement, she immediately stopped and looked me straight in the eyes, giggling and almost expecting me to know exactly what she was alluding to. And, of course, I picked right up on it.

"And out of the thirteen percent of our lives, now closer to fifteen point six percent, since we graduated, I would take this last .000002% of it over all the rest combined."

As she realized I knew the reference she was trying to make at that moment, she put her arms around me and gave me a peck on my lips.

"Garit, I have a feeling we are going to make a pretty good team, kid." I literally was about to faint from the kiss.

"Yes, ma'am," was all I could say. And smile.

What happened after that is honestly a blur. B and I spent the next few hours just talking about all the things we wanted to do in life, wanted to see. The problem is, we didn't really know what that was, so really, we just kind of kept agreeing with each other's ideas and plans.

"I want to see Paris and travel around the world," she would say.

"Oh yeah, I want to do that too!" I would agree.

Each of us not knowing how or really any way to even start going about those adventures. We just agreed that anywhere or anything was better than here. At one point, we lay down in the meadow and she started to fall asleep while resting her head on my chest. And the crazy thing was I was not even nervous about being so close to B. I felt this energy that began earlier in the night, and it just kept pulsing in me. Kept me going. Kept me calm. The girl of my dreams was falling asleep on my chest as we lay in a meadow by Miller's Pond.

"What in the hell is going on?" I said to myself. But I wasn't nervous. I wasn't scared. I felt alive. I could have died right then and there, and my life would have been completely fulfilled. Good thing I didn't, though, as it was fixin' to get a whole lot better. More complicated, for sure, but better in all regards.

Chapter 14

The past few months had whizzed by faster than a fly being chased by a Redbird. I had gotten my old job back with Mr. Stallsburg, and instead of trying to squeeze it in between the general store and chores, I was at it full-time.

Mr. Stallsburg was more than excited to hear I was ready to come back and offered me the position of Assistant to the Owner. This was a made-up position, of course, as he did not have this position while I was gone, and basically, it was the same position I fulfilled before I left. I just did it back then in a lot fewer hours and for less pay.

But it felt good having a title, and of course, the pay increase did not hurt either. He raised me to five percent of the house take each week. And that could be a lot, depending on the patrons. Most weeks, it was fairly slow, but more and more soldiers were coming through, and of course, around harvest time, things really picked up.

When I left, I was making on average two dollars per day, which was more than enough to make me very well off at my age. Now I was pulling in close to thirty dollars per week. Sometimes more. But even before I left, I had quite a bit saved up, hidden under my bed. I had not counted it since before Mother had passed, but I think I was up to around two hundred dollars. I really did not know what to do with it back then. It was way more than someone of my age should ever have and was partly to blame for my stress all the time. The work and lying were definitely more to blame but having that sort of money at a little past fifteen years old and keeping it from my mother added a lot of burden to my life.

I simply could not spend it. How? Mother would know something was up. There was no way I could make that kind of money from Mr. Dobbs and the general store. Unless I was stealing, and that's exactly what Mother would have surmised if I ever let her know how much money I had. Remember, she did not know about the saloon at all at that time. So, I just saved it. For what, I don't know, but I was stuck. All this money and no way to spend it.

But, now that Mother was gone, my friend was back in town, and B was on my arm most nights of the week, spend it I did to the point that people started wondering what on earth was going on with me. Now everyone knew I worked at the saloon, and it gave me a little bit of cover, but it got to the point that Mr. Stallsburg had to bring me in and talk to me about it.

"Garit, I know you earn your money fair and square, but people are talking. They think our games are rigged too much in the house's favor with you going around spending like you are." I had never really seen him upset before. He still was somewhat calm when he was saying all this to me, but I could tell he was worried.

"The last thing we need this town to think is that we are taking advantage of people or cheating them in any way. You're going to have to settle it down, son." I agreed. It did look suspicious, but while spending it, especially on B, it blurred any normal train of thought right out of my mind.

"Yes sir, Mr. Stallsburg, I will keep the spending down and more controlled. It's just that I have B…"

"Oh, I know, Garit. Everyone knows about you and Ms. Hahne. And everyone also knows that keeping up with her is like trying to rope a wild stallion. But your gonna have to keep a lower profile if we don't want to get run out of town."

"Yes, sir. Will do," I answered quickly. I wanted to keep my job and would never want Mr. Stallsburg to face criticism for any of my actions.

Now how I was going to pass this by B was anyone's guess. I was going to have to put on my thinkin' hat for that one.

As usual, B and I would meet for dinner around five each evening. With everything going on and my house so far away from town, it was just easier to stay around town and eat. I had even considered getting a long-term room at the boarding house, or hotel, as it was just generally easier than going home and then right back each morning. Of course, Frank would be even more worried than usual if I did that, but he and I were only passing each other each day anyways. He was up doing chores early, and I didn't have to come into town until around ten each morning. I generally only saw him on my way out. Then, I typically would not get home until around ten each night, as I would sit in for a few games of poker toward the end of my shift. Too late for him. He was usually already in bed.

But that was the great thing. Since he finally stopped drinking alcohol, he was as steady as the rock of Gibraltar. I was so proud of him. I could tell he was lonesome, though, with me gone all the time and Mother not around anymore. I tried to spend time with him, but work just started getting busier and busier, and of course, all other time was either spent with B or Pohl in town. Our farm was more of a passing burden than home anymore.

As I came out of the saloon, I had to adjust my eyes a little. It was late autumn, and although the days were getting much shorter, the sun was right at that angle that cut directly toward the saloon at about 5:00. I stood there for a moment, blinking my eyes and trying to shield the glare when all of a sudden something poked me in the ribs and made me jump two feet in the air.

"What the—" I yelled out, only to turn and see B holding her umbrella pointed toward me with her right hand and covering her laughing mouth with her left. B was always doing stuff like that to me. At first, it was funny and playful, but I tell ya, after a while, it started to get a little old.

I mean, every day, day in and day out, it was something. To the point that if you did not know any better, you would have thought she was my older sister, picking on me all the time. But she seemed to enjoy it immensely, so I just let her have her fun. Besides, I was used to it. Practically my entire life was being poked with a stick, finger, or worse, to make someone else laugh. It just got a little tiresome all the time coming from B. I still loved her, though.

We had an unusual relationship ever since the night at the pond. She kissed me, of course, and fell asleep on my chest, but really ever since then, we were more like close friends than a courting couple. I think everyone assumed we were courting. But in reality, I entertained her, she blessed me with her presence and attention, and the normal, lovey-dovey stuff was limited to holding hands or an occasional quick peck on the lips. We certainly had never gone as far as Pohl and Cora Lee; even though I was not sure what going farther actually meant.

One time, we all went out for a night on the town, and it was very uncomfortable watching Pohl and her take every opportunity to "swap spit," as we used to say. "I mean, come on, man, come up for air every once in a while," I caught myself thinking on multiple occasions. They were increasingly becoming physical, and although it made me nervous, what made it more so was the sheer delight B showed on her face when watching them behave in that manner. She could not get enough of it. It was like she was watching a carnival show or something, with oohs and aahs coming quietly out of her mouth. She was a wild one, for sure, and seeing that side of her made her even more of a mystery to me. Nervous about it but entranced at the same time. She simply thought Pohl and Cora Lee's physical touching and cuddling was a natural part of life, and I could tell she very much wanted to experiment with it. With me, though, she never seemed to want to go very far. I just assumed she was being proper.

I had seen it a million times before at the saloon. People would come in and "just watch" the poker game, but they sort of lived through the other players in their desire. Whether they did not have the money to play or would be ostracized by their family or friends if they did, they would hang back and act like they were just there for the entertainment, but really were secretly living a life of sin through someone else. They could still go about being an upstanding citizen even though, in their hidden corners, they wanted to let it all go and give in to the other side.

And so I just assumed that was B. Watch but not touch. Eat but not feast. And for that matter, I was completely okay with it. I had no idea what to do next after kissing anyway. I desperately wanted to ask Pohl, as I was sure he was an expert by then, but I just never got the time alone to do it. So, I would just marvel at B's curiosity on the subject but be complacent with the lack of participation. That should have been a red flag to me then, but I seriously did not even know any better, and having B as "my girl," even though it felt more like "my sister" when it came to stuff like that, was fine by me. At least I had B.

After dinner, B and I took the same old stroll down the main street and talked a lot about the same things we always did. It usually ended up with her seeing something she wanted. If the store was open, I would buy it for her then. If not, I'd come back the next day to pick it up. Quite frankly, I saw B for dinner and our walks, and then I headed back to work around 6:30 or so to finish the night. But it felt like I saw her all the time. I worked almost every day but Sunday. The saloon was closed on Lord's Day. I typically would still go in, though. I just had to get caught up. In reality, I saw B for about two hours every day, and it just never occurred to me that this was not okay. Or I should not say, not okay, but peculiar. What she did the other twenty-two hours of the day was a mystery to me. But a mystery that I really never thought about or wanted to solve. It just never occurred to me to think about it. I got my time with her. She acted like she was my girl during that time, and I would get a hug or quick peck on the cheek or lips at the end. More than I could ever have imagined a few years ago, so I would take it. And take it in spades.

Just the impression that B and I had a relationship, and all in the town knew it, was exhilarating. People would always refer to me not by my name, but by saying, "Oh, you're Beatrice's man," or "You're Ms. Hahne's suitor." The fact that those words would come out of anyone's mouth about me was a miracle. And I would never have thought to question any of the slight misgivings about our relationship. For once, I agreed with Frank about girls or, more succinctly, his relationship idiosyncrasies. "Treat 'em like a rattler. Give 'em plenty of space." In this sense, I had no problem giving my worries about B and me some space. Out of sight, out of mind, I suppose.

Days turned into weeks, weeks into months and my little pattern of life was pretty set. I was content. It was hard saying no to B every once in a while when she wanted me to buy her something, but I wanted to make sure I wasn't giving Mr. Stallsburg any undue grief about my spending, as we had discussed. I would do other things, though. Pick her favorite white flowers from around Miller's Pond, write her a poem, or sneak her backstage to meet some of the saloon's entertainers when they came through town. Things that first did not cost anything but second came from my heart, so I felt were much more valuable.

B appreciated all these things for sure, but if a girl was ever about the "bling" in life, it was B. She was by far the best dressed and best made-up girl in town. Very rarely did I, or anyone, for that matter, see her compromised in this regard.

One time it was raining when we were supposed to meet for dinner, and I waited at the saloon's front doors for over an hour for her to show up. She just simply never came. I, of course, got worried and rode right away out to her house to check on her. Soaking wet, I made it to her door to find her sitting in the parlor listening to a record and reading a fashion periodical without a care in the world. I asked her why she did not come to dinner or let me know she was not coming.

"And go out into this horrible weather and ruin my makeup? Garit, I tell you, you grow sillier by the day," she said.

Part of me understood, but another part of me was miffed that she just went on about her day like nothing and did not have the decency to even apologize. I knew right and wrong. I did my best to do the right thing most of the time, and this just felt wrong to me. However, I just forced it down. This was our relationship, and B was B. I did not want to cause waves. I was just lucky to be around her. But I was starting to see through the haze and mist of the B effect.

Those were my days, settled and predictable. There were, however, days that differed. Sometimes Pohl and I would get a chance to sneak off to a fishing hole, or just sit out front of his shop and talk. I really did not know how much I missed just talking to my friend. But him being here now made up for all the lost time. We were adults now, and many of life's wonders when we were younger were becoming commonplace. Girls, money, work. With everything going on in the world, we even dove into politics here and there. We felt like a couple of old men talking about the good old days and the weather most time. I loved it and I know he did too.

One day we got to talking about all the military activity. It was the winter of 1860, almost 1861, and things just seemed uneasy around Virginia. Lincoln had been elected president and the outgoing president, Buchanan, was one term in and having a heck of a time with the slavery issue in the States and territories. Virginia seemed to be right in the middle of it. Pohl and I did not really have a strong opinion about it, other than we felt people should just be free. No matter your color or background. It just seemed like the right thing. Although Mr. Dobbs and a few others in town did have negros working for them, we just never saw the slavery process fully exposed. The negroes we knew seemed happy to be doing what they did, and their owners or employers treated them mostly fair. Would push them for a fair day's work, of course, but I never saw them abuse the colored folk they worked.

It was a hotbed issue though in the newspapers, but we never really paid attention to it. We focused on women and money and not necessarily always in that order. We simply did not have time for all the other world stuff.

One day, though, as we were talking out front of Pohl's shop, a large contingent of Army troops came through town. They were headed down to Fort Loudoun in Tennessee. Most of the Army was used these days to fight or control the Indians as settlements furthered their advancement out west. But there was a growing swell of concern about some states' desire to keep slavery as a standard and the other states wanting to abolish it. It seemed as if there were more and more troops coming through town. Today, it caused us to focus on what was happening or felt like was going to happen. War.

"Pohl, what do you think about this talk of southern states going on their own, their own government?"

"Well, I have not really given it much thought, Garit. I am not sure why they would want to do that, being that we fought a war to unite and get away from the British a hundred years ago. So, we fought a war to come together, and now we want to be apart? Seems silly to me."

"Yep, but *why* is my question? I know slavery and taxes and all that stuff is being blamed, but it just does not seem like a big problem to me. I just don't see it. As a matter of fact, I see the opposite. It really seems like things are finally starting to take off. People have more money and more opportunity than ever. The saloon's weekly revenue continues to grow, and I know you have been busier than ever."

Pohl shook his head in agreement. "Boy, I have been so busy, in fact, that I have had to ask father to stay and help more and more. He was supposed to be cutting back, but I just can't keep up. But I am not going to complain about the money," he laughed.

"Me neither, friend," I responded. "I don't know, just seems like people are getting all riled up over nothing. I sure hope all the rumors about fighting and splitting, though, are just that, rumors. Can you imagine me fighting in the Army, Pohl?"

"Uhhhh, nope," he responded quickly. "You in the Army is like me in a ballerina dress; it just doesn't fit." And as he said it, we both busted out laughing, trying to picture him in that kind of outfit.

"Oh, but I would pay to see it. You in a ballerina costume, I mean," I said through my laughter.

"How much?" he asked as he elbowed me in the ribs.

"I've got a wedding coming up and need all the money I can get my hands on," Pohl continued laughing, but in a way, moving towards a more serious tone.

"Oh yeah, that's coming up, isn't it?" I said, pretending like it was news to me. The truth was it was almost all I had heard about over the past few weeks. B was in the clouds planning the wedding with Cora Lee. She was slated to be one of Cora Lee's bridesmaids. Cora Lee's sister was set to be the maid of honor, but B was hot on the lookout for how to bump her way into that position. If she couldn't be the bride, the maid of honor was the next best thing, and she wanted it. I could not get her to stop talking about it. At this point, I was willing to bribe Pohl to get Cora Lee to ask her to do it, or I was gonna go crazy. There had not been a dinner, walk, or night go by without talk of THE wedding and her role in it.

"I hope Cora Lee knows all the work and time I am putting into her wedding," she would regularly say. "You would think it would earn me maid of honor, but oh no, her lazy sister is gifted that role. She has not even helped one-bit, lazy hussy!" I could hear it right then as Pohl and I were talking. And you can bet I would hear it again that night.

They were set to be married in a little under two weeks, and I could tell Pohl was getting nervous. He would often just laugh it off, but deep down, it wasn't so much getting married to Cora Lee that bothered him. It really was the wedding itself. Knowing that he would have to stand at the altar of the church, say his vows, kiss Cora Lee and, worst of all, dance with her, all in front of everyone. That's what really had Pohl all twisted up.

Oh, and don't you think one minute that I was not adding to that situation! Every chance I got, I would remind him of it. "I can see you dancing right now, big man. It's going to be so elegant," I would poke at him. That usually would end in me either getting hit, kicked, bear-hugged, or at least warned that those things were coming.

He was really nervous. If it were up to him, they would just stay like they were now. No ceremony or nothing, just together and happy. But Cora Lee and, more importantly, her father insisted that they become a proper couple and get married. They had been courting for over a year now, and since moving away from Salem, her father was getting very insistent. Cora Lee took to the pattern of staying with B several days of the week so she could be close to Pohl and would travel back and forth to Salem by coach on the weekends. Her father wanted her to be home to attend church each Sunday, and from what I hear, it was starting to look bad that his daughter was away in Christiansburg all the time. People weren't dense. They knew Pohl lived and worked here, so as usual, the gossip mill started churning out stories. Cora Lee's father was fed up, and to be honest, I think Cora Lee was also. If she had waited for Pohl to get moving on the subject, she would be old and gray before he did. But that was just not Pohl's style.

I had half a mind that the whole "my daddy's upset" story is just that, a story to get him to move forward with a proposal. I say that, but Cora Lee does seem to be genuine and honest, so maybe not. I would understand her using that tactic, but I do find it a little out of character for her if she really did. She was just too nice and sweet of a person for that, in my opinion. Now, what seems more realistic is that B got to chirping in her ear about it and came up with the daddy story herself. Any excuse for her to be the center of attention, or at least close to it, I could see B jumping all over it. And a wedding is as good a reason as anything, I suppose.

"I just hope I don't screw it up, Garit," Pohl said plainly.

"I love Cora Lee and just want to make her happy. So, if going through all of that does, then a wedding it is."

I was proud of Pohl for saying that. This was going to be a big step outside his comfort zone, but I could also see the real desire to make Cora Lee happy. Her happiness meant his happiness. Genuine happiness. As I bid my farewell to Pohl and headed back to the saloon, that fact, I will be honest, had me feeling a little bit down.

What Pohl and Cora Lee had was real. They loved each other and wanted nothing more than to make each other happy. It was really neat to see it and be a part of it as their friend. What was getting me down was that my situation was quite a bit different. I was starting to face the reality that what B and I had was not what Pohl and Cora Lee had. But I could not be honest with myself about that right now. I did not want to give up. I did not want my life to go back to what it was. I already lost my mother; I couldn't lose B too. Not if I had any say in the matter. So, if it's trinkets, perfume, dresses, or other niceties of the world she wants, that's what she'll get. What else was I going to do with the money anyway, right?

Chapter 15

As I sat at my desk tallying up the previous day's counts, I started to notice something. Something small but a pattern of sorts that I must have subconsciously picked up on over the past few weeks. Something just seemed off.

Since coming back to the saloon, I had helped Mr. Stallsburg increase his profits not only in the alcohol and sundries sales but the table games in general. We added a roulette table right before I had to quit, and I really never got a feel for it or the profits it could generate. Evidently, it was a hit and one of the more popular games. The amount of money it ran through each night was almost as much as two blackjack tables. I was really impressed with the crowds it was bringing in when I came back to the saloon. More so, the variety of players it drew. Men, of course, were the staple of our business, but it was interesting to see that women were increasingly coming into the saloon to see shows and such.

Even more, interestingly, they were gambling. And the roulette table was their game of choice. Mr. Stallsburg and I discussed this several times, and each of us had our theories about why, but they basically all boiled down to it being an easy game to play and unintimidating. I will be the first to tell you that sitting down at a blackjack or poker table is kinda scary if you have never done it before. Everyone is typically in a foul mood, doesn't talk much, and if you screw up, the other players call you out.

That, along with the dealers. We tried handpicking them to be polite and professional, but our herd of choices was pretty small. We certainly were not the New York City or New Orleans of the gambling world. However, I had to take Mr. Stallsburg's word for it. I had never left Christiansburg. Here, we sorta too what we could get. So, polite and professional is requested, intimidating and a little rough around the edges is what we really end up with. I had even, on occasion, passed up a certain dealer or two when wanting to play, and technically I was their boss! If that tells you anything.

But roulette is something of a spectacle more than a game. Rudy was our main roulette croupier, and he was about as scary as a robin in a thistle bush, not very. I really liked him. He smiled all the time and loved spinning that wheel. Watching the black, red, white, and gold go round and round really was a sight, and Rudy knew it. He would flick that wheel around in one direction with his signature style and then the ball in the other direction, and almost everyone in the saloon would stop and pay attention. But not only that, it was also fairly easy. Easy to play in general. Sure, some of the bets could get complicated if they were inside bets, but most of the time, people just kept it simple and bet on red or black. Outside bets. Of course, those had smaller payouts as the odds were better for the player than truly betting on a certain number of red or black or an even or odd number. But I think that was the genius of the game. You could bet higher and more at risk for higher odds, but nine out of ten people would just bet on bed or black, and in their mind, they had a fifty-fifty chance of winning.

We had a European table with a single zero leaving an equal amount of red or black slots, eighteen black and eighteen red. We played into this by encouraging simple bets and relaxing the minimum level of bets required. We went from two bits to a nickel in order to encourage participation. And it worked! On a busy night, there was always a crowd around the roulette table, and by observation, people had a really good time. Of course, most lost, but it was sort of okay when they did. It wasn't a lot of money, and it was fun just watching the spectacle of it all.

But I was starting to notice something on the receipts as of late. They were leveling out. We were collecting about the same amount of money in total each week, but our weekly numbers for all other games were going up. And the thing that just was gnawing at me was the impression that more and more people were playing roulette each night. It definitely was drawing attention through casual remarks of "Roulette looks busy tonight" or just observation. More people were surrounding the table on a consistent basis. So how do the winnings not increase when the crowds are? I don't know. Maybe it was just a fluke, but I just had a feeling something was not right. I would definitely be paying more attention to it in the future.

As I was getting close to being done, Mr. Stallsburg knocked on the doorframe to my office.

"How are the numbers looking this week, my good man?"

"Pretty good, as usual, sir," I responded without looking up from my calculations.

"Well, that is fabulous. Job well done, Garit," followed, but from a female voice which caused me to look up quickly. B was poking her head around from the corner and giggling as she said it.

"What on earth, B?" I asked as I stood up from my desk and hurried toward her. Both Mr. Stallsburg and B were now in full laughter at the fun they had played on me.

"You guys go on now and get some supper," Mr. Stallsburg said. "Good day, Ms. Hahn, and please take care of this young man. He has a very bright future ahead of him," he said as he shook B's hand and turned to go back to his office.

"B, I am sorry; I didn't know it had gotten so late—"

B interrupted and said, "It's okay, silly; I just have never really been to the back of the saloon before, so I asked Mr. Stallsburg to show me around. It was fun seeing you so engrossed in your work."

"Oh, that's nothing, just tallying up the numbers and making sure the i's are dotted and t's are crossed."

"Well, you were always very good at that, Garit, I am glad you enjoy your work, and it sounds like you are as good as ever at it, according to Mr. Stallsburg. As he was walking me back here, he went on and on about how proud of you he is and how it's so nice having you back at the saloon. You seem to have found your calling, and from the looks of it, it has found you, too," she said with a big smile.

That felt good. I had never really thought about it. I liked what I was doing and was good at it. Don't get me wrong, I knew I was good at it, but putting two and two together that I liked it and it liked me was something I had never really acknowledged. And I was happy that B realized it also.

Sure, B would compliment me every once in a while, usually about my quick wit or how much money I had in my wallet, but never really about anything of substance. Nothing had really changed from the same old same old as when we were in school together except for the money, of course. She never called me handsome, which I would never expect anyways. She never really gave back to me what I gave to her. Don't get me wrong, being in her company was always pleasant. It just lacked a healthy "back and forth" of feelings or sentiments. It was usually just one-sided. Me toward her. I was starting to believe that B knew all too well that my being in her presence was a privilege.

I always felt that way as my self-esteem was constantly reminding me, but it just hurt a little to think she knew it too.

But here was a genuine observation and compliment about me from her. Maybe things are finally changing. Even if it was small, it felt good. Mother always said positive things about me. Mr. Stallsburg did also, so having those two prop me up helped. Now that Mother was gone, maybe B could fill her role. Time would tell.

As B and I fell into our usual plans of dinner, walking, and shopping, the tally issue from earlier was still on my mind. B could tell that tonight my mind was preoccupied.

"What you thinkin' about, kid?" she said innocently but with anticipation.

B was never afraid to get involved in gossip or play problem solver to your problems. She lived for that. It allowed her to again be the center of attention in the good times and bad.

She was smart. She knew how to play both sides of every situation so that she always came through it looking great to all. With Pohl's wedding coming up, it had taken a lot of the focus off other problems, but since she was not getting her way about the maid of honor position, she was starting to need other directions to focus her skill on.

"Oh, nothing," I responded.

"What is it silly, you can tell me anything?" she said as she clutched my arm tighter.

"It's really nothing. Just some of the counts were off on my weekly tallies. Or at least I think they were off; it may just be me worrying about nothing."

"Well, what kind of numbers are we talking about here, a lot?" she asked, seemingly very interested in the topic.

"No, not a lot, and maybe not even anything, just a feeling I have about it. Again, it's probably nothing."

"Well, if it has you focused on it rather than me, it's something." She looked me in the eyes, and her words rang very true. She was going to be the center of attention, and if anything was taking her spotlight away, she would not have that.

"Now tell me the whole story, all the details. And that will keep us entertained while we walk tonight, right?" she pulled my arm and kept walking.

"I suppose," I simply shrugged.

But I would be lying if I said it didn't feel good talking about me for a change. It did. I filled B in on the feeling I had about the roulette table and that I did not have proof, of course, about anything. It was just that, a feeling. But typically, my hunch about things were on point. So, I thought it deserved more investigation. B was really into what I was saying.

"Ooohh, like that Edgar Allen Poe story Ms. Thompson wanted us to read in our last year," she said at one point. "I did not like it very much then, but this intrigue you describe has left me intrigued!" she smiled as she said it.

"Maybe I can help you solve the case, Mr. Hotzmire!" she giggled but was very serious in her request. This town was, for lack of a better word, boring. B was constantly searching for excitement, and with the wedding waning, this would be her next victim…I mean pursuit. So, I fed into it.

"Well, I really don't think it's that big of a deal, but yes, maybe you can help me. What are you doing later tonight?" I asked with my eyes squinting and a little mischievous tone. She let out a wicked giggle.

"Well, I suppose I am helping solve the crime of the century. What's the plan, my good sir?"

As she and I walked, I came up with a plan for her to help me figure this out, if there really was a "this" to begin with. But it was something different than normal nights; she really was excited about helping.

And instead of her retiring home after our walk, I got to be with B a little bit more tonight. *A win-win on all accounts,* I thought.

I went back to the saloon as normal and went through my normal nightly functions, but kept a very close eye on the roulette table. Things were going like they typically did, and a small crowd had gathered around the table. They were laughing and having a great time. Nothing off at all. What was different was that I now had a spy in the midst. B was part of the crowd.

After watching for some time, she decided to make her move. I had already schooled her on the ins and outs of the game, told her how to bet, and given her some cash to use in the process. In the win-win column, she gained more of a win so far in getting to gamble with my money. But it was all part of the investigation, so oh well. She had never played before, so it was perfect. She would be new blood to Rudy, and I gave her an exact amount of ten dollars to play with.

My intention was that she lose all of it, and hopefully, the night's tally would be close to ten dollars higher than average. The crowd was about the same as usual, so it seemed to be a good idea. The first kink in the plan was that instead of losing, she won!

And she kept winning. From what I could tell without looking too obvious, she was up six dollars and had only started betting a half dollar at a time. I wanted her to be more aggressive with the bets than the typical two bits here or nickel there. We agreed that since she was new, betting fifty cents would be okay and would be a higher pot amount at the end of the night so that I could easily see if anything went missing. It's easier to skim with larger pots, was my rationale. And, in fact, my experience. But each time she would bet, she won! We agreed in our planning session that she would just act like the beginner she was and just bet on black or red. Have fun, keep it light and laugh. Like most people truly did.

And she fit right in. She was having fun. Laughing and, as usual, drawing the attention of almost the entire saloon. But as she continued to win, the crowd around her kept growing. As I said, she was up almost six dollars by now, so she had won what I had counted to be ten to twelve rounds in a row. I did have to still act like I wasn't paying too close attention in order to not look suspicious, so I might have missed one or two rounds, but I think I was close.

But now, all the attention she was getting helped me to be able to blend in much more than usual and watch more intently now. Everyone was. Even Mr. Stallsburg came out of the back and was watching from a distance. Rudy was doing his typical showboating; the other people at the table, for the most part, had stopped betting as they were fixated on B. She was eating it up. She won another spin. Up another fifty cents. She was really getting into it and, I guess, decided to up the ante. We had talked about keeping a moderate profile, but I should have known that would be impossible for B. I just figured she would lose the ten dollars fairly quickly, and we would be done with the charade. I would count the daily's tomorrow and either be satisfied that nothing was awry or have some sort of evidence that something was up.

But oh no, the B effect was alive and well, and of course, I should have anticipated that she would take it to another level. She always had and always would, I suppose. She was so entranced by the attention or the winning or the moment that she upped each bet to two dollars. Everyone let out a collective gasp upon seeing this, and even Rudy had to stop for a bit as this was highly over the typical bet.

He looked at me for approval, and I nodded. I then looked at Mr. Stallsburg with an 'I hope you're okay with this' look, and he simply nodded back. So, we were off to the races. Rudy was a little less flamboyant with his spin this next time. I think he was getting very nervous that his table was going down so quickly. We typically gave him a starting pot of ten dollars each night, and he never really had a reason to go over that and ask for more. But now, he was close to being left with three dollars or so, and B just bet two dollars. If she won, he would be down to his last dollar.

Everyone around B was growing ever so amused at this situation, and the entire saloon was now absolutely focused on her. Before letting the ball spin, B, in a move that to this day defines her to a T, told Rudy to stop mid-spin, grabbed his hand, brought it close to her mouth, and kissed the ball ever so lightly. I remember Rudy almost dropping the ball; he was so taken aback by this move.

I mean to start, B was the most ravishing patron he had ever served, he was almost going to be out of house money, and he was going to possibly do all of this in front of the largest crowd around him. Including Mr. Stallsburg, who had moved from the back of the saloon to right off to his left side near the bar. He had never done that before. But I don't think he had ever seen a spectacle such as this either. It was like I had booked the best entertainment act ever, and the place was buzzing.

Rudy finally gathered himself as the roulette wheel was still spinning and let the ball go in the other direction. B had placed her bet on red, and as soon as the ball left Rudy's fingers, the place went silent. All that could be heard was the spinning of the ball and the anticipation of everyone in the saloon almost willing the ball to land on a red number. Because Rudy had been delayed in letting the ball go by B's pre-spin kiss, the ball started to fall faster than normal. It bounced and careened off the wheel, and with every sound, it made the crowd seem to flinch.

Finally, with the last bounce and the ball came to rest in the pocket of the black seven. At that, everyone let out a collective gasp and moan as B's winning ride had finally come to an end. And on the largest bet to boot. Of all the people in the saloon that was the most relieved, it had to be Rudy. He simply closed his eyes and dropped his head. None of the usual theatrics displayed when someone won or lost, just relief. Relief that he finally broke the streak and could replenish his pot with two dollars. He was going to be back up to five dollars now. His pay was based on winnings, so technically, he was still in the hole. The chance that he could work his entire shift and walk out with nothing was very high at this point. Not to mention the ire of Mr. Stallsburg and me on how he almost cost us ten dollars. To say he was relieved was plain, but he was not out of the woods yet.

But then, his luck changed. B was setting up to do it all again. She had already placed another two dollars on the table, and the crowd was getting riled up again when Mr. Stallsburg quickly stepped up to the table.

"Well, well, Ms. Hahne, you have had quite the beginner's luck tonight. You sure don't want to stop now while you're up and have a drink with Garit and me?"

She stopped for a split second and squinted like she was thinking about it.

"Oh, Mr. Stallsburg, you worried about little ol' me taking all of your money?" she asked, at which the entire saloon belted out laughing. This gave Mr. Stallsburg some time to very coolly craft his response. Once the laughing died down, he spoke again.

"Oh, I think you have already taken quite a bit of it, don't you think?" He looked down and saw the stack of coins in front of her.

She looked down also.

"I suppose you are correct, sir," she said, then motioned to me to come to pick up her loot and walked like she was the President of the United States over toward the bar.

The crowd split like the Red Sea and let her pass. I hurried over to the table to gather up her winnings like a lap dog. But to be honest, I was way out of sorts anyways. We, meaning the house, just lost close to five dollars. We, meaning B and I, were supposed to lose to the house so that I could see if anyone was skimming. And all of us had just been a part of the most excitement around here in months. I almost forgot that B's winnings were technically my winnings since I staked her. But at this point, I could barely gain a foothold on what exactly just happened, so I just collected her (my) money and followed her as usual. Once I reached the bar, I heard Mr. Stallsburg ending a statement to B, "…on the house, of course," as he handed her a drink of whiskey.

She let out a giggle and said, "down the hatch," as she took one full gulp of the whisky and slammed down the shot glass upside down onto the bar. Mr. Stallsburg's eyes were as big as silver dollars, and not a one would be taken off of B.

She was absolutely made for this and this moment. She carried herself with a sense of "of course, I just did that" attitude. Everyone, I mean everyone, envied her even more than usual. Our plan to potentially find a thief had backfired completely. But it had morphed into a series of luck and events that would dramatically transform both of our lives. B turned around to the crowd that had now followed her over from the roulette table to the bar, just wanting to get a taste of what this magic was that surrounded her.

"I don't know about you all," she yelled out, "but that was the most fun I have had in ages."

The entire crowd started hooting and hollering in affirmation. She controlled everyone like a conductor of an orchestra. She proceeded to mingle through the group and shake hands with all her admirers. The amount of "let me buy you a drink" offers kept climbing to over twenty, probably, by the time she was done. She wouldn't have to buy her own liquor until she was eighty at this rate. All I could do was stand there in complete and utter shock. This was lightning in a bottle and by the look on Mr. Stallsburg's face, he knew it too.

The night proceeded to wind down. We all started to wake up from the hypnotic effect of B and her winning. The saloon had to stay open an extra hour or so just because it was so packed, and no one wanted to leave. So, we just kept the drinks flowing. I knew tomorrow, when I did the counts, we were going to be down. Everyone was so focused on the celebration that no one was playing any games. Heck, Rudy was so frazzled he just left at some point. No one even saw him leave. But now there were just a few people around, and I could see the staff were exhausted. Mr. Stallsburg had been keeping everyone moving forward all night, and even he was showing some fatigue. B, of course, was not even a bit tired; she, by now, was heavily drunk.

At one point, she had jumped up on stage and proceeded to lead everyone in Camp Town Races. It was a hoot. I finally got her down after I promised that I would bring her back the next night and stake her again. She lit up at that prospect, but I was not exactly sure what in the hell I was going to do. I really needed to talk to Mr. Stallsburg about all of this. Things got way out of hand and although I knew it wasn't a bad thing, it was almost too good of a good thing. Things were too crazy. You couldn't buy this type of advertising or reputation for all the gold in the world. He and I needed to talk through it all and get a handle on what would he and I would later term the "Buzzing B" effect.

Right now, I just had to get her home, and we would figure all that out later. Thankfully, Pohl and Cora Lee had been told a little earlier in the evening of the happenings in the saloon, so they had come over to join in. They got there a little before the Camp Town Races part, but late enough that they were still sober and could be of assistance to me in controlling the mob and B. I had a few too many drinks; also, I have to admit. It sure was fun. I did mention, though, to Pohl about 30 minutes ago that we needed to be heading for the door, so he was on it. He whispered to Cora Lee the plan, and she hung right next to

B so that she could start turning down the free drinks, mostly from men, of course, and not cause a fight to break out.

Cora Lee had managed to get B convinced that it was time to go and signaled Pohl, who in turn grabbed me by the arm and started leading me to the door. We all met outside on the walkway, and I swear I could hear the saloon take a deep breath out. Not the people. The actual building. I swear. It was like even it didn't know what just happened. It was all good, of course, but I was glad it was coming to an end. B was still humming Camp Town Races and was hanging on Cora Lee just to stay upright. Pohl could tell Cora Lee was growing weak, so he traded her out and now was actively holding B's weight as he looked at me with a 'what do I do now?' look on his face. I simply started laughing and walking toward the stables. The group just followed me, assuming I knew what to do or where to go.

Once we made it there, I looked around for a carriage or buckboard, anything that we could load B into so that we could take her home. There was nothing out front. As I turned around to ask Pohl if he knew if one may be in the stable or out back, I saw that Pohl had given up trying to help B walk and had completely picked her up in his arms and was just holding her as she came in and out of a drunken coma. Cora Lee did not necessarily like this arrangement but knew Pohl was the only one there that could do it. She stood right next to him and B the entire time, keeping a very nervous but understanding eye on both of them.

"Pohl, anything we can use to get her home?" I asked.

"I think maybe out back," he answered.

He was just as nervous as Cora Lee was and wanted to pawn her off into a wagon as soon as possible from the look of it.

"Ok, will be right back," I yelled. I ran beside the stables toward the back to look. Thankfully there was a buckboard back there, but we would have to hitch up a horse to it. Just then, I remembered that

Honey was still tied up out the back of the saloon. Mr. Stallsburg had built a small, 3-horse stable for him, me, and other staff that needed to set up their horses during their shift. He had water, hay, and a roof to keep them comfortable. Always having to pay Mr. Boyer to stable our horses each day was getting to be an inconvenience. It wasn't very expensive, and I still used him on occasion. Especially since I would just stop by and see Pohl anyway, but it was nice having a horse right out back when you needed it at the saloon. I ran back up to the front of the stable and past the group.

"I will go get Honey," I yelled as I went.

It only took me about three minutes or so to get there and back, but by then, B was propped up on a bench at the front of Pohl's shop, with Cora Lee doing the propping. Pohl had gone inside, and it looked like he was getting some water or something for the girls to drink as I pulled up and jumped off my horse.

"Is she ok? Everything ok?" I said anxiously to Cora Lee, who just rolled her eyes.

"Yes, she is fine, Garit. She's just too far gone and needs to sleep it off. I think it would be better if we just got a hotel room here, rather than going out to the house at this time of night. I will explain it all to her family tomorrow."

I just stood there for a few seconds, trying to think about it. B's parents were good people. They were strict at times, but as B and I had continued to be around each other, they were starting to slack off in their watchful eye. We were growing up, and I think they knew that I would never let anything happen to B. And they always saw that I treated her with respect.

But this was something of a new territory. I never really had been in this situation before. Usually, B and I separated each night, and she went back home or wherever she would go, and I just went back to the saloon. I had never had her out this late before, and for that matter, I didn't even know if B had ever been out this late before. As I stood there thinking, Cora Lee must have taken pity on me. She tried to reassure me.

"Garit, we have done this before. I mean not like this, of course, but B has stayed with me in the hotel several times when I am in town. I don't have a room tonight; I thought we would be going back to B's house, but maybe we can get one, and everything will be better in the long run. I certainly don't want to ruin my reputation by bringing her home in this condition."

Boy, was I happy someone could think straight because I was in the same boat. What on earth would B's parents think if I brought her home like this? I didn't know, and I didn't want to find out.

"I like it," I shouted back to Cora Lee and darted off toward the hotel.

Here was when having some extra money was going to come in handy. Why I didn't get back on Honey and ride over, I have no idea. I was getting pretty tired, doing all this running around, but clearly, I was not thinking straight, so run I did.

Getting to the hotel and bursting through the front door, I found no one. Lights were turned down, and it was clearly too late for new arrivals. There was a small sign that just said "ring bell" sitting next to a bell on the front table. So, I rang it kind of softly. I surely did not want to cause a scene. Although the way I entered the hotel had already done so.

I saw Emmy coming down from the back stairs. Usually, Mr. Waynegrove was the first face you would see in the hotel during the day, any day for that matter. He ran a tight ship. But after hours, it was always Emmy. To say Emmy was Mr. Waynegroves' slave was probably not the correct description. I never really knew if she was owned by him or not. Emmy was really just part of the hotel. Meaning that she was the cook, cleaner, and general all-around glue that held it together. She handled everything except for the greeting during the day as she was too busy doing everything else. Mr. Waynegrove or his wife would be the faces of the hotel during the day or at events, while Emmy conducted the other staff and herself behind the scenes. But everyone loved Emmy, and I sure did also. She was always so happy and would try (if she had the extra time) to give me grief over anything she could.

"Mr. Garit, you sure need to shine those shoes the way you shine your nickels," she would poke at me when running into me around town or at the hotel. I never really knew what she was talking about, but I just assumed it was something of a compliment and razz at the same time. Did she think I was rich or loved money or something? I never figured it out, but I liked it. Made me feel noticed by someone, and I could tell she said it out of fun, not trying to put me down or anything. Just friends joshin'. That's what she felt like to me, a friend. Although I really didn't know anything about her other than she worked and served at the hotel. I never took the time to find out more about her. I should have.

Emmy came walking down the hall toward the front of the hotel with a candle in her hand. I could see right away that although she was trying very hard to make it look like she wasn't just asleep, she had been.

"Now hold on, sir, I will be right with you," she said as she walked toward me.

When closer and the light started to fill the room, she recognized it was me.

"Mr. Garit, what on tarnation are you doing here this time of night?" she asked with a concerned look but a smile at the same time. She moved closer to me in an attempt to keep the conversation quieter than normal. She did not want to wake the other guests.

"What can I help you with, Mr. Garit" she somewhat whispered to me.

"Oh, Emmy, I am so thankful it's you and not Mr. Waynegrove tonight," I said back.

"Well, what do you need, son? Everything ok?" Emmy responded with growing concern in her voice.

"I need a room for two. Something nice. And I need it quick," I said, with the feeling I was saying it quietly, but by the look on Emmy, I was not. She just shook her head.

"Mr. Garit, you've let devil's juice get you tonight, haven't you, son? It's not good for nothin', I tell ya. You need to stay away from it. But, let me check and see what kind of room I can whip up for ya."

She went over to the desk to check on things. I was just standing there watching her when I got this feeling down in my chest. I don't know why but right then, I started tearing up. My mind pictured my mother standing there, going through the ledger, rather than Emmy. I just got this feeling that Mother was there. Watching out over me. Trying to help me solve my problems. As I saw Emmy running her finger down the page, I just lowered my head and let the tears fall. I grieved, of course, when Mother passed, and for a time after, it seemed like anything would set me to tearing up. I just really missed her.

But since Pohl and B and the saloon, I really had not thought about Mother very much in a sad way. Don't get me wrong, of course, I thought about her. But I had so much going on in my life that I never really stopped long enough to be sad. But tonight, something happened, and it all came back as I stood there in the hotel lobby watching Emmy try and help my situation. I lost track of really what was going on, and the next thing I remember, Emmy had come over to where I was standing and gave me a hug. I just let it happen. I was really more upset than I should have been at that moment. A wave of grief just came over me. I can't explain it, but it happened. Emmy just hugged me tighter.

"It's okay, Mr. Garit, whatever it is, you will be okay," she said. "I am here to help, and Ms. Emmy can fix almost anything."

She continued to just pat my back. Man, that felt good. Not in a sexual way or anything, just comforting. I had been hugged, of course, by B, but this hug felt like it was being given by someone who, although she did not know what I was upset about, had seen enough pain in her life that she just understood. I don't exactly know how long we stayed in this embrace, but it was long enough that I could tell Emmy was now getting a tad bit nervous that someone would come in and find us this way. Not that it was inappropriate, just something she would rather not have to explain to anyone. And at that moment, she didn't even know why, either, so she would have been at a loss for an explanation.

I finally regained my composure and pushed her shoulders back so that I could look in her eye.

"Thank you for that, Emmy."

"Well, Mr. Garit, everyone needs a good hug every once in a while. So I should thank you also. Now, are you okay, son?"

"Oh yes, yes. I am so sorry, Emmy, I just need a room, and my mother died and—" She interrupted me as politely as she could.

"Your mother just died?" she asked, very confused.

"No, no, Mother died a long time ago. I need a room for the girls. They can't go home, and I love her. She drank too much; I have got to get them a room. They can't go home."

At this point, I was just rambling, so Emmy took my hands into hers and looked me in the eye.

"Okay, Mr. Garit, calm down. It's way past the time of night that things make sense, so I got you. You need a room for two girls that have drunk too much, pretty much like you have, by the way." She just smiled. I just looked back and nodded.

"Ok, I got ya. I have a room that will be just fine. Now, where are these girls at?"

I just looked around like I was just coming back from another world, as in, honestly, I kind of just had. I had not broken down like that in a while, and, in combination with the alcohol, if you had told me we were in Boston, I would have probably agreed with you. Thankfully just then, I could see Pohl and Cora Lee stepping up onto the porch of the hotel. B was in Pohl's arms, completely out cold. Emmy saw this also.

"Oh, my Lord," she said, and she rushed to open the door for them. As she opened the door, she put her finger up over her mouth in an effort to have all of them stay quiet as we went through our next steps. Once they all got inside, Pohl looked at me and could tell that I had just been crying. I could see an immediate concern build on his face, but Emmy got his attention away from me with her instructions.

"Ok, you big ole buck, follow me upstairs, and let's get your two ladies settled down in their room."

Emmy led Pohl, carrying B, Cora Lee right behind them, up the main stairs and down the hallway. As the candlelight faded, I found myself just standing in the front room in the dark. Not having a point of focus, I could feel myself starting to sway a little. I knew I had to sit down soon or at least steady myself by grabbing onto something.

Luckily, I found a chair and fumbled my way into it.

I awoke to "Garit, Garit, wake up," coming from Pohl. He was bent down on one knee in front of me and slapping the side of my head. Emmy was standing right behind him and just shaking her head.

"What the…" I shouted out as I regained my focus.

"Shhhh!" Emmy hushed me as quietly as she could. "You boys are gonna get me in big trouble if you don't be quiet." Pohl looked back at her.

"I am so sorry, ma'am," he said and pulled me up out of the chair as he stood up.

Emmy then whispered to both of us.

"Now, don't you worry about your girls; Emmy is going to take good care of them. Mr. Garit, I need you to come back early, early in the morning, and pay the bill. Buck, you come back too, as I need those girls up and out of here before Mr. Waynegrove gets around. I don't think those two want their reputation soiled over one night's fun."

We both just shook our heads in the affirmative and started for the door. As we hit the porch, I just looked back and waved at Emmy. She just smiled and shook her head as she closed the door. I was walking, but Pohl was very much assisting me, and I started to laugh, thinking about what Emmy was probably saying in her mind. "These white folk has done lost their ever-lovin' minds," was ringing in my head. Pohl had no idea what I was laughing at, but I don't think he cared. He was just ready to get this night over.

"Where we going, Pohl?" I asked.

"Don't worry about it," he said as I continued to be somewhat dragged toward the stables. Right then, I had a sense of emotion come over me again. This time, not grief but thankfulness. Thankfulness for my good friend Pohl.

Chapter 16

The next morning, I woke up lying on a saddle blanket on the back of a buckboard inside the stable. The smell of hay was strong, and I could see daylight starting to filter through the boards of the east wall. My head was pounding, and my right arm was fully numb.

As I tried to move, my right arm was not helping much at all, and I was having a time trying to prop myself up to look around. Several minutes had passed since I understood where I was, and I could get my body propped up enough to relax my back against the sideboard. I could hear some rustling in the stalls right next to me and saw Honey standing there with her head over the side wall, just staring at me. I laughed a little. It really did look like she had a 'you idiot' look on her face as she stared into my eyes.

"I know, I know, Honey," I said to her as I rubbed my eyes and finally got some feeling back in my arm. I looked around and saw my coat hung up on the end of the stall, and my shoes were put neatly below them.

"Good ole Pohl," I said to myself. As I said it, the side door to the stable opened, and I saw Pohl coming through with a stressed look on his face.

"Oh good, you're up. We got to get moving," he said as he came over, pulled me out of the wagon, and set me down by my coat.

"Hold up, hold up, where are we going?" I asked, confused.

"We have to get over to the hotel and get the girls, and quick. Father's almost up, and Emmy told us early."

I just stood there. I really was not sure what he was talking about. I had forgotten most of what happened last night and obviously about what we were having to hurry around this morning for.

"Get your shoes on and follow me," Pohl said as he started for the door. Thankfully he had grabbed my coat, as I would have forgotten it. I stumbled around but managed to get my shoes on before I reached the door to go out and follow him. I must have looked like a sight, but luckily the street was mostly clear as it was very early.

The cold hit me, and as much as I like a clear, crisp day, it was pretty jolting to me that day. But it helped me wake up and come to faster than I imagine I would have without it. Pohl was walking quickly toward the hotel and looking back to ensure I was keeping up. As I got closer to him, he held out my jacket.

"Hurry, put this one on, and when we get to the hotel, stop and tie your shoes."

Man, I was happy he was here to direct me. I would still be in the wagon trying to figure out how I got there without him. As we reached the hotel, I stopped and tied my shoes. He was there to straighten me up as I stood up, tucked in my shirt, and dusted me off. I could see a few people sitting in the hotel's dining area as we made our way inside.

Once there, I also could see that Emmy was back in the kitchen preparing breakfast for the guests, but she caught a glimpse of us coming through the door and started to head our way. We stood at the front until she got there and waited to see what she wanted us to do. I was starting to remember a little about last night now, and although I was still confused about what we were doing, it felt familiar. Emmy came straight up to Pohl as if she already knew he was the composed one in the group. She whispered into his ear. At that, he went straight ahead and up the front stairs to the rooms.

As I watched him ascend, Emmy whispered into my ear, "That will be 3 dollars, Mr. Garit."

I was still a little confused, and this statement confused me even more.

Mr. Waynegrove only ever charged me one dollar per night before, so hearing 3 dollars just added to my discombobulation. But for some reason, I just trusted what Emmy had said and did not want to question it. I searched my pockets for my wallet and found it in the inside pocket of my coat.

Opening it up after last night, I was not sure exactly what I would find. Thankfully, it looked like I had held my composure enough to ensure that my money was not all spent or lost.

I pulled out a five-dollar note from the Exchange Bank of Virginia and proceeded to put it in her hand.

"Oh, no, no, no, Mr. Garit, I can't take paper money. I need coins," she said. So, I took the money back and searched my pockets. Thankfully I had some silver and hastily gave her what I had. She looked at them carefully but quickly.

"That'll do," she said and put them in her front apron pocket. Just then, I could see Cora Lee hurrying down the stairs, followed by B and then Pohl. B looked like a tornado had swept her up sometime in the night, but she still managed to look beautiful somehow. Cora Lee looked tired. Pohl looked annoyed. Emmy was looking around nervously and had already moved over to the door. As the group came down the stairs and towards the front door, Emmy shooed them away from it and said softly, "out the side door," as she pointed down the hallway toward the back stairs. Cora Lee understood, grabbed B's arm, and ushered her that way. Pohl followed close behind, and I patted Emmy on her arm and shuffled after them.

"You take care now, Mr. Garit, and keep away from the Devil's Juice now," she said as I passed her. I smiled in a "you better believe I will" way and kept on.

B and Cora Lee were back at home finally, and Pohl was back at the shop to get the morning started. I was just hoping that B's parents were not wise to any of the previous night's and, I suppose, this morning's activities. As Pohl and I said our goodbyes from the stable to the girls, we could hope that nothing seemed out of sorts. I thought them coming back this early from staying in town would be somewhat out of the ordinary, but hopefully, they could play it off. I did not know the plan for that and, frankly, probably could not even offer any suggestions at this point. I just wanted to go back to sleep. The "Devil's Juice" was still biting me pretty hard.

I finally got Honey saddled and was slowly making my way back to the farm. I suppose I could have just stayed at the hotel or in my office at the saloon, but home felt like the right place to go this morning. It seemed so much farther away than usual. Like I would never get there. Sleep is all I could think about. Good, deep sleep. I rounded the corner and finally saw the smoke from our fireplace rising in the crisp morning air.

I thought about how I genuinely loved fall, dazzled by the leaves turning all sorts of reds and oranges, but now, everything was dead. Cold and grey. Lately, I had not really even been looking at the world around me. Too busy focusing on B and the saloon to care, I guess. Sure, I would notice it being cold, rainy, or snowing, but it didn't really bother me as I had a warm place to be most days inside the saloon. And now that I was not at home as much, chores and such would not crack my pampered life like usual.

I hate doing chores in the winter. So early and soooo cold. My weak lungs always reminding me of them in the cold. Having my breakfast cooked for me at the hotel, not having to slosh through the mud, and walking on the covered walkways around town was something I had definitely grown fond of. But it was probably also the reason this morning's ride home was digging into my chest more than usual. Cold, harsh, and unforgiving is the world around me, and getting home to my warm bed has never been more entrancing in my life.

As I continued plodding towards my haven, a sadness started to build within me. The previous night's details were still foggy in my mind, but I remember breaking down in front of Emmy. *Quite embarrassing*, I thought, *but also oddly mending*. I really did not know her at all, and for her to see me like that would have been abhorrent usually. Undignified. But there was this nagging feeling of hurt within me that her hug certainly made me feel less intrusive.

The loss of Mother had caught up to me last night. It was still with me this morning and seeing the farm was starting to make it pierce deeper. But Emmy's hug had pacified me, alleviated the hurt a little, and I could not ignore it. Not because it was Emmy per se, but just because it was someone who seemed to understand the hurt. Understood the burden for a moment and held it for me. I started to acknowledge a dark truth about life. That life can give you moments of peace or joy but also supply a mountain of pain that will leave you choking on it. It doesn't care or hold back. It just is. The world only goes on with or without you. And if you are not strong enough to survive, it has no impact on the world continuing down its path. As Mother believed and I heard each Sunday in church, the world's Creator cannot be questioned. His motives are uniquely shrouded from our understanding, but then, we must have faith that they are correct and for our own good. How has my life been correct or good? I have been forced to swallow pain and sickness my entire life. I should have died when I was born, but He kept me around, weak and small, so that my life continued in affliction. For what purpose? And on top of it, He took away Mother.

"Goddamn You!" I yelled out into the air. I yelled so loud that it spooked Honey a little, and she started to gallop. I reined her back in and gave her an apologetic stroke on the side of her head.

"It's ok, girl. I am sorry about that," I said in a calming tone.

Emmy had done the same thing to me last night, just calmed me down a little when I was spooked. I needed more of that in my life. I had my work, my friends, and B, but no one had calmed me like that since Mother's passing. I yearned for it, and the sad reality that a relative stranger had eased it last night made me finally realize I was broken. Broken more than I had taken the time to acknowledge.

As I made it to the front gate of the farm, I could see Frank off in the distance doing his usual morning chores. He looked content. I had not really seen him in such a while. Really paid attention to him at all. I was too focused on the world away from the farm. My world. I was being selfish. Selfish with my time and concern for him. I need to do better with that. This ride home has given me some much-needed clarity about life.

"I should get drunk more often," I laughed.

But seriously, something was happening to me. And I was done letting life just happen to me or hurt me anymore. I had paid my dues to it already. Mother had paid with her life taken way too soon.

"So, if you want to play that way," I said as I looked up to the heavens, "then I guess I'll have to learn some new rules. Bring it on!" How foolish of me it was to tempt God with a challenge.

Frank had now seen me riding up to the house and started running my way. It somewhat startled me. I was not exactly sure what was fixing to happen. Was he mad at me, glad to see me, or drunk and fixing to jump me off the horse like the stories of him fighting in the Indian Wars with father?

He never really said much about Father. The only thing that seemed consistent was that they fought very well together. Frank was ashamed of Father's actions toward us after he left, but I always did feel that he at least gave his older brother credit for his good fighting skills. As Frank got closer, I could see that he was smiling. *So at least he's not fighting drunk, maybe just happy drunk,* I thought. It turns out he was not drunk at all. I knew that, of course, he was just genuinely happy to see me.

"Garit, what on earth are you doing out this early?" he yelled as he got closer. "I was just thinking about you, and sure enough, you are here!"

With Emmy's hug from last night and now this honest statement from Frank, I was starting to almost regret my challenge this morning to God. Maybe it's not all that bad after all. But I was now wise to His tactics; this was just a way to get me to let my guard down. "Steady," I told myself as I dismounted Honey.

I was dead tired as Frank and I ate breakfast, but I was trying to be alert and respectful of his enthusiasm while we got caught up talking. I tried, but finally, Frank stopped me.

"Garit, I am not sure what you have been up to, boy, but I have been in your shoes many times before. Go on and get into bed. I will clean up."

"Thank you, Frank," I simply said, and shuffled into my room, closed the door, and hit the bed. As I dozed off, I had a fleeting thought that I should change out of my clothes, but if they were good enough to sleep in last night, they were good enough to do the same now.

I woke up several hours later, by the look of the sunlight on my floor. My room faced the southwest, and the sunlight had gotten a few inches from my bed now, so I knew it had to be afternoon. The taste in my mouth and a feeling of molasses-like stiffness throughout my body were sure signs that I should not drink again.

Why do people do that? I thought. *I feel terrible.* And I certainly had enough regular health issues to add yet another to my life. As I lay there trying to muster up the ambition to get cleaned up, I told myself, 'the devil's juice' definitely had no place in my life. Even though it did help to bring out a new understanding of life to me last night. The reality was if I was going to fight like my challenge this morning had declared, I didn't need to be any more of an underdog than I already was. Winning against this foe was going to be hard; I had to be sharp. With that, I forced myself out of a stupor for the second or third time today and went to get cleaned up.

Thankfully Frank had already filled up my wash basin and had set out a clean towel. Having the water hit my face was just what I needed. It rocked the stiffness out of me a bit, and I finally started to feel somewhat right again. *If only it could knock out the stains from my clothes*, I thought as I looked at my 'good clothes' that B insisted I wear last night. *I don't think any amount of water and soap could do that.* They were in horrible shape.

I would just have to buy some more.

As I got changed into fresh clothes, I heard Frank out in the kitchen clanking some pots around. My head was still pounding, so any sound was louder to me than it should have been. It resonated straight to my spine.

Coming out of the room, I could see that he was just cleaning up from what looked like some stew or something he had been making.

It certainly smelled good, but I had to step outside to relieve myself like never before. I could not stop and sample the stew, or I would be cleaning up another set of clothes for sure. The afternoon sun on my face felt good. I didn't make it to the outhouse and just stopped near the fence. I faintly remember doing the same thing last night with Pohl by the stables at some point. And the relief felt the same. Amazing. I have never had to piss so much in my life. Again, a little trick life likes to play on us humans.

"Oh, I am learning life. It won't be long before I can outsmart you," I said to myself while my bladder emptied.

Coming back into the house, I had to get some of that stew. I was starving. Again, Frank was one step ahead of me, had already set a place at the table for me, and had the stew ready to go. I ate in silence and relished the homemade art of a good Hotzmire stew. I had been eating so much at the saloon or hotel. Good food, of course, but after eating the same thing for months on end, it was getting old. The stew was a refreshing change and something that I sure did miss.

Frank pretty much just left me alone while I ate, but I could tell he was itching to talk. And so was I, but I just needed to wake up a little bit more. Recover. Finally, I felt as if I could at least start a coherent conversation, so I addressed him without even turning around.

"So, what you been up to?"

I hoped this simple question would get him started on a rambling tale of life on the farm. He had a history of weaving several smaller, daily stories into a whopper of a recitation, so it would give me some more meaningful moments to just not have to think. As I listened, I would just nod every once in a while, and it kept him going. But the interesting part about it was that I found myself missing his stories as they weaved in and out. More than I thought I would. Of course, most of his statements were of modest, boring daily chores, but he enjoyed them, and it brought back memories of all our other supper talks with Mother in the past. Day-to-day stuff. Nothing exciting. Nothing fancy, just life. And a simple good life at that.

It started to make me regret cursing God earlier today. Life certainly was not entirely bad. It has its moments, for sure. But I could not let my guard down. I had to quell the faint optimism. Life no longer gets a free pass. I had to be a warrior and never let it sneak up on me again. Take the good times when I could, of course, but be vigilant to stave off the bad. It would take discipline, and it had to start today. Thankfully my condition allowed me some grace from Frank in having to be engaged throughout the evening. We sat, and I just listened most of the time, giving whatever small encouragement I could to keep him going. He thrived on the conversation. No matter how one-sided it was. And I loved him even more for it. He had no idea how much I needed this downtime.

Literally for my body to recover, but also my soul. I could feel myself growing stronger and stronger as the night went on. Even to the point that I had growing anticipation about my new "life axiom." But it would have to wait till morning. I definitely needed more sleep. I saw that Frank had talked himself out of stories, so I took that as a cue to cut the night short.

"Frank, thank you for taking care of me today, but I have to get some more sleep."

"Garit, my boy, you go right ahead. I will take care of everything out here, don't you worry," Frank assured me.

I just stood and went to hug him. Now, this was something different between the two of us, but as I had learned the night before, a good hug from someone that is genuine is needed more than you think you need sometimes. We typically hit each other, or he would bear hug me every now and then until I cried out "Uncle-uncle" to show affection toward each other. But just a basic, good hug was something absent since I was a younger child between him and me.

As I hugged him, I could tell he was somewhat uncomfortable at the start, but toward the end, he relaxed, and I sensed he needed it as much as I. Although I had to focus on my new warrior mentality, another hug wouldn't hurt, I reckon.

The next morning came sooner than I would have liked, but I did feel better and was ready to attack the world with the new attitude I had formulated the day before. Plus, I had missed an entire day at the saloon. That was almost unheard of for me. Not because Mr. Stallsburg required it, but that was just my pattern. I liked being on top of things, and it had been a nice distraction.

I saddled up Honey and rode into town right away. I didn't even eat breakfast but made sure Frank knew that I was going to miss it so that he did not get his feelings hurt. He was already getting a jump on some chores, so all was well at the farm.

As I galloped into town, I realized I had completely forgotten to worry or even think about B yesterday. I saw her briefly at the hotel in the morning but did not see her for the rest of the day. Was she in trouble with her parents? Was she still recovering from our night out? If I felt bad, she had to of felt twice as bad, as she probably had twice the alcohol as I did. It hit me that I had not even thought about her until now. I started to feel guilty about that, but the guilt was mixed with a feeling of complacency. It was more of a thought that I should have felt worse or guilty about not thinking of her rather than actually feeling bad about it, if that makes sense.

"Who knows," I said to myself. I just had to not think about it, I guess. This was my first relationship, and maybe everyone has these feelings at some point. It just was something that I felt I should not have felt about B, and it made me wonder as I rode on. As I passed Pohl's shop, I noticed his door was not open yet, so I just kept on riding. *Must be sleeping in a little*, I thought. Then as I approached the saloon, I could tell that the early staff had just started to rustle around. The lanterns were still burning on the front walk, and I could see the front doors still closed. I went around back as usual and put up Honey in the stable.

Upon entering the rear door, I passed Gus on his way out with some trash from the previous night.

"Good morning, Sir," he said as usual.

I always found it funny that a man of Gus' age called me 'sir.' Here I am, sixteen years old, getting respect from what I would guess to be a man in his sixties. Old. I just nodded back and headed further in. I should have said good morning back, but I had way too much on my mind.

I unlocked my office and plopped down at my desk to start writing down some of my thoughts. I had always done that since I was a kid. Wrote down my thoughts. Not like a journal to myself but just ideas, words, sentences, and such things I wanted to do that day or that week. It just helped keep my thoughts grounded. I had a lot of ideas. Some tame, some wild. Some were just simple changes to daily patterns or actions that would translate into bigger movements. It just was something I grew to appreciate more and more, and sometimes I would go back and read them to see what I actually got done or not. Some ideas deserved to die on that page, while others survived to live another day.

Today's list was just statements about all that I had learned in the last forty-eight hours or so. B and the ruckus she caused gambling. I wrote down 'B.' The subsequent boom in business I think she caused. I had yet to reconcile, so really had no idea.

I wrote down "Rec" for reconciliation.

The fact that I needed to pay more attention to Emmy. She impacted me the night before last. I just wrote down "Emmy?" as I did not know what all that meant yet.

Then again, my mind went back to B. Was she alright?

I wrote down "check on B." And for good measure, "Check on Cora Lee and Pohl." I also wrote down "Farewell Youth." I did not know what that meant yet, but I just heard a voice in my head saying it. So, I wrote it down.

Then I wrote "West." Again, just something that I heard in my head that I did not have a meaning or definition of what it meant yet. I just felt good about it. I felt an optimism greater than my past confidence in my abilities. I always felt that I would be great, but great at what I didn't know. Mother pushed this on me all my life. I had to be great at something to make up for my physical shortcomings, which was what I always thought.

But now, I think she pushed it because she knew that I had it in me to transcend into a better life. Take risks and win. Love. Adventure. Life. Don't wait for it to come to you. Take it or make it happen. It would have broken Mother's heart for me to leave the farm, the town, or the state to sew my wild outs. But I just had this distinct and clear feeling that even though she would have had a hole in her life and heart with me gone, it was destiny. God's will, as she would call it. "Be better and make life better for yourself and others. Don't waste it," I could hear her saying. I now realized that the voice in my head was hers. Not only had her passing removed any barriers to me going out into the world, but it had also forced me to grow up and face the reality that life was going to go on whether I liked it or not. And she was not around to protect me anymore, so I better toughen up and bend it to my will, or it will break it.

Lightning just shot from my leg up to my head. That's it! Mother was willing this to happen, and I knew better than anyone that she deserved it. Whatever forces she used to get through to me knew not to mess with her. She was a formidable force but, even more so, a deserving soul. She had a faith that would move mountains, and

177

she was being allowed to move the mountains in my way now. Fear. Self-doubt. Self-limitations. Pity. All the things that have plagued me my entire life. Not through my actions but because I was born too early, and my body failed to develop. But my mind. My mind found a way around it before and adapted well. With Mother's help, my mind was kicking the door down and barreling through it now.

As I sat there in awe of this change in attitude from such a strange series of events over the past two days, I just had this overwhelming peace about it. I can't explain it now and don't believe I ever will be able to. Or at least until I see Mother again someday. I can just see her smiling a sweet smile right now, just waiting to give me a welcoming hug and tell me all about how she came to her boy's rescue again.

I can't wait, Mom.

Sitting in my office, contemplating everything that had happened and that I hoped would happen in the future, I could hear someone walking down the hall toward my office. Mr. Stallsburg peeked his head around the corner and acted slightly startled that I was there so early.

"Garit, how are you doing this morning? I was starting to worry about you, son," he said while holding his hat in his hand and walking through the door.

"Yes, that was quite a night, sir; I had to recover yesterday," I said, embarrassed that I could not hold my liquor.

"Oh, don't you fret about it. It was a wild night, for sure. I even had to take some time away just to recover myself."

"Oh, you had too much to drink also, sir?" I asked.

"Oh yes, but more so, I was trying to figure out how to replicate it more often," he said with a gleam in his eye.

"Oh, yeah, I know. That was fantastic fun, wasn't it?" I replied, knowing that I, too, was taken aback by the night, the fun, and how the saloon was more exciting than it had been in a long time.

"I have been trying to figure it out, but why did Ms. Hahne decide to gamble that night? Did you put her up to it?"

At this point, our plan for catching a possible skim going on was so far out of my mind that I had to think back about how all this got started. It felt like our scheme was concocted weeks ago, not a couple of days.

"Well, Mr. Stallsburg, I must come clean. I did put her up to it, but for an entirely different reason than what you are thinking." I said while I got up and closed the door to the office.

He knew when I did this; we had to be getting ready to talk money. That was the only time we tried to keep things our business from the entire saloon. I explained the hunch I had about the roulette's performance, the plan that recruited B into it, and how it all went off the rails. It was a story that I could not have made up if I had tried.

"So, that is the whole story, and I hope you're not upset with me for not coming to you sooner. I just did not have any proof and thought our plan might offer some insight that I could then come to you with."

"My boy, that is a whopper for sure, but I understand your motives and am not upset one iota about it. First thing, though, do you still think we have a skimmer?" Mr. Stallsburg asked with directness.

"Well, that's the thing, I have yet to reconcile anything from that night, and to be honest, it was so crazy that even if anything was happening, I don't think I could spot it using those night's numbers. Maybe I am wrong, but I bet the numbers for roulette were way down, on accord of B winning like she did. The other games were probably dismal since no one was really playing them on account of the roulette spectacle. And I am even starting to wonder what the bar's numbers were, as it was all a blur after a certain point," I said, laughing toward the end of the statement.

"Oh, you and me both, son. Talk about going off the rails. I probably gave away twenty dollars' worth of drinks that night. I have not been that loose in years, and I tell you, it was like we were all living in a dream," he replied.

"Yes sir," is all I could say back. He was right.

We both sat there, shaking our heads and smiling, remembering the night's folly until he finally sat up straighter.

"But my daddy always said that if you can catch lightning in a bottle, then you sure would have something, and that night I think we caught lightning, son!"

I looked up and nodded in agreement. We had for sure, and I knew exactly the storm that caused it. B.

Now, what happened next is something that I look back on with divided feelings. Divided in the sense that I can't determine if that twist of fate in both of us seeing the same "lighting" at once was a good thing or not.

The next comment out of Mr. Stallsburg's mouth was neither a good or bad one. It just made sense. But what he said absolutely changed my life's direction and path for both good and bad. The sheer excitement, adventure, and wonder of it all were matched by the pain, betrayal, and loss of hope that came along with it. If I had started today with a new life's mission and attitude, the naiveness of it coming to fruition so soon caught me off guard on all fronts. My will, heart, and mind would all be tested to their absolute limits. The taunts made to our Creator the previous morning riding back to the farm had been heard loud and clear. And I should have known better since the odds are definitely in His favor.

Chapter 17

"We need to get Ms. Hayne into the saloon as much as possible," Mr. Stallsburg said with a hopeful tone as he raised his eyebrows to see my reaction. And, of course, I was thinking the same thing. But him saying it out loud just kind of rattled me. I still had not started the reconciliation, so I didn't know at that time if B's presence actually made a difference in the saloon's take or not that night, but it had to have.

"Oh, I agree, sir. I do want to make sure the numbers actually reflect our impressions—" He interrupted me.

"Yes, yes, yes. I took the liberty of running the numbers yesterday, not as good as you do, but my initial calculations show profit was up fourteen percent."

"Well, that is great, considering we lost by my last count, six dollars on roulette, and who knows how much from the bar," I said, trying to be as accurate as I could in my evaluation without seeing the numbers.

"Another area I agree with you on. The three of us drank enough that night that we should have been in the red, but we weren't. Bar was up also," he commented with a smile on his face.

"And what about the loss on roulette?" I asked curiously.

"Well, we did take a loss from Ms. Hahne's winning streak, of course. Rudy was so frazzled he didn't run another game the rest of the night," Mr. Stallsburg said, while laughing from what I could imagine was picturing Rudy's face after the game. I started laughing also. The look on his face was priceless. Mr. Stallsburg continued.

"But we made a killing on the other games that night. Everyone was floating on a cloud after all the ruckus, and just imagine if we had kept roulette up and running. I am telling you, son. We caught lighting that night. Your idea to get Ms. Hahne into play was genius. We still need to see if your hunch is true about the skimming, but we might as well make more money while we're doing it!"

We nodded our heads in agreement.

"How many nights are you thinking for Ms. Hahne—I mean, B?" I asked, hoping he had thought about a plan.

"Well, I was thinking she could come in at least three nights per week. We stake her, of course, just as you did the other night. And speaking of that, here's your six dollars back." He slid them over to me on the desk.

"Mr. Stallsburg, you don't have to do—" I protested, but he interrupted me.

"No, I am just giving you your money back as your fee."

"Fee for what, sir?" I asked, turning my head.

"Well, you have got to convince Ms. Hahne to come in three times per week. And I imagine that will be a tall task. The least I can do is give you your money back to do it, my boy." Mr. Stallsburg patted me on the shoulder as he stood up from the chair.

"And from what I know about Ms. Hahn—B, as you affectionally call her, is that getting her to do it might be the hardest part of this plan."

"Something about 'you can lead a horse to water' is coming to mind," I responded while looking down at the floor.

"Yep, I feel for you, son, but if anyone can do it, it's you," he said while turning to open the door.

"Besides, I know how having her here more often will make you all the happier. We just have to stay away from the bar when it does, my good man," Mr. Stallsburg said while rubbing his head like he was recalling our previous night's endeavors.

"I will leave you to it to work out the details, son," he said as he left to walk out front, I assume to get some coffee.

As I sat there thinking about our plan, it again occurred to me that I had not even talked to B since that night. I don't know if she would even contemplate doing it again. I know she had fun up to a point, but after a while, it all became a blur, and she got entirely too drunk. She might be sworn off the whole thing by now. I had to find out, but it was just past 7:00 am and too early for me to venture out to her place. But I knew someone who was up and probably knew the story. I sprung up from the desk and headed over to Pohl's shop.

As I rounded the corner, sure enough, I could see Pohl's door open and him stoking the fire in his forge. This part of his job I always envied. He and I were alike in our enjoyment of tending a fire. But this morning, I could see on his face some perplexing emotion. Like he was not getting the desired temperature from the fire or something else was bothering him. As I bounded onto the step, he turned to see it was me.

"Garit!!! Where on tarnation have you been?" he asked, setting his tools down and coming over to meet me.

"Recovering at the house," I said quickly back, hoping he understood my meaning.

"Oh, I am sure you were. I was afraid you rode all the way to Tennessee with how drunk you were when you left me yesterday. I was about to send out a search party," he said with a smile.

"Oh, give me a break. I just needed some time to rest and think a little," I said, hoping he would understand. "But enough about me, how are the girls doing?"

"Don't you mean, how is B doing?'" he shot back.

"Uh, well, I mean both of them. But now that you say it, yes, how is B doing? Seemed like she took the brunt of the evening, from what I remember," I said, kicking the anvil, trying to look impartial, but in reality, was hanging on every word Pohl had to say about it.

"She is a little worse for wear but will be okay. I was kinda shocked to learn from Cora Lee that this was the first time B had ever gotten drunk before. I just always assumed she had before," he said, shrugging.

"Oh no, she and I just don't really ever drink. Not sure why. We just don't," I said, shrugging also. "But she is, okay? Her parents aren't mad or nothin?" I asked, trying to get more information out of him.

"From what Cora Lee tells me, they made up some story about staying up too late with some last-minute changes to the wedding and some bad beef causing all the problems," he said, smiling. "Her parents were none the wiser. Yesterday I went out to check on them after bringing them home early that morning. Cora Lee was definitely tired, but B was up and prancing around like nothing ever had happened. I am serious, Garit. She looked like it was just another day, and the previous night had not even happened. That girl is something," he finished.

"So, she was not mad or nothin'?" I had to press him further.

"No, she seemed happier than usual and wanted to know if we all wanted to get together tonight for dinner. I told her I had not seen you yet, but I am sure it would be ok."

"Absolutely, that is a great idea," I responded.

"How about we meet up around 5:00? I assume they are coming back into town anyways around that time, as usual?" I asked Pohl.

"Yes, I think that was the plan. I just wanted to make sure you were good to go. I was getting a little worried," Pohl said while he poked me in the ribs.

"Stop it. Of course, I am okay. You think I can't handle my liquor?" I asked while trying to poke him back. I failed, of course. His reflexes and mine were different.

"Well, I am glad you're okay, Garit. That was some night," Pohl said while going back to his forge.

"Speaking of weddings," it just hit me. "You all good with it? Need anything from me?" I asked.

"Garit, you have already done so much, my friend. We are good. I just can't wait, but I also can't believe in a few days, I'm gonna be a husband. Who would have thought it?" he said, poking the fire.

"Well, all I can say is that Cora Lee is a lucky girl. She is getting the most eligible bachelor in Christiansburg and, on top of that, his best friend as well," I said, beaming with pride.

I was truly happy for Pohl. He looked like he was really warming to the idea of being married, and Cora Lee really was a match for him. He was always awkward around girls, to begin with, but not Cora Lee. The first time I met her, I could just sense that Pohl was completely smitten and felt comfortable around her. And her also towards him. Two peas in a pod. I had agreed to use the saloon for their reception after the wedding and even went as far as saying the cost was all on me. Again, what was the point of having all the money in the world if you can't spend it on things to bring others joy? I wanted to make Pohl and his new bride happy. His coming along in my life definitely made my days better; it was the least I could do to repay him. He put up a rebuttal at first, but I persuaded him over time. And besides, he really did not have the extra money to spend on something like that anyway. I just told him it was my wedding gift to him.

"So don't expect anything else," I joked. He just smiled.

"Thank you, Garit, you're a great friend."

But, back to this morning. I needed to think through my proposal to B, and it looked like I had just gained some extra time to do so. With that, I slapped Pohl on the back as he pushed some coals around.

"See you at five," I said as I hurried out the door. I had to get back to the saloon and look at the books, come up with a plan of attack, and see how my new life mantra would play out. A big day was in store for all of us.

As I looked up from my desk, it looked like it was almost midday. I had been so busy going over the numbers that I had lost track of time. I was actually getting a little hungry, so I decided it was good to make a trip to the front and see what was on today's menu. I made the menus, so I should have known, but I really didn't even know what day it was, to be honest. The past few had been a blur.

"Friday?" I said to myself as I glanced at the calendar on my way out of the office. As I made my way to the bar, I noticed that the saloon was more full than usual during lunchtime. A lot of men were reading the local newspaper and were seemingly riled up at whatever it contained. I grabbed a newspaper that was on the end of the bar. It read "Texas Secedes." Reading this out loud to myself must have scared my hunger pains away. I just turned around and went back to my office to read the story.

You see, this was a big deal. Something that I had hoped and prayed would not happen. The Abolitionists had been growing in strength over the past few years, and Lincoln had been elected a few months ago. This was a huge issue for southern states, and Virginia was caught in the middle. South Carolina seceded in December, followed by Mississippi, Florida, Alabama, Georgia, and Louisiana. We all were waiting on who would be next, and that day, it was Texas.

I don't talk politics with many people. My job is to create a good time, not have everyone getting in a fist or, worse, a gunfight about politics. We tried to keep talk of it to a minimum. But you could tell that everyone was really getting worked up over what was happening in our country. Again, with Mother's passing, work, and B, I really had not waded into it yet or had time to get too deep into the reasons or meanings of what was happening. And it all happened quite quickly over the period of just a few months. No doubt, though, when someone had too much to drink, their night of fun and frivolity would often turn to "Damn that Lincoln!" or "Damn those Yankees!" statements.

We at the saloon had taken the position of neutrality and would often just politely ask the person to simmer down or escort them toward the door. Getting them home was more of a pressing issue at that moment than a war between states. No violence equaled more profit, in our opinion. We liked it that way. But now, with this headline, it was going to get tougher and tougher to keep the peace. This was a big event and everything going on was really starting to make me worry about the future. Life has a funny way of playing tricks on you. In the past three days, I had gone from happy-go-lucky and lucky just to be here with B, getting ready to celebrate a wedding, to seizing my future as of this morning.

What if there was no future? This was starting to be too much. Too much up and down. Frankly, I was starting to get fed up with it all. I had B to worry about, Pohl and Cora Lee, Mr. Stallsburg, The saloon, The country, and I were stuck in the middle of it all. The one thing that I could not handle on top of all that was war. I don't know much about it personally, but from reading about the Indian Wars, Mexican War, and of course, the Revolutionary War, none of it was good, and my having physical issues made it even worse. Then you add to that the stories that Frank would sometimes tell.

If we were headed for war, I wanted nothing to do with it. Plus, I personally did not agree with the reasoning behind it. Slavery. With everything I had been through in my short life, I could not imagine having to be a slave. Life was hard enough as is. And Mother always said, "God doesn't care what skin color you are; he made all of us beautiful in our own way." I reckon if God made us, why is one better than the other? God doesn't make mistakes, and you can't tell me that just because one person is from Africa and the other from America or that geographic location coupled with skin color gives one the right to own the other. This is something that logically just does not add up. Mother always called me a pragmatist. I look at things for what they are, not what someone says they should be. Whether in the saloon or the world, I was rock steady in that approach. I just wished the world felt the same.

I had to shake this off. I just really did not have the time to think about it much deeper. I needed to get ready to talk with B. I made the decision to send a messenger out to her place just to make sure we were still on for dinner tonight. I had done this a few times before, mainly to let her know I was going to be late or, in the rare instance, had to cancel. But I had never done so to make sure we were still getting together. It was almost like clockwork anymore, but since I had not really seen her since Tuesday night, I really did not know what to expect.

I handed the note to Jed, the young man that cleaned up around the salon.

"Ride straight out to Ms. Hahne's and give the message to only her. Wait for her response on the porch and come straight back to me here." I told him. Jed nodded his head and ran out the front door to the stable to get a horse. I again looked around the saloon. More people had shown up, and several were seated around a side table listening to someone speak. I could tell they were talking about the latest headline, but I was surprised to see Mr. Stallsburg was in the group. He looked worried. I could also tell that he was not really partaking in the comments, just listening. Going from each comment to comment with anticipation. We had talked about all of this before, but he just shook it off.

"There won't be enough states that secede to make a fuss," he'd said. Again, I just stayed on the edge of the conversation, but this sure looked like a fuss to me. Seven States now. Seven was a lucky number, but right now, by the look on Mr. Stallsburg's face, seven was starting to lose its shine. I stayed close to the bar and pretended not to be paying attention to the group. Asked the bartender about today's inventory. Walked over to the gaming tables and inspected them like I normally do. But to say some of the comments from the group were ignored would be a lie.

"And we're gonna be next, I tell ya," one man said as some in the group just looked down and shook their heads. Others raised their fists and appreciated the comment. Mr. Stallsburg just looked pale. This was really getting to him, I could see.

And then another man raised his voice.

"If the Yankees want a fight, by God, we will give 'em one!"

And now, a majority of the crowd agreed and raised their fists higher.

I took this opportunity to step out front and get some fresh air. Today felt like it was growing colder than the last few days. I was sleeping in a stable two nights ago, so I was happy it had been a little warmer than usual. With no coat on today, though, the February cold had crept back in. I just started walking back and forth on the porch of the saloon as I got the chills. I was not sure if they were from the cold or the thought of war.

It was probably because I was nervous about seeing B. Again, I was not sure how she felt about everything that had happened over the past two days. But more importantly, how she would react to me asking her now to do it multiple times a week.

The fresh air was good, but I had to get back inside. As I walked back to my office, the group was now growing louder and louder. I could see that Mr. Stallsburg was now standing and trying to get everyone to calm down a little. He knew as I did that all of this talk would be bad for business. He was doing his best to walk the thin line of "well, who knows what's going to happen? Anyone up for a game of poker?"

I wanted to step in and help, but I had enough going on in my world. I didn't have time for the rest of it. I made it back to my office without getting pulled into the fray and found my coat. Put it on and sat in my chair to focus a bit. I went ahead and started putting away my reconciliation work from that morning. I really had not found anything of suspicion. All the numbers were skewed anyway. I resigned to feeling that I would have to just keep looking on more normal nights of operation. Plus, Mr. Stallsburg's' estimates and my numbers were pretty close to each other. Why keep pulling at a string that might not even be there in the first place? I cleared off my desk and started to jot down some talking points for B. As I opened my notebook, I saw what I had written down just a mere six hours or so ago.

B
Rec
Emmy
√ on B
√ on Cora Lee – Pohl
Farewell Youth
West

I was amazed at how, in the past six hours, all the things I had written down just this morning had taken on a deeper meaning. This morning

I was simply worried about my friends and having a self-discovery moment about the future of my life. Now, all these notes had such a higher meaning and more poignant message. All of them became so much more serious if I followed them with "if a war breaks out."

B. What happens to her and me? Reconciliation of the saloon's books. If war breaks out, will there even be a saloon left?

Emmy. A war for her freedom! That would be wonderful. But what pain and suffering would she and her people go through? I couldn't imagine.

Pohl and Cora Lee. My God, they are set to be married in less than a week. And I can promise one of the first to be drafted in a war would be Pohl. Strong and capable Pohl.

Farewell Youth; that was the understatement of the ages. I was kind of proud that I had written that down, but now, how right could I have been? The life I had been living this past year would not even be a fleeting thought if, in fact, a war broke out. And I thought things could not get worse than losing Mother. There's that pesky life again, throwing things at you out of the blue.

West. I had no idea why I would have written that down this morning. Was it a small idea, daydream, or foolish boy's wish to see the rest of the country, maybe? I had really never thought about it before but probably more of a curiosity. I mean, anywhere other than Christiansburg was a curiosity. But this almost seemed like a premonition or something now that war was looming on the horizon. West. That would be the only place to go in order to escape the darkness of war. But it, too, was full of dark and murky things. Stories I had heard over the years had never played it out to be anything other than hard, lonesome, and full of peril. Sure, men would come through the saloon all the time, saying this was their last drink for a while as they were headed out west to find their fortune. Mr. Stallsburg even told me one time that a man came through and said that after he struck it rich in California, he would be back to buy the saloon. He never saw him again. But the stories of people coming through town headed out west were many. Even several local families got caught up in it. Packing up all they had and left. Most never to be heard from again. A few would make it back every now and again. Most were broken and battered with a hollow look in their eyes. So, with every story of fortune and fame out west, there were, in actuality, none that we had heard ever came true. But I had written down West this morning, and that had to be paid attention to.

Just then, Jed came running into my office with word back from B.

"Ms. Hahne told me to tell you she would be here tonight for dinner and that you'd better be ready because she has a lot to talk about," Jed said while trying to catch his breath.

"Is that all she said?" I asked, trying to get more of a clue of what all the talk would be about.

"Something about 'ungrateful and unbecoming?'" he said, confused as to the meaning.

"She said 'ungrateful and unbecoming.' And that's it? What else along with that?" I asked, with a sense of urgency and panic, to be honest.

"She was saying all kinds of words and so fast that all I could catch and remember were ungrateful and unbecoming," Jed said. "They were the longest words, and both started with U, so I assumed those would be the most important words to remember and make sure you heard them.

I appreciated Jed's honesty and desire to help, but only those two words, without the context of others, were making me very nervous.

"Okay, okay, Jed. Thank you for relaying the messages. How did she look?"

"Well, she looked like she always does, sir. Pretty," he said, not really understanding the question but hoping his answer was correct and would make me happy.

It did not. Not in that I was upset with Jed, but with the lack of detail and true nature of how she really looked. Any clue of her appearance, composure, or expression on her face could have helped me in trying to figure out the last two words meaning. But 'pretty' did not give one iota of direction as to what I could expect when she showed up tonight. I just sat there trying to figure it all out, saying "ungrateful and unbecoming" over and over under my breath. Poor Jed. He did not know what to do next, so he just stood there with his hands in his pockets and head down. After I repeated everything in my mind a few times, I finally came to.

"Oh, Jed, I am sorry," I said, tossing him a two-bit coin from my desk.

"Thank you for running out there today. You really helped me out."

He simply caught the coin, turned, and said, "yes sir," as he hurried out the door.

I think him seeing me so worked up over his message made him very keen on getting out of there and fast. Poor kid, he was just the messenger. But then had a nervous chuckle at the fact that I, too, would be the messenger this evening when talking to B about the proposal. And now, the whole saying about "don't shoot the messenger" had a whole new meaning to me. I was wading into something this evening that sounds like it will be tougher than I thought. But this whole day has gone like that, so what could I have expected?

"Farewell Youth" just seemed to be jumping off the page of notes to me once again. I just looked at it, shook my head, and said to myself, "Oh, to be young again," and shrugged. I wanted excitement and shouted to the world to bring it on yesterday, I just did not expect it all to come so fast and include B in the equation. With that, I proceeded to clean up my office and start the countdown to 5:00 pm. It felt like the war had already begun in my life. A war of new and old. I have to admit; I started to miss the old one already.

Chapter 18

As I came out of my office toward the front of the saloon at 4:55 pm, I really did not know what to expect. Would B be waiting for me at the front like usual? Would the group of men talking about possible war be gone or have grown larger? All I could do was try and keep my composure and try to be as calm as possible. I really felt the burning back in my chest again, and frankly, a little sick to my stomach. But life was marching on so, so must I. I made it to the front and had not seen B yet.

"Oh no," I said to myself but just then, she pushed open the swinging doors and glided right in. Because I was already at the front, it took her off guard a little.

"Oh Garit, you're ready to go?" she said, somewhat confused.

"Uh, yes, I suppose so. Is there something you want to do before we leave?" I asked, not knowing really what I meant, but just trying to interpret her statement.

"No, no, I just…I just thought I would have some time to look around. The other night was such a blur that I kind of lost my orientation of the place," she said with a small smile.

"Well, of course, of course, I understand. I need to go check on something anyway, so I will be right back," I said as I retreated toward the rear of the saloon.

She seemed pleased at this break in time, so I continued. I don't know why I did it, but it felt like the right thing to do and would give me some more time to pull myself together. But at least one thing had come to light. She didn't seem mad at me, so I suppose that is one thing going right so far.

As I entered the back of the saloon, I stopped and sat on some crates around the corner. I just needed to catch my wits. The burning in my chest was still present and rubbing my chest seemed to help it a little.

"What in the hell Garit?" I said to myself, replaying what had just happened. I had no idea about most of what I had just said, and running off to hide in the back brought back memories of me doing the same thing as a child when running from Willy in grade school. I thought those days were behind me. But running from danger was something I had gotten very good at in my life, so today should not have been a huge surprise.

But running from B? Something had profoundly changed in the past few days. Sure, B frightened me but not in that way. More of an "I hope she likes me" kind of nervousness, not scared. And we had gotten so close over the past year or so that I was starting to get down on myself that I had run away from her just now. For what? Because she might be upset with me about the other night? I really didn't know if she was, to be honest. She didn't seem upset with me just now. But again, that feeling of uneasiness started to come over me. Uneasiness about our future together. Something had been nagging at me the past couple of days. The fact that B was in my thoughts, but not like usual. I would obsess about B normally but the past couple of days, she was more of a side note than the main storyline.

Nothing really happened between us. We had not had any foul words with each other or anything. She just got drunk, and so did

I. The side effect was that we didn't see each other for a day or so, and for the first time in as long as I could remember, I was okay with it. Typically, I would fret about not seeing her. It would occupy a significant part of my thought process. But she wasn't as much, now. Of course, she was still in my thoughts, but there seemed to be more of a practical reason why. I still needed to convince her to be at the saloon a few nights a week as part of the plan. Made sense I would be thinking about that. But something had changed in the fact that it was the saloon that needed her, and I was not waiting with my normal eagerness to see her.

And at that moment I heard a sort of loud "clap" in my mind. It kind of shook me, and things were all starting to make more sense. The last year or so had been great, having B on my arm most nights and doting on her, but did I really love her, or was it just pride? Me being prideful that I had the most beautiful girl in my presence, the one I had adored for almost my entire life. Did I really enjoy her company or was it all for show?

As I continued to unravel my relationship with B in my mind Mr. Stallsburg came out of his office and up to me.

"Garit, you okay, son?" he asked, wondering why I was sitting on a pile of crates rubbing my chest.

"Uh, yes, sir. I guess I am not fully recovered yet from the other night," I said trying to deflect.

"Okay, you sure?" he asked again.

"Yes sir, I will be fine," forcing myself to stand up and take a deep breath. "I guess I am a little nervous about the B plan also," I said, again trying to deflect the attention away from me.

"Well, don't you worry about that, Garit. With all this war talk, I am not sure her coming to the saloon is that important after all. If this gets any worse, we won't have a saloon to worry—" he stopped himself. He caught himself getting ready to say something that both he and I knew might be the truth, but both of us did not want to say it out loud. He cleared his throat and patted me on the back.

"If asking her about our plan has you this nervous, Garit, don't worry about it. We can do that anytime. You just take her out for dinner and have a good time. Life is too short to worry like you are."

I appreciated this parry in conversation. The fact that the burden of me asking B tonight was off the table. It seemed as if I had a lot more to figure out about the two of us than I thought.

"Thank you, Mr. Stallsburg. We will figure it out, sir," is all I could say. I did not really mean B, I meant the war and how all of us would be affected by it if it really did happen.

I think he also knew what I meant and just shook my hand.

"You bet, son, now go have a good time tonight, there's always tomorrow, we can worry then." He said with a smile.

As I came back out from the rear of the saloon, I could see that B was not waiting in her normal station from all the dinners before but was standing over by the roulette table. I could not see her face, but it looked as though she was talking to herself and using her finger to count something. As I got closer, I could faintly hear her saying, "Fifty cents on red, fifty cents on black," and each time she would raise one finger on her hand.

"Trying to add up all the money you won off of us the other night?" I asked as I drew closer.

"Oh, you know me too well, Garit, yes. That night seemed ages ago, and when I looked in my bag yesterday I had over sixteen dollars! I was shocked at all that money. I could not believe it! So, I was just going back over in my mind each step as I want to try and understand it better."

"I bet it was a heck of a night for sure," I responded. And I was starting to sense that B was not upset at all with me. She seemed pensive but happy. Like she, too, was just trying to reconcile all that had happened in the past few days and how she should feel about it. As she finished counting all the bets she had made and that she had, in fact, won six dollars, she turned to me and held up her hands.

"You see, Garit, you are not the only one good at arithmetic!" Her fingers displayed six upright, and she smiled.

"Well, you actually did a little better than that. I did the books this morning."

She just laughed and spun around with delight.

"I can't believe it, Garit. It was so much fun."

"It was," I said in response as I took her arm and started toward the door.

"Well, we have to celebrate tonight, don't we?" she said as we stepped outside. "And since I have all this newfound wealth, I will even buy our dinner with it," she said very proudly and with her nose turned up toward the sky in a regal gesture.

I laughed out loud.

"You are buying dinner? Now, this is a special occasion," I said as she tugged on my arm. I had to add, "You remember Pohl and Cora Lee are coming with us, right?" smiling and making sure she understood that dinner would not just be the two of us, or more specifically, would be more expensive than usual. She just nodded her head and pulled me toward Pohl's shop.

"Well, alrighty then," I said and went right along.

As we walked, I could sense that she was happy and proud of herself. Almost as if she had a bigger place in the world than just a few nights before. In fact, she even seemed like she was holding onto my arm tighter than ever. Most days, we got into a general routine of me telling her how my day went, asking how hers had gone, and her intently looking into the windows of the shops as we passed by for things I could buy her later. The most drama would be when trying to decide what main course we should eat. That was about as suspenseful as what day it was when there typically were only two choices. To say our time together was boring would be a stretch, but to say it was exciting would be one, also.

Tonight, it felt different. Like B was truly happy to be with me instead of the other way around. She was just acting different, and as we walked, could not stop talking about her winning, having fun, and drinking way too much. It was almost like she was rescued from her normal, routine life and had found another source of excitement. I felt happy for her. But it was another kind of happiness. Not happy that I was with her, or might even be the reason she was happy by suggesting she come play roulette, just happy to see us talking about something else for a change. I could see that her winning the other night had empowered her somewhat. Like she felt a sense of delight in her prowess at roulette. I, on the other hand, was more realistic and would describe it as dumb luck. But she seemed to think it was her keenness or sharpness that caused her to win. And I did not want to take anything away from that, so I just went along with it. I had seen it so many times before. Luck is on someone's side one night, and then the next night, they leave with nothing. There always was a sense of cheer in seeing someone so happy when they are up. Their eyes sparkle, their smiles much easier and more welcoming. I felt good for them. I really did. Life is hard, and seeing someone winning at it is fun.

But I also knew the reality of life would come back to roost, and it happened sooner rather than later, most of the time, up one hand and down another. That was gambling. But seeing B up tonight felt good, and I was just happy to be a part of it. Especially with the anxiety I was having the past few hours about what I thought I was going to find tonight. I couldn't help but wonder what Jed was talking about, with the words ungrateful and unbecoming he had relayed to me from his message. Her mood seemed completely opposite of what I was expecting, and I just had to know why Jed told me she had said those words earlier. As we got closer to Pohl's shop, I stopped her.

"B, when I sent Jed out to give you my message, he came back and said that you would be here tonight and that I should be ready to talk about the other night."

"Yes, I did tell Jed to tell you that," she replied.

"But what I don't understand is that he also said you said the words 'ungrateful and unbecoming' in the same message; he didn't understand, though, in what context. He's just a kid."

"Oh, don't mind that, Garit. I was just rambling on about how my mother had gotten on to me the previous day about staying out so late and then coming home with alcohol on my breath. She really laid into me. I am sorry the messenger boy heard me say that. I was really just talking out loud to myself, I should have clarified."

"Ohhhhh," I said while nodding my head. "Now it all makes sense. Jed told me that, and for the life of me, I could not figure out what he meant. I thought you were going to be sore at me and was nervous about meeting you tonight."

"Now, Garit, you're always so nervous, but you don't need to fret. I had a great time the other night, and although I drank waaaay too much, it was the most excitement I have had in ages. In fact, when I relayed the message 'we have a lot to talk about,' I meant that. We do. After dinner, I want to talk further, but let's just have a nice dinner with friends first tonight. We can talk about that later," she said as we arrived at Pohl's shop.

Cora Lee was sitting inside on a small stool, and I could see Pohl getting cleaned up at his wash basin just behind the anvil. Cora Lee looked very pretty. More pretty than usual to me. Of course, she was pretty, but tonight it just caught me a little more. She looked so...*pleasant* is really the only word I can describe it as. Happy. And I guess she had the right to be. She was getting married soon, and what bride would not look this way leading up to her marriage day? As we stepped inside the shop, B started to make an announcement.

"Hear ye, hear ye! Sir Garit Hotzmire and Lady B graciously invite Lady Cora Lee Hazle, soon to be Lady Starp and Sir Pohl Starp, to a humble celebration dinner in honor of Lady B's prowess at the royal game of Roulette!" At which she could not hold her fake accent any longer and broke out in a laugh. Cora Lee just looked up at her like she was crazy but started laughing, also. Pohl just shook his head.

"Oh, B, you're nuts."

We all had a good laugh for a few seconds. I spoke up.

"Oh, and Lady B has graciously offered to pay for said feast with her gambling proceeds, I should add!"

At that statement, Pohl yelled.

"Oh, now I know B has gone crazy, paying for dinner?" as we all kept laughing. It was a really great moment. No worries about the war, the wedding, or our friendships. Just the four of us at that moment were happy.

How quickly things would change.

As we sat through dinner, recapping "the coming of age," as we had now affectionally named it, it was nice hearing everyone's take on it. Especially since a lot of it was a blur to me past a certain point. Pohl and Cora Lee had not participated in drinking very much that night and, because of that, had all the fine details of how it played out. It was hilarious watching B's face light up when Pohl would tell all of us some of the things she had said or done. It was like she was experiencing it for the first time, as she truly did not remember. Nor did I do most of it. Pohl was even getting into it and reenacting some of the night's follies. At one point, he stood up from the table and got into the character of B. He gave her this funny little walk and started to sing, "Camptown ladies sing doo-dah, dooo da…" He stopped there as he really did not know the words, but him going through the motions and acting like he was B was a riot.

I had never seen him like this before. Not hiding in the shadows or shy but right out there, doing a small skit of the night's events. It was great. Cora Lee even got into it and jumped up and pretended to be me.

"One more round for the road," she said, acting like me drinking a shot of make-believe whisky. She even hunched over a little to mimic my size. I just shook my head in embarrassment, not of her acting skills but of my obvious, grandiose, and excessive behavior.

"Yes, sorry about all of that, folks. I got a little away from myself. Thank God you two did not get pulled into it as well. I bowed my head to compliment Pohl and Cora Lee's restraint. They both just laughed and bowed back. They were great friends, and we were lucky to have them.

As they sat back down, I wanted to get the night back under control. I don't think the hotel dining room could handle another round of impromptu skits recounting our famous night. It was fun, though, seeing Emmy laughing in the kitchen to herself as we told the stories one by one. She knew even more than we did, I suppose, about how the night ended. Her saving our backsides the next morning as she did. As I raised my drink, the others followed, and B spoke.

"To what are we toasting, my good man?"

"To Great Friends, To Great Loves, and To Coming of Age!" I said as we clanked our glasses together.

"Here, here," Pohl added as we did.

Each of us took a drink, and then Pohl and Cora Lee kissed each other on the cheek. I looked at B with a 'want to join 'em?' look, and she nodded. A kiss on the cheek followed, and I could not think of a better time or place to be. All felt right with the world. Or at least this part of the world did. The rest of it seemed to be getting ready to burn down. But out of sight, out of mind, I suppose, as we were all living in that moment. Caught up in the company and stories.

As we finished our dinner, I was curious if B really would follow through with her offer to pay for tonight's dinner. As Emmy brought the ticket to our table, I went ahead and moved my hand toward her as she knew I always paid; thus, she walked up to my right side.

"Oh no, you don't, Garit," B said while clambering for the ticket from my left. I was surprised she was actually going through with it. I could tell Emmy was not sure what to do, so I interjected.

"Ms. Emmy, my lady, has offered to pay for our dinner tonight, so you may hand the ticket to her," as I motioned toward B.

Emmy put her hand over her mouth, trying to hold in a laugh, and handed over the ticket to B. That's what I loved about Emmy. She was just so happy all the time. Getting her to laugh was pretty easy actually, and I loved doing it. Emmy did a little curtsy-type movement and quickly walked back to the kitchen. I could tell she was trying to be polite and not laugh at our expense, but I could overhear her telling the other staff about how funny it was seeing a woman pay the bill. That was just not customary at all. And I must admit, seeing B rummage through her purse, pulling together the money to pay the bill, was a sight to see. I had not seen her pay for anything in so long, or really ever, for that matter. She looked at the bill and then back at the coins in her hand as she counted it up. She then stopped and looked up at me with a look of 'help me.' I moved closer to her so that I could ask quietly

"Everything okay?"

"How much do I leave for gratuity?" she asked in an innocent tone. She really didn't know. Why would she? I don't think she had ever paid for her own meal before. That's the truth. I looked at the bill.

"Two bits will be plenty."

She laid all the coins down on the table and looked up with an expectation for all of us to recognize her unselfish gesture. To which we all commenced in clapping our approval. I rarely saw B get embarrassed about anything, but our clapping did just that.

Her cheeks flushed, and she said, "Y'all cut that out!"

We just kept clapping, of course, to drive it home. She then stood up.

"Fine, be that way," she said as she turned to head out the door.

We all just started laughing, including her, and got up to follow. What a great time we were having.

Once outside, Pohl turned to B.

"Well, B, thank you for a lovely evening and dinner, but I really need to get Cora Lee back home. I promised her father that she would be back in Salem first thing tomorrow. She has a big few days ahead of her, pulling everything together for the wedding. We are going to get a head start tonight and stop at her aunt's in Shawsville."

We all understood this and, of course, agreed. Salem was about twenty-five miles away, so traveling the whole way this late at night and in February would not be wise. I could see that B was happy that they were going to be leaving us sooner than normal, and I was also. She and I had a lot to talk about.

We bid each other farewell and gave everyone hugs before they set off to the stable to fetch the wagon. B and I just kind of stood there for a moment, watching them walk away. They both looked so happy. So, looking forward to their next chapter in life. They strolled off into the distance, arm in arm, with Cora Lee's head resting on Pohl's upper arm as they walked. True love. What a great thing to witness. I wanted to say something but didn't want to spoil the moment, and was not sure how to get it started. And I had the feeling she didn't either.

We waved again as Cora Lee looked back and then turned to each other

"Garit—"

"B—"

We said to each other at the same time. We both laughed.

"You go first," I said.

Her going first would allow me some time to find the right opportunity to bring up the saloon plan. Plus, I had been itching all night to know what she needed to talk with me about. It was rare that she would make such a run-up to what she had to say. She usually just blurted it out. That was B. Not shy about anything. So, to see her nervous about discussing something was definitely new.

"Garit, I have been really thinking about how to ask you what I am getting ready to. You know me, and being hesitant is not my normal behavior, but I am just not sure what you will think about my idea."

Now I was really getting anxious. What on earth was she about to ask me? It must be something big.

"Well, I guess just come on out and say it, B. I won't bite, I promise," I said, and she smiled. I took her arm and eased her into walking back toward the saloon. It was a crisp night, and I did not want her to get too cold while we talked.

"Ok, here goes. The other night was such a new experience for me. And it was exhilarating. I mean, it was so much fun playing in the saloon and seeing your world from the other side. You get to be around that every day; I can't imagine it. I have seriously underestimated your role and life inside the saloon. I did not know how it all worked before but playing, winning, and being with everyone that night really felt right to me. Does all that make sense?" she asked me while looking into my eyes.

"Well, yes, I suppose. For me, it's just an everyday occurrence, but you have never seen that side of it. Now, the drinking, not so much," I wanted to clarify that to her.

"Oh, of course not, Garit. I am not really talking about the drinking. It was fun, don't get me wrong, but a proper lady would never do that too much, of course," she said, trying to downplay the fact that she pretty much drank Mr. Stallsburg and me under the table.

"But the spectacle and excitement that night is something that I rarely feel anymore, and it was glorious," she continued.

I just shook my head in agreement. I did know what she meant. All of us did. Hence Mr. Stallsburg's and my plan to get her to come in more often. She continued as we walked.

"I was just thinking; you gave me the money to play the other night. Staked me, as you say, with ten dollars, and I won so much the first night that if you let me use the original money and we go back and do it again tonight."

"You mean go back and play in the saloon tonight?" I interrupted her just to make sure I was following correctly.

"Yes, go back and play again tonight. I had so much fun, I was just thinking we could do it again. But this time, keep the drinking to a minimum. Not sure I could handle another night like that so soon," she said while placing her hand over her stomach.

"Trust me, I understand," I said back, doing the same action.

My stomach was still giving me fits as we walked. Half nervousness and half the result of that night.

"Can we please, Garit?" she asked quickly, as if she did not want to get off the subject.

"Well, of course, I don't see why not B. In fact, that's what I wanted to talk with you about. Mr. Stallsburg and I both talked, and you do what you did the other night really could be a good thing for business. Just the atmosphere and laughter alone were enough to draw more and more people in. Drinking, for shows, or gambling, it does not matter. The more we can get in, the better it is for all of us who work there. And you were amazing the other night!"

"Oh, Garit, you're embarrassing me."

"No, I mean it. I have worked there for a while and have never seen anything like it before. You lit the place up. I think you being there would do it again for sure."

To this, she smiled ear to ear and hugged me right on the spot.

"Oh, Garit, I was so worried that I caused too much of a ruckus and that you would not want me coming back. I am so happy you are okay with it. I have been worried sick about it!"

"Of course. I am not your father B, you can do whatever you want, I just want you to be happy. And if coming in to gamble or see a show is what you want, then it is something you should be able to do," I said, holding her shoulders in my hands. I could tell that this really made her happy, and she jumped forward and kissed me with the biggest kiss she had ever before. All I could do was melt in her arms and think to myself, "is this really happening?"

When she pulled away, she looked up at me.

"And you will stake me again?"

"Of course, B. You already have my ten dollars; use it again, and let's go have some fun!"

At which she again popped forward and gave me another kiss. Then she shouted.

"I love you, Garit Hotzmire!" and pulled my hand in hers as she started almost running to the saloon. I could do nothing but follow.

As I did, I said to myself, "this has to be the strangest day I have ever had." From how it started to now, it had given more ups and downs than a water well pump. But going out like this tonight. Getting kissed twice by B, her saying she loved me, and now running to go have another night of fun with her by my side at the saloon. I am not sure how it could have gotten better. It was magnificent.

Chapter 19

"I am so proud of you, son," Mr. Stallsburg said as he slapped me on the back the next morning. "I can't believe you got her back in, and you did it so soon! To see that same lightning in a bottle happen again, wowzer. I can't believe it, Garit! You are amazing, my friend. Thank you for getting it done; I couldn't have done it without you," he concluded.

I just shrugged.

"That's my job, Mr. Stallsburg."

He just shook his head.

"Boy, I know your mother probably would not approve of it, but if she could see you now, I think even she would not be able to hold back her emotions."

At that statement, I felt proud and sad at the same time but tried to play it off.

"She does see it, or at least I hope she does," I said, looking down.

"You bet she does, son! And sorry for bringing up a sore subject, but you have done so well and deserve to be told that," he said with some emotion in his voice. "I miss her also. A lot more than I have even let on to you before. I never told you this, and I hope you're okay with it.

I was falling for her," he said while motioning for me to sit down. I knew that this conversation had just taken a deeper turn so followed his direction.

"Garit, you have no idea how I felt for your mother. She was a very special person, and frankly, I was falling in love with her. Now, I have no expectations that she felt the same about me. Your mother was a stern one for sure, but in her own way, she was beautiful, and I loved her for it," he added, looking down at his hands in his lap.

Almost as if he was finally released from a great burden he had been carrying around for years. I could tell he wanted to tell me this for a long time, but the time just never was right, I guess. All of it started to make sense, though, now. All the banter back and forth between them. Him taking a special interest in me. Him riding out to the farm to make sure Mother was not mad at him for hiring me the first time. All of it.

"Wowzer, it all makes sense now," I said out loud.

"Yep, I thought you would have caught on to me sooner than now. You're such a bright young man, and with you and Ms. Hahne being in a relationship, I just figured you would be able to see right through me."

I just sat there for a moment and took it all in. Mr. Stallsburg had always been upfront and honest with me. Or at least I thought he had been. I never had any reason to think differently, so this must have been a big deal to hold back. He loved Mother? I felt kind of like a dunce, not figuring it out before he told me. It was right there in front of me.

"Mr. Stallsburg, honestly, I am shocked in one sense, but in another, I am not. Mother was a special lady once you got through the hard exterior. I am just sad that she never knew your feelings toward her. She was taken way too soon."

"Well, Garit, I have another secret to divulge. She did know."

"What?" I exclaimed back at him.

"I wrote your mother a letter soon after she found out about you working here the first time, and she got onto us. I was so ashamed that we had lied to her, that I had lied to her. I mean, how was it that I could attend church each Sunday with her, and hold something like that from her? It was not right and is now one of the greatest regrets in my life. I justified it by not wanting you to get in trouble, but it was just me being a coward. I knew how she felt about the saloon, how she felt about me. But I was taken by her and did not want to drive anything else between us. Lo and behold, I had done just that by hiring you and then lying to her about it. And for that, I am truly sorry to both of you. I should have known better."

"It's okay, Mr. Stallsburg. I lied too. This is not all on you."

He patted me on the knee.

"Well, after she found out, I had to tell her the truth, the whole truth. So, I wrote her a letter a few days after we all last met at your house. I just could not live with what I had done to her. I wrote a letter asking for her forgiveness, and I told her that I loved her in that same letter. I had Jed take it out to your place. It was a terrible decision, and I should have known better. Your mother would have expected news of that magnitude to be told in person. I can almost see her scolding me now for not having the courage to say it to her directly."

We both chuckled a little at imagining her scolding Mr. Stallsburg. She did it quite often.

"And yet again, I was a coward. I thought a letter exclaiming my sorrow for lying and my love for her would mend the rift. Boy, was I stupid. I never did get an answer, though. I am so mad at myself for not coming out and doing it in person. At least I would have known her answer. Two days after sending it, well, we both know what happened."

A tear had started to form in my eye as I thought back to that day.

The day Mother left me. The day a snake and God stole her from me. Mr. Stallsburg knew how much it would hurt for me to be brought back to that day, but I understood why he had to tell me. He lost someone he loved that day, also.

I was surprised at how much attention and help he had given to me in the days that followed. And I don't think I could have even had the funeral without him taking most of it off of me. I just figured he knew I was just a kid and needed help. Now to find out he was doing what any good man would do for the woman he loved was restoring. It was good to see someone care for my mother the way he did. And not expect anything in return. She was gone.

"I will never know if I even had a shot at deserving her love, but I am comforted in her knowing how I felt and for finally telling the truth. I am just happy to have been a small part of her life and hopefully can be a larger part of yours from now on."

I finally looked up after wiping the tears from my eyes.

"Thank you, Mr. Stallsburg, for everything you have done for me. And I think Mother may have had some feelings for you also."

Mr. Stallsburg's eyes got big, "Really, you really think so?" he asked quickly back.

"I do. Mother had a tendency of giving the people she cared about the most the hardest time. Call it being difficult or controlling; I just call it her way. It was hard to understand at times, but I think it was just her way of showing affection. And from what I remember, she liked to give you a harder time than most," I said, hoping it would give him some resolution.

And it was the truth. Between Uncle Frank, Mr. Stallsburg, and me, Mother made quite a habit of fussing at all of us. I really do think she had feelings for Mr. Stallsburg and was happy that he told me about his feelings toward her. To know that in her final days she knew she had an admirer, or really, much more. Someone who loved her, other than me and Frank, made me feel warm. She deserved that. And kind of explained how quiet she was those last few days. I think she was still upset, of course, with the both of us, but probably was working through Mr. Stallsburg's letter as well. That made me smile. Her finding out someone loved her. I hope it made her feel special. Not just needed. Wanted by someone other than me and Frank.

As we both just sat there, taking in all that had been said, I finally stood up.

"Mr. Stallsburg, thank you for loving my mother. She deserved it, and I am sorry you never got your answer from her. But I think if she were here today, she would give you a big hug. The kind only Mother could give."

He stood up while I was saying it, and I could see the emotion welling in his eyes also. As I finished saying it, I opened my arms in a motion to hug him. He needed it, so I followed through. He simply said, "Thank you, Garit," as I ended it. "Now, let's see how last night's numbers stacked up and if our plan worked!"

I simply said, "yes, sir," in a way to get both of us out of a somewhat awkward conversation. He left my office, and I dove right into the numbers. But a few moments later, I had to stop myself and smile. Mr. Stallsburg loved Mother? I shook my head. Now I knew for a fact the world had gone crazy. And I just dived back into the books.

After I finished looking into the numbers, the premise that they would be up proved true; sure enough, we were up twelve percent last night. B did not have near the winning streak she had the first night, but she somehow still managed to come out ahead. That girl amazed me! Last night she never got on a hot streak as before, but she stayed patient and ended up clearing four dollars. But again, what we were hoping for came to be. All the others around her felt better and had a better time. And the saloon once again just had a buzz about it that made people loosen up their wallets, and it translated into higher pots, purchases, and house winnings. And to top it all off, B even tried her hand at blackjack. I will say, she had a long way to go, but everyone, from the dealers to the players, genuinely had a better time with her at the table. Our experiment was working.

Afterward, B was again filled with excitement and was really not ready to quit for the night. But, after our first episode, we had learned some valuable lessons, and both agreed it was better to bring the night to a close rather than wake up the next morning feeling like we did. We still had to work out some of the finer details, but Mr. Stallsburg and I agreed to stake her ten dollars each night she played and get her a hotel room for the nights she did so that she would be safe and not have to ride home so late. And the best part, any money she won and ended up with at the end of the night above the stake, she got to keep. So, if she ended up with fourteen dollars, she gave the ten dollars back to me and kept the four. If she lost all the ten dollars, she walked out with nothing, but really nothing of hers personally was lost.

Looking at the deal, I wished I was in her position. Essentially getting paid to gamble. But in a way, I was. Her change to the atmosphere brought in more players and, in turn, put more money in Mr. Stallsburg's and my pockets. Things were going great so far. It had only been two times since she started, but things were on the up and up for sure.

The talk of secession and war was still on everyone's mind, though, and the talk was becoming more of a small roar. It seemed as if everyone was talking about it, and with most items of this sort, anxiety was starting to grow throughout the town. I was thankful that our new strategy with B was taking my mind off it somewhat. I was, however, worried about Pohl more and more. I could see that the talk of war was beginning to weigh on him and his wedding was just a few days away now. I made a point to stop by his shop more and more. Both yesterday and today. I knew he would be getting nervous in general, so I wanted to be there for him during this time. I would stop by on my way to work, head over around lunch, and then again on my way to dinner each night with B. This gave me several chances to check in, but also times when B would not be with me so he and I could talk openly if needed. I figured I would keep doing this up until the day or so before the wedding and then leave the poor guy alone so he could get some rest. Pohl had already planned it with his father so that he could have some time off the day before the wedding, his wedding day, and the day after.

Pohl's father was hard—as hard as the iron he hit all day long. To get him to give even one day off was a miracle, but even he had to acknowledge that the boy would need some more time off. This morning when I went by, Pohl seemed fine, but I could tell he had a lot on his mind. He was trying to hide it, of course, but he couldn't hide it from me.

"What you thinkin' about, big guy?' I asked, hoping he would let me help.

"Oh, nothing, Garit, just normal stuff, I guess."

"Normal stuff?" I asked, really wanting to know. "Come on, Pohl, tell me what's bothering you. I know something is," I continued to press.

"Well, all right, but this stays between you and me, you hear!"

I just made a motion of crossing my heart with my finger and smiled.

"Garit, I am serious," he said while making a fist and acting like I would have to eat it if I told anyone.

"Pohl, don't worry, I won't tell a soul, I promise," I tried to reassure him.

"Well, okay then. I am not nervous about getting married and such. I love Cora Lee, and she loves me. I am just worried about what happens afterward."

"Oh, you mean like when you two have children and such?"

"Well, yes and no. Of course, I am worried about the future and all this talk of war, but really, I am talking about what happens directly after the wedding," he said in a manner like I should know what he meant. I was still a bit confused.

"Well, your father said you could have the next day off, didn't he?" I shrugged my shoulders, trying to show I really did not know where he was going with all of this.

"Garit, you dummy, I am trying to say I am nervous about having relations with Cora Lee on our wedding night!"

"Ohhhhhhh," I said, finally understanding what he was talking about.

"I have never done it before, and I am not sure I know how," he said shyly.

"Man, you would have fooled me. I guess I just assumed that you had done it before, uh, not with Cora Lee, of course, but some other damsel in distress while you were away!" I said, laughing a bit as I said it.

"Why, you little...Garit, I am really being serious! Cora Lee and I have messed around a little, but we are both virgins, and I can't bring myself to ask her if she knows what to do. I don't."

"Pohl, listen, you know as well as anyone that I am a virgin also, so not sure I can be of much assistance but.... I have seen it happen before out back of the saloon. It doesn't look that comfortable for either person to me, but then again, doing it up against some crates in the ally is probably not the best example," I again said with a chuckle and smirk.

"Garit, cut it out, I am really nervous about it, and I can't think of anything else. What if I don't do it right or something? What if I hurt her? I sure would never want to do that!"

"Ask your father, you big dummy!" As I hit him on the arm and said it, I knew what kind of response that would get me. Of course, he started after me and chased me around the anvil two times before finally catching me and putting me in a headlock.

"Garit, stop messing around! I'm not going to let you go until you give me some real advice. And asking my father is not the right answer!"

"Alright, alright, I hear ya! Let go, and I will…let go, I tell ya, and I promise to help!" I felt his grasp starting to ease up a little.

"You promise?" he asked again as his arm tightened again around my head.

"I promise on my mother's grave," I yelled out.

Immediately he let go and pushed me to the ground.

"Garit, don't put that on me. Don't you ever bring your mother's passing in on stuff like this. That's not right!"

With this statement, I could tell he was really upset with me. As I sat there on the dirt floor of his shop, I immediately shot back to the time Willy had me on the ground, beating me like usual, and Pohl came to my rescue. But this time, Pohl had put me on the ground. And I deserved it, I suppose. First of all, I was razzing him about something he really seemed concerned about. And second, I put Mother's death in the middle of our fuss. I should not have done that. It was not right of me to do. He was correct. But it still brought back bad memories of him pushing me down as he did. It shocked me, to be honest. He had never done anything like that before. As I sat there licking my wounds, he just went back to the forge and poked the coals. He did not say anything for a while, and neither did I. I finally got up and dusted myself off, regained my composure, and walked over to him.

As I did, I thought about how this last week has been the craziest I have ever been a part of. Of course, Mother's passing was a shock and was terrible, but I have seen more things change pretty drastically in my life over the past week than ever before. Sure, there were some exciting things, but some were very scary and heavy as well. Now, this. My best friend pushed me to the ground and was legitimately upset with me. Again, I deserved it, but something about it just felt wrong. He was taking out his nerves on me, and this was unlike Pohl. I had to tread lightly as I had never seen him like this before.

"Pohl, I am sorry for saying that. That's not what I meant. I wasn't putting any of that on you. It just came out. Really, I meant nothing by it. I'm sorry." I could tell he was calming down, and he looked up.

"No, Garit, I got away from myself. I am the one that should be sorry. I shouldn't have done that. I am just really nervous about stuff, and all this talk of war is adding to it."

I just nodded my head as I knew what he meant. I had been trying to ignore it also, but the news was like a rattler in the shadows waiting to strike. Everyone was talking about it and not just the normal talk. People seemed really serious this time. I was getting worried for sure.

"I know, Pohl, I feel the same way. I am sorry I should not have messed with you like that."

Pohl put his hand on my shoulder and just said, "never again, friend, we gotta stick together, and I promise I will never hurt you again."

"And I will never razz you when I know you're being serious, I promise," I returned. "Now, let's solve your problem about the wedding night. Hear me out. I really don't know what to tell you, Pohl, but people have been doing it for thousands of years. I think you both will be just fine when it comes to it. Just get naked under the covers, and it will naturally just happen." Although I tried the best I could, the picture of them getting naked made me crack, and I started to laugh again.

"Why I oughtta—" as Pohl grabbed me again, but this time with much less force, I knew I would be ok, so I laughed even harder. We both just started laughing then, and it was really a good moment between us. I think it really helped him loosen up a little.

"Yeah, I guess you're right. I just love her so much and want to do right by her."

"You will, Pohl, you always have, and no matter what, I know, and more importantly, she knows that you would never hurt her and just want to love her. You will be fine, I promise on my—" he quickly looked up.

"Don't you say it, Garit!"

I just smiled.

"Not to bring you down, but do you miss her?" Pohl asked a few moments later.

I just took a deep breath in and shrugged.

"Yes, more than you can imagine."

"Man, I am sorry, Garit, I really am. I can't imagine someone I love dying so quickly like that. I am sorry she went that way. And sorry you are alone."

"Well, I'm not," I shot back. "I have you, B, Frank, and a soon-to-be sister, Cora Lee!"

We both just smiled, but that last name brought us back to the fact that he was getting married very soon. I think it made him nervous again.

"Yeah, and if you can get it right, you might even be an uncle yourself someday."

I just shook my head as if to say, "I don't want to picture that."

Just then, there was a knock on the front door frame of Pohl's shop, so he hurried up to the front. He was met by a mounted rifleman, and several other US soldiers lined up behind him, holding their reigns.

"How can I help you, sir?" Pohl asked.

"They tell me you're the best shoer around these parts. Have time to work on our horses before we head out in the morning?"

"You payin' with Virginian dollars or silver coins?" Pohl asked before committing to the job.

"We have been out west most of the last year, so we have silver and Spanish coins, whichever you prefer."

"Well, to get it all done by morning will be a tall order, but I will do my best. Let's do silver," Pohl answered

The soldier looked at another a few horses back and yelled, "Silver!"

The soldier hopped off his horse and brought a small bag forward and handed it to him, saying, "Here you go, Captain."

I had lost my hat somewhere in all the scuffle from before, so I started looking around the shop for it. I found it over by the forge, and good thing I did. It was starting to get singed a little from the intense heat. As I made it back to the front, Pohl was telling the soldiers where to tie up their stock and where they could find a place to eat and stay. This gave me a perfect opportunity to butt in and welcome them to town and over to the saloon.

"Men, we put together a mighty fine dinner at the saloon. I am sure you will find it to your liking, and we have a full assortment of table games to make your stay here less boresome," I said while pointing down the street and toward the saloon.

The other soldiers seemed very keen on this, but all looked to the captain standing next to Pohl for their next move.

"Boys, no play, no dinner. Put your gear in this here backboard, and we will head out to camp double-time. You know the place." He looked back at Pohl and asked him if taking the buckboard was okay.

"Yes, sir You have a lot of gear so go right ahead, just have it back by sunup tomorrow. I have a need for it, then."

"Thank you," the captain responded and turned to signal his men to start loading up.

"Well, if you change your minds, the name is Garit Hotzmire, Assistant Manager of the best saloon in Virginia; stop by and see me anytime."

I could tell the other soldiers were disappointed in their superiors' orders but went straight away with unloading their gear. I just kept walking and waved at Pohl.

"I will come back later, and we can continue our conversation, Pohl." He just nodded.

As I walked, I thought all this work could be good for him. Would keep his mind off the wedding, and in particular, the wedding night. Although, all this talk about relations was sure getting me wound up and curious also. I was honest when I told Pohl that I did not know what to do either and had only seen it in the ally a few times.

As I walked, I couldn't help but think about B and how doin' it with her would probably cause my heart to stop. I mean, if I got a shooting pain in my chest when we just talked, what would happen if we were in bed together? I would probably just roll over and die right there. What in the heck was I going to do if she wanted to do something like that? We had kissed, sure, and that was great and all, but what if she wanted to go further?

I started to feel Pohl's anxiety. I had to figure this out. But who on earth would I ask about a subject like this? Frank thought all women were rattlesnakes. I couldn't ask him. Pohl obviously knew as little as I did. I thought about Mr. Stallsburg but got a little sick to my stomach now knowing he 'loved' Mother. No way in hell could I ask him and not think about him and Mother doin' it. That's just gross. Who else? As I made it to the saloon, I had to set aside my internal discussion as I noticed there was a large crowd gathered again inside, and things sure seemed contentious. *What else can happen this week?* I walked through the doors.

As I made my way over to the group, I once again saw that Mr. Stallsburg was right in the middle of the action. As I stood and listened, it seemed as if the soldiers that had visited Pohl's shop were the root cause of this uneasiness in the saloon. I did not really understand why, as soldiers coming through town was a regular occurrence. Christiansburg was one of the larger towns on the way to or from Tennessee, Kentucky, or other surrounding states. No debate that it was happening more often, but no one seemed to be that alarmed by it before. Why now?

"Those yanks want to shove their politics down our throats, I tell ya," one man shouted while most of the others shook their heads in agreement.

"Lincoln's not even the true President if you ask me," another shouted.

Mr. Stallsburg tried to calm everyone down by saying the same thing I was thinkin'.

"Gentlemen, soldiers coming through town is something that's always happened. Why is it so upsetting now?"

"Because there is going to be a war this time!" someone shouted out.

Again, everyone nodded their heads in agreement. Mr. Landry spoke up.

"I heard that we are next to secede, and if we go, there surely will be trouble for all of us. The militias are already trying to get my boys to join them, and they are itching for a fight."

I knew the Landry boys from school. They were some years behind me. I can't imagine someone that young fighting in a war.

"You can't be serious, Mr. Landry," I blurted out. The entire group turned and stared straight at me with scowls.

"Oh, I am serious, son. Twelve, fourteen, and fifteen-year-old boys are being recruited to fight against the yanks and Lincoln. It's the truth, and with everything going on, I think I'm going to let 'em."

Everyone let out a collective gasp and a "yeah" at the same time.

I really don't think they knew what to say. Were they for or against an upcoming war? I think in the conversations prior to this one, most were just blabbing, but this time felt different. More serious. The thought of friends of mine, boys, going off to war took this whole thing to a different level in my mind. This past week sure has been upended, but war was a game-changer. I needed to get away from the group and think a little, so I headed back toward my office. Mr. Stallsburg could see that I was a little out of sorts, and he left the group and followed.

"Garit, things are getting a little bit more serious now with all this war talk. You, okay?"

"Yes, sir, I suppose, but with everything going on and now this, I am starting to feel a little overwhelmed. And, if war breaks out, what's going to happen to us?" I said, uncertain.

"Well, son, war is something that I hoped none of us would ever see again. And fighting other countrymen, that's the worst kind of war, I suppose. I don't know what will happen, but nothing about war is good, that I do know," he said, trying to comfort my anxiety but at a little bit of a loss himself. "All we can do is try and keep things moving forward as normal until something happens and then stick together if and when it does. We are going to need each other."

With my physical stature the way it was, the last place I needed to be was in a war. I simply would not make it, and Mr. Stallsburg knew that as well as I. He needed me to keep things going at the saloon, and I would need his protection in return. But at this point, I had no idea how that protection would play out.

"Let's just stay calm and see how this next month or so goes. And pray that no other states secede!" he added, trying to be as hopeful as he could.

"I agree, sir, but with everyone up in arms about it, it sure seems like things are going to go downhill fast."

He just nodded in a manner that confirmed he, too, thought this was the beginning of the end.

"Listen, just concentrate on the wedding. Your best friend is getting married, and all this other stuff should not be of concern right now," he said, trying to be as enthusiastic as he could.

"Yep, I suppose you are right. Thank you, sir, for talking with me," I said back in an effort to conceal my growing fear.

But he was right. I needed to push that down and concentrate on Pohl and Cora Lee, we were two days away from the big day, and they deserved my attention for sure.

"Speaking of that, I better head down to the bar to make sure things are all set for the reception," I said as I hastily made my way back out front. I did not want Mr. Stallsburg worrying about my mindset, so I just needed to change the subject. I think he was happy I did also, as he, too, needed to regroup and wrangle his thoughts.

As I walked, I couldn't help but notice that the group was still in the saloon. Albeit a little quieter now, but still talking about all the political happenings going on. I just had to try and ignore it.

"Dub, everything looking good for the wedding reception coming up?" I asked, trying to sound normal.

"Yes, sir, I have all the items you requested ready to go. We do need more whisky, though, as, for some reason, we are running short this week," he said while winking at me, trying to be polite about all of us drinking half of it ourselves a few days ago.

"Yes, yes, don't remind me," I said as I smiled and rubbed my head. "I will head over to the general store and see if they have any extra in stock. We can purchase until the next shipment comes in from Richmond."

I needed any excuse I could get to get out of the saloon for a while. Hopefully, the group of men would be gone when I got back, and things could go halfway normal today and tonight in the saloon.

It had been a while since I last had a reason to visit the general store.

Since quitting and then going to work for the saloon full-time, I did my best to steer clear. Not that there were too many bad feelings between the Dobbs and me, it all just got a little lopsided back then, and I felt pretty bad about how it all went down. I would just usually send Jed over for any needs of mine or the saloon so that I could save embarrassment. But I had to face the music at some point, and getting out of the saloon was what I needed at the moment.

As I walked in the front door, I could see Mrs. Dobbs bent over and counting some fabric bolts near the back and Mr. Dobbs at the counter looking at some papers. Mrs. Dobbs did not look up when I entered, but Mr. Dobbs did immediately, and I saw a smirk come over his face.

"Well, well, if it isn't Mr. Hotzmire that is gracing us with his presence this fine afternoon!" he said loudly so that Mrs. Hotzmire and I would hear for sure.

I did sense a hint of sarcasm in his comment, but also, I think that he was actually happy to see me. I knew this would be something of an awkward visit, but I was already in the mix of things, so I might as well go along with it.

"Mr. Dobbs, it's been a long time for sure. How are you all doing?" I said back, to give some space to his first comment.

"Why yes, it has, Garit. I was beginning to think you were too good for us lowly townspeople with you doing so well at the saloon," giving me a larger hint that he was still a little sore about me leaving as I did. By this time, Mrs. Dobbs had stood up and come over to the counter to join us.

"I can't believe my own eyes, Herman. Is that really Garit standing in our store?" Mrs. Dobbs added with a little kick.

"All right, all right, I know it's been a long time, and I am truly sorry for how I left in such a rush, but can we call a truce?" as I stuck out my hand to shake Mr. Dobbs.

"Oh, I reckon we can do that, son. You were going through a lot back then, I suppose. Just razzing ya and giving you a hard time like the old days," Mr. Dobbs said while shaking my hand in return.

I had never really appreciated Mr. and Mrs. Dobbs before. Yes, they had given me my first job and were always there to help me if I needed it. I definitely had taken for granted their kindness, though. It just was hidden behind their pension for running a tight ship, I suppose. I just smiled.

"I sure hope you both are doing well. I really do. And Mr. Dobbs-looks like you have a pretty big order on your hands there," I referenced the paper that he was looking at when I came in.

"You bet I do, Garit. Some soldiers from out west just came through and placed a big one for sure. They said they were headed south to Fort Sumter and needed to stock up on supplies."

"Fort Sumter, huh? Well, at least they will get to see the ocean," trying to keep the conversation light.

"Oh yes, and a beautiful ocean it is. Mrs. Dobbs and I visited down there back in '55; a beautiful place to see," in an effort to reciprocate the light conversation.

"What brings you in today, Garit?" Mrs. Dobbs then asked. She was always the "get down to business type," so it was fitting.

"Well, we are a little short of whiskey this week, and our next shipment from Raleigh is not due for another six days or so, and I was hoping you might have some extra we can purchase to get us through."

"Well, I'll be. The saloon needs our help for a change, Herman. Isn't that something?" Mrs. Dobbs said with a raised eyebrow.

You see, this all went back to when they wanted to start selling some of their wares in the saloon. Nothing too much, just simple things like perfume, aftershave, and such. Some of the pricier items that they thought might be good for our patrons and would open up some space in the general store for other items. I was all for it, as I could see the benefit to both of us, but Mr. Stallsburg said that having that stuff for sale in the lobby would take away the dollars people would have to drink and gamble. Why would we willingly allow those products to take business away from the saloon? I saw his point, of course, but I did not think it would harm us that much in the long run. Plus, we would get a commission on each sale, as I had worked it out with Mr. Dobbs. But he was the boss, so I abided by his wish. Of course, I was too chicken to tell them myself, so I sent Jed back the message that we would be declining the offer. I would have done the deal just to try and keep the peace between the two establishments, but oh well.

"Yes, Mrs. Dobbs, we need some help from you this time, and I sure hope we can get it," I responded.

"Well then, let's talk about your lobby and our proposal again, shall we," she shot back, knowing this might be their chance to rekindle the conversation.

"Oh yeah, I remember Mr. Stallsburg saying something about that at one time," trying to deflect the final decision to him and staying out of the fray.

"Yes sir, he turned us down flat, and I am not sure we shouldn't do the same to you about the whisky in return," she replied.

"Well, I know Mr. Stallsburg had his reasons, but maybe I could bring it up again. And I would sure appreciate you selling me some bottles if you have some extra. You see I am hosting Pohl's wedding reception in a few nights and just want to make sure I have enough for all the friends and family," I continued. Just trying to get back on track and hoping the obvious grudge they held about the past would not rub off on me in the present.

"Oh, so this whisky is for Pohl's wedding, you say?" Mr. Dobbs intervened. I knew I had to play the Pohl card as Mr. Dobbs always really liked him when he and I would visit the store when we were kids. I don't know why; he just took a shine to Pohl and would always ask me about him after he left for Salem. With the disposition they were both giving me, I figured bringing his wedding up might be the only way I get the whiskey out of them. And it worked. Mr. Dobbs immediately let the past fall away.

"Well, if it's for Pohl's wedding, I can't see how we won't oblige and sell you some of our whisky. Under two conditions."

"Oh yeah? Let's hear these conditions," I said, chuckling.

"Well, the first one is that Mrs. Dobbs and I don't recall getting an invitation to said wedding and reception. Is that correct, Mrs. Dobbs?" he asked innocently to her.

"I think you're right, Mr. Dobbs. I don't remember seeing any invitation come our way, must have gotten lost or misplaced?" she asked in a bewildered tone.

"Being that your Pohl's best friend and all, I am sure you can take care of that, can't you, Garit?" Mr. Dobbs asked.

"Of course, Mr. and Mrs. Dobbs, please accept my verbal invitation to attend both the wedding and reception. I will make sure to have a formal invitation sent over right away. Now, let's hear this second condition."

Both Mr. and Mrs. Dobbs looked at each other and smiled. I think they were genuinely excited to attend, as I don't imagine they get invited to most things around town. They kind of had that blunt propensity about them, much like Mother did, now that I think about it. That's probably why we got along so well over the years. I was used to it. Most townsfolk were not, though, but being the largest general store in town, they just had to deal with it.

"The second condition is that, due to us sacrificing our stock and possibly having to turn down other sales until our next shipment comes in, a neighborly but commensurate markup in price, I think, is warranted, of course."

And there it was. When it came to making an extra nickel or so off some opportunity, the Dobbs would do so in a heartbeat. Money was their focus, and clearly, they had not lost it during this conversation.

"Of course, of course, whatever is needed to make sure my best friend has all he needs on his big day!" I responded. I wanted to keep the focus on Pohl. "How many bottles can you spare?"

"Oh, let me check the stock and see," Mr. Dobbs said as he went to the back, leaving Mrs. Dobbs and me there alone.

"Sure is a fine winter we are having, isn't it, Mrs. Dobbs?" I said, trying to keep us on the right path until I had the whiskey paid for and in my hands.

"Oh yes, really nice that we have not had all the snow like usual," Mrs. Dobbs replied politely. What happened next was a little unexpected.

"Garit, I never really got to tell you this, but Mr. Dobbs and I are both very sorry about you losing your mother the way you did. And we both talk about it often, how you did such a fine job with her funeral. No matter the past, we are both very proud of you and how you have managed since losing her. It must be hard…" she stopped herself. This was very unlike Mrs. Dobbs to show any emotion or real kindness at all. But, because I knew her ways, I also knew that she meant it and was being very kind.

"Thank you, Mrs. Dobbs, that really means a lot to me. You and Mr. Dobbs have always been good to me, and I am grateful that you both aren't holding too much against me that I had to leave so suddenly. I really was in a pickle and, unfortunately, dragged you both in with me."

Mrs. Dobbs just nodded, and I could tell she really wanted to let me have it for pulling them into the lies I told and how I left, but she was showing grace and restraint. I had never really seen her do that before. As good as it was hearing all those kind words from her, it also made me feel like a real dud for how I have treated them. At that point, Mr. Dobbs had come back out from the back and was holding a crate of six bottles.

"Well, it looks like we are a little low ourselves, but for Pohl, we can make a sacrifice. Hopefully, we will have more coming in on the same shipment from Raleigh as yours, so we will be back up in a jiffy. How does four dollars a bottle sound, Garit?"

Now, his whiskey was about five grades below our whiskey, and he knew that I knew that all too well. He also knew that I knew they paid around a dollar fifty a bottle, even with the shipping costs added in. So, he knew that I knew the four-dollar price was sticking it to me quite a bit, and normally I would have put up a fuss and negotiated or passed on the purchase altogether. But, with what Mrs. Dobbs had just said and, honestly, what I deserved from them, I just smiled.

"Absolutely, Mr. Dobbs, and I am grateful for your Christian souls in my time of need."

They both just smiled back as I told them I would send Jed back with the money, invitation and to pick up the crate shortly. As I turned and headed back toward the front door, Mr. Dobbs just nodded.

"Nice doing business with you, son! Come back anytime!"

I just gave a half smile again and continued my walk of shame back to the saloon. One thing I was good at in life was taking my lumps, and they both just gave me a whopper.

After giving Jed my handwritten invitation, money, and instructions to bring the crate of whisky back to my office and not the bar, he handed me a note from B. He told me it arrived earlier while I was out. I went to open it, but I stopped, instead concentrating on the group talking of war still in the saloon. Although it had grown smaller, I could hear a higher sense of fear in their comments. I just could not escape the overbearing theme that war was on the horizon, and as much as I tried to ignore it, I had to really start thinking about the what-ifs surrounding it.

What would happen to the saloon? What if Pohl and I got called up to fight? What would B and Cora Lee do? What about Christiansburg as a whole, would there even be a town to come back to? All things that I truly had no idea how to even begin to answer. I had never even seen war before. I was sixteen, for God's sake. I had not even seen that much of anything in my life.

My mind immediately went back to Pohl and I's conversation this morning. He and I have never even had sex before. I mean, come on! And sure, I have had to live through some hard times with my health issues, Father leaving and Mother passing, but those were all things that really only affected me. Not everyone. Not my friends and the people I care about.

And the time had come that I really must be honest with myself; I wouldn't last two seconds in any kind of fighting. I'd never even ever learned to shoot. Mother, Frank, Pohl, or Mr. Stallsburg have always just either done things or looked out for me. And I suppose I could add the Dobbs to that list. Seriously, I was really in trouble if a war did take place. I wouldn't make it. And as strange as the last week or so had been, this last realization that I wouldn't make it through the war created a different emotion in me. Of course, I was scared and nervous, but I immediately thought back to the other morning, riding Honey back to the house. I had felt that God was unfair or that the world was fighting against me all the time. So, adopting the mantra of "it's me against the world" was fitting. The improper factor in my equation though was that I ignored my physical flaws in that boisterous moment. Mentally, put me up against anyone, and I would have a fighting chance. Physically, I nor my new mantra would even begin to have a fighting chance. A child left in the middle of the woods, full of wolves, was the picture I had in my mind. Add in a world at war, and that child regressed to an infant really quickly. I simply was not equipped for this. So, what other options did I have? B's message pulled me back from all my thoughts, so I finally opened it to read.

Garit,

I won't be able to attend our dinner tonight. I am just too busy getting prepared for the wedding, and we also have had some unexpected visitors come in from out of town. I will see you tomorrow.

B.

I truthfully was not that upset she was canceling. It would give me some more time to think through things. And I really didn't feel like having to entertain her. My mood was just in a different place this afternoon. I closed my office door and settled in to strategize. All night if I must. My life might literally depend on it.

Chapter 20

As I got to Pohl's door I could barely breathe. Running in the morning winter air was even harder than normal for me, but I had to get to him quickly. I had it! I knew what to do, but this was too big even for me to think through alone. I had stayed up late into the night thinking it through, and I simply had to have his opinion about it all. I had told myself I would hit his shop at daybreak but had overslept, and it was now closer to ten in the morning.

I stood just outside the door, trying to catch my breath, but could see that the captain from yesterday was back, and talking with Pohl toward the rear of the shop. Pohl's father was also with them. It seemed like they were having a pretty serious conversation. I wondered if Pohl was upset that the soldiers did not get the wagon back to him by the agreed time. He had to use it to pick up supplies in order to have the next few days off for his wedding. That made sense, but from the way Pohl was moving, it looked like he was much more upset than it should have made him.

Pohl's father noticed me and shook his head in an attempt to tell me, "Now is not the time, Garit." I just nodded and stepped back out front of the shop, and continued to catch my breath. Several minutes passed, and the soldier came toward the door and shouted back toward Pohl and his father.

"Now, I must notify Ms. Hahne." He walked past me to the wagon waiting for him.

"B?" I said out loud as he did, and he stopped, looked me up and down, and then continued.

"How do you know B?" I then asked him directly.

He did not seem happy with the question, climbed up onto the wagon, and told the other soldier to move out without answering.

"Why does he have to go and talk to B?" I said out loud, hoping Pohl or his father would fill in what I was missing. I stepped back inside to talk with Pohl about it and could see his father had both hands on Pohl's shoulders and was talking very intently to him. Pohl just was looking down and nodding. This did not look good. Did he mess up the soldiers' job up or something? What was going on? What I didn't know then was that my taunting of God was going to be answered without mercy, for I could not believe what happened next.

Pohl's father left out the rear door of the shop. This seemed unusual to me. He always made it a point to say hello to me, but today it was like he was avoiding me for some reason. Pohl then came toward the front of the shop, and once I could see more clearly, he looked like he had seen a ghost or something. He was pale, hollow. Like life had been pulled out of him. Not the typical strong, straight, and tall Pohl.

"Pohl, what is going on? Are you okay?" The sight of him and all that had occurred was really starting to worry me. As he got even closer, I could see the tears in his eyes.

"What in the world, Pohl? What is it?" I pressed.

He just shook his head as if he was trying to regain his wits. Like he had been kicked in the head by a mule or something and was just coming too. I just stood there and let him come back for a few moments.

"Pohl?" I asked softly, and at that moment, his eyes came back into focus on mine.

"She's gone, Garit. Cora Lee's gone," in a tone I had never heard from Pohl before. Defeated but also scared. Pohl wasn't afraid of nothing. I have seen him do things over the years that most grown men would run from, and he did not even blink. Heck, the only time I even saw him a little bit afraid was when I would try to get him to talk to Cecilia back in grade school. He really didn't like that, but this was different. He was really acting frightened.

"Cora Lee's gone? What do you mean, Pohl?"

"There was a fire, her family's house is gone, and she did not get out in time," Pohl explained as his voice cracked a little.

"What the—a fire?" is all that I could say.

We both just stood there in shock for a moment. Pohl's father came back into the shop and over to meet the both of us. I was glad he did, as I did not want to be pestering Pohl with questions, but I had to know more. Also, I wanted to ask why the captain was here. It had just seemed strange that Pohl would have received word of Cora Lee's death from him.

Pohl's father saw that I was baffled and that Pohl was in no condition to be questioned. He pulled me aside and explained that the captain had been notified by a squadron stationed in Salem to be on the lookout for Virginia Militia members and of the news that they had burned down the house of a family that had supported Lincoln. Since his battalion was in the general area, they dispatched a rider early this morning to inform him that, in the process, Cora Lee had been killed. Her parents, brothers, and sisters made it out, but Cora Lee had gone back into the house to save her wedding dress from burning and did not make it back out.

By this time, Pohl had sat down on a stool with his head down in both of his hands. He was crying but not loudly. Pohl's father further explained that the captain stated the Militia was starting to target Lincoln sympathizers and that this was not the first incident. Over the past two months, things like this had been on the increase amongst the southern states, and the soldiers expected it to continue.

I had to stop for a second and think back. I knew Pohl, and I really did not have an opinion about Lincoln getting elected. We both certainly agreed that slavery was wrong, but we weren't part of any faction or anything to be against it. But I never heard Cora Lee say anything too much about it either, so why was her family targeted, I had to ask.

Pohl's father further explained that Cora Lee's father had been a strong supporter of Lincoln's election and because he had taken part in the election process in and around Salem, he was singled out by the Militia to leave Virginia. Evidently, they have been threatening him for some time now, and whatever the reason, last night, they acted on it by burning his home down. They allowed the family to get out before doing so, but Cora Lee broke free and ran back inside.

"Oh my God," I said as I looked at Pohl again, and by now, he had somewhat regained his composure, and I could see anger filling his eyes.

"Pohl, I am so sorry," was all I could say. I mean, what else could be said? He had just learned that the love of his life and the woman he was going to marry in just days had died. And at the fault of a Militia? "What the hell is going on?" is all I heard myself saying out loud. Pohl heard it, stood up, and looked at me.

"I will give them Hell for what they have done."

His father and I just both stood there, not really knowing what to say as Pohl walked past us, out the front of his shop and beyond. Pohl's father put his hand on my shoulder.

"Garit, he is going to need you now more than ever, son. Please go and help your friend."

Upon hearing that, I just nodded and went to follow Pohl to wherever he was going. When I made it outside, Pohl was already mounting up on a horse and looking like he was going to ride straight to Salem to find the people who had done this. I had never seen Pohl this angry or determined before. I just ran over to the horse and grabbed the bridle to stop it for a moment. As I did, Pohl jerked hard on the reins.

"Garit, leave me be!"

I could not. I had to talk with him before he did something stupid. I really did not know what he was doing, but I did not like the look on his face, so I had to try and calm him down.

"Pohl, where are you going?" I shouted, just trying to hold on to the horse's bridle the best I could.

"Garit, this is none of your concern. Let go, dammit!"

"No, tell me what you are going to do first!" I pleaded with him.

I could see that for a split second, he was conflicted. He wanted to tell me, but the rage was overwhelming his code of friendship. He took his right leg and pushed me off the bridle and down to the ground with one swift kick.

"I'm sorry, Garit, I just don't need you!" he shouted while galloping off and around the corner. I just sat there in the dirt in total shock. Not only was the pain that Cora Lee had been killed starting to set in, but this was the second time in that many days that I had been pushed to the ground by my best friend.

Seriously, what the Hell was going on? I couldn't take much more of this. The world was going crazy, and taking my best friend with it. As I picked myself up and dusted off, Pohl's father came out of the shop to see what all the commotion was about. He could tell that I was really upset with what had just happened, but also, he had to find out where Pohl was going. He helped me steady myself.

"What did he say? Where is he going?"

To which I could not answer. I simply shrugged as I was trying to figure it out myself.

"I heard him say, somethin' boy. What was it?" he insisted.

"Something about doing it on his own, sir, that's all I remember," I honestly said back.

"Well, that's what I was afraid of," he said as he quickly went over to his horse, mounted, and took off in the same direction that Pohl had ridden.

I just stood there, trying to make sense of all that had just happened. In just a matter of minutes, the excitement to tell Pohl my idea and this earth-shaking news had collided in a manner that frankly had left me in a stupor. I really did not know what to do next. I had spent last night coming up with a plan to save us all, and now Cora Lee was dead, and I might have just lost my best friend as well. I felt numb, but a question lingered.

"Why did the captain say he had to tell B all of this?" I said again out loud. I just shuffled back to the saloon to try and make heads or tails of everything. Again, life was playing tricks on me. I was learning the hard way that it could take the best-laid plans you make for yourself and throw them in the shitter faster than you can say the word shit.

I made it back to my office and just needed to sit down for a second to gather my thoughts and process everything. As soon as I did, though, the crate of whiskey that I had sent Jed to pick up was sitting on my desk in front of me. The whiskey was intended for Pohl's wedding reception. I just started to tear up right then with the pain of knowing Pohl was out there, filled with rage. But more so, pain that his world had been suddenly taken from him. It was not fair. I closed the door so that no one would see me breaking down. At that moment, it seemed a tidal wave of grief overtook me, and I just sobbed for what seemed like forever. Trying to be quiet but uncontrollable. Similar to what happened a few nights ago with Emmy in the hotel. As if all the pain associated with my life, Mother's death, and Cora Lee's, along with all this stupid talk of war building up inside me, was coming out again. But this time, much greater.

Then the guilt started to build. I should be beside Pohl right now, helping him work through whatever he was set on doing. But of course, I was too weak to stop him or fight to go along. Too weak for anything. The pain and guilt were starting to manifest into self-loathing. I thought I was so smart, so sharp, and full of plans, but in reality, I was nothing. Nothing to a world that only respects strength. Nothing but a gnat waiting to be squashed.

And with that thought, I truly was at my lowest point ever. More money than I had ever had in my life, B more invested in me than ever, but still empty. More defeated than ever. I was worthless in the eyes of the world, and even my best friend cast me off into the dirt. He knew I could not help him. I just ended up in the dirt, no matter how hard I tried.

The world doesn't need me. This feeling was one I recognized but now seemed to have a tighter hold on me. All the struggles with life this past week were really nothing new. I had experienced it all before, but back then, I always had Mother to bring me out of it. I would get down about my circumstance, but Mother would pick me back up and give me something to focus on other than my condition. But the world had taken her. It had allowed evil to spring up and take her from me, just like evil had taken Cora Lee. The world does not care; it just takes. The strong take from the weak, and I am part of the weak. It will surely take me sooner or later. *Maybe I should save it the trouble,* I thought. The beast that devours everything eventually will miss its final meal on me. I will outsmart it at the bitter end and go out on my own terms.

And just as I was to the point of falling over that cliff in my soul, I heard a voice in my head. Faint but growing louder. It was building; as if getting closer to me. *Go. Go,* is what it kept saying.

"Go?" I said out loud. I did not understand what it meant. "Go?" I said again out loud to myself. I just shook my head, trying to either get it to leave me be or shake some meaning loose so that I could understand it. As I opened and closed my eyes several times, trying to force the water from them and focus, the voice started to fade, but I could not get my eyes to cooperate. I felt dizzy. All this emotion, coupled with my lack of sleep last night, started to take control of me. I really was trying to fight it, but I could feel my head slowly falling to my desk.

I came to and somehow ended up on the floor behind my desk. I had a set of blankets there from the past nights I had stayed at work way too late to ride home or ramble down to the hotel. How long had I been like this, I wondered, as the sunlight had fallen to a faint glow in my office. I sat myself up and just stared at the whiskey bottles in front of me on my desk. They contained the past. The remnants of what could have been. A future party, celebrating love, family, and friendships that were now splayed out and rotting with the world's vultures fighting over the last scraps of them. Pohl's future was taken without mercy. And I could do nothing to help or change the path of it. Again, I sank further into my self-pity.

"What the hell?" I said as I grabbed a bottle from the crate, opened it up, and took the biggest swig I could stand. I took another and tried to forget everything once more.

A knock on my door stopped me from taking a third. A quarter of the bottle was gone by now. I corked it and put it back into the crate as I hurried around and tried to get put together.

"Uh, who is it?" I asked as I was lifting myself off the floor.

"Sir, it's me, Jed. Just wanted to make sure you saw the whiskey and let you know that the pretty lady is here for you."

"Oh yes, thank you, Jed, I see the crate right here...and tell B I will be right out, just finishing up some work," I said, hoping it would spare me a few minutes to pull myself more together.

"Yes, sir. I also have a message from Mr. Stallsburg, sir."

"Uhh, okay. What is it, Jed?" I responded.

"He left this morning but told me to tell you he will be back tomorrow. He had to go to pick up some supplies," Jed continued.

"Ok, Jed, thank you, and again, please tell B that I will be out in a minute," I shouted back as I still needed time to compose myself.

"Yes, sir," he said, and I could hear him walking back toward the front. As I looked around the office, I focused on the mirror and went over to make sure I looked okay. I could barely see with the light so low, but even so, I saw that my face and eyes were red and swollen. There was a wash basin and rag sitting right beneath it, so I hurriedly dunked the rag in the cold water and pressed it onto my face. It felt good, and I just let it do its healing while I stood there trying to compose my thoughts.

I was starting to get a warm feeling in my gut, surely from the whiskey.

"What is B going to think about all of this?" I wondered out loud.

And then I remembered the captain. He was going to go tell her what had happened. That still seemed like an odd statement to me, coming from him. Maybe Cora Lee's parents wanted her to know due to the wedding? I didn't know but soon would have the opportunity to find out. And in a way, I was relieved that she might already know about Cora Lee rather than me having to tell her the horrible news myself. With the dark thoughts I had been having, explaining it to her might pull deeper darkness back into me. I was obviously too weak for that at the moment.

I finally felt well enough to leave my office and head toward B at the front. As I came through the hall, I could see B seated at a far table along with the captain.

"What is he doing here?" I said as I continued to walk toward them. The whiskey starting to have an effect on me, but I tried to keep my composure. As I came closer, the captain stood up and waited for me to arrive at the table.

"B, I am so happy you came tonight," I said as I reached for her hand. She was just looking down at this point and did not reciprocate the gesture. Instantly this told me she already knew about Cora Lee.

"B, I am so sorry, this must be so terrible for you," is all I could say, seeing that she was visibly upset.

"Mr. Hotzmire, I think you should take a seat, son," the captain said while pulling out the open chair next to him rather than the one next to B.

I just looked up at him and back at B, confused, but took the seat next to B without concern for his suggestion. I sat down. I wanted to talk directly with B, but the captain was interjecting his presence at the table quite rudely, in my opinion. Something didn't feel right, and I started to get really annoyed that he was here. I finally asked him directly.

"What are you doing here, and what in the world is going on?"

The whiskey seemingly gave me some false courage and directness.

"Son, there is a lot to talk about here, so I would ask that you stay calm in an effort to not upset Ms. Hahne any further."

"Stay calm. I am not even sure how to respond to that statement. Cora Lee is dead, and my best friend just tore out of here to God knows where without me," I said, a little louder than I should have. Again, the whiskey was starting to talk for me, but with everything going on, I was okay with it.

"Son, I asked you politely to stay calm, and you are not obliging me, so I will say it again, stop being difficult and let me tell you what is going on," the captain said, having a hard time holding his composure.

This whole time B was just sitting there with her head down and looking very upset. Not saying a word.

"Okay, Okay, please help me understand what is going on!" I said sarcastically but yielded, pulling my hands back from B's direction.

"Son, as it seems you already know, Ms. Cora Lee Hazle was killed yesterday evening when her house was set afire by a Militia looking to drive out her father from Salem. Now, I have also informed Ms. Hahne of any details I have been told about the incident, as I know them to be very close friends. And seeing that you, Ms. Hahne, and Mr. Starp are friends, thought that you should also be brought details about the incident."

"Yes, Pohl and I are best friends, and I was to be his Best Man for the wedding," I said, confirming his statement.

Upon hearing this, B started to cry a little harder.

"Now, I can't imagine the pain that both you and Ms. Hahne are experiencing right now, but I feel I should also inform you that Mr. Starp came into camp this afternoon and enlisted in the U.S. Army. Doing so with the sole purpose of finding the perpetrators of this heinous crime and bringing them to justice."

"Pohl enlisted?"

"Yes, and he will be joining my unit with our reassignment to this region of Virginia once he returns from his initial training. No matter what is going on in our nation, law and order must be maintained. These Militias are growing in strength and are starting to cross the line throughout the south," the captain explained.

I just looked at B. Although she was still upset, she had raised her head and was looking at the captain as he talked.

"Pohl's blacksmithing talents will be a valuable asset to our ranks, and his influence on others in the region will be of great help with recruitment."

I could feel the whiskey was having an ever-growing effect on me, but with this revelation, I was being rocked back to sobriety quickly. I absolutely could not believe what I was hearing, and the sheer rapidness of it was overly cruel. One minute to the next is like living in a nightmare.

"Where is Pohl now, and when will we see him again?" is about the only thing I could think of to ask while I let it all sink in.

"He has already left for training, and typically it lasts just over a month. But I have requested him to be trained just outside of Salem with my battalion leader, as we will be needing him sooner rather than later. We lost our last blacksmith at Fort Riley a few months back. And having him in the Salem area will hopefully allow him to gain details and knowledge of the Militia we are now all searching for. He will have to show great restraint during this process, but that was the deal I made with him for enlisting, and I am a man of my word."

I just nodded my head as this all seemed to make sense, knowing Pohl the way I did. Pohl would find them for sure, and when he did, only God himself would be able to save their souls. B finally broke her silence.

"Oh, Garit, this is all so devastating. I really don't even know what to do," she said as she dabbed her tears with a handkerchief.

"I don't know either, B, but whatever we do, we have got to get out of here to do it," I said with directness.

She looked at me, confused.

"Out of here? The saloon or Christiansburg?"

"Both. Before all of this happened, I had figured it out B, figured out what we all had to do. I was on my way to tell Pohl when…"

I just couldn't say it again. Couldn't say Cora Lee had been killed. It would be too painful to hear again so soon. B just looked at me with sadness in her eyes. The captain once again tried to take our attention away from each other by taking his hat off and placing it on the table.

He followed by saying, "Mr. Hotzmire, as you probably might be wondering by now, me coming here with Ms. Hahne is not quite within the protocol. Gathering you and Ms. Hahne together to divulge the details of Ms. Hazle's death and Mr. Starp's enlistment and plans for his training is outside my typical constraints of sharing information. The actual reason for this meeting is that I believe it is time for the truth to be told to you about Ms. Hahne and me."

"What? Ms. Hahne and you?" I stammered as I looked at B. "B, what is he talking about?"

I could tell B was rightfully upset with what had happened to Cora Lee, but what was going to be said next was holding a higher place in her current apprehensiveness. Grabbing her hand, I asked again.

"B, what is he talking about?" She turned her head away from me and started to cry.

"Mr. Hotzmire, please take your hand off of her," the captain snapped, but I ignored him.

"Right now!" the captain further insisted.

Immediately I wanted to stand up and slap him across the face for even assuming he had a place in our relationship, but as always, the thought would be just that, and no action, for I knew my body could not back up a reaction like that.

I just took my hand back and eased into my chair while trying to stay calm. He began to expound that he and B had met last summer as his unit came through town on their way to a station out West. They camped outside of town as usual, and it just so happened to be near B's farm. During that short time, they established feelings for each other but did not act on them, as he was leaving so quickly for his post. They had agreed to start corresponding with each other by letter, and in doing so, their feelings for each other had continued to grow over the past few months.

He went on to describe that, toward the end of his deployment, her letters had stopped reaching him. This gave me optimism that B had regretted their relationship and had chosen ours to continue. Our relationship appeared to be growing stronger over the same time frame. My optimism was short-lived, though, for he continued his story by saying that he assumed the letters not coming was due to simply moving around too fast for them to reach his camps. And upon receiving orders to relocate to Fort Sumter, he had taken a non-direct route through Christiansburg in an effort to see her again. This whole story was producing question after question within me, but I just sat there and tried to stay calm. Listening and watching as B and this captain started to smile at each other like two little schoolkids on different pews in church. It was starting to make me sick to my stomach.

The captain continued his narrative that, once making it back to Christiansburg, he immediately set his sights on camping near B's farm again so that he could determine if she still had feelings for him. And she confirmed that she did. Because of this, he explained he was set to ask her father for his blessing for them to be married. But the news about Cora Lee came before he had the opportunity to. When he said the word 'marriage.' I could feel my body shrink even further into the chair. I looked directly at B.

"B, is this all true? You have feelings for him and are going to marry him? What…what about us?

She looked like she wanted to answer me, but the captain intervened.

"Mr. Hotzmire, we are here today to confirm our intent to marry and to request that you no longer attempt to contact Ms. Hahne for anything more than friendship from this point forward. I understand that this must be a shock to you, and on a terrible day to hear such news, but it is our intent to be married within the month.

"And on behalf of myself and the US Army, condolences on the loss of Cora Lee, but please know that we will find the vermin behind it post haste. Now, please excuse us, as I must get Ms. Hahne back home so that she can grieve for her dear friend accordingly. Good evening."

That was it. A well-executed lecture that finished off my chapter with B and started another for both of them. I could do nothing but watch them stand up, him taking her hand and leading her toward the door of the saloon. I had now progressed from anger to complete and utter shock. Too shocked even to move, but truthfully, too emotionally crushed to do anything about it anyway. As I sat there taking in all that had just happened and replaying the words in my head, B walked back into the saloon alone. She approached the table and sat down again.

Looking straight into my eyes, she began to speak.

"Garit, I can't imagine the emotions you are trying to deal with at the moment, but I just could not leave without you knowing that I do care for you. I did not expect my relationship with Charles to ever develop any further than just playful flirting and letters. It was supposed to be just letters. He's in the military, for heaven's sake. I didn't even expect ever to see him again. But he came back, and with everything going on, it's clear that I need a man that can protect my family and me. Father says war is coming, so I am doing what he and I both think is right. I care for you deeply, but he can protect me in ways you just can't. I am so sorry, and I hope that someday you can understand and forgive my actions."

I just shook my head and lowered my stare from hers. I had so much I wanted to say, but my spinning brain could not even put together words to form sentences. Literally, for the first time in my life, I was left utterly speechless. Fractured would be an understatement. B could see this and just put her hand on my knee.

"I am truly sorry, Garit. You will still see me around, though, and we can still remain friends." She then stood up and walked out the door again to her awaiting new benefactor.

I continued to sit at the table, trying to process all that had just happened, had happened earlier today and, really, this entire past week. My head began to hurt. A pain that was unlike any other pain before. Deeper, more pulsating. As I rubbed my head, trying to soothe it, Jed came over to the table.

"I am sorry to bother you, sir, but I have another message for you."

I did not respond.

"Sir?" he said again and shook my arm.

"Yes," is all I could say in response.

"I told you earlier about Mr. Stallsburg being gone for a couple of days, but he also left you this note and told me to give it to you. Your door was closed earlier, but here it is now. I hope you're not sore with me about it being delivered late," Jed said in a hopeful tone.

I did not look up or respond, so again he just said, "Sir?"

I continued to just sit in silence, not acknowledging his presence, so he finally just tucked the note in my left jacket pocket and backed away slowly.

Even being as young and uneducated as he was, he knew something was very wrong. Thankfully, he did not press the issue any further. I just needed to sit and process everything for a bit. As I did, the comprehension that Mr. Stallsburg would be gone for a few days started to take hold. I supposed that was good. I would have some time to not have to talk through all of this with him. He always gave good counsel, but these topics were just too raw for me to address at the moment. I started to see people filing through the front door of the saloon, and it was starting to get busier, as evenings typically did. I could not let anyone see me this way, so I retreated once again to my office. But this time, the whisky would stay in the bottle. I really needed to think straight now.

As I closed my office door, I noticed that someone had lit my lantern and put some more wood in my stove, as usual, each night. The light and warmth felt good. I huddled up close to the stove, and its warmth penetrated even deeper into the coldness that had taken up refuge within me. Rocking back and forth allowed my blood to start flowing and retake my extremities. I bet I was as pale as snow, based on how I felt. It wasn't that the saloon was exceptionally cold, just that the shock of what just occurred had left my body fighting itself. I had the same reaction just hours ago, and when Mother died, so I was beginning to learn through forced repetition its effects. I then remembered the note Jed gave to me earlier, so I pulled it out of my pocket in an effort to take my mind off of all of it for a moment.

Garit,

Leaving for Roanoke to get supplies for the reception and a special surprise for Pohl and Cora Lee. I will be back in time for the Wedding. Keep the saloon steady, and I look forward to the celebration!

F.

"Well, that didn't help," I said to myself in a pitiful tone. As the warmth continued to do its thing, I started to envy Mr. Stallsburg. Envy that he did not know what I did at that very moment. He was just headed out of town to pick up supplies, excited about the wedding and oblivious to the change in plans awaiting his return. Oh, how I wished I were him right then. I just lost what was left of the world around me, and being anywhere but here seemed the right place to be.

Chapter 21

I woke the next morning on the floor of my office again, shivering from the cold that had continued to plague me since yesterday. I stared at the slight hint of fire in the stove and was grateful for the lock on the door. Last night I locked it and the rest of the world out. At some point, Jed had come by to turn my lantern off but could not get in, so I went on about closing down the saloon with Dub as usual. Thankfully, he had brought in some extra wood from out back before I barricaded the door, as it helped me stay warm throughout the night.

At some point, though, I stopped filling the stove, as I just was done. Over everything and giving up. Hoping that God would see fit to take me out of my misery while I slept. Acting on it myself, rather than waiting on God to do it, did seem somewhat valiant though, in my twisted, jumbled thoughts. No longer having to be at the world or God's will for my destruction. To further inflict pain on me as He had, for whatever reason, felt necessary to do so intently since the day I was born. And now He had obviously declared war on me personally. To be fair, though, I did challenge him earlier this last week. But ending my life would give me the chance to have the last word and right now, that was enough to make me content. To win in fact. I was always competitive, and this would be the final game to play and be victorious at that.

Mother saved me again from my dark thoughts, though, as she always had done before. I clearly remembered last night, us riding back from Church one afternoon on a beautiful spring day, full of life. She looked around, bringing the wagon to a stop.

"To think that God made all of this for us, all this wonderful beauty, for our pleasure, and some people prefer to waste it all away by killing others or themselves, seems pointless to me. What good does that bring?"

Mother then just flicked the reins and kept driving toward home. It was such a slight moment, one that a child of my age then should not even have paid attention to. But I did for some reason, and mother was using it to save me now. The memory was so clear. So real to me that I could not ignore it. It had to be coming to my aide. I could always count on her. But the world…God had taken her from me.

"Damn you."

I could curse God but letting my Mother's words fall on deaf ears would be something I would not allow. She would have given anything for me, so I will gladly give this to her. I desperately wanted to see her again someday, and I feared that killing myself, although winning my match against God, would likely result in losing any chance to see Mother again. That was too high a stake for me to gamble.

I lay there for what seemed to be another hour or so before I started to have somewhat of a breakthrough. If I was at my end and had no fear of death, then I was in a no-lose situation. I just took the house odds of winning out of the picture, I simply did not care if I lost. Losing was winning, in my strange new twist of philosophy. As long as it was not self-inflicted, I had no fear of death or leaving this earth. Really. I had nothing left to live for, but in a curious turn of fate, could move forward without fear of death or loss. In fact, me dying got me to the one place I hoped it would, back with Mother and off this good-for-nothin' world.

My entire life had shaped and molded me into what I had become, lying on a cold saloon floor. Unencumbered and apathetic. Free to let life just happen, damn the consequences. I didn't care. As I sat myself down at my desk, I was amused at my new understanding or, should I say, comprehension of life and the ties that typically bind someone. I had none of them. Father was gone. Mother was gone. Pohl had left. B had chosen another over me.

And as I went over it, again and again, all that had happened, B leaving me for the captain, in reality, didn't hurt as bad as I thought it would. Shocking yes. Out of the wild blue yonder, for sure. I was rightfully angry at how all transpired, but the fact is, it started to feel more like a weight was being lifted off of my back. I felt physically lighter somehow. Free. Now, I really only had Frank and the saloon as burdens, and in reality, either one of them would be perfectly fine without me around. I had quite a bit of money saved up and no one to spend it on anymore. I then felt even more emboldened in this newly formed outlook.

"I can literally go anywhere in the world. No one can stop me, and I will never let a War catch up to me."

I simply could be the master of my own destiny. That was the one factor missing from the other morning when I challenged God to bring it on. I had collateral damage around me then. People that I could hurt by my actions, but now, they were all gone. This continued realization still caused me pain, of course, but there was plainly nothing I could do about it, and not one iota of it was my fault. They all left me, just like everyone always does. I should have expected it. I thought I was smarter than that, but it took wishing I was dead to really enlighten not only my brain but my soul. Everything had changed last night, as

I lay on a cold floor, forcing my heart to forget all the noise. Emerging better, stronger, and more focused than ever before. And taking advantage of this new me would be my life's greatest feat so far.

As Mr. Stallsburg was gone, I went to the bar and checked on things in an effort to keep everyone calm. I had not even thought about the saloon or how it was operating since yesterday morning. They all probably thought I was going cuckoo anyways by my actions, but I am sure by now they all had heard about Cora Lee, Pohl, and even B. Heck, how could they miss B's revelation to me? We were sitting smack in the middle of the saloon when it occurred. As I approached the bar, Dub was there early, and I did not expect him to be. Typically, Gus would be opening up.

"Well, Garit, I was not sure you were ever going to come out of your office. I sure am glad you did, son. I took the liberty of making some coffee just in case," Dub said as he offered me a cup.

"Thank you, Dub. I need this more than you know," I said as I sat down and enjoyed the warmth. The simple and hearty smell of a good cup of coffee.

"Son, I just want to say how sorry I am for everything that has happened to you. Damn shame about that girl and your friend. And I know it's not your main worry, but we all sure were looking forward to the Wedding and Reception tomorrow. It's almost too hard to comprehend."

I just took another sip of coffee and nodded. I really did not know what to say.

Was I sad? Of course. Should the world stop due to this tragedy? Yes, it very well should. But it wouldn't. People will just say things like, "I'm so sorry for your loss," or "You will continue to be in our prayers," but none of that would actually help. In fact, all it would do was remind me of all that had happened, and I didn't want to think about it anymore. What's done was done. I did feel it appropriate to hide my disdain for these types of comments, though.

"Yes, it's a shame what happened, Dub, but what can you do?" I said.

I didn't hide it well enough, I suppose. My comment caught Dub a little off.

"You okay, son?" he asked, genuinely concerned about my current state of mind.

"Yep, my life has been turned upside down, shattered, you might even say, but we still gotta go on, and go on I shall, just like everyone else," I said. I stood up and turned to go. I added, "Thank you for the coffee, Dub, and please tell everyone that we will be open for business as usual tonight. No longer closing down early for Pohl's bachelor party. And I suppose the same for tomorrow night. No wedding, no reception." I said as I headed back to my office.

I knew that he would be even more alarmed by that last statement, so I did not even want to give him the chance to respond. I could see his reflection in the mirror at the end of the bar as I walked, and sure enough, he just stood there shaking his head at my remark. I didn't care. I didn't have to care for the first time in my life.

Once back in the office, I set about burning any notes and lists that I had made over the past few weeks. So many pieces of paper planning out what would have been. What could have been. Wedding plans, reception plans, plans for taking Pohl out on the town tonight before his big day. Plans that would never be realized and had been burned up, just like the paper was doing now. I started to feel bad, watching the fire grow larger and larger for Cora Lee.

Sweet Cora Lee. What a terrible way to die. And of anyone, she surely did not deserve that. She was harmless and joyful. Someone that made this world a better place and politics, or more accurately, men who allowed something as meaningless as politics to take over their thoughts, had killed her. Although I was livid about how all this transpired, the thought of Pohl exacting his revenge on them made me happy. They deserved to die. They deserved worse than hanging. And hopefully, Pohl would burn them to the ground just as they did her. I picked up a few more scraps of paper, and the list that I had created just a few mornings ago was on top.

B
Rec
Emmy
√ on B
√ on Cora Lee – Pohl
Farewell Youth
West

I smirked as I started to read it.

"Don't have to worry about one or four anymore, I reckon. And how true is number six? Number two, might not even do that anymore." But then I got to numbers three and five. Both those items immediately changed my tone.

The reality was that, based on everything going on, Emmy would have a lot to worry about, and she did not deserve that. Just because of the color of her skin. I had internally put her on the same level as Cora Lee, harmless and joyful. Probably even more joyful than Cora Lee, but without any means to a future other than being a hotel cook, and if the south has its way, slave for life.

"That's not right," I said out loud. Pohl's name on the list I just skimmed over. He was hurting right now, but he knew what he was doing. I didn't need to worry about him for now. Then seven.

"West," I said out loud. And I had to sit down as this one had changed meaning so much in the last day that it was almost too hard to grasp. I was running to Pohl's shop yesterday to tell him my big plan. The plan that could have saved us all from war, from losing our friendships and loves. Had I only thought of it sooner! But it vanished as soon as I hit Pohl's doorway. Gone into vapor before it even had a chance to live.

West. Colorado. Denver, to be more exact. The great wild west and on the edge of the most glorious mountains man had ever seen. Or so I was told.

A few months ago, some French prospectors had come through the saloon and commenced telling stories of the great Rocky Mountains. Or *Montagnes De Roche*, as they called them. That sounded much more exotic. Describing mountains so tall that God himself would have a hard time stepping over them. Of trees and rivers and wildlife so plentiful that few have ever seen a country so ample and ripe. And right on the edge of it was the growing city of Denver. Shops, saloons, and commerce that, due to the mountains in the distance, were a natural stopping point for settlers and dreamers headed through them and beyond. The nightlife was plentiful, and the day was filled with clean air, adventure, and riches to be had by anyone wanting to brave the risk. I was entranced by what they were talking about.

But Mr. Stallsburg called it all ballyhoo. He said that there's nothing but Indians, grassland, and Black Legs out west. I remember so surely because I had to ask what a Black-Leg even was. But the picture those men painted that night had stuck with me. It seemed like a place we all could go and make our fortune and outrun the war. It wasn't even a state. Just part of a vast, mostly undiscovered distant land.

My plan was to get everyone to agree to leave after the wedding and give it a try. I had enough money saved up that I think we could have gotten there. I could have helped Pohl open a blacksmith shop, I could have gotten a job working at any local saloon, and Cora Lee and B could love the both of us each night. What a life! What a plan! Until it, all was torn apart.

256

"But did it have to be?" I wondered out loud.

Going without all of them would be riskier, of course, but I could move faster, I reckon, and the train goes all the way to St. Joseph, Missouri. Maybe even further by now. I also learned that the mail route from there to Denver through Kansas territory was regularly traveled by pioneers and the Army. The stories of Indians raiding wagon trains seem real, but surely, I would be safe. Just tag up with other groups or the Army on the march and head west. And, if I left in a month or so, I would be traveling during the early spring months. Sure, still cold a bit, but getting warmer each day.

I could be set up and working by early April or even sooner if things went well. As I considered this revised plan in my mind again, it took on an even more exciting appeal. I would not have anything or anyone slowing me down. If I made it to Denver and it was not everything the Frenchies had said it was, I could just keep going, I reckon.

"Wow," I said out loud. As I looked back down at the list, I had no need for it anymore. More directly, I had no need for anything written on it anymore. So, into the fire, it went. In fact, everything that was on my desk was picked up and thrown into the fire. It didn't have a hold on me anymore. Responsibilities. Who needs them? And I almost stopped myself from saying what came out next, but at this point, I really didn't care. Looking up, I spoke.

"God, I don't care anymore. Kill me or save me. Either way, I am going to live my life my way until then." And at that moment, a spark traveled back into my veins. Like the first time B ever kissed me. I was back. Returned from my cold, self-imposed exile. I hurried up and gathered all my stashes of cash throughout the office. Stuffing it in my pockets and saddle bag. And immediately, I stopped.

"Honey!" I had been so preoccupied with what was happening to me and everyone around me I had completely forgotten about Honey. "Oh, my Lord!" I jerked open my office door and ran out the back. As

I rounded the corner, I saw that our stable was completely empty, and Honey was nowhere to be found. "Shit," was all I could say as I turned and ran back into the saloon and up to the bar.

"Dub!" I yelled as I came in. He jumped up from down behind the bar.

"Yes sir," he said quickly and with a tone of worry.

"Where's Honey at?" I demanded in a manic tone.

"Uh, uh, I don't know, sir; I just figured she was at your place," he said nervously back.

"Shit," I let out again, and tried to think back over the last day or so and what could have happened to her.

Just then, Jed came walking through the front door, hands in his pockets, without a care in the world. I frightened him as I shouted.

"Jed, where's Honey?" He almost fell down, trying to react.

"Uhhhh…took her to the stable, sir, just like I always do when you forget about her," he said, not knowing if his honest answer would get him in trouble.

I loved that about Jed. In fact, I had started teasing him lately by calling him "Honest Abe" after President Lincoln because they were both known for telling it like it is. Or at least that's what the paper says.

"Well, by God, son, you have saved the day once again," I said as I ran toward him.

He started to cower down like I was going to hit him or something, but I just grabbed both his arms, lifted him back up straight, and yelled.

"That's my boy!" As I let him go, I reached into my pocket and slapped a silver dollar into his hand.

"Sir, you need me to go fetch her and pay for the boarding with—" I interrupted him.

"Nope, this is for you, and you alone, son. Thank you for everything you always do for me. In fact, here's another, for just being you, Jed." I pulled another coin out and slapped it in his other hand.

I will never forget the smile that came across his face at that moment. He was so happy, and I, too, was happy I could share this with him. So happy, in fact, that I immediately turned around and saw Dub standing there with his mouth wide open trying to figure out what in the world had gotten into me. I just started laughing uncontrollably at the sight and made my way over to where he was standing. I laughed even harder as I approached the bar because he seemed to wince back with every step I took toward him. I think he was genuinely scared of how crazy I was acting. Nevertheless, he stood his ground, and as I got to the bar, I grabbed his hand and slapped a coin into his as well.

"Dub, you have always been a pleasure to work with, and I highly appreciate your sense of humor, "I shouted as I almost fell down laughing.

Dub had the sense of humor of a dry toad, but I always tried to get at least a chuckle out of him. It never worked. The face of stone that man had. At this point, even Jed was laughing. I don't think he knew why or what for, but he just laughed, as mine must have been contagious.

"Garit, what in the world has gotten into you, son?" is all that Dub could say.

I stopped for a moment and made a face like I was thinking really hard.

"I have no idea, Dub, but life stinks one minute, and then the next minute, some crazy person gives you a Silver Dollar." I was laughing as I completed my statement. Dub just stood there in shock at my behavior.

"Well, tally ho, gentleman, I have a horse waiting in the stable for me." I headed out the front door and onward to fetch Honey. As I hit the boardwalk, the chill of the morning slapped me right to attention. I knew it was cold, but this cold, I didn't care. I had to get to Honey and get home fast because adventure awaited, and I was bound and determined to make it wait no longer.

Once again, as I made my way home on Honey, I looked at the world around me and just smiled. Days ago, I was half drunk, cursing God and the World for picking on me, and now, I should have been in the exact same state. You could argue that my current situation was way worse than the other morning. At least then, Cora Lee was alive, Pohl was still here, and B, although drunk and probably passed out in her bed, was still mine for the moment. Leagues away from where I was presently. I was elated. Chipper. Up. I actually started thinking, "maybe there really is something loose in my head." But the benefit of being in this state of mind was I didn't care. Carefree. At ease and calm for the first time in my life. This feeling was intoxicating. No need for spirits; this was even better. No matter how cold the wind blew or misfortune, the world felt like it shoved my way; I felt impervious to it. It really was the strangest feeling, but who was I to question it? I just took it in, and it felt like it fit me like a finely tailored top hat. Like I had finally caught up to it after all these years. It was just waiting on me to get here. I spurred on Honey with this feeling and started to gallop the rest of the way home. And home was right around the corner for now.

Opening up the front door, I could see Frank sitting by the fire and warming up after, I presumed, he had been out taking care of the morning chores. His coat was buttoned up, and he even still had his hat on.

"Garit, I thought I heard someone riding up," he said with a wide smile.

"Yep, and boy, am I happy to be home, Frank. It's cold out there," I responded.

"Oh, it is for sure. I have been sitting here for twenty minutes just trying to thaw my feet and hands out from this morning." And with that, I had to stop and tell him how much I valued him

"Frank, I know I have told you this before, but I want to make sure you really know how much I love you and appreciate you keeping the farm running. I never worry about you or this place, and in one sense, that is not right. In another, it's right as rain."

"Okay…you're welcome?" he said, not knowing how to really react to my words.

"No, I mean it. Ever since Mother left, heck, even before that, you have carried my weight and yours and kept us on track. Never complaining, never asking for help. Just doin' what you do day in and day out. I have taken that for granted, and for that, I am sorry."

"Garit, I am not really sure what you are talking about. I just want to make myself useful around here for you and An…" he caught himself before he said Mother's name.

"Frank, it's okay. I sometimes forget also that she is gone," I said, trying to make him feel better.

"Well, I sure do miss her, and sometimes I imagine her walking right through that there door and getting onto me for wearing my boots on the rug. I would gladly take a scolding if she were here to give it," Frank said in an honest, childlike way. I had made my way over closer to the fireplace now and took a seat next to him.

"Frank, me too, but we better still take our boots off. She might just come down from heaven and swat our hides anyway!" I said, trying to ease the seriousness and get him to laugh. It worked, and it felt really nice to hear him laugh again.

"What I really came out here to do was to gather all my earnings and tally up how much I had."

"Well, I haven't touched it, just like I said I wouldn't, so it should all be there, fair and square," Frank assured me.

"Oh, I have no doubt, Frank," I said as I hopped up to head to my room.

"Oh, by the way, I might be taking a trip soon, but don't you worry, I will explain it all before I go," I added on the way.

"Sounds good, Garit. I look forward to hearing about your plans."

As I entered my room, I just shook my head in wonder at how Uncle Frank never really got worried about much or upset at hearing something like that. If someone had told me they might be leaving soon on a trip, I typically would want to hear all the details and how it would affect me right away. Uncle Frank had none of that. He just assumed it was what you needed to do and kept his focus on the farm and keeping it running. I wondered how he would take the news of me going on something longer than just a trip. I am not sure if I would ever come back, to be honest. I had convinced myself I did not care about anything anymore, but I couldn't ignore the fact that I did care about Frank. I was not sure how my leaving for good would play out between us. I would worry about that later. Right now, I must focus on my resources, and cash on hand was the most important.

I pulled all the money together, counted, and stacked it. And then did it again just to make sure it was correct. I was surprised at the amount. It was less than I had thought it should be. This kind of hurt my ego a little, as I always prided myself on having a running tally in my mind. Three hundred fifty-seven dollars and a few odd cents. *Sure seemed like I should have more than that,* I thought. *I suppose spending all my money on B and getting prepared for the wedding took more than I thought.* Also, I knew I had not paid myself out of the saloon for the past two weeks or so, and I estimated that to be another thirty dollars. I would find out tomorrow morning for sure.

But even three hundred and eighty-seven dollars was less than I thought I would need to head out west. It was a lot, but it might not be enough. And I would want to leave Frank with something. I knew he had money after Mother died, I gave him some of her savings. I was surprised at how much she had managed to save up over the years.

A tidy little sum, but only enough to weather out a bad crop or two. Besides, it would be wrong to just pick up and leave without making sure he had a good nest egg, just in case.

I had to make more somehow and fast. The thought of postponing my trip was out of the question. War was on the horizon and God was just itching at the chance to cause me a delay, illness, or some other life-changing event. He'd thrown everything else at me so far, though, so not sure what could be left. But I didn't want to give him too much time to come up with something. I could hold out for a few days, maybe a week, but every minute I fought against the clear direction I should be traveling, would be a minute too long. I had some things I could sell but nothing of real value. B always insisted that any companion of hers had to be well dressed and appointed, so she would regularly coerce me into not only buying nice things for her but nice enough things for me. Nice jackets, shoes, or hats would come in handy out west, I imagined anyway, so selling them might not be the best idea.

And, for that matter, who would even buy them around here? I did have some silver cufflinks, a silver chain, and a pocket watch. But again, who would buy them? I could see them helping me get employment once I got to Denver.

I was already going to have my age fighting against me, might as well look the part at a minimum. I really did not have that many other valuables, and Honey, she was coming with me. I wouldn't even consider leaving her behind. So, what else could I do?

I sat there contemplating my options, and finally, gambling sprang to the front of my mind. Yep, that was it. I had always played it safe before, but now, what did I have to lose? I should go all in and show everyone and, more so, myself, what I am capable of.

"Well, Garit, you think you're so smart. Put it to the test," I continued to challenge myself. And why not? Living without fear was my secret power now. One that I might as well let out of the bottle quickly before I lose it. Ok, that is what I would do. Tonight, at the saloon, I would have full control, so I was going to make it count. Nothing shady or against Mr. Stallsburg, just honest gambling against others. I would take their money, not the houses. So, I had to play poker, and I had to get into the bigger games. The nice thing was that I had been playing more and more after the crowd started to fade, and the other players knew me and my style. Tough. Calculated. But safe. I never bet too aggressively, and I would always bow out when the pot got a bit larger than normal. I mean, it would be wrong of the saloon's assistant to win the big pots all the time. People would start talking, and business would suffer. But winning a little here and there never caused much of a ruckus. More of just entertainment, really, to most players. I think they enjoyed playing with someone of my age but also really enjoyed it when I lost to them. Gave them a sense of retribution, winning money from a "company" man.

"Well, let's see how they like it tonight."

Chapter 22

As I entered the saloon from the front, things felt very different. I suddenly wasn't counting the players, people sitting at the bar or other usual factors in gauging whether the saloon would have a good night or not. It was just me, looking for a game. Optimistic, like most who had walked through that door before me.

It was nice. The colors seemed brighter, the music sounded better. I wanted to try and stay in this mood but also realized that I could not make it through the night without conducting a little bit of normal business. Mr. Stallsburg was gone, so I went ahead and walked toward the bar first to speak with Dub. Plus, I was curious about how he would react to me after our fun this morning.

"Dub, how's the evening going?"

"Uh.... well, it's pretty slow on account everyone thought that we would be closed early for the private event," he said, being careful how he said the last part, not knowing how I would react to it.

"Understandable," I said without emotion. And as I looked around, I had to finally turn back on my assistant mentality and count the patrons.

"Yep, only seventeen in-house. Down around a dozen or so from usual."

"Yes, sir. I sent Jed around town to make sure everyone knew we would be open as usual, but everyone sure is shaken up by all that's happened." He looked at me with eyes that knew I knew what he meant.

"It's okay, Dub, a lot has happened for sure, people just need time to process it all," I said, showing no emotion, for I had none left anymore.

"Listen, I am going to take a night off and just relax a little. I need some time to think, so just act like I am a normal patron and give me some space. Is that okay with you?" I pressed him.

"Of course, son, with everything you have been through, you don't even have to explain it. I will also make sure the rest of the staff knows as well."

"Thanks, Dub." I tried to act downtrodden to sell the ruse a little bit further.

"You bet, son, have a good time."

I walked toward the poker tables. The crowd was truly down, but there were two tables in play tonight. One with four players and the other with two. I just stood and watched for a few minutes, and everyone looked to be acting the same toward me as usual. That was good. I did not want to spend the entire evening recounting how many things I had lost over the past two days. The past was the past, and it was better staying there.

I then walked back to the front to check on Rudy at the roulette table. A few patrons were there, having what seemed to be a great time. Rudy was playing into the fun as usual. As I got closer, Rudy just nodded his head and kept on at it. That was probably the only real thing that I was going to be sore about when I left. I never got the bottom of my hunch that someone was skimming. It was like an itch that I just could not quite scratch, and it would bother me for some time, I imagined. But then again, it was only a hunch, and if I hadn't figured it out by now, then so be it. I turned and headed back to the bar and was hit with the realization that I should have been at the bar with Pohl right now. Toasting to his upcoming marriage and razzing him about all the things that come with it. I had planned for his father, B's brothers, our friend Thomas and I all to have the bar to ourselves. Closing early to the rest and just celebrating life, love, and the future. What a change in events. What an upside-down world it has now become. Still, I felt this need to make a private toast to him and Cora Lee.

"Dub, can I get a shot of the finest bourbon we have on hand, please?"

"You bet, Garit. Coming right up," he responded quickly, as the bar was his domain, and he was quite good at it.

I sat down away from the others already seated and placed my hat on top of the bar beside me. Kind of a makeshift stand-in for Pohl.

"Dub, make that two," I called out to him. And he just simply nodded in affirmation.

I thought for a moment about all of the losses. But had to also acknowledge the self-perceived gains that came with it. It helped, but I already missed my friend and to sit here without him seemed wrong. The greatest writer in the world could not have written a more unstable last forty-eight hours. I just shook my head in amazement. By then, Dub had returned and set both glasses down directly in front of me. Wiped his hands with a rag and proceeded back to the other end of the bar. I appreciated his discretion and awareness that I needed to be alone. I moved one of the glasses over to in front of my hat. It was Pohl's glass. I picked the other up, made an internal toast in Pohl's and Cora Lee's honor, and clanked my glass against his. Drank mine down in one mouthful.

"Whoooo!" I let out once it settled in my stomach as it burned badly going down. All the others at the bar, including Dub, just nodded and smiled. They could recognize my fledgling reaction.

"Well, I don't know if that was good Bourbon or not, but thank you, Dub, for serving it to me," I yelled down to him with a wave. Again, he just nodded and smiled while he cleaned a glass with his rag. The other glass just sat there in quiet reverence.

"Pohl would have liked it," I said quietly, referring to the bourbon. But also, I suppose, to the celebration of him we would've been having right now. Pohl was a good man. A good friend. And would have been a great husband.

After several more minutes of just sitting there at the bar and reflecting on Pohl and all that had happened, I noticed that the poker table with four players was now down to three. I guess that was my cue to go over and commence my plan. Picking up my hat, I saw that Dub had now come back down.

"Want to make it another round, Garit?" to which I just shook my head.

"Nope, one is enough for me tonight, Dub, and I am going to leave this one here for Pohl." Dub understood the meaning behind that statement.

"You bet, Garit. I will keep an eye on it until he gets here." He winked.

"Thank you, Dub, thank you for everything," I said and walked over to join the game.

As I got closer, I could see that Mr. Nelson, Mr. Fuller, and Mr. Evans were playing with a fairly large pot in front of them. I guess the other player that had left had bowed out as it was too much for him. I think it was Mr. Hamilton. He was smart to do that. The other three left to play were pretty salty at poker and had a higher pain level when it came to losing greenbacks. All three of them were in a little bit higher league than other players. Played more regularly and all known to be careful but placed larger bets than most could handle.

This was the perfect group to set my sights on. George, the dealer, was also a preference to me as he was stern with the rules and careful with his shuffling and card work so that no one thought one player or the other was getting "too lucky" if he won several hands in a row.

I was focused on Mr. Nelson, though, as he was the wealthiest player of the three. He would bet big, often the maximum, in an effort to push other players deeper or bluff his hand. He ran the local sawmill and had other interests throughout town as well. Rough, hard-working, but hard playing. I had gotten to know his style pretty well over the years, and if I needed the pot to get into the higher amounts I was looking for, he was the man to take it there. I approached the table, and George just looked up at me, then back down at the table.

"You in, Garit?"

"If the table will have me."

The other players just looked back at me and nodded. I waited to sit down, though, until this hand was over, and with a flip of the hole card, Mr. Nelson had won against both of the others. It was a modest pot; I estimated around twelve dollars total. Bets at the saloon on this table were fifty-cent and one-dollar limits. We just did not have the clientele to warrant any higher than that. The other table was twenty-five/fifty cents, so it gave a good option to new players or regulars. I have heard that in New Orleans, typical limits were one to two dollars and could be even higher, but we just did not have that kind of play here. One time we increased it to those levels when we had an invitation-only tournament, and the players whom we invited could handle it. But for everyday play, it was just too steep. Occasionally if a game got going hard or someone was trying to show off, a player would ask to increase the limits, but I or Mr. Stallsburg typically would not allow it until the fourth card was dealt. It just didn't happen much, as our rules already allowed for doubling or tripling the high limit raise on each card after three. So, a player could raise up to two or three dollars if wanted. That almost always took care of any limit raise needs.

I remember once, though, that some fancy out-of-towners came through and got Mr. Nelson into a large pot by asking to raise the limits and tripling the raise each bet. All the players at the table agreed to the terms, so we obliged. That pot got up to seventy-eight dollars, which was the largest anyone had ever seen before. Mr. Nelson lost that hand, but it was nice for the saloon because our take on the pot rake was five percent for the tournament. We made almost four dollars on just one hand. And the other pots that night were still way above average. A good night for us indeed, and Mr. Nelson even won back most of what he had lost, so everyone went away satisfied. Not a winner, but not a loser either. Just challenging and aggressive play. For a seasoned poker player, that's almost as good as a big night winning. Almost. Everyone, of course, is chasing the thrill of the win but having another player or two at the table that can challenge you is fun when you play a lot like the group here tonight.

As I sat down, I said hello to everyone and thanked them for letting me play. I tried to make it seem like I just needed to take my mind off of everything, and I didn't have to explain much, as everyone had already heard the news. Either from general gossip around town or from Dub telling George to treat me like a regular patron. I was not the assistant tonight, in essence. As we started to play, things were going fairly normally, and each hand was helping to do what I intended it to do. Take my mind off things but give the impression that I really did not care if I won or lost.

That's one thing I loved about poker. You needed some skill, of course, but you could be anyone you wanted to be at the table. Aggressive, timid, careful, or wild. Each hand could be a different act in the show, and you could adapt as you saw fit. You can't control the cards being dealt to you, but you absolutely could control your reaction to them and the other player's hands. It was acting. It was all show. You want to be stoneface and show no emotion, fine. If you want to act like this last card held every ounce of silver you had to your name on the line, so be it. And voila, you just happened to pull out another silver dollar for the next hand with a "where did this come from?" expression on your face. It was an exhibition, a drama, or a comedy act. Whatever you wanted, and in essence, leveled the playing field across the entire spectrum of players. You could be the poorest man in town, but play like you owned a Railroad. Or vice-versa. Hard to do that anywhere else in life.

As we continued to play, Mr. Evans won the first game, Mr. Nelson the next, and I was just down about three dollars. I either checked or bet the minimum each time. I just wanted to blend in and keep a low profile. Thankfully there was not much talk at the table except the occasional request for another drink. Another reason I was glad that these three gentlemen were players tonight. They just liked to play; this was not social hour for them. As we went into the third game, mine started with a good hole card and door card. King of spades down and king of hearts up. Mr. Evans had the highest card showing so he had to post the bring-in. Basically, a starting bet for all others to follow. Mr. Fuller matched it, and Mr. Nelson also matched it. I went ahead and also bet the minimum just to ease into the game. So far, a fifty-cent bet with another twenty-five cent ante in the pot for me.

The third card, or third street, was dealt to each of us. Two cards showing, and one face down. The pot was already up to three dollars, and that was why I chose this table. It also showed that the other players were here to play, not just waste away another night. Another fact I hoped would help me tonight was that whenever Mr. Stallsburg or I would play, the other players somewhat upped their game. A nine of diamonds to me and no other face cards down the row except for Mr. Nelson receiving a Jack of clubs. Again, a good sign for me. Since

I had the best face-up hand showing so far, the action was to me, so I again bet fifty cents. Mr. Evans just had low-number cards showing, so he contemplated folding but decided to bet the minimum, another fifty cents in the pot. Mr. Fuller had a slightly better hand but also bet the minimum. Mr. Nelson had the second-best hand showing compared to me, so he raised the bet to a dollar. We were now up to five fifty even before the fourth card was dealt. Perfect. Fourth street is dealt, and I still had the best hand showing with a King, so I matched Mr. Nelson's last bet with a dollar of my own. Mr. Evans had nothing, so he decided to fold. Mr. Fuller had decent face cards but not enough to beat me so far, from what I would tell. Surprisingly he also bet a dollar, and then Mr. Nelson had to either fold or bet the same. I already knew he would bet based on the cards; I could see so another dollar in the pot. Pot up to eight fifty. *Now we are getting somewhere,* I thought. Nothing too crazy, but not everyone just calling or betting the minimums. George then dealt the fifth card, and I landed another king. Mr. Fuller a ten of hearts and Mr. Nelson another Jack. I was showing a pair of Kings with a ten and six. Mr. Fuller's best face card was the ten, but he also had a seven, eight, and four. Mr. Nelson was showing a pair of Jacks with a five and two.

The bet was to me as I still had the best hand showing, so I bet another dollar. Mr. Fuller appeared to have nothing higher than a possible pair of tens if his hole card was also a ten. And going up against two better hands on the table, I was sure that he was going to fold. He did not; he bet another dollar as well. That threw me off, but maybe he knew something I didn't. Mr. Nelson had the last play before we all had to turn our hole cards over, and he hesitated a bit before making his decision. Looking back and forth between mine and his hands. I thought he would immediately fold as my hand showing two kings was clearly the high hand, no matter what hole card he pulled. But he also did what Mr. Fuller had done and matched the bet of a dollar.

I just shook my head, not understanding why. I looked at George, and he had the same reaction. George then proceeded to speak.

"Gentleman, please show your hole cards," he said as each of us turned them over almost at the same time. I had a two of clubs, Mr. Fuller a ten of diamonds, and Mr. Nelson an eight of spades. Confirming I had won the round with a pair of Kings. I wanted to smile and boast about winning, but I just looked at both of them with a questioning look on my face. They both smiled and looked at each other and back at me.

"Garit, I understand you have had a rough few days," Mr. Nelson said, "so Mr. Fuller and I agreed to let you win the first one no matter what. But you won it fair and square, so we just chipped into the pot a little to make it interesting." At this point, Mr. Fuller started chuckling and slapped Mr. Evans on the knee.

"Evans, you were supposed to stay in no matter what. Why'd you bow out like that?"

"Well, I thought we were all going to fold on the fourth street," Mr. Evans said and hit Mr. Fuller back on his shoulder.

"Dagnabit, we were, but when Garit was holding the pair of kings, we thought it would be fun to mess with him a little and keep going," Mr. Fuller said back. Mr. Nelson and George were just laughing and taking it all in while I just smiled and started shaking my head, finally understanding why the bets kept coming.

"You guys really got me going there," I said to all of them, and I could tell they got a kick out of fooling me.

"Well, that will be the last of the easy ones tonight, son. Let's play some poker!" Mr. Nelson said, and we all let out laughing while George took the house's cut and gave me the balance. A little under eleven dollars. Not bad for a start, and an even better understanding, it contained some charity dollars from the rest of the table. I turned to all of them while George began shuffling the cards.

"Thank you, gentlemen, your charity to me will be returned by me buying the next round."

I turned around toward the bar and shouted.

"Dub! Set these three rabble-rousers up with a shot of that fine bourbon you served to me earlier. In fact...empty the bottle, and another if needed, for everyone else in the saloon, but save the last glass for Pohl. All on my tab, sir."

To that statement, everyone in the saloon let out a yelp and raised their glasses to me as a thank you. As I soaked in the appreciation, I thought, although the goal of tonight was to make as much money as I could, this might be the last night I have in this saloon, and it just seemed the right thing to do. The saloon and its people had been good to me over the years. Accepted me even at my age and always showed respect to me, Mother, and Mr. Stallsburg. Even tonight, they were allowing me to just be one of them and blend in a little. It was the least I could do, buying them a round. Plus, I would have spent the same amount or more during the original plan for tonight, Pohl's bachelor party.

"What the hell, let's have some fun," I said to the rest of the table as George dealt another set of cards to each of us. The night went back and forth between all of us at the table. Pats on the back after the free drinks arrived and fun teasing throughout each round. It was truly a good time, and I think not only what I needed but what everyone needed after a tough week. I was even winning a few rounds here and there just to keep up my goal but losing a few also, which I probably shouldn't have, but these were my friends.

I had assumed my feelings for people would have died right along with my faith in God, but I guess a little of each still existed. Real hard to turn it completely off in one day, I reckon. We continued playing into the early evening, and I was content with the way it was going. I was happy. As happy as I would let myself be under the circumstances.

That all changed faster than a bolt of lightning across the midnight sky. For who walked in and stood right behind me (without me noticing) set my skin and soul on fire.

Chapter 23

The bet was to me, and I had a pretty good hand showing, so I felt good about stepping up the bet to Mr. Evans. But, when I looked at George and saw that he was not watching me or the table and he was looking at something behind me, I knew something was wrong. I slowly turned in my chair to look, and what I saw took my happy mood and trampled it into pieces.

B was standing there with her captain, arms hitched and dressed to the nines. I did my best not to show any emotion, but how could I not? I tried to shield it by bowing my head down, but it could not hide my right fist clinching and the low rumble that emitted from my throat. I took a deep breath, trying to relax, and sat back up straight in my chair, turning my back to both of them in the process.

"Now, Garit, is that any way to treat your friends?" B said with a slight giggle. To which I replied without even turning my head.

"Most of my friends are dead or gone, B. And that sorry son of a bitch you're with will never be my friend."

Everyone at the table's eyes went as big as saucers, for they could not believe what just came out of my mouth. Not only because I was likely the smallest and weakest person in the room, but I was also insulting a US Army Captain in the process. Plus, I was typically the person who greeted everyone in the saloon with respect, manners, and etiquette, as it was literally my job to do so.

As everyone tried to process what had just occurred, the captain shot back.

"Son, I will forgive that normally fatal slip of respect toward me, as I know you have had a trying and regrettable series of days. But, let it happen again, and I will have to be somewhat less forgiving."

Everyone in the saloon that heard what had been said let out a gasp. We didn't have much violence in our place normally. Sure, a few unwise, drunken words were said here and there but typically, nothing that could not be handled by me or the staff intervening and calming all parties down. We did have one fistfight between a couple of cowboys a few months back, but that was really due to something that had happened between them way before they entered the saloon. A little alcohol just brought to the surface the animosity they seemed to still be carrying with them. Nothing big, and we just guided them out front onto the street to continue their quarrel. I know everyone liked to tell stories about two poker players resorting to gunplay because one felt like he was cheated or something, but we really never had that type of element here or any incidents like that before. Just a good, clean, and safe place to have fun and get a drink. We prided ourselves on that, and over the years, it had managed to stay that way. But this type of talk and coming from me, for crying out loud, was waaaayyy out of character. No one knew what to do next, so I broke the silence by saying, "You're probably right, sir. I apologize for my disrespect. George, let's continue our game, shall we?" without turning my head, not even an inch to speak to the captain directly.

I felt a tinge bad for George as he didn't know what to do. Here I was, his boss, but I was supposed to be a "regular joe" tonight, but then I had turned into a disrespectful civilian insulting a captain in the US Army. I had put him in a bit of a pickle for sure. He finally just shrugged his shoulders and went back to what he knew best, dealing poker.

I could tell by the silence all around me that B and the captain were still hovering behind me, but I didn't care, really. If he wanted to take out his pistol right now and shoot me in the back of the head, at least, it would be a quick and unexpected death. I wouldn't thankfully see it coming. If he wanted to drag me out of my chair and arrest me for insulting an Army man, then so be it. I guess my thirst for adventure would start by seeing the inside of a jail cell first. Have never seen that before, so it would be something different, at least. Or if B felt a bit of relief at her choice by seeing her new captain protect her honor by him slapping her old beau across the face, then so be it. Again, I didn't care. But, from the sound of them walking back toward the bar, it seemed as if my penalty for being mouthy would be postponed or maybe even acquitted. The other players sitting with me seemed to be squirming in their seats about what to do next, except for Mr. Nelson. He just stayed cool, calm, and collected throughout the whole event. I gained a little bit more respect for him for doing so. He was a tough old dude. I looked around the table and saw that Mr. Fuller had the high card.

"The bring-ins to you, Mr. Fuller," I said calmly.

I don't think he even knew what his card was yet, to be honest, as he just blinked his eyes a few times and almost had to force his head down to look.

"Uhhh...I fold," is all he could muster.

Mr. Nelson looked at his card and then back at me and put a dollar in the pot. I saw what my card was, but at this point didn't care, so I just slid a dollar toward the pot in an effort to hopefully move the attention back onto the game. Mr. Evans was looking straight at the side of my face this whole time. He was the closest to me, so it was easily felt and seen by me. He finally turned his head back to his card and slid another dollar in the pot.

"That was the greatest thing I have seen in a long time, Garit," he said. I will gladly pay you a dollar for that kind of action anytime."

Mr. Nelson actually chuckled at that statement, and it was good because it seemed to calm everyone down, including me. George dealt the 3rd street around, and things felt like they were back on course. He did keep watching me, though, to see if I would turn around to glance at what B and the captain were doing. But I just kept my head straightforward and my mind on the game. Of all the people at the table, he knew all too well how I was infatuated with B, at least up until now. He would often tease me about how I followed her around like a little puppy dog, to the point that I would hear him let out a little bark anytime he saw her and me together. And we were together almost every day, so the barks started to become normal. I didn't mind, though, as I could put up with a lot of teasing or small remarks here and there as it was an affirmation that I was the one on B's arm. I would sometimes say back to him if B was not in earshot:

"Sure is nice, being the runt of this litter," as he only wished it could be him instead of me. Everyone did. But nope, it was me, at least up until today. As George laid down the 3rd card for all of us, I took the lead with the best hand showing. An ace and a ten. And accordingly, the bet was to me.

"How about I kick it up a little? I will go two dollars," I said as I slid it into the pot.

Mr. Evans immediately folded and then looked at Mr. Nelson to make the next move. He was showing a king and a jack, so his chances were a little better than mine actually of getting another face card or having one in the hole. He matched my bet. George dealt out the final cards, and thankfully, I gained a jack, and he an eight of clubs. So, just looking at our face cards, I had the stronger hand. Not by much, but stronger it was. I then felt I had to keep going aggressively, so I raised the bet to three dollars. He raised his eyebrow a bit at that and started to tap his finger on the table. I had paid enough attention over the years that this tell meant he was struggling with which way to go.

Based on the table cards, I had better odds of winning. Certainly not by much, though. If he got an ace on the next turn or had one in the hole, he would win. For that matter, if he got another king or jack, he could take it also, most likely. This hand was putting the definition of gambling to the test. One more card and no real clear indication of where the odds would lay best. But I also knew that Mr. Nelson was a gambler through and through, so he did exactly what I knew he would. He slid three dollars into the pot same as me. Both Mr. Evans and Fuller were shaking their heads and brimming with skepticism. George just took it as his cue to deal the fifth and final card. A ten of hearts to me and a seven of diamonds to Mr. Nelson.

There it was. A definite advantage to me with a pair of tens. You would have thought Mr. Nelson would have sunk back in his chair a little, but no, he sat firmly and still. Knowing that my odds were significantly higher than his, I had to slide another three dollars in without hesitating. And with that, he did the same. Mr. Fuller and Evans almost jumped out of their seats in exasperation with this move. Mr. Fuller even said out loud, "Oh no, Bill," in a futile attempt to tell him something he already knew. He had the losing hand as it stood now for sure. Mr. Nelson didn't flinch. George then spoke.

"Gentlemen, please reveal your hole cards."

And we both flipped them over at the same time. Revealing a three of clubs for me and a jack of hearts for Mr. Nelson. The table just erupted in gasps, yells, and hollers as Mr. Fuller and Mr. Evans both jumped out of their seats and could not believe that Mr. Nelson had come back from a certain defeat and won the game. The entire saloon was now paying attention to our table and the commotion that we were causing, including B and her new beau.

I just leaned back in my chair, tipped my hat to Mr. Nelson, and smiled ear to ear. That was fun. But more than that, it told me that Mr. Nelson was most likely going to stay in, bet harder and higher, for the rest of the night.

Also, on a more spiteful side of my brain, I was happy that I was able to show B that she wasn't the only one that could cause the saloon to be livelier. I had some tricks up my sleeve as well. Of course, this directly challenged her newfound prowess at the roulette table, so in an attempt to show her new man her abilities, she tried to steal the show and started her now well-known routine at the roulette table. The captain, left at the bar, holding her drink, turned and followed well behind her. *Who's the puppy now?* I thought and let out a small but noticeable bark. I don't think either of them heard it due to our distance and continued celebration of Mr. Nelson's turn of luck. But George did, and he knew exactly what I meant by it and just shook his head while smiling. After our table started to calm down, I turned to Mr. Nelson.

"Nice game, sir, that one could have gone either way, but you held in there with me. I appreciate the gamesmanship."

He just nodded and said, "Thank you, son, that was fun."

Although he and I had started to increase the bets and the action, Mr. Evans decided to join back in due to all the fun we were having. Mr. Fuller decided to take a break for a while and just watch the event from the sidelines. I thought another patron would step in and take his seat, but no one did, so George began to shuffle, and we prepared to play. We were fully into the third street before B's magic started to take hold. I could hear her laughing and carrying on, but mostly, I could see people starting to wander over to that area of the saloon in hopes of watching the spectacle and having some of the exuberance rub off on them.

I can't fault her for that talent, she was great at it, and I knew it made her happy. I did wonder, though, where she got the money to gamble with. Who staked her? I certainly did not, and Dub did not have the authority to, even though he knew about our plan and was in charge tonight. Did she actually use her own money, or did she wrangle her funds out of the captain? Either way, I was just happy it wasn't mine. My funds had bigger and better plans tonight, and B was, for once, nowhere in them.

We continued to play, and it got to the point that even though Mr. Evans was hanging in there, it always really came down to Mr. Nelson and me pressing the pot. The game was now moving faster due to only three players, and my winnings were roughly up to around thirty-nine dollars. Not bad for a few hours playing and a little over ten percent of all the money I had in my stash. I will admit my goal when coming in was to walk out with another hundred in winnings that night. That would put me close to five hundred dollars total. A much better amount to leave some for Frank and head out to Colorado.

That would be a tall order, though, to set the player to take the record for one night, but still a large amount. I really needed one more player, though, to step up and play. Three was good, and four was better. I figured we had seven, maybe eight more games at the table before it started to get late, and one by one, players would peel off. I would have to win around nine dollars a game to meet my mark. Odds were, that was not going to happen, so I either had to win some big pots or get more money into the game. I might be able to do the first, and I could work on the latter.

As we entered the fourth street on our game, the pot was growing. Other than the minimum bets, we had graduated to starting with the big bet followed by regular two-dollar and three-dollar bets in between. That was good. I was able to score a couple of face cards so far, so I was feeling pretty good about my odds of winning this one.

And as I had planned, I took it. Another fifteen or so in my stack.

But how it helped me even more was that by now, watching B spin a little ball around the roulette table while holding her drink was starting to bore the captain. I could pick that up the first time I met him. All business, no dilly-dallying was his style. Plus, he liked attention probably more than B. Him standing by at her back as a glorified drink keeper was not his style. And when I took a peek back in their general direction to see if my hypothesis was correct, sure enough, he had started to creep our way, setting down her drink on the nearest table. Boy, I was glad I could read people. This was going to get very interesting. I could hear his footsteps grow ever closer, although he was doing his best to sneak up on his prey.

But I knew this saloon inside and out, and very few people actually heard the saloon when it was empty. Quiet. The floorboards could pretty much project exactly where a person was walking to or from, and I was a literal virtuoso in translating the creaks and craws of the floor. I had heard them a million times while sitting in my office doing numbers or orders. With just me, Gus, or Jed in most mornings. The saloon was my partner tonight, in every which way she could be. As he got closer, I started to talk a little more and a little louder. Started to add some grandiose descriptions to the games we had competed in tonight and how great my fellow players' instincts had been. If I knew the captain, he wanted to show everyone two things tonight before he left. The first being that he was not just brawn but brain, and the second, was that he had to be the most admired man in the entire saloon, heck, the entire town, by midnight. He already had B pledged to marry him, the US Army dress uniform, and medals. He just needed to add to his haul, beating the greatest minds in the saloon in an improvised battle to the death. Figuratively, of course. It almost seemed too easy, like leading a fly to a picnic. But no matter how the night was going in my current favor, I still had to win. And poker is a finicky lady, for sure.

"Well, captain, I did not see you watching our game," I said when I turned around to a loud laugh from B. "Play any poker much out on the range?"

"Well, since you asked, I happened to be the best player in my class at the United States Military Academy or West Point, I should say. And I have been known to play a game or two when set up in camp," He responded. *Hook.*

"Well then, fancy a quick game or two with us, civilians? Maybe we will learn a thing or two from you," I said, looking around at the other players and egging them on to agree.

"I agree," said Mr. Nelson. "Would love to learn some Yankee card tricks and would love even more to add some Yankee money to my winnings. *Line.*

"Well, sounds like a game I would like to participate in while teaching some Yankee wisdom to you all," the captain replied.

He turned slightly and spoke loudly to B.

"Dear, continue having a good time, of course. I am going to sit in for a chance to educate these fine gentlemen on how five card stud is played by the civilized region of our great nation." *Sinker.* I had him on the line, and by pulling him in, was going to be just what I needed to reach my goal. I hoped.

Mr. Evans jumped up

"Sir, let me be the first to say thank you for protecting our settlers against those savages out west. My sister and her husband wrote to me just last month saying how they were saved by a group of soldiers defending their wagon train headed to Oregon last summer. Not saying it was you, of course, but it was the US Army, so to me, you are all heroes," he said, and he pulled out the chair next to me for the captain to take a seat.

"Well, thank you, sir," the captain responded. "It may or may not have been my unit. We do that on a regular basis, but regardless, we in the Army are one, and it is our duty to protect all citizens from any sort of injustice, attack, or savage."

I thought that the captain, whether a blowhard or not, must help people, so maybe I should show more respect, but then he kept talking.

"Whether from the West or South," as he sat down.

Definitely a blowhard. And I could tell Mr. Nelson was thinking the exact same thing. Mr. Evans didn't notice that last part, I don't think, as he continued to smile and exchange pleasantries with the captain. I don't think Mr. Evans would have liked the last comment either, but his not hearing it allowed the captain to think he had an ally at the table with him, would make him more comfortable and probably stay longer. Now for the real fun of the night to begin.

I kept hearing cheers and laughter from the roulette area, so knew that B was just doing her thing and keeping herself occupied. This was good, for that was the one thing I could not control in this situation. B. If she got bored and wanted to leave, I don't think even the captain's desire to put us in our place would have been enough to keep him seated. What B wants, she usually gets. Trust me, I know from experience. But she was happy for now, so we had to get playing.

"Gentleman, since we have such an esteemed new player at the table, how does everyone feel about raising the limits? Nothing drastic, of course, but I have heard through the grapevine that up north, most saloons have two-dollar minimums and four-dollar maximums. Is this true, captain?" I inquired like I really was interested.

"Uhh, yes. In fact, around Boston and New York City, they have three-dollar minimums with little to no regard for maximums if all the players at the table can stand for it. And most of the people I play with can, of course."

"What a doofus," I continued to shout inside my brain.

"Well then, let's oblige our friend here from the northland and do the same, shall we?" Mr. Nelson said and looked around the table, urging us to agree.

"Absolutely," I responded. "Seems to be the proper thing to do in honor of our visitor, don't you think, Mr. Evans?" I continued.

"Oh, I agree. A little rich for my blood, but I will hang in as long as I can. You never know; pots that high will be good for my station if I win one or two." He smiled and prepared to get into a more serious playing style.

The captain then added, "But, I have noticed something about your style of playing down here; you never look at your hole card until you reveal it at the very end. Up north, we look at our hole card, hiding it from the other players, of course, as soon as it's dealt. That way, we know exactly what kind of hand we are dealing with moving forward."

"I also know that to be true, as Mr. Stallsburg and I have discussed changing our game to that style. In fact, we almost did a few weeks ago but decided to wait a little longer. We were going to open up one table for that sort of play and keep another table in the more traditional style. How does everyone tonight feel about accommodating our guest with not only higher limits but the Hole card openness play?" I asked calmly.

I had to pretend to be calm, as inside, I was jumping like a cricket in hopes that they would all agree. Mr. Stallsburg and I only hesitated because each player knowing their hole card gave them a distinct advantage over our current style. Most of our players liked the good ole traditional style, and it kept the better players more in line with newer, more inexperienced ones. It, in a sense, kept the game more honest. No one knew what card was in the hole, so it was gambling, truly gambling to bet on a fully unknown hand. Knowing the hole card from the start was essentially a whole new kind of game. I loved it, and in fact, I was the one trying to convince Mr. Stallsburg to adapt one table to that sort of play. He was more of a traditionalist and argued to keep it the same

As I looked around the table to see if anyone objected to this proposal, Mr. Nelson just smiled from the corner of his mouth a little and nodded that he was in. Mr. Evans was a little more hesitant to agree quickly, as I am sure he was still feeling a little out of water with the new limit rules we just implemented.

"Well," he finally said, it does sound like a new way to experience good table play. Let's do it."

The captain just smiled and was proud that his suggestions had both been adopted, thus reaffirming his self-perceived superiority complex to the rest of us. Arrogance will get you far in life for sure, but tonight that same arrogance would hopefully lead him straight into my trap. So far, it was working.

"Well then, George, you have heard that all players are in agreement toward these new table rules," I said. Then, turning back to the bar, I yelled.

"Dub, you okay with us changing the limits and hole card rule just for tonight and just for this table?"

I asked, as I wanted it all to be above board and right as rain for the saloon. He seemed to understand the question and the terms.

"Yes, sir, I will make sure to check on the table throughout the night, but the saloon agrees."

"Well, there you have it, gentleman, let's all learn a new thing or two and get to gettin'." I nodded to George to start dealing.

As George dealt out the cards, I could tell that each player other than the Captain was hesitant about looking at the hole card. We had been playing the other style forever, and one of the rules was to never look at your hole card until the dealer told you to reveal them or you would be kicked out of the game. Do it again, and you would be kicked off the table for the night. It was a serious infraction. And precisely why I wanted to change one table to that style. We were increasingly seeing people coming in from other parts of the country that played that way, and here we were, getting kicked out of games. Once you develop a habit, it's hard to stop it and your unconscious thought or action just happens. So, forcing yourself to actually look at the card if you were just learning the new style was kind of an issue. What once was off limits is now not.

I could see that Mr. Evans was hesitant about moving forward, but Mr. Nelson looked like a bull in a China shop, trying to see his hole card but not letting others see it also. He slowly picked it up, cupping it in his right hand, and brought it way up close to his face, almost touching his nose. George had to stop and remind him that he could not remove a card played from the table once it was down.

"Well, how in the hell am I supposed to see the card then?" he retorted gruffly.

I interjected.

"Watch how the captain does it, sir," and urged the captain to show all of us hayseeds how to effectively see the card but not remove it from the table.

The captain obliged and showed everyone how to just slightly pull up one corner of the card with one hand and shield it with their other. Nothing too hard to do, but something that just had to be learned, and perfected through repetition.

"There, we are all learning new things already," I said, trying to lighten the mood.

Mr. Nelson did not lighten.

"Well, that's fine and dandy if you can see that far; you younguns don't have the kind of vision or lack of vision that I do," he again protested.

"How about this, fellas, does anyone object to Mr. Nelson pulling his card up from the table and looking more closely at it?" I said while looking around.

Everyone seemed to be fine with it, and I could see that this was making Mr. Nelson more comfortable with the game.

"Alrighty then, amended rule for this game only tonight, hole cards may be removed from the table to be seen by Mr. Nelson only," I said while looking at each player and nodding my head so that they would nod back understanding the rule. All complied.

"George, you heard it, third new rule for this table, for tonight only," I clarified to make sure he understood.

"Yes, sir."

I was starting to get fidgety at all these delays in getting started, so I did not even bother to inform Dub of this change, we had to get moving, and time was slipping by.

"Ok, it seems as if Mr. Evans has the bring in, let's bet," I prodded, but about fell out of my chair when I realized none of us had put in our antes yet, as we were all discussing these new rules.

Even George missed it.

"Stop! We forgot our antes!" And as soon as I said it, everyone at the table just let out a "come on, let's get on with it" moan.

"How about since we raised the limits, the ante is also raised from twenty-five cents to one dollar? It will keep things simple and clean," I said.

Again, everyone seemed to agree, and this time I just nodded to George, and he just nodded back.

"All right, ante up, gentlemen, and the bet goes to Mr. Nelson," George directed to all of us.

We all slid in our dollars and waited for Mr. Nelson to bet. Of course, this early in the game, he just bet and moved on. The action was to me, and with now knowing my hole card, I had a queen and a ten, pretty good cards, so I also added two dollars. I did not want to be too aggressive as I had yet to see the captain's playing style or prowess.

Play it safe but stern, I told myself, as the bet was to him. He also just slid two dollars more into the pot, and we were ready for our third card. George commenced to laying them down, and as he did, I was adding up what was already in the pot. Twelve dollars already. Now we were getting somewhere.

The third card did help me. It was a jack, and I was working on a straight with what I already had. A hard hand to get, but again, all my cards were fairly high so getting somewhere. I was showing a one—jack. The captain was showing a three–nine. Mr. Evans an eight–jack and Mr. Nelson a queen–four. I had the high-showing cards, so the bet was to me. I went ahead and just added another two dollars to the pot. Again, trying to be safe but pushing just a little bit. The captain folded right off as his was the low hand on the table. This disappointed me, as his dropping out so early would not allow me to see his style. Oh well. Mr. Evans bet two dollars also, and Mr. Nelson the same. Pot up to eighteen. Fantastic. George now laid down the fourth street, and I received another queen. Although the other players only saw my ten–jack–queen face cards. Mr. Evans pulled another eight, and Mr. Nelson pulled a seven. Mr. Evan's hand was now the highest with a pair of eights. He bet another two dollars, and Mr. Nelson started to tap his finger again, so I knew he was not sure his hand could take us. He hesitated for a minute but then folded. The bet to me, I knew I had the better pair, but what if Evans had another eight in the hole?

"Looks like you are working on a straight there, Garit," he said, as my ten-jack-queen could have been.

"Well, who knows, Mr. Evans? Wait, I do, now that we can look at our hole card," I responded, and everyone smiled.

"With that in mind, I think I will raise," I said as I slid three dollars into the pot.

Turning a little more aggressive in my play. Twenty-three dollars in the pot. George dealt our fifth and final cards, and I received a nine, Mr. Evans a three. This is where it got hard. I was showing a possible straight, but Mr. Evans had a known pair of eights, maybe even three of a kind, not knowing his hole card. The odds of that were low, but it was a possibility. My possible straight would beat a pair and three of a kind, so it at least looked daunting to Mr. Evans, but he knew getting a straight was really hard. Odds were against me. And what if I had another jack or queen under my hole? That would beat his low pair. Since he still had the highest hand showing, the bet was to him. And since we were on the fifth street, and I had previously bet three dollars, if Mr. Evans were to stay in, three dollars was the lowest bet that could be made now.

He looked back and forth at both our hands and finally slid three dollars into the pot. He almost didn't, though, and I would not have blamed him. This was a tough hand to read. Of course, I had to either fold or match, so I matched. Twenty-nine dollars in the pot.

"Gentleman, please reveal your hole cards to the table," George said, and we both flipped over our cards. Thankfully Mr. Evans had a king, and I beat him with a pair of queens. Mr. Evans let out a sigh, and I waited for George to take the saloon's rake from the pot and slide it to me.

"Wow, that was a good one, Mr. Evans. If you just would have gotten another eight, jack or three, you would have gotten me good. Tough bet, but I would have done the same thing in your shoes."

Mr. Evans just nodded, and so did Mr. Nelson. The captain did not and just pursed his mouth a little, just watching me win a fairly large pot. I could tell it was bothering him that he had not prevailed, and of anyone at the table, I was the one who did.

God, I love pride, I thought, as it would be his undoing over the next few hands.

The games continued. Mr. Nelson winning another. The captain winning one, and I winning another as well. Based on my rough math, my winnings were in the fifty-five-dollar range, and my true net was probably around thirty-eight, maybe forty dollars, counting losses and my own bets coming back to me.

Not enough.

Mr. Evans had not won a game in a while, so he was starting to look pretty thin in his stack. I could also tell that Mr. Fuller wanted to jump back in, but with the new bet and ante levels, was not quite sure if he could handle the action. He was a casual player, really. Just for fun and probably did not have the twenty or thirty dollars to lose if a game or two got larger. But, who knows, he might, and so be it, if he wanted to get back in. Thankfully Mr. Nelson leaned over and whispered into Mr. Evans's ear. I assume he was telling him that if he needed to back away or take a break to go ahead. No one would fault him for it. Again, another reason why I respected Mr. Nelson. He was a hard gambler and an even harder person, but he did tend to keep a lookout for other players when they were extending beyond their playing or financial abilities. He didn't judge; he just counseled so that someone wouldn't be ruined. He was a fairly private person, but I had overheard a couple of conversations over the years in which he talked about losing it all and having to start back over several times in his life. I don't think he meant gambling took everything; I think it was more business ventures, ranching, or other hard luck situations that cleaned him out. But he always got back on his horse and built it up again. He was tough and had the backbone to do that. I also think this honed his skills in knowing who didn't have it in them to lose everything and turn it around. Plus, Mr. Nelson didn't have anyone else counting on him. Sure, he had businesses and investments, but no wife, children, or other wards needed him to provide for them. Mr. Evans did. He had a wife and a young son. Sometimes you might not want the advice but having someone there to at least give it to you is a good thing. And Mr. Nelson was doing just that for Mr. Evans now. Mr. Evans must have taken it for what it was, good advice as he stretched his arms out in front of him, cracked his neck, and spoke to the table.

"Boys, I think I am going to take a break and stretch my legs a little." We all just nodded, and he gathered his money and stood up, walking towards the bar. Typically, when a player took a break, the dealer would just take their stack, leaving just a coin or one bill in their position and holding the rest of it in a stack to his right. Keeping it safe until the player returned. If you were out and not just getting a drink or running to the outhouse, you collected your stack and took it with you. This allowed other players to know the spot was open.

In this case, George looked around and saw that others did want to jump in, including Mr. Fuller, but no one made a move just yet.

"Ante up," George said and started to shuffle. This was the cue to all around that no one else could join the game. The cards went round to each of us still in, and I could hear the saloon was definitely getting quieter. Looking back toward B, she had stopped playing roulette and was sitting at a table directly behind us, drinking what looked to be her third or fourth drink. A lot for her.

When she noticed I was looking at her, she just did a half-smile and then looked away. I guess I should have expected this type of behavior from her, but it still hurt. What had I ever done to her? I treated her like royalty. A princess. Always respecting her time and talents. I literally gave her anything she wanted and introduced her to so many things she would have never done on her own. And I do still feel that we had genuine fun together and feelings for each other. Sure, the prettiest girl in town and the runt of the litter seemed a little far-fetched for a "they lived happily ever after" story. But it was headed down that trail.

At least, that is what I thought before today. We were friends. Maybe not lovers. Maybe not headed for the alter but Friends. With a capital F. That meant something to me. But based on this last interaction, maybe not so much to her. Was she really that shallow? Was I just mesmerized by her that I did not ever notice it? No. Although the past week or so had been rockier than the Rocky Mountains, I started to have my doubts about B. We had fun, we got drunk, we laughed, and we kissed. But I also had periods of time when I did not think about her or wonder about how she was doing. She simply was not occupying my head and heart like she typically had. I think that was partly why I was feeling so down lately. God and the world had given me more than enough reasons other than her to be down. But, hidden back in all the muck and mess of this week, a small realization that she probably did not love me and was keeping herself amused by me like a cat playing with a bug. Swatting me here and there and always keeping me on my toes, running for my life.

Right then, I realized she was holding me back. I thought she was elevating me to new and more adventurous heights, but no. She was actually preventing me from thinking about anything other than her. Her wants. Her pleasures. Her agenda. My desires had been wrapped up in her. They had nowhere else to look or search. Content with being contained. Until things started going horribly wrong, and I was forced to examine my life, my situation, and giving them a chance to break away a little. Bubble up to the top and feel some sunlight. And once they did, they started to grow and move and nudge me into thinking deeper about Mother's death, Cora Lee's death, and Pohl abandoning me for his rage. All terrible and depleting events on their own. Together, unimaginable. I had no other way to go but down.

But loss had brought a stillness to my life. Stillness and desolation so that I could notice my own will and needs. To acknowledge my own thirst and hunger for life beyond Christiansburg. Beyond B. I didn't need her anymore. What I needed was one more big win tonight to solidify my aptitude. My capacity. My power. To leave and fulfill my destiny for however long God saw fit. To live without strings, concerns, or fear. Things I have no need for anymore.

As I snapped back to reality, I saw George just looking at me with concern. He had been saying something to me, but I did not comprehend what it was.

"Garit, you okay?" he said louder.

"Uh….yes, yes, George. Bet to me, you said?"

"Yes, the bet is yours, Garit," he responded. I looked down at the table and realized I had not even looked at my hole card yet. I looked at the other hands and then at each of my opponents, who were sitting there staring at me like I had mud all over my face.

"You all right, boy? Or is it getting past your bedtime?" the captain said, eliciting laughter from B and a few others around the table.

Mr. Nelson just stayed stone-faced as usual, but I got the slightest hint from the corner of his eye that he wanted to show this no-good Yankee what we were capable of.

"I'm in," I said as an answer to George and the captain's questions. And to Mr. Nelson's silent declaration.

"And how about we make this really interesting, fellas? I have not looked at my hole card yet. Everyone agree with that?" I said while looking around the table.

Everyone nodded, and George confirmed.

"Yes, I can confirm you have not looked at your card," he said as a supplement to my statement.

"Ok, then how about I keep it that way, and we play a little bit of a combination game this round? You both know what you have; I don't. But I am so confident in my skill and fate that I will play just like that for the rest of the game. George, kindly take my hole card and place it next to you."

George did, and I looked back to Nelson and the captain for their reaction. Both were not exactly sure why I was doing this, but not going to pass up an opportunity to embarrass my audaciousness and win some money in the process. Especially the Captain.

To do it in front of B would be the pinnacle of the night. The cherry on top if you will.

Mr. Nelson again smirked. He was way too smart not to know what I was doing.

"Your funeral, son," he said simply and tipped his hat. At that, the captain turned around to his fiancé.

"B, come on over and see what is fixing to happen to your friend Garit here. Mr. Nelson and I seem to have been underestimated by this young man's rashness. I, for one, take that as disrespect to my abilities. But I am also keen enough to take that as an advantage on this field of battle. You will want to see this up close and personal." He patted the chair next to him. As she stood to take the seat, he turned back to the table.

"If that is okay with you, gentleman, that she joins us as a spectator rather than a player?" and looked to all of us for approval.

"Of course, of course, I don't mind one bit. Anyone else?" I said while looking at George and Mr. Nelson. They just shook their heads and shrugged.

"Sure," Mr. Nelson added. "Will be nice not to have to look at all you ugly bastards for a change," and everyone just smiled or chuckled at his jest.

B sat down and said, "Oh, this is all so exciting, and thank you for inviting me to play, dear."

The captain cleared his throat.

"Oh no, dear, you're just going to watch the big boys play. Dealer, where were we again?"

And with that simple statement, I saw a flash of anger spill over B's face.

No one told her no. And I used to let her play, gamble, and have fun. But her new knight in shining armor would not. *Such a pity*, I thought. But more so, she knew it, too, and for this, I was glad. This perfect example of a man she thought would be the perfect match for her was just like every other entitled bastard. Who never had to fight for anything in life. It was just given to him through good genetics, health, or being born to good stock, much like B herself.

But we others, that had to fight and claw through life just to survive and still be looked down upon for our inferior looks, weakness or health had a different view. We actually had more respect for others and hope for their ascension up, and often was their cheering section in doing so. Not the Captain. He wanted to keep the dirt under his feet, right where it belonged. Women's rights. Colored rights. The inferior's rights. He talked a big game, but his soul was as dark as most others in his same position in life.

With B sulking a bit next to the captain but him not giving it the slightest care, we were off. The bet was to me, and of course, with the fact that I did not know my hole card, I was at a huge disadvantage. But I had a king showing, the highest card on the table, so I bet four dollars, the maximum for a first bet. The captain smirked and, of course, matched it without hesitation. He was showing an eight, but so early into the game he had to match it. Mr. Nelson did the same. With our antes and bets so far, the pot was already at fifteen dollars. The next cards were dealt, and I gained a ten. The captain an ace, and Mr. Nelson now had one queen and a ten showing. All good cards, and all giving incentive to each player to stay in and bet. Since The Captain now had the high card, he was the next to bet. This new ace gave him a big bump in confidence, and I think he wanted us to think he had another ace in the hole. He smiled largely and looked at B.

"Watch this, dear," he said and slid six dollars into the pot. A good move and one either Mr. Nelson or I would have done also under the circumstances. I just nodded my head, and the bet was to Mr. Nelson. With him showing a queen–ten, he had a good initial hand also, so he matched the bet. And, of course, I had to stay on course. I just had a feeling it was time, and my wits were confirming my hunch. Another six dollars in the pot from me took it to thirty-three in total. And we were just hitting the fourth street. George dealt the next cards, and I took a jack, the captain an eight, and Mr. Nelson a seven.

That did not help him much with what I saw showing, but the eight to the captain did. This gave him a pair of eights, ace high. I now had another straight forming, but without knowing my hole card, it was truly a gamble. The captain was still showing the high hand with a pair, so he was first to bet this round. He looked at B again, who at this time was still interested but also was still upset about him not allowing her to play, but not wanting us to know.

I knew.

I also knew that she did not want to embarrass him by throwing a fit and risking any shine to come off of her new showpiece in him. If he scolded her or immediately cowered to her demands, he wouldn't be the highest model of a man she wanted everyone to believe he was. He just patted her on her knee and slid another eight dollars into the pot. Since the maximum bet had been moved to four dollars, he could double it on this round. He could actually triple it according to the rules, but eight dollars made just about the same impression as twelve would have to the audience and to us. Besides, being too aggressive might give away that he has an ace in the hole for sure.

I just did not know yet, as his tells had not been totally exposed to me in the short time playing tonight. Mr. Nelson took a deep breath, though, as the bet was to him. He had a fair hand but definitely had the worst of the three so far.

But he was not a folder, so I had a feeling he would stay in at least until he saw the next card. So, eight dollars into the pot once more. The bet was to me, and I could feel the excitement growing around the table and saloon. We were up to forty-nine dollars in the pot, and I still had to bet. Again, with a possible straight showing, I had to stay in, so I moved eight dollars forward, and as I did, several people around gasped. This was getting serious. Fifty-seven dollars in the pot and one more card to go. B sensed the drama building from around the room and started to perk up. I don't think she really knew that this amount of money was not usual or at what juncture we were at in the game. She was just responding to the energy now surrounding all of us. George then dealt out our last and final cards, and I shuttered a little when the queen of hearts came my way.

I was legitimately looking at a straight. The second time tonight. What were the odds? I cared, but I didn't. It was exciting, and all who knew what that queen meant to me around the table cheered.

B looked around like, "What? Is that good?" But the Captain looked over to me.

"Great card, son, but mine's pretty good, too," as another eight had landed in front of him.

Another level of energy was just achieved when the crowd noticed that also. Mr. Nelson had landed another queen. Not near as good as our cards, but still good, depending on what his hole card was. He could have the final queen and be holding a high three of a kind. The captain had three of a kind showing also, but they were eights. Not as good. Me holding a possible straight would win the game unless the captain had another eight or an ace as his hole card. Four of a kind or a full house would beat Mr. Nelson's hand and mine, even if I had a straight.

"Wowzers," Mr. Fuller said from behind us. "Now I am glad I

decided to sit out of this one."

"Yep," agreed Mr. Evans, "this one is way too rich for my blood, and I would have fainted by now had I stayed in," to which everyone in the room laughed. B started to laugh just because everyone else was. Just trying to be in the know and secretly scheming to get the attention back on her. She tried again.

"Oh Charles, this is so exciting and fun. Let me give you a kiss on the cheek for good luck." She raised her lips to his cheek and gave a long but delicate kiss to her mighty Captain. He just smiled and relished in the jealousy of almost every man in the saloon. I understood that but had suddenly become immune to the effect.

My mind was on the game and on my heart rate. I could feel it building but was trying to stay calm. I could not show my nerves, or so I thought. It might actually help me with my ultimate goal, getting the pot up higher. So, I feigned a bit of shaking in my hands, knowing that it would get The Captain's attention for sure.

"Son, everyone gets a little scared on the battlefield; I have seen it thousands of times. I always tell my soldiers the fear will be gone soon enough, though. You will either be dead or be triumphant, and if were not triumphant, I will see to the first option."

B just said, "Charles, that is so morbid, stop it," and swatted at his arm. Mr. Nelson took that statement differently.

"Captain, I have seen all kinds of leaders in my life. And you, sir, rank down at the bottom based on that remark. If a war does break out between the North and South, I feel better knowing leaders like you will be leading the troops against us."

At first, B thought that was a compliment. But looking back at the captain, I could see his facial expression showing contempt.

"Ms. Hahne, I think the gentlemen are just a little upset with how I will be taking the battle, the pot, and you all home with me tonight," he said. And she just continued fawning over her hero.

Everyone else in the saloon shifted a little on their feet as it was starting to get contentious. Entertaining, for sure, but with a tinge of uncomfortableness mixed in. I brought it back to center.

"Well, it appears that, yet again, the bet is to you, Captain, as you have the best hand showing and may even have the best hand of the night. What'll it be, sir?"

He looked over to me, down at his cards, and back over to Mr. Nelson.

"I think you're right, son. I might have the best hand of the night, indeed. How about all in? Is that something this little saloon recognizes?" the crowd gasped, and George could do nothing but look at me.

"Why yes, our little itty-bitty saloon does recognize that bet and will gladly accept it," I said while nodding to George to allow it to take place. In truth, we tried to stay away from all-in bets as it would typically lead to one or more players losing all they had in one fail swoop, and that typically led to altercations. We didn't like altercations, so did not typically allow them. Typically. Mr. Stallsburg and I had the authority to allow it, and if we knew the players well and they were customarily cordial and calm when they lost, we would. Mr. Nelson was one of those allowed players. I was one who had the authority to approve it, so, in essence, was one also. We did not know the captain's affinity for behavior in defeat, but I sure did want to see it. I had a hunch Mr. Nelson would too.

George understood my approval, and by now, Dub had come over and was standing right next to George as he knew the stakes were getting high. George looked at Dub, Dub nodded, and we were all in.

Everyone erupted with commotion. This was a rare sight, and no one really knew how much the captain had in his stack. As the talk and turmoil swirled around us, George counted up his stack and had Dub confirm it just to be safe.

301

"Fifty-seven dollars and two bits," George said out loud. The crowd's animation grew even more. This quite possibly was the largest bet anyone had ever placed on one hand of five card stud in this saloon. And better yet, it looked like at least one of us would be sure to follow it. As Dub tried to calm down the crowd, B tapped the captain on his shoulder and whispered into his ear. His eyebrows went up immediately, and a large smile came across his face. She was smiling ear to ear herself as she settled back down into her chair. The captain raised his voice a little to project over the crowd and turned to George.

"Is the lady allowed to add money to my bet?"

The crowd went silent, and George again just looked at me. I, in turn, looked at Mr. Nelson and then to Dub.

"Of course! We have taken this game to a whole new height already; why not take it all the way to the clouds?" I turned around and raised my arms to the rest of the crowd.

They ate it up, and all started jumping, dancing, and laughing in anticipation of this never-before-seen folly. B stood up, pulled a wad of money from between her dress and bosom, and handed it over to George's now quivering hand.

I swear to God I heard someone fall and hit the ground from fainting at this sight, but everyone in the saloon absolutely went into a frenzy. This night would be talked about until this place was long gone. It was wonderful! As George and Dub counted B's addition, I just shook my head in admiration of how B could change a funeral into a party by doing something so small. She was a force to be reckoned with, and I respected her for it. I could not help but smile and tip my hat to her in a slight attempt to let bygones be bygones. She just smiled back and batted her eyes in an attempt, in her own way, to say she was sorry for all that had happened to me and between us.

Dub confirmed the count, so George yelled back out of above the fray, "Eighty-two dollars and two bits is the bet to Mr. Nelson."

Everyone gasped and again broke out into hysterics. Dub again was trying to get everyone to settle down when Mr. Nelson yelled out to the crowd.

"For crying out loud, shut your mouths so I can hear myself think," and it caused exactly what he intended it to.

He was gruff, and everyone knew it, so they immediately jumped in line and simmered down. He looked around the room as it stilled.

"Thank you," he said in a graveled voice. He was getting tired. It had been a long night, and with this last bit of turmoil, it was starting to wear him down. He took a long hard look at the pot. A longer and harder look at both our hands and looked at the captain.

"I don't think you have a full house," he told him. Then he turned to me.

"And I don't think you have a straight. Therefore, I will wager all I've got to prove it," and pushed his stack over to George to count.

There was a slight roar, but he quickly looked around the room, just waiting to pounce on the offenders, and everyone settled right back down.

George and Dub counted up the stack.

"Forty-nine dollars, even," George announced and pushed it into the pot. Everyone wanted to jump out of their skins, but Mr. Nelson's stare just kept everyone in check. I didn't want to add any stimulation to the crowd but had to ask.

"George, what does that put the pot up to?"

He had gone to writing down everyone's contribution so far since it was growing so large.

"One hundred eighty-eight dollars and two bits," he announced.

With this, the crowd simply could not contain itself any longer and erupted once again. Mr. Nelson just shook his head and threw his hands up in the air like there was nothing he could do about it. I just started laughing and wished that Mr. Stallsburg could be here to see this. I looked around the room at all the smiles and laughter filling the saloon and was just happy.

I then looked further back, and unbeknownst to me, Mr. Stallsburg had come in through the front door and was standing with several others behind us. Blending in. He had gotten back early from his trip and, I imagine, was transfixed by what was going on in his saloon when he arrived. His eyes met mine, and we both just smiled. He nodded his head to me, and I nodded back. Shrugging and turning back around to meet my fate.

In an all-in bet, it is exactly the way it sounds; it's *all in*. If you only have one bit, you put it in the pot. If you have more than the highest bet in play, all you must do is match that. I had a pretty good pot in front of me but decided to let fate be my muse tonight and started counting my stack. As I did, Dub started to move people back from the table as the surge had started to crowd all of us pretty well. I had right at forty-one dollars from the initial count of my stack, so I looked to George.

"What was the captain's bet again?"

He confirmed it was eighty-two dollars and two bits.

I just nodded and proceeded to pull some money out of my inner jacket pocket. I had a pretty good wad of it, so I took my time counting it out. I didn't have to match his bet; I could have just put in my entire stack and moved on.

But tonight was about proving something. Proving to me I could do it. Proving that I had what it takes to push myself harder and higher. And proving to B that I was the better man after all. Plus, I knew this night was special when my arithmetic in my mind told me I needed another forty-one dollars and two bits to match his bet. Exactly double what I already had in my pot. *What are the chances of that?*

I just peeled off another dollar and laid down forty-two total to cover the two bits.

"I bet eighty-three, even," I said and pushed it into the pot. The amount of buzz and noise around me had now surpassed anything that it had been before, and I started to tune it out as I moved forward a bit on my chair. This was a huge gamble, but I had enough money that I could lose it.

Of course, it would be a small setback, but nothing I could not work or gamble my way out of. Besides, this was probably the only chance I would ever have again to let caution fly to the wind and be in the presence of a lot of friends and people I cared about. If I was going to do it, better to do it here than in some strange saloon in a strange town. With a pot this big, I was likely to be robbed of my winnings somewhere else or robbed of what I had left over after all the saloon just saw the extra greenbacks I had in my wad. At least everyone here had my back. Everyone but the captain.

So, this was it.

Just then, a shot rang out, and everyone jumped or fell to the floor.

As I turned around, Mr. Stallsburg had taken his pistol out and fired one round through the roof to try and get everyone to settle down and bring order to the place. No one could believe it. He had shot his own saloon! And I suppose he had the absolute right to do so. As everyone waited for him to say something, he finally spoke very calmly.

"I just shot a hole in my own roof to get everyone to settle down and let us finish this wonderful game. Please don't make me regret doing it when I have to climb up there tomorrow to fix it."

Everyone busted out laughing, including the captain. But the crowd was quick to bring it down so that we could all finish the game, as Mr. Stallsburg had just suggested. Everyone just turned back and focused on George to lead the next move. He looked around, then looked at us.

"Gentleman, please reveal your last card to the table."

It seemed like everyone in the room took a deep breath in. Customarily all players would turn their cards over at one time. But my card was over next to George, so I could not, and the other two players saw this and hesitated.

Mr. Nelson spoke up.

"Let me go first, then the captain, and then George. Your turn, Garit's, over." He looked toward all of us to get an agreement. We all nodded.

He turned his card over to reveal a queen of spades, giving him three of a kind. Not only three of a kind, but in a higher suit than the captain's three eights. It was stupendous and a great hand. As everyone looked at the table, they also noticed a very rare event.

All of the queens had been dealt during this game. Mr. Nelson had three of them, and I had the fourth. On top of that, two hands were showing three of a kind. Amazing. And for those who played five card stud, they knew the odds of this were very low in any game. The captain then reached out and placed his hand over his card. He turned to B and spoke simply.

"Well, you win some, and you lose some," he said as he turned over a two of clubs, and the whole saloon erupted. Mr. Nelson had beaten him, and the only other hand that could have possibly beaten me if I had a straight was now gone. For if he had flipped an ace or an eight, I couldn't have won no matter what card I had in the hole, and he would have beaten Mr. Nelson at the same time.

Again, the saloon went crazy. I seriously thought Mr. Stallsburg was going to have to fire his pistol again to get people calmed down, but they seemed to have this animal instinct come across them to hush and be still all or their own.

For I still had one card to turn over, and no one, including me, knew what it was. At this moment, Mr. Nelson thought, and everyone else also assumed, that he would be taking home the largest pot ever in the history of this saloon. And probably Christiansburg, or heck, all of Montgomery County, for that matter. I settled back into my chair, looked over at B, and spoke very simply and from the heart.

"I hope you two have a wonderful wedding, marriage, and life. I really do."

She just smiled a sad type of smile.

"Thank you, Garit. They broke the mold when they made you. I sure love you, kid."

The entire saloon started to go deadly quiet, and I nodded my head for George to flip my last card over. As he prepared to do it, I stood up, adjusted my hat, and turned to walk back toward Mr. Stallsburg, a few feet away.

No matter what card George revealed, I had won. I had won the respect of everyone I cared about. I had also won because I knew B finally realized that I was the one man that could have given her everything she ever wanted, including love and respect above all. And, I had beaten the captain. Maybe not in this last game, as I still didn't know what my final card was, but in the real game, I was playing. I had stood up to someone stronger and better than me by all measures this world sees as important. But I think the world is wrong about most of that; it just doesn't know it yet. And most importantly, I had won a sense of satisfaction and peace, knowing that I could and did, play a fair game with very good players and could now leave Christiansburg with my head held high. Rather than riding out on a dark, cold February night, running from my past and prepared to die in the process if necessary. Completely alone and broken.

As I met Mr. Stallsburg and we shook hands, the saloon literally shook as everyone gathered around the table jumped, stomped, and yelled. George had flipped my card to reveal an ace. He yelled out, "A STRAIGHT, ACE HIGH!!!"

I won the game. Unbelievable. But I knew what everyone around me did not; I had already won the game that really mattered.

To Be Continued...